S0-AUY-582

Summer Fancy

by

Anne Avery

A TOPAZ BOOK

TOPAZ

Published by the Penguin Group
Penguin Books USA Inc., 375 Hudson Street,
New York, New York 10014, U.S.A.
Penguin Books Ltd, 27 Wrights Lane,
London W8 5TZ, England
Penguin Books Australia Ltd, Ringwood,
Victoria, Australia
Penguin Books Canada Ltd, 10 Alcorn Avenue,
Toronto, Ontario, Canada M4V 3B2
Penguin Books (N.Z.) Ltd, 182–190 Wairau Road,
Auckland 10, New Zealand

Penguin Books Ltd, Registered Offices:
Harmondsworth, Middlesex, England

First published by Topaz, an imprint of Dutton Signet,
a division of Penguin Books USA Inc.

First Printing, July, 1997
10 9 8 7 6 5 4

Copyright © Anne Holmberg, 1997
All rights reserved

 REGISTERED TRADEMARK—MARCA REGISTRADA

Printed in Canada

Without limiting the rights under copyright reserved above, no part of this publication may be reproduced, stored in or introduced into a retrieval system, or transmitted, in any form, or by any means (electronic, mechanical, photocopying, recording, or otherwise), without the prior written permission of both the copyright owner and the above publisher of this book.

BOOKS ARE AVAILABLE AT QUANTITY DISCOUNTS WHEN USED TO PROMOTE PRODUCTS OR SERVICES. FOR INFORMATION PLEASE WRITE TO PREMIUM MARKETING DIVISION, PENGUIN BOOKS USA INC., 375 HUDSON STREET, NEW YORK, NEW YORK 10014.

If you purchased this book without a cover you should be aware that this book is stolen property. It was reported as "unsold and destroyed" to the publisher and neither the author nor the publisher has received any payment for this "stripped book."

This book is dedicated to all the pioneering farmers of the Lower Arkansas River Valley, both men and women, who turned rough prairie into productive farm and ranch land that continues to produce the watermelon and canteloupe that are special treats of summer.

Chapter 1

Friday, March 17, 1893

Got the melon seeds today from Mr. Swink. Seemed strange hearing an important person like him call me "Mr. Jeffries."

He's done a lot in developing these Rocky Ford watermelons that are bringing such high prices. Showed me a picture of these new, sturdier cantaloupes he's been raising the past few years. Hard to believe, a cantaloupe that can be shipped so far, but there was the picture and Mr. Conner, down at the depot, told me they shipped tons last year. Back East, to St. Louis and Kansas City and the fancy hotels in Cincinnati and Lord knows where else. New York, too! The market just keeps growing and that means good chances for my crops this first year.

I asked Mr. Swink if what I'd heard was true, that a man with irrigation and good bottomland like mine could really do as well as that article I cut out from the Cincinnati paper said you could. Seemed hard to believe, but Mr. Swink, he threw back his head and laughed. Guess he could see I didn't really believe in all those wild promises, even if they did bring me all the way out here to Colorado.

"Mr. Jeffries," he said—I didn't have the courage to ask him to call me Zeke—"Mr. Jeffries, you just plant your seed, then stand back, because those melon vines will be poppin' out of the ground faster than you can blink."

Well, that's an ~~exajera~~ that's a tall tale, of course, but with all the sun out here and the cold water from

the Arkansas River that'll be coming into my fields,
it's easy to see that crops should grow real well here.

Month and a half now since I climbed down off
that train. Doesn't seem possible, so many changes.
Sometimes I'm not sure my head is all that steady on
my shoulders yet. Selling the farm after Mama
died . . . well, I can't explain it, but I'm not sorry I
did it, even if half the county did think I'd run mad.

A man has to have dreams, but I intend to make
mine come true. I'm not going to be like Daddy, going
around with his head in the clouds and forgetting to
plant his fields on time.

A new start's the thing, getting away from Ohio and
everything. You have to leave the past behind. That's
what I decided when I buried Mama. Daddy, he just
hung on despite all those years of failure and that
didn't do anything but kill him. Then Mama went and
there wasn't much left to stay for that I could see. I
didn't figure on hanging around long enough for that
old farm and the past to come around and kill me, too.

Now I'm getting foolish. Well, it's late and no sense
wasting good kerosene just so I can have enough light
to write in this old journal. There's plenty of work
waiting for tomorrow. More than plenty. I took a good
look at that steam traction engine Mr. Frellerhof sold
me. It's only ten years old or so, but it's in worse
shape than I thought. I'd planned on using it to open
up some new fields as well as for the regular plowing,
but that will have to wait now. I can't do it all with
just my two teams of mules and me.

I'm going to have to look around for some help.
Don't know how much luck I'll have, though. Sure
can't afford to pay much, and there's plenty of better
opportunities for a man out here. Enough I can't think
why anyone would work for me.

Well, Mama always said sufficient unto the day,
which she said meant not to worry about what's down
the road, because the Lord would take care of it, anyway. Then again, she also said the Lord would provide. Can't say I ever thought He did too well along
that line—not in all the years I knew her to say He

would, at any rate—so I can't see much reason to go trusting in Him handling that sufficient business, either.

Friday, April 7, 1893

I reckon I'm in trouble now, and no help for it. I finally had to say I'd go to the church social on Sunday.

I told Mrs. Smith I didn't want to go, but she's a mighty persistent lady, even if she is no bigger than a minute. Her and Hiram—Mr. Smith, that is—live on the next farm over but one, and she's been trying to drag me to church with them ever since I moved in. I thought I'd been doing pretty good holding her off with one excuse and another. Figured she'd get tired of asking before I ran out of excuses, but it didn't work that way.

She came over on Wednesday. Day before yesterday, that was. Said she wanted to remind me that she'd take any extra milk once my Delphi freshened but that was all an excuse. She sold Delphi to me in the first place so she knows she won't be dropping her calf for another couple weeks yet, and we've already talked about the milk often enough for our jaws to have gotten sore from the chattering. Mine anyway. Mrs. Smith's are a tad more toughened up.

Anyway, she spent about a minute flat on the milk, then, before I got half a chance to plan what kind of excuse I could try this time, she just charges right on to the matter of the church social invite. Tried to tell me I'd meet lots of nice people. I headed her off on that one by saying I'd already met a passel of nice people. Darn near tripped over them every time I went to town, there were so many, I said.

I thought that was a pretty good reply, but it didn't hold her long.

All the ladies would be bringing food, she said. There'd be so many good things to eat, I'd probably have trouble walking once I'd finished. I said I really appreciated the thought, but I didn't dare risk it. All that good food after so many months of my own cooking was like to prove fatal, I said.

Well, that stopped her for a minute or two, but nobody ever said Mrs. Smith didn't have spunk. She just came charging back with a half dozen more good arguments about why I should go.

In the end, I held her off, but it was a close-run thing. I figure that little skirmish cost me a month's worth of good excuses, minimum. Trouble was, I didn't have any idea just how determined that little lady could be. If she'd been in charge of the Confederate army, I doubt even General Grant could have licked her.

I found that out when Hiram drove up this morning looking like a hound dog that had just been whupped. "Zeke," he says to me, his voice sort of raspy, as if it hurt him to talk. "You gotta go to the social."

Of course, I told him I didn't *want* to go to the social, but he just shook his head and said, "*I* know that. But Mrs. Smith don't know that." Hiram always calls her Mrs. Smith, even if she *is* his wife. "*She* thinks you're just shy or scared or something, and she's making *my* life miserable because of it. Says I'm supposed to convince you to come along. For your own good, she says."

Well, I knew then it was pretty serious. When the ladies start talking about a man having to do things for his own good, then you just know he hasn't got a prayer, even assuming he's on good standing with the Lord, which I'm not going to try and claim. And this *is* a church social we're talking about.

Now, it's no use saying that just because I'm six feet four and strong as they come that I can stand up to a lady like Mrs. Smith, because I can't. Hiram's an inch or so taller than me and he must weigh a good thirty, forty pounds more, and Mrs. Smith can't weigh a hundred soaking wet with all her petticoats on. You'd think that kind of difference in size would settle the matter, but it didn't take me ten minutes first time I met them to figure out who was tougher.

"That bad, huh?" I said, feeling pretty shaky.

He nodded, real sad, like a hound that not only got whupped, but got his favorite bone taken away, just for good measure. He said, "Worse. She hasn't hardly given me any peace since day before yesterday when she come home from visitin' you. I don't know if I got the courage to go back and tell her if you don't agree to go to the social."

"Hiram," I said. "*You* know and *I* know that the only reason Mrs. Smith wants me at that social is she's planning on fixing me up with one of her single lady friends. Or maybe more, depending on how I take. I *know* how these ladies work, Hiram, and so do you."

He sighed, real deep and long, then said, "I tried to hold out, Zeke, honest I did, but she was worrying it so this morning, she cooked my eggs till they was tough as old leather. And I like 'em soft with the yellow running into everything."

Then he looked at me out from under those droopy eyelids of his, just like a hound that's begging to have his bone back, at least. "You *gotta* go to that social, Zeke. As a favor to me. I just can't stand to have tough eggs two days in a row, and there's no telling what she'd do to the beans if she got *real* upset."

It was my turn to sigh then, but I just couldn't let a man down who's been as good to me as Hiram has. "All right," I said, none too enthusiastic. "But don't you go blaming me if I make a fool of myself and upset the ladies, Hiram. I always do, and I don't expect this will be any different."

I'm hoping I was wrong on that prediction, but I don't think I was.

Had to go into town this afternoon. Coulter broke on the plow, so I took it into the blacksmith's along with some parts from the traction engine I needed fixed. Seems like I just keep finding more and more on that thing that needs to be done. Finally had to break down and order some parts from back East, though it sure hurt to do it. The darned things will cost me a good nine dollars plus freight. If the money keeps going out at that rate, I'll have to ship twice the number of melons I planted, just to break even.

Anyway, while I was waiting I wandered around some. Started to turn into Hodgeson's Emporium, but there were two ladies standing there at the counter and I ended up backing out faster than I went in. Automatic. Don't know how I'm going to manage the social if I can't face a couple of strangers in a general store.

"These are the very finest facial creams, Mrs. Carter, I assure you." Samuel Hodgeson, sole proprietor of Hodgeson's Emporium, extended two bright blue bottles for inspection. "There is no finer manufacturer of quality beauty products than Maison Riviere"—he pronounced it Maysawn Riveeairee—"and these have just come in direct from New York."

As Delphi Carter leaned across the wide store counter to study the bottles' labels, Sophronia Carter shifted her laden market basket from her right hand to her left and sighed. Her feet hurt, her corset pinched, at least five hairpins were sticking into her scalp, and the day was unseasonably warm, but none of these arguments would be sufficient to persuade her mother to abandon her absorbing discussion of health and beauty products once it was well launched.

Delphi Carter had begun a quarter of an hour ago with an animated debate on the relative merits of Peruvian Wine of Coca versus a Nutritive Beef, Iron and Wine Tonic as a remedy for the physical exhaustion brought on by stress and overwork. Since her mother was the picture of robust good health, and the most strenuous activity in which she regularly engaged was sticking her nose into her neighbors' business, Sophie couldn't quite see the need for either restorative—but there was no dissuading Delphi Carter. The tall amber bottle of Nutritive Tonic now stood at one side of the counter along with a roll of Jaynes' Sugar-Coated Cathartic Pills and a blue-paper-wrapped can of Bromo-Vichy, which Mr. Hodgeson had assured them was an excellent cure for Nervous Headaches, Neuralgia, Sleeplessness, and Over Brain Work.

From patent remedies, the discussion had moved on to the even more absorbing topic of beauty aids.

"This Creme Incomparable is a marvelous addition to Maison Riviere's Eau de la Jennesse," Mr. Hodgeson said, delicately waving first one blue bottle, then the other, under Delphi Carter's nose. "Of course, *you* don't really need such aids, Mrs. Carter. Why, just the other day Mrs. Hodgeson was saying to me that she didn't know how you managed to keep your complexion like you do, considering our dry western climate."

Sophie's mother beamed and shoved back her shoulders, which made her stays creak and her impressive bosom thrust out even farther than it already did.

"It *is* a trial, Mr. Hodgeson, I assure you," she said with a heartfelt sigh. Her fingers fluttered at her breast, delicately hinting at just how much a trial it was. "Although I do flatter myself I've managed better than most. Mr. Carter, may heaven rest his soul, always said my complexion was a great blessing and that I should take care to protect it. 'Delphi, my love,' he'd say to me, 'you be sure to take care of yourself. A beautiful woman is a joy for a man's eyes and you're a true wonder.' That's what he'd say."

"I don't doubt it, Mrs. Carter. Indeed I don't." Mr. Hodgeson's heavy eyelids drooped in soulful appreciation of Mr. Carter's perspicacity.

Delphi Carter was clearly fighting against the urge to preen. She settled for lightly brushing her fingertips across her smooth pink cheek. "I've found, however, that a judicious use of Dr. Rose's French Arsenic Complexion Wafers is a great preventative against whatever damage our weather might cause. You might suggest them to Mrs. Hodgeson, if she is concerned."

Her smile turned to a ladylike frown as a new and less pleasant thought occurred to her. She glanced at Sophie. "*Some* people are wise enough to take a well-meant suggestion."

Sophie pressed her lips tight together and turned to scowl at a poster advertising Geyserite Medicated Soaps, patented February 3, 1885, and manufactured *only* in Denver, Colorado. The central design, which looked more like an exploding volcano than a geyser, roused a certain sympathy in her. She'd been fighting against the urge to let off steam all morning, herself.

Against her mother's wishes, Sophie had ordered her new summer suit to be made in a practical brown broadcloth. Worse, she'd chosen unfashionably narrow lapels and none of the decorative trim and braid that so appealed to her parent. As if that weren't transgression enough, her four new shirtwaists were similarly neat and practical, and completely lacked any of the heavy pleating or ruffling that might have helped disguise her hopelessly flat chest.

The plain brown straw hat she'd chosen had been, literally, the last straw for her mother's already abused and overburdened sensibilities. At sight of it, Delphi Carter had launched into yet another diatribe on Sophie's deplorable inattention to the finer points of feminine dress and beauty, and she hadn't calmed down yet.

It wasn't her fault she hadn't been blessed with her mother's womanly charms, Sophie reminded herself rebelliously. If she could have, she would happily have traded a few excess inches out of her five feet ten inches for a corresponding increase in her bust measurement. But that wasn't possible and she saw no sense in trying to pretend she was anything except what she really was: a tall, thin, rather plain spinster of twenty-six who looked even taller, thinner, and plainer when compared to her buxom and eminently feminine mother.

The silence might have stretched uncomfortably, but Mr. Hodgeson was too experienced a salesman to let the sudden tension between his best customer and her daughter divert him from a profitable sale.

"Well, I'll be sure and tell Mrs. Hodgeson about those arsenic wafers, Mrs. Carter," he said with respectful enthusiasm. "I thank you for the suggestion. Your comments on such matters are always so *very* helpful and informative, you know. That's why I thought you would be an excellent judge of the quality 'of these new products here. Just in from New York, as I do believe I mentioned."

Diverted, Delphi turned back to the more immediate concern of just how much benefit might be obtained by trying the proffered beauty creams. Ever since her daughter had grown into a rather lank and unpromising womanhood, she'd found it increasingly difficult to ignore the unwelcome hints that her own youthful beauty was fading. Patent medicines, expensive beauty creams, and the surreptitious use of face powder and rouge had all come to occupy a central spot in her limited range of interests, second only to her preoccupation with her daughter's worrisome unwed state.

"Well, Mr. Hodgeson, since you ask." She sighed delicately, as if in recognition of her responsibility to the less well-informed women who might come after her. "I *suppose* we could try one or two of them. Sophronia is occasionally troubled by the dryness, you know, and with my delicate skin, I am peculiarly sensitive to the sun."

Rather than explode like the soap poster, Sophie bit her tongue, spun about on her heel, and, head high, marched down the aisle toward her favorite spot in town—the small glass case at the back of the store where Mr. Hodgeson's collection of books was displayed. A few minutes spent in the presence of books never failed to calm her too quick temper; although the way she felt right now, she might well have to spend an hour or two buried in the store's shadowy depths before it would be safe for her to reappear.

She rounded the display of farm tools that occupied the center of the floor only to discover, to her dismay, that she was not alone.

A thin, grimy boy of about ten, dirty hands pressed flat against the glass, stared hungrily at the clothbound books primly arrayed before him, just out of reach.

Sophie stopped short. She'd seen the boy around town before. From a distance, he'd appeared to be in need of a bath and clean clothes.

Closer inspection revealed that one bath wouldn't

be near enough to remove the dirt ground into his
hide, and his clothes didn't have a chance of surviving
a washing, even if they hadn't been too small and too
full of holes to be worth saving. Bony elbows poked
out of tattered shirtsleeves. Scrawny ankles showed
three inches below the ragged edge of his pants. He
was barefoot and the soles of his feet were so thick
with calluses that Sophie doubted he could wear a
regular pair of shoes, even assuming he had them,
which she doubted.

He hadn't heard her approach. He was too intent
on the books to be aware of anything else.

There wasn't much for him to see, really. Just the
titles on the spines of the three or four dozen cloth
and cheap paperbound books lined up side by side
along the shelf.

From her own frequent investigations of the case,
Sophie knew it contained books by novelists as diverse
as Mark Twain and Edward Bellamy, as well as some
of her favorite romantic novels like the ones penned
by Mrs. Southworth. There were stories by Harry
Castlemon and Horatio Alger for boys, and some of
the Fireside Series for girls. What puzzled her was that
the boy didn't seem to be concentrating on the novels,
but on the manuals and handbooks at one end.

Sophie edged forward, curious to see more clearly.
A floorboard creaked beneath her, startling the boy.
He jumped away from the case and whirled to confront her, eyes wild beneath a broom-corn thatch of
dirty yellow hair.

"I wasn't doin' nuthin'."

Sophie smiled encouragingly and set her basket on
the floor out of the way. "I didn't think you were."
She glanced at the books, then back at him. "I like to
look at them, too. My favorites are Sir Walter Scott
and Mrs. Southworth. What about you?"

She asked out of politeness and because she
couldn't think of anything else to say. Tatterdemalion
boys like this one seldom spent enough time in school
to learn to read, let alone read anything as difficult as
a novel.

The boy hesitated, eyeing her uncertainly, but the case with its precious cache of books was stronger than his doubts. He edged closer and peered through the glass.

"That one," he said, pointing. "An' that one."

Sophie leaned closer, trying to make out the titles. *"A. B. C. Of Electricity?"* She frowned. Surely she was mistaken.

"An' *Electricity Simplified.* I saw 'em in Mr. Sobeck's office when he let me come in one night when Ma was busy and it come on to storm real sudden."

"Wouldn't your mother let you into the house in a storm?" Shock at his casual statement temporarily drove out Sophie's surprise at both his choice of reading material and the fact that he'd found shelter with the town's irascible telegraph operator, who lived for his telegraph and the electrical gizmos he was always experimenting with.

The boy shrugged. "She had company. *You* know. An' I don't like to stay around when she does."

Sophronia stiffened, suddenly uncomfortable. She knew who the boy's mother was now, though she'd never gone near the tumbledown house at the far edge of town where "Mrs." Peabody conducted her sordid "business." Even the most redoubtable members of the Ladies Missionary Society had refused to have anything to do with her after she'd driven them away by swearing and flinging empty whiskey bottles at them.

If the boy noticed her reaction, he gave no sign of it. Sophie hated to think he might have learned to take such reactions for granted.

"Mr. Conner, the stationmaster, he don't much like me hangin' around," he said confidingly, "but the station was closed and it was snowin'. Mr. Sobeck, he showed me how his telegraph worked, and this light he's got rigged to a battery, and stuff like that. Didja know you don't need oil for a lamp? There's a newfangled kinda thing called a 'lectric light bulb. You heard about that?"

He waited just long enough for Sophie to nod encouragingly before plunging onward. "Bright as day, purty near. An' you don't hafta scrub no chimneys! Well, that's when I decided *I* wanted t'be an engineer an' put 'lectric lights in everybody's houses, an' maybe have 'lectric trolleys and cars like Mr. Sobeck said they got in Pueblo an' Denver. An' telephones! I could build telephones, too!"

Excitement shown in the boy's blue eyes, bright as the electric lights that had caught his young imagination.

Sophie smiled, inexplicably touched by his eagerness. "That sounds like a wonderful plan to me."

He looked as if he hadn't eaten a decent meal in weeks. He certainly hadn't seen a bath in all that time. Yet even dirty and half starved, he'd been lured into Samuel Hodgeson's store by books he probably couldn't read even if he'd had the money to buy them.

No, she corrected herself a moment later when he turned back to study the contents of the glass-fronted case. It wasn't the books that had drawn him here, it was a dream. An impossible dream.

And if there was one thing Sophie Carter understood, it was impossible dreams.

Her mother's voice, raised in a peremptory command, jerked her out of her thoughts. "Sophronia, come here. I want you."

Startled out of his reverie, the boy shrank back against the edge of the case, suddenly wary.

"It's my mother," Sophie reassured him. Her odd feeling of kinship with the boy grew stronger. Delphi Carter often had the same effect on her.

"I'll be back," she told him, and surprised herself in saying it.

Without stopping to see if he'd wait, she turned on her heel and headed back to her mother, who wasn't at all fond of waiting.

"I've made my selection, Sophronia," Delphi informed her grandly. "Mr. Hodgeson and I decided it would be best if I tried all of them. Except, of course, for the hair tonics and the freckle remover. It would be impossible for me to judge such things since my hair is naturally luxuriant and I have *never* had a freckle in my life."

Delphi's right eyebrow arched in a silent reminder that her daughter, regrettably, had been known to display a freckle or two whenever she heedlessly exposed herself to the sun.

Sophie refrained from rising to the unspoken challenge, but it wasn't easy.

Mr. Hodgeson, wise in the ways of his customers, kept his attention firmly fixed on the column of numbers he was toting up. The effort might not have been so notable if he weren't perfectly capable of adding the figures in his head faster than most people could manage with paper and pencil.

When Sophie remained silent, Delphi reluctantly continued, "I've told Mr. Hodgeson that you will settle the bill. I have decided to drop in on dear Mrs. Bassett. There are a few matters I wish to discuss with her regarding the Ladies Missionary Society."

"Yes, Mother."

"You may feel free to go on home when you are done here. I don't know when I shall return."

Sophie just managed to keep from balling her hands into fists. "Of course, Mother."

Rather than risk losing her temper in public, she looked away. Anywhere, just so long as she wouldn't be forced to see the all too familiar disappointment and frustration—disappointment and frustration with *her*—that glittered in her mother's eyes. Her gaze swung to the front of the store . . . and stopped.

Standing in the open doorway, head and shoulders haloed in sunshine, was the hero of all the romances she had read so avidly, over and over and over, then tucked away at the very top of her closet, where her mother would never find them. His perfectly sculpted features, half hidden in shadow, highlighted by sun, were those of a man destined to dare great things and suffer untold agonies for the sake of the woman who claimed his heart. His broad shoulders were wide enough and strong enough to bear the burdens of the world, yet he would, Sophie knew instantly, be gentle

and infinitely loving when he at last drew his love into
his arms and bent that perfect head to kiss her. He
was Ivanhoe and Ben Hur and Rochester and every
other tormented and wildly romantic man of legend
who had ever driven a heroine to despair, then opened
her soul to a passionate, spiritual love that tran-
scended time and space and. . . .

And he was gone.

Sophie blinked, then swallowed uncomfortably. Her
cheeks flushed.

Fool. Silly, romantic, unrealistic fool. She'd let her
mother upset her and now she was seeing fantasies,
right there in the open door of Hodgeson's Emporium.

She reluctantly turned her attention back to her
mother, but dropped her gaze to the wide plank floor
so no one could see her confusion . . . or her shame.
It wasn't until her mother was out the door that she
realized she's been holding her breath, fighting against
the sting of tears.

Ever discreet, Mr. Hodgeson waited until Delphi
Carter sailed past the front window and out of sight
before announcing the results of his calculations.
"That will be five and a quarter, Miss Sophronia. That
is, if you don't want anything else."

"I don't think so, thank you," Sophie said, then
remembered the boy by the bookcase and her abandoned market basket with her day's purchases of meat
and vegetables.

With a quick apology, she retreated to the shadowy
depths of the store, grateful for a moment alone to
regain her composure. She had more time than that.
It only took an instant to determine that both boy and
basket had disappeared.

The corner of Sophie's mouth twitched upward, in
spite of her. Her mother liked to be of use, and she'd
clearly provided the distraction the boy had needed
to slip away without Mr. Hodgeson spotting him. Sophie tried to imagine her mother's expression if she
ever learned that her little speech had cost her her
shopping basket and her dinner. The mind boggled.

She glanced at the row of books. They were all

still there, the romantic novels at one end, the electric handbooks the boy had yearned for at the other.

Sophie's heart skipped a beat.

She'd been right earlier. It wasn't books, but dreams, that were locked away behind that glass. All it took was a dollar or so to bring them out. But no matter how much she wished it were otherwise, hers would always remain nothing more than wishful fantasies. The boy, on the other hand, still had a chance of turning his into reality.

After a moment's foot-tapping deliberation, Sophie returned to the front counter. "Actually, Mr. Hodgeson, there are a couple of items I'd forgotten."

The shopkeeper beamed. "That's not a problem. What can I get for you?"

"I need a market basket"—Sophie pointed to a woven basket with a hinged lid that hung from a hook overhead—"and the copy of *A. B. C. Of Electricity* that's in your case."

Mr. Hodgeson's eyes widened, despite their drooping lids. Then he blinked. "Miss Sophronia?"

"I've decided to take up science, Mr. Hodgeson. Who knows? If I find it promising, I might be back for more."

Chapter 2

Well, I did it. I made a fool of myself, just as I knew I would, sooner or later. Only thing is, I would a whole lot rather it had been later.

Hiram and Mrs. Smith took me up in their buggy this morning. Right off, Mrs. Smith looked me up and she looked me down, and that's when she got the first doubtful look on her face.

I'd put on my only suit, but Mama bought that suit when I was seventeen and Daddy died, so I'd have something fitting for the funeral. It's a good suit with lots of wear left in it, but I've grown an inch or two and filled out a tad in the eight years since then. I had it let out when it looked like we were going to have a funeral for Mama, too, but the pants and the sleeves still run to high water and there's no denying it's good and tight all over. Makes me sweat a bit whenever I go to sit down, wondering if I'm going to be able to stand up again and still be decent.

My hair didn't please Mrs. Smith any too much, either. I'd tried to trim it up a bit with shears. I didn't have any proper scissors since I'd given Mama's pair to Miss Becky before I left because she'd always admired the silver-plated handles. I'd used the window in the kitchen for a mirror. I didn't feel I'd done too bad, considering, but I didn't have any brilliantine to slick things down with proper and I have to admit there were a few rough edges. Not to mention that cowlick at the top that I can't seem to settle no matter how hard I try.

Then there were my boots. I don't have any proper shoes, but I'd done what I could with my best pair of work boots. Even polished them twice with spit to get a good shine. I didn't think they looked too bad, but Mrs. Smith frowned something fierce and I could see that I hadn't quite come up to scratch, as far as she was concerned.

At least she can't say I didn't *try* to keep out of it.

Actually, she didn't say anything at all. About the way I looked, I mean. She had plenty to say about everything else, and every dozen words or so she got in a pitch for one or another of her lady friends I could tell she was aiming to sic on me.

She told Hiram and me about Miss Neumann and her wonderful dried apple pies and about Mrs. Talbot's daughter, Annie, who took the prize for elocution at some fancy ladies seminary back East last year. She had quite a bit to say about a Mrs. James, who had been widowed young but was working hard to care for her elderly father and was an upstanding example to the community of dedication and sacrifice and true Christian womanliness. According to Mrs. Smith, this Mrs. James was a woman a man could depend on. I took that to mean I'd have to be pretty fast on my feet if I was going to keep out of her way. There were a few others whose names I can't remember now. Enough so I knew it was going to be rough hoeing, no matter how hard I tried to keep out of the field.

Of course, I didn't say anything, but I couldn't help staring at the back of Hiram's head because it was his fault I'd landed in the whole mess in the first place. He didn't say anything, either, just tended to the horse and the road, but I could see the back of his neck getting redder and redder, so I felt some better. At least he was sorry for what he'd gotten me into. Not that it did either of us much good.

It was only when we were coming up to the church that he seemed to come awake. "Zeke," he says, real casual like, "I'm gonna let Mrs. Smith off at the door so she don't get her skirts dusty, but I'd sure appreciate you helping me tie up the horse and carry in the food."

Well, Hiram didn't need any help from me with the horse, and Mrs. Smith had only packed one big basket of food, which Hiram could have carried just as easy as me. I knew it and Mrs. Smith knew it, but before she could say anything, he'd pulled up in front of the church. Of course, I hopped right down and helped Mrs. Smith climb out, then hopped back in quick as a jackrabbit with a coyote on its tail, in spite of that tight suit. Hiram drove off before I'd even gotten settled, which made me plop down with a jerk, but I figured he must have something pretty important to tell me in private for him to risk getting Mrs. Smith riled like that.

He pulled up in the field by the church and twisted 'round in his seat. He was looking a mite wild-eyed and nervous, so I quick turned to look where he was. All I could see were the folks trailing in to church. "I just had to warn you, Zeke," he said, swallowing hard. "Spotted 'em coming down the street and figured you needed to know."

"Know what?" I asked, real puzzled.

"See that lady?" he asked, pointing to a mighty impressive middle-aged woman marching down the street.

I had to admit I did. If I hadn't been so nervous about Mrs. Smith and her plans, I would have noticed her first thing. Would have been hard not to.

First off, she was wearing a hat that must have had at least two stuffed birds on it, if not three, not to mention a big blue bow and a couple dozen flowers. Hat like that stands out in a crowd. I hoped we didn't end up sitting behind her in church, because it was so high even Hiram wouldn't have been able to see over it if he was sitting down.

But that wasn't all you noticed about the lady, though I'll admit a real gentleman wouldn't have been thinking such things. If she'd been a plow horse, she would have needed an extra big collar—she had one of the biggest, deepest chests I'd ever seen on a woman. She carried it thrust well out in front of her and was following it very determined like. She couldn't hardly help it, since it was aimed straight at the church door. It wasn't that she was fat, mind you, because she wasn't. But she *was* built mighty solid.

"That lady," says Hiram, "is Mrs. Julius T. Carter. I thought you oughta know. She's a widow lady and she's so bound and determined to get her daughter, Miss Sophronia, married off that she won't let any bachelor in town who's not a drunk or in jail get by without a howdydo. If she ever gets you backed up to the fence, so to speak, well . . ." He didn't say what would happen, but he shook his head real sad and sort of tsk tsked, and then he scrunched up his forehead as if it pained him even to think about it.

It wasn't until he mentioned the daughter that I noticed the tall, slim lady following after Mrs. Carter. Have to admit, any man would tend not to notice her if her mother was around. She was dressed in brown and there was a small brown bow on her straw hat, but no birds or flowers or anything. The hat sort of blended in with all the brown hair she had piled up on top of her head. She didn't wear any of the fancy curls that ladies seem to like these days, and her suit was real plain, too. Neat and trim, but plain.

Most of all, though, she hadn't been blessed with her mother's bosom. Fact is, she was pretty near flat as my best plowed field, and she didn't seem to have made much effort to hide that fact because her jacket was plain and neat, but didn't have any of those fancy ruffles and folds and whatnot that the ladies usually wear, especially the flat-chested ones. As if a man couldn't tell the difference.

As I say, a real gentleman wouldn't have noticed, but I've never made any claim to being a gentleman, even if Mama always said the girls chased after me because I was polite as well as good-looking. Mama was confused about a lot of things, and it never did surprise me to know she was confused about her only son along with everything else.

Well, I didn't want Mrs. Carter and her daughter

Sophronia—now *there's* a name!—to think I was staring. Wouldn't do to attract the ladies' attention if I
didn't have to. So I turned back to Hiram and said,
"I don't recall Mrs. Smith mentioning Miss Sophronia
this morning."

Hiram twitched a bit, then he swallowed and said,
"She didn't. Mrs. Smith and Mrs. Carter, well, they
don't quite see eye to eye on some of the doin's in
the church. Had quite a discussion a few weeks back
about who was goin' to head up the Ladies Missionary
Society. Mrs. Smith had some pretty fixed notions
about what she was going to do when she got picked,
but Mrs. Carter, she stepped in and said *she* was the
one rightfully oughta be the head, seein' as how she'd
already done so much for the Society and all. Guess
they got into it somethin' fierce, judgin' from the way
Mrs. Smith banged around in the kitchen afterwards,
though I *did* try to stay out of it. Not that it did me
any good. Got a good earful and then some about the
wickednesses of Mrs. Carter, what with her pretensions and her *dis*ruptive influences—that's what Mrs.
Smith called 'em—in the Society. Took me nigh on an
hour to figure out the Society ended up electin' old
Mrs. Bassett, in the end."

Well, I could see how that sort of thing could upset
Mrs. Smith. I could also see how I would be in a whole
heap worse trouble than I already was if I got caught
in the cross fire. When the ladies start taking potshots
at each other, any man with an ounce of smarts knows
enough to keep out of the way. Providing he can, that
is. Sometimes a man gets dragged into the fighting no
matter what. The only thing he can do then is keep his
head down and run like the devil first chance he gets.

I have to admit, I gave some serious consideration
to cutting and running. It was only a bit above four
miles back to the farm. Not too bad a walk if I got
going right away. I suspect Hiram guessed what I was
thinking, because he quick handed me the basket of
food that'd been tucked in under the seat and suggested I take it right in before Mrs. Smith got to wondering what had happened to me.

I noticed he didn't include himself in Mrs. Smith's wondering, but, then, he's been married to her a good while. More than enough time for a man to figure out what's what, and whether or not he's the one in his wife's sights. And we both knew it wasn't Hiram Mrs. Smith was aiming at this time 'round.

My luck held awhile. By the time I found Mrs. Smith in the church hall, folks were gathering in the church proper for the service so she couldn't do more than fuss at my being slow and thump that basket down in a spot right near the center of the table where you couldn't miss it. Then she led me around to the church and shooed me into a pew just as if I was a hen she was chasing into a coop. Hiram joined us right after. He was looking almighty innocent, considering, but Mrs. Smith was too busy spying out where her lady friends were to notice.

Got through the service all right. Reverend Wembly gave a fine sermon, though I don't exactly remember what it was all about. He has a deep voice that just boomed around the church and he could thump and shout and wave his hands in a way that made a body sit up and take notice. Mama would have had a fine time, but all I could think of was the social afterwards. Didn't help any that every now and again I caught some young lady sneaking a peek at me, just as if I was a prize pot of jam at the county fair and she was wondering how I'd do spread on her morning toast.

It was after the service when we all started filing into the hall that the trouble started.

Sophie spotted him the minute he walked into church three steps ahead of Adelaide Smith. Her heart skipped a beat and threatened to spring into her throat and choke her. There was no mistaking that compelling profile.

She caught her breath and took a second look.

It was all she needed.

Her shoulders drooped, her heart settled firmly back into place, and she let go the breath she'd been holding in a little sigh of disappointment.

He was the man she'd spotted in Hodgeson's doorway on Friday, but that was the end of it. No romantic
hero she'd ever read about wore suits that were a size
too small or looked as if he cut his hair with a pair
of shears. And not one of the heroes in her books
would have allowed Adelaide Smith to herd them into
a church pew like that, just as if they didn't have any
more sense than a sheep.

Rather than risk being caught staring, Sophie sternly
fixed her gaze on the back of the pew in front of her.
At least her mother was engaged in animated discussion with Mrs. Joerring on her other side and had
conveniently forgotten about her for the present.

She ought to be glad the reality hadn't matched the
fantasy. Ever since she'd spotted him on Friday, she'd
had a hard time keeping her mind off him and on her
work. If someone came to the door, she expected to
see him standing there. If she looked out a window,
it was with the mad, unacknowledged hope that he'd
be waiting for her, devotedly guarding the house until
she appeared.

The nights had been worse, lying awake in the dark
with the vision of a man cast in sunlight and shadow
etched on the backs of her eyelids, tormenting her
with impossible longings and a sharp, physical discomfort that was almost past bearing.

She *ought* to be glad to come to her senses, but
she wasn't.

Ever since she'd first read the story of King Arthur
and his knights, Sophie had dreamed of one day meeting her own Sir Lancelot, someone brave and bold
and handsome who would take her up before him on
his great white horse and carry her off to his castle,
where they would live happily ever after. Never mind
that there hadn't been a happily ever after for
Lancelot and Guinevere. In her fantasies, things always worked out right.

Of course, in her case Merlin would have had to
step in first to work a little magic. Fairy-tale ladies
were never tall and thin and awkward, and they certainly were *never* flat-chested or plain.

Fairy tales. Sophie's mouth tightened in self-disgust. They were children's stories for children, yet she'd never quite managed to outgrow her secret belief that somehow, just for her, they would someday all come true. But they hadn't come true and they never would and she knew it.

Sophie clasped her hands tight together in her lap, fighting against the sudden urge to hit something.

She'd turned twenty-six in March. Twenty-six! All the women she knew who were anywhere near her age were married and mothers, while she had never even had a beau, or been squired to a dance, or let a man steal a kiss or two when nobody was looking.

There'd been reasons, of course. Her father had fallen ill with consumption when she was sixteen. That's when he closed his bookkeeping office and they moved to Colorado where the dry air was supposed to help his condition.

For a while, he'd appeared to get better, but eventually his illness had gained the upper hand and he'd stayed home to sit in the sun, wrapped in blankets and coughing up blood into one handkerchief after another. Delphi had bathed him and dressed him and helped him with his personal needs, but it was Sophie, just turned twenty, who stayed by him through the long hours of the day, reading to him, talking to him, or simply sitting quietly while he slept. At the last, Sophie had held basins for him as he'd vomited great gouts of blood, day after day until there was nothing left in him and he'd died, glad to go and be done with the suffering.

At the funeral, Delphi had fussed because Sophie had grown thin and her gown was too drab and had hung on her in an unbecoming fashion. Sophie had been too tired and too frightened to care. She had loved her father and she had done her best for him, and her best had not been good enough. Not anywhere near good enough.

She'd been doing her best for her mother ever since. Taking care of the house, managing the cooking and the cleaning and the washing, investing the savings her

father had left them so that their funds had grown
instead of dwindling as they would have if left in
Delphi's careless, spendthrift hands. And none of that
had been good enough, either.

In Delphi Carter's eyes, the only achievement wor-
thy of a woman was to attract men and, eventually,
to marry one of them. Preferably the handsomest and
richest one available.

In that one, essential area, her daughter was a failure, and Delphi Carter had made no effort to hide
her disappointment. Eventually she'd stepped in and
tried to remedy the situation.

Sophie had never found the courage to tell her
mother that her determined efforts to find her a husband had only made matters worse. Her unmarried
state had become a standing joke around the county,
and single men with whom she might otherwise have
at least been friends now steered clear of her for fear
of falling into Delphi's clutches.

But this man . . .

Reluctantly, Sophie raised her head. He was sitting
two rows in front of her and a little to the left. The
angle gave her a clear view of his broad shoulders and
the back of his head with its raggedy ruffle of hair.

His hair wasn't black, as she'd thought. More a deep
mahogany-brown. His botched efforts at a trim had
left a cowlick at the crown that bobbed a bit whenever
he moved. Every now and then he turned so she
caught a brief glimpse of his profile. And every time
he did, she felt her breath stop in her throat.

Forget the bad haircut and the straining seams of
his suit. Forget his awkwardness and his obvious discomfort at being here. He still looked like a hero
straight out of her secret fantasies. The only difference
was, he was real and he was sitting just a few feet
away from her.

Sophie knew the instant Delphi spotted him.

Reverend Wembly was smack in the middle of a
stirring exhortation to righteousness. Delphi, as usual,
was engaged in inspecting her neighbors and assuring
herself that not one of the ladies was as stylishly

dressed or as elegantly coifed as she was. Her roving gaze latched onto the stranger just at the moment he turned his head. At sight of that striking masculine profile, Delphi sucked in her breath and leaned forward for a better look.

For the remainder of the sermon, Delphi almost squirmed in her seat with eager curiosity while Sophie grew more and more tense, dreading what lay ahead.

The sermon ended. The congregation stood and patiently began filing out as the sound of shuffling feet and conversation filled the little church.

To Delphi's disgust and Sophie's immense relief, Adelaide Smith took full advantage of her strategic superiority. Before Delphi could work her way through the press of people that separated them, Adelaide dragged the man off and began introducing him to friends who just happened to have a daughter or two in search of a husband.

The daughters looked pleased, the parents looked interested, and the man . . . well, Sophie had seen cows at the slaughterhouse that looked happier than he did.

Despite Adelaide's advantage, Delphi was determinedly working her way toward him through the crowd. Sophie didn't say a word. She didn't dare.

Instead, she slipped into the slowly moving crowd when her mother wasn't looking and headed for the hall that was built onto the back of the church. Someone Upstairs had been looking out for her. Sophie had promised more than a week ago to help with setting up for the social. It gave her the perfect excuse for escaping while escape was still possible.

Like just about every other woman present, except, perhaps, her mother and old Mrs. Trowbridge, she'd brought food to serve at the social. This time it was honey-cinnamon bread, something sweet and just a little bit different from what everybody else would have fixed.

Thinking of the bread and the praises it usually earned her, Sophie sighed. If the way to a man's heart was through his stomach as some of the ladies claimed, she'd have been married years ago. Unfortunately, it hadn't worked that way for her. Her cooking had earned her enthusiastic praise from everyone who had ever tried it, but the bachelors were just too scared of Delphi to ever consider coming back for seconds.

Not that she was going to waste time fretting about it now. Taking care to avoid the broken board on the fifth step that someone or other from the Maintenance Committee was always going to replace and never got around to, Sophie climbed the outside stairs to the hall and darted inside. She didn't want Delphi spotting her before the hall got so crowded that introductions to strangers became difficult, if not impossible.

A good dozen ladies were in the hall ahead of her, busily engaged in laying out the food on cloth-covered trestle tables arrayed along one wall. They went about their work with a smooth efficiency that spoke of long practice with similar gatherings, but while their hands were busy, their tongues were even busier.

"My George says he's a hard worker and making real progress getting that old farm into shape. Has to be lonely, though, on his own like that."

"He needs a wife. You can see that right off. All you have to do is look at that suit!" A chorus of giggles signified general agreement on the subject of the suit.

"Adelaide said she just about bit her tongue off trying to keep from commenting on his haircut." More giggles.

"I thought about offering to trim it up for him, but with a man like that . . . why, I just might forget I was married! I don't think Jason would approve at all!" The giggles dissolved into raucous laughter.

Sophie tried to ignore the conversation, but these were her friends. They might not know anything about her fantasy lovers, but they knew she was single and plain and that her mother was capable of making her life a misery when it came to the subject of men.

Amabelle Marlen, a friend who was only recently married, gave her a knowing wink. "Did you see him, Sophie?"

Sophie feigned ignorance. "See who?"

"See who? See who, she says!" Amabelle exclaimed, glancing at the others as if inviting them to share her amusement. They did. "Why, who do you think? That handsome young man that was sitting just two rows in front of you in church. Don't tell me you didn't see him, because I know better. I saw you looking at him."

"Not half as hard as Delphi was!"

Sophie wasn't sure who had spoken and hadn't the slightest idea how to respond. Not that it mattered. The women were laughing too hard to hear anything she might have said, and her cheeks were burning so hot she couldn't draw breath to speak, anyway. The only thing that saved her was the arrival of Reverend Wembly, closely followed by members of the congregation who had had more than their fill of prayers and now wanted their fill of food.

Within a matter of minutes the hall was filled with folks lining up to make their first pass at the laden tables. A small herd of boys jostled for position at the head of the line, but a couple of stern threats to make them wait until everyone else had seconds proved sufficient to quell their antics. The old folk and mothers with toddlers and babes in arm were catered to special as Sophie and her friends took turns filling plates and taking them around, then laying out even more food on the tables when the first disappeared as if by magic.

Sophie tried to keep her mind on the job at hand, but it wasn't easy. *He* was there, backed up against the far wall with a heaped plate in his hands and a gaggle of glowing, unattached women clustered so close around him that he'd never in a million years have a chance to eat anything. He hadn't even had to go through the line. There'd been more than enough unattached females willing to do that for him.

From the panicked, pop-eyed look of him and the way he was constantly running a finger under his collar, Sophie guessed he wasn't exactly enjoying the experience, even if he *had* managed to make Annie Talbot giggle.

But, then, maybe he didn't know about Annie's awards for elocution and the dignified way in which she usually conducted herself. Not that "dignified" was quite the way Sophie would have described Annie's behavior right now. Downright silly was more like it. On the other hand, she wasn't being any sillier than Marla May Purvis or Susan Stevens, and she was *much* better behaved than Eliza Neumann had ever dreamed of being.

Sophie frowned, then hastily tried to cover the expression by ducking down to retrieve a rag doll that Clara Randall's baby had dropped. Not that it did any good.

As she returned the doll, Clara shifted her baby and leaned so far forward that Sophie could see the pins anchoring the hairpiece of crimped bangs she wore. With a quick glance toward the man against the wall, Clara said conspiratorially, "It's absolutely *shameful*, the way those girls are carrying on." A twinkle of amusement in her eyes softened the disapproval as she added, "But I can't hardly blame them. He's the best-looking man in three counties, and that's counting my Joe."

Sophie mumbled something, she wasn't quite sure what, but Clara wasn't listening. "*You* should be over there with them, Sophie, not tending to old married ladies like me. Just go on over and introduce yourself. Take some of your honey bread, special for him. Can't do any harm and it might do some good."

Sophie fled.

Unfortunately, there wasn't much of anywhere she could go, so she claimed the safest spot she could find, a corner at the far side of the hall behind the serving tables. There the people coming back for more kept her hands busy and provided an effective barrier between her and the man who had quickly become the chief object of interest for every woman in the hall.

From her vantage point in the corner, Sophie inevitably heard all the gossip that was making its way through the assembled crowd. Most of it focused on Mr. Zeke Jeffries. Within a quarter of an hour, Sophie knew all she needed to know about his work habits (good), moral standing (upright), financial standing (poor but expected to improve), and his farming prospects (excellent).

Nobody bothered to wonder if he was interested in finding a wife. That was simply taken for granted. Speculation focused instead on which of the young ladies who presently surrounded him had the best chance of landing him, and whether or not one of the other available females who hadn't come to the social might grab him despite having lost the initial advantage.

Sophie almost found herself feeling sorry for him. She would have, too, if she hadn't been so worried about what her mother was up to.

There was no denying it. Adelaide Smith had outmaneuvered Delphi. She'd deployed her troops with consummate skill, backing Zeke Jeffries into a corner, then surrounding him with every eligible young lady of her acquaintance with the foresight to have attended the social.

Any woman of sense would give up and leave the matter of introductions for later, but not Delphi. Sophie knew her mother well enough to know that even now Delphi must be plotting an attack to counter Adelaide and her assembled forces.

Sophie didn't wait around to find out the details. The first chance she got, she slid from behind the table. Zeke Jeffries was nowhere in sight—probably buried behind a wall of women—and Delphi and Adelaide were at opposite ends of the building. It ought to be safe enough for her to slip away for a while.

With quick, brisk steps that made her skirt flip out in front of her, Sophie marched toward the hall door. From out of the corner of her eye, she spotted her mother headed in her direction, eyes glittering jaw set, and as intimidating as one of those massive traction engines under a full head of steam.

Sophie reached the screen door first. She pushed it open and charged out, not caring if it banged closed behind her.

She was just starting to step off the top of the wooden porch when her brain finally told her what her eyes had been focused on from the instant she'd stepped outside.

Zeke Jeffries, back turned toward the door, was standing on the lowest step. At the sound of her hasty exit from the hall, he jumped and whirled around, just in time to catch her as Sophie's foot hit the broken board on the fifth step, her ankle twisted under her, and she pitched head first into his arms.

Chapter 3

Sophie had read enough romances to know what happened when a woman fell into a man's arms. He caught her and clasped her to his manly breast, holding her safe, then bent his head to gaze soulfully into her brilliant blue eyes. Or emerald green eyes. Or maybe rich amber. The color didn't matter, so long as he gazed into them soulfully. It was at that point that he fell madly in love with her, of course, his tormented soul having seen the possibilities of love and trust and devotion latent in her bewildered, virginal gaze.

That was the way it worked in books, anyway.

That was not the way it worked for Sophronia Carter.

As Sophie plummeted downward, Zeke threw his arms up in a clumsy effort to fend her off. He was too late. Her forehead caught his nose a vicious blow. His head snapped back, throwing him off balance just as the rest of her weight hit him full force. With an explosive grunt, he pitched backward off the step like a bull calf at the end of a rope. His right hand struck Sophie in the side with lung-jarring force. His left grabbed her arm, dragging her down with him to the unmusical sound of seams shredding.

"Oof!" said Sophie as she landed on top.

"Aarrrrgh!" cried Zeke. His body curled in on itself protectively. His face turned redder than a firecracker, almost rivaling the bright red blood suddenly spilling from his nose. With another unheroic grunt, he threw her off him and scooted away like a crab in its death throes. He managed to get about two feet before he collapsed again, groaning and gasping for breath with his legs drawn up toward his chest and his hand clamped over his gushing nose.

From behind Sophie, the screen door to the hall banged open.

"Sophie, my love! Are you all right?" Delphi's usually dulcet tones had turned shrill, curdling Sophie's blood with the promise of worse to come. "What happened? Look at your clothes! Sophie, how *could* you?"

Sophie groaned and wondered if it was possible for a woman her size simply to melt into the ground and disappear.

Delphi's skirts swirled into view. Sophie tilted her head back to look up at her mother, only to find her mother wasn't looking at her. One glance at Zeke Jeffries' handsome, anguished face had stopped Delphi in her tracks. When it came to a choice between comforting her only child, or soothing the agonies of an eligible male, Delphi had her priorities, and it wasn't Sophie who came up on top.

Delphi's feminine charm reappeared with a rush. "Oh, Mr. Jeffries!" she cooed. "You poor, poor man. Are you all right? Is there anything I can do to help?"

Zeke sat up awkwardly. "I'm fine," he muttered from between bloodstained fingers. It actually sounded more like, "Arm phrine," but Delphi graciously ignored his lack of clarity.

"Oh, dear," murmured Delphi sympathetically. "Oh dear, dear, dear. Sophronia didn't really mean it. I'm sure she didn't."

More voices sounded from behind Sophie. The hall screen door banged open, a herd of feet clattered down the steps, and another dozen skirts swept past Sophie in a flurry of feminine lamentations. No one even paused to verify that Sophie had survived. They all gathered around their fallen knight instead.

Abandoned, Sophie cautiously propped herself up, her legs inelegantly splayed in front of her. The movement brought a wave of dizziness. Her ribs ached where he'd hit her and her forehead throbbed where his nose had struck her. Or she'd struck his nose, depending on how you looked at it.

Sophie sighed and closed her eyes, waiting for the dizziness to pass. At the sounds that signaled the emergence of yet another agitated body from the hall, she opened them again hopefully.

Adelaide Smith sailed over Sophie's outstretched legs without breaking stride. "Mr. Jeffries! Whatever hap—? *Mrs.* Carter! I might have known I'd find *you* here!"

Sophie squeezed her eyes shut. She couldn't bear to watch the coming carnage.

"Why, of *course* you should have, Mrs. Smith," Delphi said sweetly. "Unlike some, I'm *always* more than willing to help those around me who might be in need. Though if you and your church Maintenance Committee had seen fit to replace that broken step, which has been a problem for I'm sure I don't know *how* long, then my Sophronia would never have fallen and poor Mr. Jeffries—"

Sophie's eyes snapped open. *Poor Mr. Jeffries!* What about poor Sophronia?

"—wouldn't be sitting here like this, with his nose gushing and his nice suit gone all to tatters." Delphi drew herself up indignantly. If Mrs. Smith had been standing any closer, Delphi's swelling bosom would have knocked her over.

"Well!" Adelaide ruffled up like a banty hen itching for a fight. Her lack of inches, both vertically and horizontally, didn't seem to bother her any more than they would have bothered the hen. "I haven't noticed anyone else having problems with that step. But, there! What would you expect, knowing Miss Sophronia?"

Sophie glanced around for a hole to crawl into.

Zeke Jeffries tried to croak something from behind his bloodied hand. Not one of his dozen would-be rescuers paid the slightest heed. Their attention was avidly fixed on Delphi and Adelaide.

Delphi sniffed. A very loud, indignant sniff. "If I were you, Mrs. Smith—"

Sophie forced herself not to listen. With a groan,

she got shakily to her feet and tottered over to the knot of women around Zeke Jeffries.

"Excuse me. Excuse me please," she said, shoving her way between Adelaide Smith and her mother. Moses probably had an easier time with the Red Sea, but the two combatants eventually—and very reluctantly—drew apart, their eyes still darting daggers.

Sophie ignored them. "Mr. Jeffries?"

He squinted at her over his bloodied hand, then winced and hunched his shoulders, as if he expected her to launch herself against him.

A fine, brave man indeed, Sophie thought disgustedly, and immediately felt better about her own undignified tumble. "I'm very sorry for landing on you like that. I forgot about the step and when it broke . . . Well, I *am* sorry."

She leaned down and held out her hand, then immediately withdrew it, flustered. He'd used his right hand to cover his battered nose.

"S'aw'right," he mumbled. He tried to heave himself upward, but the unpleasant sound of his pants ripping scotched that effort. His face flaming, he slumped back down on the ground, a miserable, tattered object of pity.

Sophie sighed. So much for romantic heroes.

"Well, I should hope it's all right!" Adelaide Smith declared indignantly, rounding on Sophie. "Falling on him like any hoyden, knocking him over and making his nose bleed and ruining his good suit, to boot. Fine welcome to a newcomer, Miss Sophronia!"

"I didn't—!"

"My daughter would never—!"

Adelaide charged on. "I can see, can't I? The poor man probably didn't even have a chance to finish his meal and now look!" She gestured toward her hapless guest.

A dozen pairs of female eyes obediently looked.

The "poor man" shrank under the barrage of combined curiosity and eager female compassion. "Mizz Shmiff," he said plaintively from behind his gore-grimed hand. "Mizz Shmiff?"

Sophie half expected him to tug at his patroness's skirts.

Adelaide ignored him. Sophie had presented her with an undreamed of opportunity to embarrass her greatest rival for the leadership of the Ladies Missionary Society, and she wasn't about to throw opportunity away.

"A disgrace. That's what this is. A disgrace and an embarrassment, and I trust you're suitably ashamed, Miss Sophronia. Terrible, to let a thing like this happen. And a guest, too. As if the physical assault weren't sufficient."

Delphi's chest expanded as her lungs drew in air. Lots of air. "Physical assault! An accident caused by your not living up to your responsibilities, Adelaide Smith! If my poor Julius were still here, he'd tell you. Why, I've no doubt he'd be considering an action at law for dereliction of duty and . . . and reckless endangerment." She brought that last out with gusto, obviously pleased at the ominous legality of the words. "And to go blaming *my* Sophie for *your* mistakes. Well!"

"Action at law!" Mrs. Smith's voice turned shrill. "Action at law! Are you threatening me, Mrs. Carter?"

There was no stopping them now. Sophie didn't try. Instead, she knelt beside Mr. Jeffries—no use worrying about a little more dust, considering she was already covered in it from head to foot—and pulled her handkerchief out of her pocket.

"Here," she said, extending the neatly pressed and folded square of cambric. "Take this. And pinch your nose, don't just cover it. It will stop the bleeding sooner."

Zeke eyed the handkerchief, then her, then reluctantly did as he was bid.

Sophie knew how she was supposed to handle this. She'd read about it often enough. A proper, romantic heroine was fluttery and feminine and ever so gentle as she tended the hero's wounds—all received in a valiant defense of her honor, of course—and soothed his weary brow.

The trouble was, Zeke Jeffries' brow looked dirty, but not in the least bit wearied; there wasn't a whole lot she could do about an unromantic nosebleed; and, rather than having been rescued from a dastardly villain, some ungenerous souls might consider her guilty of assault and battery for having injured Zeke in the first place.

Romance was for books. Real life, at least for her, was plain-Jane practicality and she might as well get used to it.

"When you get home, soak that shirt in cold water," she said, grimly ignoring the argument between her mother and Adelaide Smith being waged above their heads. "After a couple hours, rub some good mottled German laundry soap into the blood spots, rinse it out, then soak it again in blueing, just to be sure." She frowned at his dangling coat sleeve and added, "I don't think there's any way to salvage your suit."

The suit's owner stared at her over the rapidly reddening handkerchief with the same kind of wide-eyed wariness he probably gave any stray madwoman he happened to meet, regardless of whether she'd physically assaulted him or not.

Sophie was about to suggest he try a cream laundry soap if he lacked the mottled German, when a well-modulated female voice broke in.

"Oh, Sophie! What a thing to be worrying about when you can see the man is in pain! As if he cared about his suit right now." Annie Talbot, petite, buxom, blond, and beautiful, suddenly materialized on the far side of the circle that enclosed Zeke Jeffries. She carried a bowl heaped with what appeared to be damp cloths, the perfect touch to complete the picture of womanly, nurturing charm.

At her appearance, Adelaide and Delphi broke off in mid-cry and turned to stare, clearly disconcerted.

Annie ignored everyone but the wounded man at her feet. With polished, maidenly grace, she knelt beside him and set the bowl on the ground.

Probably wouldn't even get dust on her skirts, Sophie thought sourly, and barely managed to keep from scowling.

"Here we are, then, Mr. Jeffries," Annie said sweetly. "When I saw what happened, I couldn't help but think you'd need something more than a handkerchief."

Zeke smiled. A rather weak, watery smile, to be sure, but he definitely smiled. Sophie rocked back on her heels and tried hard not to glare at either one of them.

"I thought a wet cloth might be better," Annie said. "I brought others so you could clean off the . . . the mess."

She blushed prettily, then delicately picked a cloth out of the heap and handed it to him. He instantly clamped it over his nose.

"Ahhh," he said, closing his eyes appreciatively. "T'ank yoo."

"Not at all." Annie picked up another cloth and leaned toward him. "Here. Let me make you a little tidier. But first . . ." Grimacing in distaste, she plucked Sophie's stained and sodden handkerchief out of his hand and held the wretched article out to Sophie. "I assume this is yours?"

Sophie gingerly took it by an unstained corner, then rose to her feet. Given the look of grateful adoration that Zeke Jeffries was bestowing on Annie Talbot right now, she was strongly tempted to toss it back in his face.

Or maybe in Annie's. She wasn't sure just which.

The blond lady's voice was balm to his suffering soul, her delicate touch that of a ministering angel. Zeke wished he could remember her name, but she'd been one of a horde of young ladies who'd corralled him in the hall and he'd been too gut-tearing scared to do more than nod when they'd been introduced. As it was, he'd considered himself lucky to get away with his skin intact.

Lucky, that is, until Miss Sophronia Carter dived

head first onto his nose, then kneed him in the groin as she landed. The woman weighed a ton and came equipped with more sharp angles than a box of angle irons.

On the brighter side, the golden creature dabbing at his face right now was doing her best to make him feel better—and her best was mighty good. A man appreciated a little feminine sympathy and attention now and again, even if he was sitting in the dirt with his best suit in tatters and his pride lower than the dust on the seat of his britches.

Little enough chance he'd get either sympathy or attention from Miss Sophronia. Once she'd given up lecturing him on his laundry, she'd shooed away the gawkers and sent Mrs. Smith in search of Hiram and the buggy, but her apology had been as lame as a three-legged mule. Now she was towering over him like an angry scarecrow that had scared off the crows and was starting to work on driving away the corn, too, just for the hell of it. To look at her, you'd think *he'd* been the one landed on *her*!

At that moment, Hiram came driving around the corner of the hall. Mrs. Smith was sitting beside her husband, stiff and straight as the wrath of God and clearly twice as riled.

Hiram pulled to a stop about five feet away. "You all right, Zeke?" he asked, leaning out of the buggy, eyes wide and Adam's apple bobbing nervously. He made no move to climb down and help. Probably didn't dare leave Mrs. Smith in the buggy alone for fear she'd drive off without him.

"Just fine, now you're here, Hiram." Zeke grinned weakly. "I appreciate your bringing the buggy around." Now he wasn't pinching his nose, his words sounded only a little bit furry and thick.

Beside him, Miss Sophronia stirred restlessly, as if she wanted him to quit jawin' and get on with it. The angel plopped the soiled wash rag in the bowl, then wrapped her hand around his arm.

"Let me help you, Mr. Jeffries," she breathed into his ear.

Zeke jumped. He'd never had an angel blow on his ear. It was a mighty unsettling experience, especially under the circumstances.

"I can manage, ma'am, thank you," he said, and tried to scootch backward a foot out of her reach. He was pretty sure his drawers were showing through what was left of the seat of his britches and he wasn't too anxious for anyone, let alone her, to be checking out the condition of his underwear along with everything else.

"He has a bloodied nose, Annie, not a broken leg," Miss Sophronia said tartly. Zeke couldn't help thinking, if she'd been a sour cherry pie, she'd have made a man's mouth pucker for sure.

Zeke felt a little safer once he had his rump firmly planted on the buggy's hard bench seat. He also felt a whole lot more capable of facing the angel and Miss Sophronia since the buggy let him look down on them instead of staring up from somewhere around knee level. Not that he should be thinking about things like knees when it came to the ladies, of course, but he couldn't deny it had been a tad unsettling.

"Miss Annie." He nodded. "Thank you for your help. Miss Sophronia."

"You will take care of yourself, won't you, Mr. Jeffries?" Annie the angel said in a voice so sweet and clear it was almost like hearing church bells chime to listen to her.

"Er . . ." said Zeke, discomfited by those wide blue eyes staring up at him with such intensity.

"I imagine Mr. Jeffries is perfectly capable of taking care of himself, Annie," said Miss Sophronia, coming up behind the angel.

Zeke couldn't help noticing how she towered over the petite blond, without much of any curve to soften the long climb from her toes to the top of her head. And yet . . .

He blinked, and looked down into those gold-brown eyes, and for the first time he wondered if maybe she wasn't feeling even more embarrassed than he was. There was something fragile in those brown depths, like the frightened, uncertain gloss in a jackrabbit's eyes when it was trying to decide whether it was safer to stay put, or run like hell.

Miss Sophronia Carter wasn't one to run, it seemed, for she edged closer to the buggy and stared up at him. Zeke swallowed uncomfortably. Her eyes might reveal her uncertainty, but the rest of her was as stern and straight and stiff as before.

"I truly am sorry for falling on top of you, Mr. Jeffries," she said primly. "It was all my fault, but it was *not* intentional."

Annie the angel giggled, then immediately pressed the tips of he fingers to her mouth to stop her smile. Her big blue eyes sparkled enchantingly.

Mrs. Smith, who'd shifted around so she could keep a sharp eye on affairs, sniffed loudly. "I should hope not!"

Hiram's neck got a little redder and a little shorter as he hunkered down on the seat, but he didn't say a word. He'd had far too much experience with his wife's opinions even to try.

"No, ma'am," Zeke said, trying to ignore the charming picture Miss Annie made, standing there in sunlight that was the same bright gold as her hair. "I didn't figure you'd planned it. That step could've broken under anybody." Miss Sophronia's hair didn't glow at all. It was mostly hidden under a brown straw hat, and what wasn't hidden was pulled up so tight a man couldn't help wondering if her scalp didn't ache from the strain.

"Well, I imagine you'll want to get on home," Miss Sophronia added, stepping back from the buggy, chin high. She didn't exactly turn away, but she shifted so Zeke couldn't see her eyes, just the thick, unexpectedly lush lashes and the delicate flush on her cheek.

"Yes, ma'am," Zeke said, relieved.

"Humpf!" said Mrs. Smith.

Hiram straightened on the seat, obviously relieved. "Get up!" he said, flicking the reins to set his horse in motion.

"Will we be seeing you next Sunday, Mr. Jeffries?"

Annie the angel cried as Hiram urged the horse into a trot.

Zeke pretended he didn't catch her question.

"You're always welcome, you know! Come back anytime!" she called after them. Her voice carried clearly over the rumble of the wheels and the rapidly widening distance between them.

Zeke caught a glimpse of her waving good-bye, just as if they were family and she was sorry to see them go. A dozen paces behind Annie, Miss Sophronia stood watching them like a tall, brown shadow somehow lost in the sunshine that surrounded her.

To Zeke's amazement, they were a full three blocks away from the church before Mrs. Smith started scolding.

Chapter 4

The townsfolk hadn't had such a juicy bit of gossip since Franklin Frederick, the town's leading ne'er do well, had run away with the new schoolmarm a year earlier, and they made the most of it. By Monday afternoon, the town was buzzing.

Sophie's friends were more than willing to share the news of her notoriety. They dropped in by ones and twos all day long, just to keep her updated.

The worst was when Annie Talbot and Eliza Neumann showed up with Marla May Purvis in tow and Delphi, who had refused to talk to Sophie, invited them in for iced tea and cookies.

Annie ignored the food and drink in favor of recounting, for everyone's benefit, exactly how hard and strong Zeke Jeffries' muscles had been, and how big he'd seemed when she was standing right there beside him.

"He's just like a hero out of a romance," Annie said dreamily. "Tall, dark, and handsome. Why, I bet he'd even be able to lift *you* in his arms, Sophie, for all you're so much bigger—er, *taller*—than the rest of us."

Sophie blushed and the others giggled.

"And he has the most beautiful eyes!" Annie added. "Like the aquamarines in Mother's necklace, and *you* all know how pretty *that* is. If you can get him to open them. I swear, I don't think he even tried to until Mr. Smith came around with his buggy. You'd have thought I was an ogre and going to eat him up, he was so nervous!"

"He was just scared of Sophie!" Eliza Neumann

objected, ever ready to defend her friend and perfectly willing to sacrifice Sophie in the process. "His wits were still rattling around in his head. After all, first Sophie landed on him like a sack of flour, then Mrs. Smith and—"

Too late, Eliza remembered who their hostess was. She bit her lip and colored up, then added, "and all the rest of us sort of surrounded him, clucking over him as if he were dying or something. I'll bet he was just embarrassed. And you have to admit his suit was an absolutely awful mess! *I'd* hate to be caught with my clothes torn like that. And in public, too!"

"I kept watching him when we were in the hall, before he managed to sneak away," Marla May admitted with a snicker. "I couldn't help wondering if he was going to bust through the seat of his pants right there! Did you ever *see* a man in a suit that tight?"

"And that haircut! I've seen *sheep* that were better trimmed! Though I've never seen one that looked that good!"

"You should have just dragged him off while you had the chance, Sophie. You're the only one of us big enough to do it!"

And so it had gone, until Sophie had wondered if she could convert and join a nunnery. Preferably one in darkest Africa, where she could wear a veil and no one would have heard of her.

It didn't help that, for the second night in a row, she dreamt of a man with aquamarine eyes who devoured her with a thousand hungry kisses, then swept her up into his arms and carried her away to his magic castle, which, for some odd reason, had cows grazing out in front and watermelon vines growing over the ramparts.

Tuesday, April 12, 1893

Hiram dropped by today to apologize again for dragging me to the social. I told him not to worry. At least with my suit turned into a pile of rags, there's a pretty good chance I'll be able to steer clear of any more of these affairs.

Something had been puzzling me, though.

"Hiram," I said. "What I can't understand is why none of the men came out to razz me, what with me like a fool sitting in the dirt and all."

He choked, and then he stuttered a bit, and then he came out with the truth.

"The womenfolk wouldn't let 'em," he said. "Jeff Talbot told me his wife threatened him with beans and rice for a month if he embarrassed you and turned you off their daughter. You know, Annie, the one who cleaned you up?"

I remembered Annie just fine. A fellow would have to be half dead not to.

"Seems the other fellows got warned, too, one way or another," Hiram said. "It was just the ladies allowed to slip out, and if it hadn't been for Miss Sophronia drivin' 'em away, Lord knows if you'd ever've got to your feet without causin' a scandal."

"Oh," I said. There wasn't much to say after that, but I couldn't decide if I should be grateful, or nervous as a bull calf at a roundup when the hands are planning on a feast of roasted bull oysters after.

Hiram looked at me long and mournful, like a man at a good friend's funeral, and then he said, "The ladies have staked you out as prime property, you know. You don't drink and you don't smoke or chew tobacco. You're a hard worker with a good farm, even if it has been let go somethin' awful. You're the best-lookin' feller in three counties, accordin' to Mrs. Smith. And you're single."

He pushed out his lower lip and shook his head real sad like. "Zeke," he said. "You haven't got a prayer."

Now, I'll admit the situation looks grim, but I can't agree it's totally hopeless.

One good thing about that social, I made such a fool of myself even Mrs. Smith seems to have given up on me. Haven't seen hide nor hair of her since they dropped me off after.

Mainly because she pretty well covered matters on

the drive home. She had some mighty unkind words to say about Miss Sophronia, and a whole lot more against Miss Sophronia's mama. She had a few disapproving words for me, too, of course, though I could tell she was holding back mighty fierce in case she said what she was *really* thinking.

Once she'd said her piece, however, she quieted down some and kept her comments on safer topics. Such as how it was a pity Mrs. Todd couldn't make a potato salad a body could eat, and that Mr. Granger had taken back to the bottle, despite poor Mrs. Granger's best efforts and some substantial praying from the ladies of the Christian Women's Temperance League.

Other than bachelor men like me who are trying hard to steer clear of the ladies, nothing stirs up a woman more than a man who's fallen off the straight and narrow. Oh, and babies. But babies, thank God! don't require so much from us menfolk. Ladies like Mrs. Smith will give us credit for having started 'em in the first place, but they don't think much of our ability to deal with 'em after. Which suits most of us just fine, leastwise till they're over that dirty diaper and spitting-up stage.

Anyhow, all I have to worry about is Mrs. Smith getting her matchmaking instincts warmed up again. I don't have any intention of falling off the straight and narrow—there's too much work around here for that nonsense—and if I can keep clear of Mrs. Smith and her flock, I won't have any cause to worry about babies. Or young ladies with their matchmaking mamas.

"He'd make a fine husband for my Sophronia," Delphi Carter informed her guest. "A real gentleman. I could tell right off, first thing I met him. But now . . ."

Even safely out of sight in the kitchen, tending to the midday dishes, Sophie could picture her mother's grim expression.

"It's all that Adelaide Smith's fault," Delphi continued. "If she and her church Maintenance Committee had gotten that step fixed like they were supposed to, my Sophronia would never have fallen like that.

Certainly *not* to throw herself at a man like that Adelaide is suggesting. Scandalmonger, that's what she is, and not a scrap of decency in that scrawny little body. Though it *does* grieve me that a fine young woman like my Sophronia hasn't got a husband and children, and her turned twenty-six last March. It's a worry. I know you'll appreciate just how much a worry it is, Mrs. Bassett, what with your four daughters and all."

Sophie tried to keep her attention on the dishes, to no avail. Nothing could drown out Delphi's complaints. Her mother had been on a perfect tear ever since Annie Talbot had left on Monday, and that was two days ago. If not for the timely arrival of Mrs. Bassett, the president of the Ladies Missionary Society, Delphi might be ranting at her yet. When roused, Delphi Carter could outtalk a politician, and there was no doubt Delphi was roused.

If it had been on any subject other than her daughter's feminine failings, Delphi would have been enjoying herself mightily. But Delphi was *not* enjoying herself, and neither was Sophie, though her sufferings had little to do with her mother's incessant lectures and lamentations. She was already accustomed to those.

No, what troubled her was her body's insistence on reminding her how it had felt being pressed close to a man like Zeke Jeffries, even if it was only for a few seconds. Waking or sleeping, she was haunted by potent memories that made her heart beat faster and her skin grow warmer until Sophie was afraid she might break out in a sweat just thinking about it. Memories of the firm, masculine curve of his chest, the flat solidity of his belly pressed to hers, the long, powerful reach of his thighs.

Even the most descriptive of her favorite books had never gone into near the detail that her memory—or her imagination, she wasn't always sure which—was so willing to produce. And if the books were missing that kind of information, Sophie couldn't help wondering what else had been left out.

Of course, at her age she had a pretty good idea

how things worked between a man and a woman, and she'd once seen a man's . . . er . . . apparatus when she'd unexpectedly come across a stranger relieving himself against a tree west of town. She hadn't meant to intrude, mind you, but what was a body to do when she'd been berry picking and she comes up through the brambles to find a stranger standing on the side of the road not five feet from her with his pants unbuttoned and his member out there for all the world to see?

Evidently he'd been so intent on his job, he hadn't heard her thrashing around in the underbrush. When she abruptly emerged, he'd yelped, then swung away. But he hadn't been able to stop peeing, which meant he'd cut a pretty impressive arc along the side of the tree and over the roadside weeds as he turned. Soon as he'd finished, he'd given himself an anxious little shake, then buttoned up and climbed back on his horse and lit out for parts unknown. She'd never seen him in town since, and Sophie couldn't help wondering if the embarrassment and the fear of running into that wild woman in the brambles had convinced him to stay away.

Not that it had anything to do with romance, of course, but it had been a memorable experience. Other than her friends who'd had to take care of their little brothers, which didn't really count, Sophie didn't know any women who'd seen a man's member until they actually got married. And then they tended to titter and blush and say archly, "*You'll* find out when *you're* married," in response to all questions, as if they were determined to keep their friends as much in the dark about such matters as they'd been before their wedding night.

Which might have been all right if Sophie were sure she'd *have* a wedding night. Unfortunately, she wasn't at all sure she would. Prospects weren't good, and with the word spreading that her mother pounced on every promising bachelor who came within reach, she was afraid she'd died a spinster, always wondering what it would be like for a man to make love to her.

Well, no use repining, Sophie thought, stacking the last of the pans. Until she'd landed on top of Zeke Jeffries, she'd thought she'd come to terms with reality. One minute's accidental intimacy—an intimacy he'd made clear he hadn't appreciated—couldn't be allowed to upset her peace of mind.

The scrawny calico cat that had kept its nose in a bowl of canned sardines for the past ten minutes looked up as she moved away from the sink. "Meow?"

"What's the matter, Adelaide?" Sophie asked, bending to scratch behind the creature's ears. "You can't possibly want more sardines."

The cat insisted she did, in fact, want more sardines. She rubbed against Sophie's skirt, then returned to her bowl, shoved it hard with her nose, and "meowed" again. The little lift at the end of the "meow" indicated that a drop of milk wouldn't go amiss, either.

Sophie had found Adelaide, the Cat in the alley over three years ago, half starving and badly battered from a fight that had left one ear with a permanently tattered edge. She still looked flea-bitten and malnourished, even though she ate enough for four cats and no self-respecting flea would be caught dead on that scruffy hide.

It was Delphi who had insisted on naming her Adelaide, the Cat—including the comma and the capital "C." The cat, according to Delphi, was just like her namesake: scrawny, ugly, and argumentative.

Sophie put Addy out, despite the cat's plaintive insistence that starvation was imminent.

She had other, more important things to worry about right now than an alley cat's demand for more sardines. Things like a visit to the bank that she'd been putting off, and trying to find one scruffy, towheaded boy and give him the book she'd bought for him.

The first gave her a perfect excuse to get out of the house. If she was lucky, no one would never find out about the second.

The minute Sophie walked into the bank, the two clerks behind the wrought-iron tellers' grills looked up. They looked at her, then they looked at each other, and then they turned back to her.

"Good morning, Miss Sophronia." Somber Mr. Thorn actually permitted a faint twinkle to appear in his pale eyes.

"Mornin', Miss Sophie. Fine day," stocky Mr. Finley said. His grin was so wide that his fat gray mustache stuck out like a scrub brush.

Sophie's heart fell. They'd heard about the social, then. It shouldn't have surprised her—they'd have had a steady flow of gossiping customers since Sunday, and Mr. Finley's second son's wife was an enthusiastic member of the Christian Women's Temperance League, whose membership included Annie Talbot's mama. Given Delphi's penchant for gossip, she should have known just how fast juicy tidbits could make the rounds of a small town.

Still, in this case a little more ignorance on their part would have been bliss for her. Her only hope, Sophie thought gloomily as she signed for the withdrawal, was for some scandal to come along and divert everyone's attention.

The minute she had the money, Sophie tucked the folded bills into her handbag and fled. She hoped she was mistaken, but she'd almost swear it was grim Mr. Thorn she heard chuckling as the heavy oak doors of the bank closed behind her.

Sophie made a deliberate point of pretending she didn't see the knowing smiles exchanged over the cash register between Mrs. Purvis and the grocer, Mr. Goveneur, when she sailed into the latter's store five minutes later. She had a harder time ignoring old Roger Makepiece after he spotted her from his favorite spot between the cheese board and the cracker barrel.

"Miss Sophie!" he cried, loud enough for everyone in the store and half the loungers on the street to hear. "You're looking mighty pert. Taken any dives off any steps lately?"

A snicker, suddenly choked off, came from somewhere behind the potato bins. Most likely the stock boy, but Sophie couldn't be sure.

She ignored both the snickerer and the sudden quiet from around the cash register. "Why, no, Mr. Makepiece," she said with forced calm, "I haven't. These days, I'm a little more cautious of broken boards than I used to be."

Roger wagged his head in mock dismay. "That's no way to do it, Miss Sophie. No way at all. You know what they says, don't you? Practice do make perfect."

"Do they?" said Sophie, desperately trying to pretend she wasn't in the least affected by his teasing.

" 'Deed they do!" the old man said, and snickered. "And if you need some help practicin', Miss Sophie, you just tell me. I'd be right happy to help."

"Have a piece of cheese, Mr. Makepiece," Sophie said politely, repressing an almost overwhelming urge to hide behind the pickle barrel.

"You had oughta give that cheese to Zeke, you know," said Mr. Makepiece, mashing his toothless gums together in a trollish grin. He tilted backward in his chair and cocked a thumb toward the rear of the store. "He's back there. Hidin', most probably, though could be he's just havin' a hard time decidin' does he want the sack of flour with the pink roses, or mebbe the one with them blue flowers would be prettier. Mighty particular about his dish towels is Zeke."

Caught between mortification and an unexpected excitement, Sophie froze. She was vaguely conscious of someone choking up at the cash register. The snicker from behind the potato bins was rapidly turning into an outright chortle, and Roger Makepiece looked so pleased with himself it was a wonder he didn't pop his suspenders. All of that faded compared to her sudden and intense awareness of the stillness at the back of the store.

Zeke Jeffries? Here? Her good sense said run. Her body, suddenly gone dizzy and slightly weak in the knees, insisted she stay.

"Zeke? You there, boy?" Roger called out. "Come on out and say hello to Miss Sophie proper like." When the silence stretched, he added, " 'Less'n she climbs up on a chair or one of these here counters, I don't imagine she can get the height she'd need to fall on top of you. I do believe you're safe."

"Mr. Makepiece!" Sophie protested, flushing scarlet.

The floorboards at the back of the store creaked, then a tall, broad-shouldered shadow emerged and came toward her cautiously. Zeke Jeffries stopped a safe distance from her. Sophie couldn't decide if he deliberately kept the cracker barrel and three stacked cases of canned sardines between them or not, but there was no denying his lack of enthusiasm. Or his wariness. The latter stuck out as plain as prickles on a porcupine.

Wary or not, he was as breathtakingly good-looking as ever. The cowlick at the crown of his head still waved defiantly, but every other trace of the absurd had disappeared when he'd discarded his celluloid collar and shredded suit. Dressed in a rumpled, sturdy blue work shirt, bright red suspenders, and plain work pants, Zeke Jeffries was . . . well, magnificent didn't seem too strong a word. Not too strong at all. The simple, unpretentious clothing fit him surprisingly well, emphasizing his raw strength and solid size in a way that was reassuring, rather than intimidating, and providing an almost unsettling contrast with the sculpted perfection of his face.

Sophie forced herself to look away, swallowed uncomfortably, and felt her heart suddenly slide back into place and start beating again.

"Miss Sophie, you remember Zeke Jeffries, don't you?" Roger said with a totally spurious air of polite inquiry. "Zeke, this is Miss Sophronia. I do believe you were introduced proper at the social, but you might have forgotten some, what with that rattling your brain box got afterwards."

"Miss Sophronia," Zeke said at last.

His voice sound a little stiff and about a half octave higher than normal. Assuming she'd ever heard him speak in a normal tone, which was doubtful.

"Mr. Jeffries," Sophie said. "You . . . your nose? It's all right?"

He shifted his weight from one foot to the other and back again. "Just fine." A pause. "Thanks for asking."

Around them, the store had grown quiet as a church before the sermon. Sophie had the uncomfortable sense that everyone there was watching them, wondering when—not if!—she'd launch herself at him. As if she'd *ever* deliberately behave like that in public. Why, she didn't even flirt like some of the young women she knew!

That thought wasn't as comforting as it might have been. It was too harsh a reminder that she didn't have any cause *to* flirt.

"That's good," she said instead. "About your nose, I mean."

"Yes," said Zeke.

Another apology about now was probably called for, but she'd already apologized twice and Sophie was darned if she was going to try for a third time. Not with so many curious ears turned her way!

"Well," she said. "Good to see you again."

"Yes," said Zeke.

If the avid ears in the room didn't fall off out of sheer boredom, it certainly wouldn't be her and Zeke's fault, Sophie thought.

The floor creaked loudly as Zeke shifted his weight once more. "Well," he said. He cleared his throat. "Guess I'd best get back to business."

Mr. Makepiece chuckled wickedly. "Did you decide on them yellow flowers, or the blue ones?"

Zeke frowned at him hard enough to melt wax.

Sophie blinked, startled by the big man's unexpected fierceness. Under that shambling, gentle exterior was a bit more spirit than she'd thought.

"Me, too," she said brightly, then winced. Her mother wouldn't have approved of so egregious a grammatical slip. "I'd better get going, that is."

Zeke looked relieved.

"Well," Sophie said, and backed up two steps, just far enough to trip over a crate of onions someone must have maliciously set behind her when she wasn't looking.

Roger Makepiece cackled in delight, then brought his chair back to all fours with a thump. "If you two are goin' to be jawin' away like this, I'm going to need some extra nourishment just to make it to dinner. Want a cracker, Zeke? Or would that maybe stop up your windpipe so you couldn't keep rattlin' on like you are?"

Sophie slunk toward the front of the store, as far out of Roger's range as she could get. Though she tried to tell herself she really wasn't interested, she found herself straining to catch the sound of Zeke Jeffries' footsteps as he retreated to the back of the store, out of sight.

It didn't take her long to select the few items she wanted. Mrs. Purvis, primed with the latest word on Sophie's nonexistent relationship with Zeke Jeffries, had already shot out of the store. As she set her purchases on the counter, Sophie tried not to think of where Marla May's mother might have been headed. The number of eager gossips in easy reach of Goveneur's Groceries was simply too large to calculate without giving yourself a headache.

"That it, Miss Sophie?" Mr. Goveneur wiped his fingers on the vast apron wrapped around his substantial middle and eyed her over the tops of his steel-rimmed glasses. When Sophie nodded, he added, "You don't usually do your shopping on a Wednesday, do you?"

Sophie jumped, startled by the unexpected question because she'd been trying to listen for movement at the back of the store. "What? Oh, no. No, I don't. This is for old Mrs. Franklin. I haven't been out to see her for a while and I thought I'd just take her a few things.'

When she'd grabbed the book on electricity, it had occurred to Sophie that she'd need an excuse for wandering around the less reputable side of town in case somebody spotted her. Fortunately, the Widow Franklin came ready made, so to speak. Both Sophie and Delphi visited her a couple of times a month and her tumbledown house wasn't all that far from where Sophie was really headed.

"That's nice of you, Miss Sophie," the grocer said, beginning to tote up the items she'd selected. "You just tell Mizz Franklin hello for me, will you?"

"I'll do that, Mr. Goveneur," Sophie said. "I'll do that."

The creak of the floorboards warned her that someone was approaching. Someone far too massive and sure on his feet to be either the stock boy or Roger Makepiece. Sophie decided not to wait for Mr. Goveneur to wrap up her purchases in a neat bundle. She began throwing them higgledy-piggledy into the string bag she'd brought, heedless of the grocer's open-mouthed surprise.

"Just remembered. I have to run a quick errand for Mother, first," she fibbed. "Bye!"

Sophie was almost a block down the street before she realized to her dismay that she'd grabbed up the grocery bag, but left her handbag on the counter. She hesitated. She could always pick it up on her way back home; Mr. Goveneur would keep it safe for her. Then she remembered that the *A. B. C. of Electricity* was in the handbag. She *had* to go back for it, whether she wanted to or not.

Rather than charge in and risk running into Zeke Jeffries, Sophie peeked through the front window first. With the afternoon sun shining bright, she had to cup her hands around her face to see much of anything inside, but Zeke was large enough she figured she wouldn't easily miss him, regardless.

The way looked clear. Mr. Goveneur was bent over the counter making some notes in a ledger book, but there was no one anywhere near him. Either Zeke had left or he was at the rear of the store, far enough away for her to be able to safely retrieve her handbag and run.

Relieved, Sophie pulled open the screen door and sailed right in—and smack into Zeke Jeffries. She jumped back at the same time he did, but he dropped the three cans of tomatoes he'd picked off the top of the display in the other front window.

Sophie gave a little cry of dismay, bent to retrieve the fallen cans, and promptly banged heads with Zeke. He clapped a hand to his bruised forehead and jerked upright and out of danger. She staggered back two steps, her hand firmly clapped over her mouth. *No sense making a bad situation worse by cussing and having Delphi hear about it.*

The thought made her feel slightly sick to her stomach. Delphi would hear about this additional embarrassment, one way or the other . . . and she'd probably hear it before Sophie even got home.

Sophie stared at Zeke and wondered how difficult it would be to move to Montana. "I'm so sorry."

" 'Scuse me, ma'am."

"I didn't mean—"

"Should've been watching where I was going." He didn't take his eyes off her as he gingerly stooped to retrieve the cans he'd lost.

"No, it's my fault, I—"

Mr. Goveneur chuckled. "You come looking for this, Miss Sophie?" he asked, holding up her handbag.

"I— Yes. I didn't mean— That is, I forgot—" Sophie abruptly abandoned all attempts at explanation. *"Thank you!"* she said, and grabbed the bag and ran.

Chapter 5

"My, my, my." Mr. Goveneur shook his head and stared at the screen door through which Miss Sophronia Carter had disappeared. "Don't recall I've ever seen Miss Sophie so flustered."

He shoved his spectacles up his nose, then held on to them while he tilted his head back a fraction and peered across the counter at Zeke, frowning slightly.

Zeke suddenly felt like he was six again and old Preacher Eames had caught him with a frog in his pocket at Sunday School.

"Hmmm," said the grocer. He brought his head back to an even keel and let go of his glasses, which immediately slid down to the very tip of his nose. "Most times, Miss Sophie's the nicest, politest, best-mannered lady you'd ever want to meet. Not like that mother of hers. Missus Carter is a terror, even if she is one mighty fine specimen of womanhood."

"Mmrrmm," said Zeke. He suddenly realized he'd retrieved only one of his three cans of tomatoes. Blame it on Miss Sophronia. His wits had gone begging the minute she walked in the store, and now they looked to be coming back empty-handed.

He bent with awkward haste to pick up the closest can and set it on the counter. He had to get down on his hands and knees to retrieve the third, which had wedged itself behind two squat barrels of dried beans. By the time he got to his feet, Zeke's face was uncomfortably flushed. With any luck, Mr. Goveneur would put the red down to his crawling around on the floor and wouldn't realize it was really the thought of Miss Sophronia that was responsible.

Of all the fool things, to find himself blushing over a spinster lady who bid fair to make him the laughing-stock of the entire town! Yet there it was, plain as the nose on his face . . . or the red on his cheeks.

He'd tried—Lord knew he'd tried!—to put her out of his mind, but he hadn't been able to forget those soft, gold-brown eyes that had looked up at him there in the churchyard. Miss Annie had been prettier, sweeter, and a lot more gentle, precisely the kind of lady any man of sense would fix on if he could, yet it was the memory of Miss Sophronia's eyes with their fear and those long, long lashes that came back to pester him when he least expected it.

And then he'd gone and made an even bigger fool of himself by cracking heads with her and dropping the canned tomatoes. Just when he'd thought he was safe, too.

There he'd been, rooting around in the shadows at the back of the store among what Mr. Goveneur called his "farinaceous goods," trying to decide if he'd be better off with a bag of Aunt Jemima's pancake flour, or whether he should try the unfamiliar, and less expensive brand of self-rising pancake flour, instead. His mama had sworn by Aunt Jemima's and disapproved of self-rising flours on general principles, but there was no denying his last batch of flapjacks had been a mite flatter than they should have been.

Caught in the middle of a dilemma like that, he'd been almost grateful that the jangle of the brass cowbell over the door had interrupted his cogitations.

He'd looked up and there she was, standing in the open doorway with the sunlight streaming in behind her, highlighting her slender figure and setting the few wisps of hair that had escaped her hairpins to glowing like spun gold. Of course, on Sunday he'd have said she was thin, not slender, but he hadn't been at his best then, and Hiram had put the fear of God and Mrs. Carter in him so he wasn't prepared to be generous. This time, he'd had plenty of opportunity to study Miss Sophronia from a safe distance, and there was no denying her waist tucked in and her hips curved

out in a mighty tempting way. Nothing blatant and
bold, like Miss Annie's curves, but definitely tempting—and all the more appealing for being a bit more
of a secret, so to speak.

Miss Sophronia didn't bustle around like most ladies
did, either. Instead, she'd kind of . . . floated into the
store. He'd have sworn that even the floorboards
didn't creak when she crossed them, though Goveneur's Groceries had darned near the noisiest floor of
any place in town.

Even though he'd been admiring her from the safety
of the shadows, Zeke had to admit he'd been hoping
she wouldn't come far enough back to find him. He
certainly wouldn't have ventured near her if old man
Makepiece hadn't teased her something unmerciful,
then dragged him out from the shadows like that. Miss
Sophronia had looked to be holding her own despite
her embarrassment, but the minute she'd clapped eyes
on him she'd gone red, then white. Plain as the nose
on his face, she'd hoped never to see him again.

He certainly hadn't helped matters any. Polite conversation never had come easily to him, but it had
been downright impossible when conducted under the
amused stare of Roger Makepiece and within earshot
of Mr. Goveneur and his customer. Not to mention
the stock boy, who had finally run out the back door
rather than risk being clouted for laughing out loud.

What with all his fool stammering and stuttering,
Zeke figured Miss Sophronia had him pegged as a
half-wit, at the very least. And probably bad-
tempered, to boot, given the way he'd behaved when
she'd clobbered his nose on Sunday. It hadn't been
her fault that step broke when it had, but, looking
back on it, he guessed he hadn't been any too
understanding.

And yet, just thinking of her, Zeke could feel a
stirring in the middle of his pants that had been plaguing him off and on for days now. Ever since Sunday,
in fact. Or at least since that particular portion of his
anatomy had recovered from Miss Sophronia's sharp-
kneed assault on it.

"Trying to think if you forgot something, Zeke?"

Zeke jumped, startled out of his thoughts, and stared blankly at the grocer. "Beg pardon?"

The grocer grinned. "I asked if you'd forgot anything. Other than me, that is."

"He didn't forget you, Josh. You're too ugly for that." Mr. Makepiece sauntered up to the counter. His words were for the grocer, but his bright little eyes were firmly fixed on Zeke. Or rather, on Zeke's pants. "I suspect Zeke, here, had his mind on other things."

For the second time that morning, Zeke blushed, then edged closer to the counter where matters wouldn't be quite so obvious. Since he couldn't think of any good comeback to the old man's suggestive comment, he stared at the pile of foodstuffs he'd assembled. Something nagged at him, insisting he was forgetting something, but he hadn't the faintest idea what that something might be. After a moment's fruitless effort to remember, he shrugged and pulled out his wallet.

"Guess that's it, Mr. Goveneur."

"I don't see no sack of flour there, Zeke," Mr. Makepiece said. "Or couldn't you decide between them roses and the blue ones?"

Flour! That was it. He'd been trying to decide between Aunt Jemima's and the self-rising when Miss Sophronia had walked in and rattled his brains. Just the thought of her was enough to get things stirring again.

"I forgot. I need some pancake flour," he told Mr. Goveneur, shifting from one leg to the other uncomfortably. "That self-rising kind."

"Flour ain't the only thing around here that's what you might call self-rising," Mr. Makepiece said, eyeing the front of Zeke's pants respectfully. "Myself, I'd have said you were doing purty well on your own, but there, you never can tell about the younger generation, can you, Josh?"

When Zeke, scarlet-faced, finally escaped from the store five minutes later, the two men's laughter was still ringing in his ears.

* * *

By the time she left Mrs. Franklin's after an hour's exhaustive chat, Sophie had almost managed to put the thought of Zeke Jeffries out of her mind. Almost.

Not that it mattered. After today, he'd run like a rabbit with hounds on its tail if she so much as came within hailing distance. He'd be a fool not to. Heaven only knew what further bodily harm she might inflict on him, otherwise.

Sophie forced away the thought and concentrated on where she was going. Rocky Ford wasn't that big, but she wasn't often in this part of town. There were no street signs to guide her through the maze of small clapboard houses that shouldered in between store-houses, livery stables, and other odd and sometimes dirty businesses scattered along roads that were more like rutted wagon tracks than city streets.

Sophie didn't have directions to the boy's house, but she thought she could identify it since Delphi had complained at such length and in such extensive detail about the way his mother, Mrs. Peabody—the "Mrs." was commonly considered a sop to propriety rather than a title honestly earned—had treated them when the Ladies Missionary Society had come calling.

She'd never have said it to her mother, but Sophie had come sympathy for the woman. A drunk and a fallen woman she might be—she was certainly an unfit mother—but no one deserved to have so large a contingent of the Society inflicted on her without warning, especially not when the members were at their most righteous and her mother was leading the charge.

After a half hour's futile search, Sophie was almost wishing her mother was leading *her*. She'd found any number of gray, weatherworn houses, but nothing to indicate which of them was the one she sought.

The lack of identifying marks was a disappointment. She'd been hoping for the infamous red light that was often mentioned when the ladies were whispering among themselves. Or perhaps a sign that gave its true nature away by its pretensions, like "Mrs. Peabody's Parlor." Sophie wasn't sure what she'd expected, but she'd certainly expected something. The house's anonymity was a sharp disappointment.

Either she would have to ask directions from someone, or she'd have to give up and go home.

The idea of revealing, even to a stranger, that her destination was the house of a scarlet woman wasn't particularly appealing, but Sophie didn't like giving up, either.

After a minute's consideration, she decided to ask directions at a nearby blacksmith's shop. The place had a solid, prosperous air about it, and the sleek, if mismatched pair of mules hitched to the wagon parked out front indicated a respectable clientele.

Sophie edged around the mules—she'd never had enough experience with farm animals to feel she could trust the brutes—and marched up to the open doors of the smithy.

With the bright sun outside, the gloomy interior of the tin-roofed building seemed black and oppressively hot. Sophie could make out the rough outline of the unheated forge and a couple of workbenches, but not much more.

"Hello?" Her voice echoed. Sophie nervously ventured farther into the shop. "Anybody here?"

"The smith's around back, ma'am," said a pleasantly deep, masculine voice from the doorway behind her. "I'd be glad to fetch him if—"

Sophie turned. "Not you!"

Zeke Jeffries froze in his tracks. His eyes went wide with shock.

"I mean— That is, I didn't mean— Oh, dear!"

"Were you— Uh, were you looking for me, ma'am?"

"Absolutely not! I was just— That is—" Worse and worse. Sophie took a deep breath, tightened her grip on her handbag, and tried again. "I'm looking for a . . . a house and I wanted to ask directions. From the . . . the smith. I had no idea, none whatsoever, that you were here. Not an inkling. Really! I—" She choked and swallowed all the rest of the words that wanted to tumble out, in spite of her resolve.

"Oh."

Zeke apparently couldn't think of a thing to say after that. He shrugged uncomfortably and looked away. He looked at the wall of the smithy, the door frame, the ground—anyplace except at her. He shoved his hands in his pockets, then evidently remembered that a gentleman didn't do that in the presence of a lady, and immediately pulled them out again and stared at them as if he wasn't quite sure where they'd come from or what he was supposed to do with them now.

Of one thing he seemed to be certain, however— he stayed right where he was, safely out of reach.

If it hadn't been for the smith finally appearing from around the side of the building, they might have gone on forever, standing and staring at each other like a pair of witless pigeons.

The smith, a grimy, solid barrel of a man with massive muscles and hair as black as the iron he worked didn't seem to notice anything amiss. He grinned and waved some sort of metal contraption. "Haven't had a chance to work on those parts for that crazy traction engine of yours, Jeffries, but I found your coulter. Good as new. Trouble was, I set it down with another batch of work and couldn't find it right off. You'll be knowin' how that is, I fancy. Though how *you'll* be managing all you've planned with just you, a plow, and that ugly pair of mules is something I can't figure, since it's sure you'll never get that engine going."

Zeke, clearly relieved, edged around Sophie as cautiously as she'd edged around the mules. "Grateful to you, O'Boyle. How much do I owe you?"

Mr. O'Boyle didn't pay him any attention. He bowed and flashed Sophie one of the widest, whitest smiles she'd ever seen. "Patrick Dwayne O'Boyle, at your service, ma'am. And what might I be doin' for you, then?"

Sophie smiled uncertainly, still too flustered by Zeke Jeffries' presence to think straight. "I . . . I'm afraid I'm lost. I thought perhaps you might help."

"Of course! Patrick O'Boyle has never disappointed

a lady in distress. Never! And what might it be you're looking for?"

"Well, I . . . That is . . ." Bad enough to tell a stranger, even a charming stranger like Patrick O'Boyle, where she was going, but she wasn't too anxious for Zeke Jeffries to hear as well. She took a deep breath and thought fast.

"I'm looking for a little boy. Towheaded. Very thin and scruffy. About this high." She held her hand out, palm down, to indicate the approximate height. "He lives with his mother somewhere near here."

"A boy?" O'Boyle cocked his head to one side and regarded her doubtfully. "There'll be any number of little boys hereabouts, ma'am. Would you be knowin' his name, perhaps?"

She'd hoped he wouldn't ask that question. "Well, no, actually, I don't. He's interested in electricity," she added hopefully.

Zeke had taken advantage of the diversion to deposit his coulter in the back of his wagon. Being a sensible man, he stayed right where he was, safely out of reach, waiting for his opportunity to pay his bill and run.

O'Boyle scratched the side of his rough-shaven jaw and looked bemused. "Might you be knowin' anything more about the lad, ma'am? It'd help to sort him out from the rest of the little boys, you see."

Sophie reluctantly forced her attention away from Zeke. "I believe his mother's name is Mrs. Peabody."

"Mrs. Peabody!" O'Boyle straightened up as fast as if she'd hit him. "Now what would you be wanting with a lady the likes of Mrs. Peabody?"

"I don't want anything with Mrs. Peabody," Sophie snapped, embarrassed and painfully conscious of Zeke Jeffries staring at her as if she'd suddenly grown two heads and a tail. "I want to talk to her son."

"Are you a teacher, then? Or maybe a lady from the church?" O'Boyle frowned, then added, "Though usually the church ladies come more in a flock, so to speak, bless their hearts."

"I'm neither a teacher nor am I the representative

of any church," Sophie said with forced dignity. "I have a book for the boy, that's all. But I can't give it to him unless I can find his house, so please, if you know where he lives, could you tell me how to get there?"

"Well, now," said Patrick O'Boyle, clearly at a loss. "Well, now."

"Well, what?" Sophie demanded. "Will you tell me, or won't you?"

O'Boyle frowned. "Tellin' you is just what I won't be doin', ma'am. Mrs. Peabody's is no place for the likes of you, book or no book, and that's the truth."

This time it was Sophie's turn to draw herself up straight and stiff. "Then I will just have to ask elsewhere. Thank you for your time, Mr. O'Boyle. I'm sorry to have troubled you."

Before she could take two steps, Zeke Jeffries was blocking her path. "Patrick's right, ma'am," he said with an apologetic grimace. "Mrs. Peabody's is . . . it's . . . well, it's no place for a lady."

"Indeed? I assume you are sufficiently acquainted with the place to know?" An instant after they were out, Sophie regretted her words, but it was too late to take them back.

The red on his face almost matched the red on hers. "No, ma'am. That is to say . . . The fact is . . ." Zeke floundered to a halt. He frowned at her, then sighed. "You're dead set on going, I can see that, but that still doesn't mean you should be visiting there."

"Are you afraid Mrs. Peabody will attack me?" Sophie demanded with asperity. "Or, perhaps, her son?"

"No, ma'am." He hesitated, as if debating whether to explain himself further, then reluctantly added, "But that's not to say that some fellow who's . . . erm . . . visiting, so to speak, might not step outside the limits of what's right and proper. Not knowing, you see, that you and she aren't . . . er . . . acquainted."

That stopped Sophie cold. She hadn't even considered the possibility that she might be mistaken for a loose woman. She'd never had problems with men getting fresh with her, gentlemen or not.

Sophie couldn't help it. The thought of anyone not blind or dead drunk mistaking her, lanky, too tall, plain, spinster Sophie, for a woman of easy virtue, was simply too absurd. After the strain of the past few days and her humiliating display in Goveneur's Groceries, she simply couldn't take anymore—and she certainly couldn't take it seriously. She burst out laughing.

Zeke stared at her, then stared at the smith, clearly at a loss on how to deal with the madwoman in front of him. His sober expression made her laugh so hard that tears formed and her sides hurt.

"Oh, dear," Sophie said at last, fighting for control. "I'm sorry, Mr. Jeffries. I know you're being kind, but that . . ." She gave a little hiccup. "That really was quite a silly suggestion."

She took a deep, steadying breath, and dabbed away a tear that lingered in the corner of her eye. "Now, if you'd be so kind, could you *please* tell me where I can find Mrs. Peabody's house?"

Zeke crossed his arms across his broad chest and frowned even harder. His frown changed to an expression of puzzled frustration when Sophie refused to look away. He shook his head like a bull baffled by the defiance of a scruffy terrier, and turned to look at O'Boyle, who'd been watching the exchange with obvious interest. Instead of finding support, Zeke evidently discovered a solution, for his frown disappeared and his eyes lit up.

"I'll tell you what!" he exclaimed, turning back to Sophie. "Mr. O'Boyle will be glad to see you get there and back without any problems!"

"I'll *what*?"

Sophie was just as shocked. "That's ridiculous!"

"Patrick's a good man," Zeke urged. "You can trust him to get you there safe and see you home again."

"That I'll not! I've a customer coming and I've promised to meet him here, faithful. Why don't *you* go with the lady?" O'Boyle demanded.

"Me?" An instant before, Zeke had been bright red beneath his tan. At the suggestion that he should be the one to accompany Sophie, he paled until there was almost no tan left. "I couldn't leave my mules. Besides—"

"Your mules will be fine right where they are. You must know where the place is as well as any man. When the lady's delivered her book, you can collect your wagon, pay me the four bits you owe me, and take her home. That's not so much trouble, now, is it? Not when a pretty lady needs your help."

"But—"

Sophie didn't wait to hear Zeke's objections. She didn't want to, nor did she need the humiliation of listening to the two men arguing about who would be inflicted with the responsibility for escorting her.

"Thank you," she said with haughty dignity, "I'll ask directions elsewhere."

She was halfway up the block when Zeke caught up to her.

"Ma'am?" he said anxiously, stumbling in a deep rut. "Miss Sophronia?"

Sophie didn't turn her head. "I said thank you, Mr. Jeffries, but I do *not* need your help."

"But . . . But it's not proper, ma'am. *Believe* me."

He said it with a conviction that shook Sophie. What kind of depraved place was she walking into? Delphi hadn't said anything other than it was shabby and run-down, but if—

No! There was nothing indecent about what she was doing. Ill-advised, perhaps, but *not* wrong!

"I am going to give a little boy a book, Mr. Jeffries, nothing more," she said with determination, clutching her handbag and the book it contained closer to her. "Nothing terrible will happen to me and if, by some absurd chance, some man should mistake me for . . . That is, if someone should be rude, I'm quite sure I can take care of myself, thank you very much."

She was almost stomping now, angry, embarrassed, and resentful that, once again, the Fates had conspired to make her look a fool in front of Zeke Jeffries. Zeke was stumbling along beside her, puffing in the effort to keep from twisting an ankle in a rut and trying to reason with her at the same time. Out of the corner of her eye, Sophie could see people standing in shop doors or on sagging porches watching them go past obviously amused at what they probably mistook for a lover's spat.

"Miss Sophronia? Miss Sophie? If you'd just listen to me, you'd see—"

Sophie halted and turned on him, furious at him for making her feel a fool. "I will *not* listen to you, Mr. Jeffries. If you do not desist from this . . . this unwelcome attention, I will scream. Or I shall hit you. And *this* time it will be deliberate!"

He gaped at her, stunned by her unexpected attack.

Sophie ducked her head and stormed past him. She desperately wanted to weep from mortification, but she wasn't willing to do it in front of witnesses. She wasn't willing to do it in front of *him*! That was all that would be needed to ensure she never had the courage to face him again. Not if she lived to be a hundred.

"But, ma'am!"

Furious and fighting tears, Sophie swung around to confront him. Her foot in its stiff, high-heeled boot hit a ridge of dirt and twisted, then slid into the deep rut on the other side. She staggered, cried out, and pitched forward into Zeke Jeffries' arms.

Maybe it was the practice, but this time he caught her.

He staggered slightly, but his strong arms closed around her, easily encircling her. He pulled her close against his broad chest, then shifted, regained his balance, and somehow—Sophie was too dazed to be sure just how—lifted her free of the rutted track and set her down on flatter ground.

It was a mad, foolish thought, but for an instant— just an instant!—she hoped he wouldn't let her go, that he'd go on holding her and . . .

The thought thrilled through her, shocking and utterly irresistible, all at the same time. Reluctantly, Sophie stiffened, preparing to be set free, almost ready to stand on her own.

Bur Zeke didn't let her go, and he didn't ease his hold on her. Inexplicably, he pulled her closer against him.

"Oh!" Sophie said, and blinked at the collar button in front of her nose. "Oh, dear."

His shirt was coarse, warm from the sun and the heat of his body. Through the rough cloth Sophie could feel the hard line of shoulder bone and the unyielding curve of hard muscle across his chest. She could hear the erratic beat of his heart.

Strange. Didn't men's hearts keep the same one-two beat a woman's did?

He was so solid, so comfortingly substantial, so reassuringly *large*.

And he was warm. His body, his arms around her back, his breath that caught the edge of her cheek as he breathed out . . . the simple heat of them sent her own temperature soaring.

"Are you . . ." He sounded a trifle breathless. "Are you all right?"

It took a moment for Sophie to collect herself sufficiently to reply. "I . . . think so."

It was a lie. She couldn't possibly be all right if her heart was pounding hard enough to hammer its way out of her chest. Nor was it normal for the blood to be racing in her veins, or her breath to come in quick, excited little gulps, or her muscles to melt until she wasn't at all sure she'd be able to stand on her own if he let go of her.

If only he would kiss her . . .

The thought snapped her back to an acute awareness of exactly where she was and what she was doing . . . or wasn't doing, which was standing on her own, as any lady would be expected to do when in public.

"Thank you," she said, so faintly he had to bend his head to catch it.

She should have pulled free of him, right then and there. Any proper lady would have.

But Sophie didn't pull free . . . and he didn't make any effort to release her. Instead, he bent closer still, as if he expected her to say something more, and Sophie found herself staring at him, memorizing the intimate details of his face.

His lashes were short, thick, lush like sable. Annie had been right. His eyes *were* the color of aquamarines, but she'd neglected to mention the faint circle of darker blue at the edge. He had a dimple beside his mouth, Sophie realized, so small it was almost invisible unless one were as close as she was. She could see the pores of his skin and the faint, rough stubble of his beard, though he'd obviously shaved that morning. She could see the minute patch of day-old beard he'd missed, just there, under the curve at the back of his jaw, and the—

"Oh, my!" she said, and clumsily shoved away from his chest. It wasn't easy. Her hands where pinned between them and her handbag bumped against her side because its handles had slid up over her elbow.

"Sorry. I . . . That is . . ." he said, and awkwardly helped her stand on her own.

"That's all right. So silly," she faltered, and shakily checked to see if her hat was still firmly on her head. She wasn't sure why.

He stared at her, then hesitantly reached out and shifted her hat a tad back toward center. For an instant they remained like that, his hands lifted, his fingertips at the edge of her hat, scarcely touching her hair. Then he abruptly snatched his hands back and rammed them in his pockets.

"Sorry. It's . . ." He cleared his throat uncomfortably. "You pushed it out of whack."

Her scalp tingled where he'd touched her.

I wonder what it would feel like to run my finger across his chin, along his jaw? she thought, and blushed.

"All my fault," she said, and briskly slapped at her skirt. Not that her skirt was at all dusty or disordered, but she couldn't think of anything else to do that would enable her to avoid looking at him without being rude. "So clumsy. I should have been watching where I was going."

He didn't say anything, didn't move. Sophie glanced up, embarrassed by his silence, and found him watching her, his big body suddenly taut with tension. His mouth was slightly parted, as if he were having trouble drawing in sufficient air. His eyes were wide and fixed on her, the pale blue of the iris almost swallowed up in the black of the wide, round pupil.

His stare wasn't the kind that comes from curiosity. It wasn't rude, either. But it *was* profoundly unsettling . . . and Sophie, to her surprise, found she liked it very much.

The thought sent an odd charge of energy shooting through her, like fizzy bubbles through ginger beer after it's been shaken hard.

She smiled, only to have him duck his head and turn away. "Hadn't we best be going, ma'am?"

He couldn't have brought her back to reality more effectively if he'd doused her with a bucket of ice water. They'd covered half a block before Sophie remembered to say, too stiffly, "Thank you."

Zeke glanced at her out of the corner of his eye, then as quickly looked away. "You're welcome, ma'am." He cleared his throat again—Sophie could see his Adam's apple bob—and said, "Awful rutty road."

"Yes." *Scared to face me,* Sophie thought, suddenly depressed. If Annie Talbot were here, for sure he wouldn't be avoiding *her*.

Sophie restrained the urge to give a good, swift, *hard* kick to a stone that lay in her path.

If Annie Talbot were here, *Zeke* wouldn't be here. They'd probably be sitting on Annie's front-porch swing, so close their arms touched. He'd be smiling at her and sipping the lemonade she'd squeezed specially for him, and she . . .

Sophie sighed. No use thinking about what Annie would be doing. Annie didn't have to *do* anything to attract a man's attention; men swarmed on her like bees on honey, regardless.

And Sophie drove them off just by standing in one place. Or falling on top of them.

"Maybe . . ." Zeke said hesitantly, breaking into her thoughts. "Maybe you'd best take my arm." He blushed. "Because of the ruts, you know." Awkward as a marionette, Zeke held out his arm, elbow crooked.

Sophie stared at him in surprise, then relief. Maybe she hadn't driven him away after all.

"Thank you," she said, and cautiously slipped her hand through the crook of his elbow.

"Mind that rut," Zeke warned, and, hand pressed tight over hers, led her to a less uneven strip of ground. The move meant he had to walk in the weeds, but he didn't seem to mind.

Sophie floated all the way down the street and around the corner, but she came back to earth with a thump when Zeke stopped in front of a peeling gray picket fence.

"Urmm," he said, and cleared his throat nervously. His smile was gone, wiped clean off his face. "This is it." He gestured at the tumbledown cottage behind the fence. "Mrs. Peabody's."

Sophie's grip on his arm tightened. "Oh," she said, and was conscious of a vague disappointment.

There wasn't anything remarkable about the house or the tiny, weed-choked yard. A couple of scrawny hollyhocks at one corner of the house bore testimony to a time when someone had considered the place something more than mere shelter. Nothing had been done to the place for some time and now the paint was peeling, the roof was missing a few shingles, and the crude wood porch was sagging, as dull and de-crepit as the rest of the place.

Sophie couldn't see anything that would identify the place as a local attraction. She really would have liked a red light. She'd heard about cities that had entire neighborhoods classified as a red-light district, which sounded interesting. Rocky Ford couldn't boast such a distinction since Mrs. Peabody was the only "working" woman in town. At least, so far as Sophie knew.

"Something the matter, ma'am?" Zeke asked, frowning down at her.

"You're sure this is the place?" Sophie said doubtfully.

He stiffened. Sophie could feel the sudden tension in his arm, sense it in the rigidity of his body.

"Erm, yes, ma'am. I'm sure," he said, and blushed.

Silently, Sophie cursed herself for a fool. At the time, she hadn't thought it strange when he hadn't had to ask Mr. O'Boyle for the directions to Mrs. Peabody's. And thinking about it now, it wasn't. Strange, that is. He was a good-looking young man in the prime of life—and he was unmarried. Of *course* he would know where Mrs. Peabody's was!

Disappointment stabbed at her, but she resolutely ignored it. Zeke Jeffries' private life was his concern, not hers.

"You want me to, er, leave the book?" Zeke asked.

"No. No, thank you. I'd like to talk to him myself. If he's home," she added, as she realized she hadn't considered that possibility, either.

Nothing ventured, Sophie thought, letting go of Zeke's arm and pushing open the gate. The gate was in serious need of oil for its hinges.

The squawking gate didn't bring anyone to the door, and neither did Sophie's first timid knock. Sophie strained, trying to catch any sound from within, but everything was still and silent. Even the big cottonwood that shaded the tiny yard didn't stir.

Zeke stood at the gate, face tight with embarrassment and clearly uncertain whether he ought to remain where he was, or stand by Sophie's side on the step.

Sophie knocked again, louder this time. And this time a chair scraped across a wood floor, followed by the heavy thump of someone lumbering toward the door. The door opened silently and a whiskey-roughened voice demanded, "Who is it?"

"Ms. Peabody?" Sophie asked, trying to make out

the details of the dark head she could dimly see outlined by the light of the room behind her.

"I ain't interested in no churchin', so you can just git and stop wastin' my time."

"I'm not from any church, Mrs. Peabody. My name's Sophie," Sophie thought it wiser not to mention her last name, in case Mrs. Peabody connected her with the Mrs. Carter who had tried to storm the barricades earlier. "I've brought a book for your son that I thought he'd be interested in."

She held up the book so the title was clearly visible, though she was careful to keep it out of reach in case Mrs. Peabody decided to grab the book and slam the door in her face.

Mrs. Peabody leaned forward, squinting against the light in an effort to read the cover. To Sophie's surprise, the woman wasn't much older than she was, and her face wasn't the hardened, booze-roughened visage she'd expected. Mrs. Peabody might actually be pretty if she cleaned up and took the time to brush her hair and iron her clothes. As it was, her dull brown hair trailed down her neck in straggling hunks, as unwilling to submit to the discipline of a hairpin as she was to public opinion, and her wrinkled and stained percale wrapper hung on her slim figure like a laundry sack waiting for laundry.

"Thomas don't need no books," Mrs. Peabody announced at last.

Thomas. If nothing else, at least now she knew his name. "He was very interested in this one," Sophie said.

"Is that so?" The woman peered out at her suspiciously, ready to slam the door if she tried anything. "How would you know? An' who are you, anyway?"

"I'm just a friend. And I know he was interested because he pointed it out to me at Hodgeson's Emporium last week," Sophie explained. "I happened to come up to the book display when he was looking at it. We got to talking and . . ." She shrugged. "I bought it, but he was gone before I had a chance to give it to him."

Evidently the mention of Hodgeson's Emporium triggered a memory because Mrs. Peabody snarled, "I don't know nothin' about no baskets!" and slammed the door in Sophie's face.

Chapter 6

Sophie couldn't help grinning. She hadn't said a word about baskets. She hoped the two of them had enjoyed the pork chops. They'd been the best the butcher had in stock.

"I'm not here about a basket, Mrs. Peabody," Sophie shouted through the crack. "I just want to give Thomas the book."

Not a word. The little house was completely silent. Zeke shoved the gate open, clearly prepared to come to her aid, but Sophie waved to indicate he should stay where he was. She wasn't quite sure what the etiquette for visiting a whore's house while accompanied by one of her customers was, but she'd just as soon not strain the conventions that far.

She waited until he reluctantly shut the gate and retreated a little way down the road, out of direct sight of the door and half hidden by the cottonwood. Satisfied, Sophie turned back to the house.

"Mrs. Peabody?" She rapped on the door. "Mrs. Peabody! I know you're there. I'm not here about the basket, and I'm *not* going away until you tell me where I can find your son and give him this book."

A minute ticked slowly by before Mrs. Peabody decided to open the door again. Just a tiny crack, smaller, even, than the first time she'd answered.

"You ain't from the school board, is you?" Mrs. Peabody demanded suspiciously.

"No, I'm not. Though I do occasionally get drafted to teach Sunday school."

"Sunday school!" Scorn squirted through the crack. Mrs. Peabody, evidently roused, swung the door wide.

"Don't need no Sunday school, neither! And I sure as hell don't want none of you fine church ladies comin' 'round here tellin' me how to raise the boy. No, nor lead my life, neither!"

"I'm not trying to do anything of the sort!" Sophie snapped, her patience worn through. "Here!" she added, thrusting the book at the woman. "See for yourself! There's absolutely nothing in that book to which you can possibly object."

Mrs. Peabody grudgingly accepted the book. "How can I be sure 'bout that?"

"Just take a look at the pictures. If you're like me, all that stuff about electricity and ground wires and resistance won't make any sense. But Thomas is interested in it. It will make sense to him." From the way she was handling the book, Sophie was pretty sure Mrs. Peabody couldn't read, but there was nothing to be gained by insulting the woman.

Mrs. Peabody frowned hard at the cover with its fancy scroll work and neat letters, then at the spine, then casually flipped through a few pages before reluctantly handing the book back to Sophie.

"I s'pose it's okay, if Thomas wants it." She nervously wrapped one arm around her middle, propped her other elbow on it, and started gnawing on her knuckles while she stared at Sophie as if she expected her to turn into a frog right in front of her.

Sophie calmly returned her stare.

"Why're you goin' to all this trouble for the boy?" Mrs. Peabody demanded at last, clearly at a loss. "You ain't got no need to get involved with him and that book musta cost a whole dollar. Mebbe more. So why're you botherin'?"

What explanation could she offer, Sophie wondered? Not the real one, that in Thomas Peabody she'd recognized a fellow dreamer. That she'd seen the longing in his eyes, felt the passion stirring in his scrawny, dirty little body.

"I . . . I just thought he'd like it," she said at last, knowing that it must sound as lame to Thomas's mother as it did to her. "I read. A lot. So I understand about wanting to own a special book. And he wanted to own this."

Was that sadness she saw flickering in the pale gray depths of Mrs. Peabody's eyes? Sophie wondered. Was it shame? Or some other, far more complex mixture of emotions that encompassed both, and more besides?

Tentatively, Mrs. Peabody reached out and slowly ran the tip of her finger along the edge of the book that Sophie held. She refused to meet Sophie's questioning gaze, but Sophie could see she was chewing on her lower lip and her brows were furrowed as if at some thought that hurt. Badly.

"He ain't never had much," she said softly, so softly Sophie could barely hear her. "I s'pose it won't hurt none for him to pretend about this, too."

She drew back her hand, but she continued to chew her lower lip and stare at the book, as if it offered answers to questions she was too afraid to ask.

Abruptly, like a dog shaking off water, Mrs. Peabody shook off her strange, sad mood. All her earlier anger and hostility came back with a rush as she stepped back, away from Sophie.

"He's out back cuttin' firewood," she said curtly, indicating with a jerk of her head where "out back" was. "If you can catch him, I guess you can talk to him. He don't cotton to strangers much, though. Might be he'll hightail it before you can get three words in crosswise."

Sophie beamed, undaunted. "Thank you!"

"But don't you go botherin' him too much," Mrs. Peabody snapped, just as if Sophie had suggested the two of them spend the rest of the afternoon lying around in the shade and drinking lemonade. "He's got work to do and he ain't got no time to be wastin' readin' or dreamin' about what he can't have."

Before Sophie could respond, she took another step backward, half disappearing into the shadows behind her, and slammed the door in Sophie's face.

*   *   *

Zeke could just see her through the branches of the cottonwood, standing on that rickety porch like she dared anyone to say otherwise. He'd thought about objecting, but Miss Sophronia was a determined lady and no mistake.

He could still feel the slight pressure of her hand where it had laid on his arm. She hadn't worn gloves, which was unusual for a lady as prickly about the proprieties as she was. Come to think of it, though, she couldn't be all *that* prickly if she hadn't objected to him holding on to her for as long as he had, or if she was willing to march up to Mrs. Peabody's, bold as brass, all so she could give a book to a boy whose name she didn't even know.

Truth was, she seemed a good deal less embarrassed to be here than he was. Probably because she didn't have anything to be ashamed of and he . . . well . . .

Zeke squirmed, remembering the night he'd come all the way into town with the intention of paying a visit to Mrs. Peabody. He'd been driven by a hungry fire in his belly and an aching loneliness that wouldn't quit, and he'd been absolutely sure he could go through with it until he pulled up in the street not too far from where he stood now.

He'd sat there in the dark and the cold for what must have been an hour, maybe more. It had seemed like eternity, and all of it spent on the edge of hell.

Physical need, curiosity, a desperate urge to talk to a woman, even for a little while—they'd all twisted through him like vicious snakes, biting at him and making him writhe. Nobody had passed him in all that time, no one had entered or left the little house, yet he'd been achingly self-conscious and desperately afraid of being caught out, of making a fool of himself.

A man his age, he was afraid they'd say, and still a virgin? He could almost hear the raucous laughter that would greet that kind of information. Most of his friends had had a fling or two with a fancy woman long before they got married. One still had his flings, even after he'd married his childhood sweetheart and had three children. Like a drunk that wanted to reform but couldn't give up the bottle, he'd told Zeke he couldn't give up the thrill of doing something he knew he shouldn't, regardless of what he stood to lose if he got caught.

But *he* didn't have anything to lose, Zeke had told himself. *Except your self-respect,* a whiny little voice in his head had insisted.

Even now the memory of that struggle bit at him, wounding him anew, until Zeke had to grab hold of the fence to keep from running.

While he'd sat and suffered through the battle between his conscience and his demons, Zeke had watched the lamp-lit windows of the cottage. The cheap muslin curtains had hidden details, but they hadn't been able to block out the shadowy image of a woman, the lamp behind her, crossing in front of the windows every now and then.

She'd had her hair down. Zeke remembered that vividly. Once she'd raised her arms above her head and leaned back, as if she were stretching out the kinks in her muscles. He'd avidly studied each movement and prayed that she would remain where she was for a little longer, and all the while his imagination tormented him and his body burned and ached for the release that only a woman could grant him.

In the end, it wasn't his conscience or any of the stern moral principles his mama had tried to drill into him that had made him turn away. It was shame, pure and simple.

The minute he got home, before he'd even unhitched the mules, he'd filled a bucket full of water from the pump in the yard and then he'd poured every icy drop over his head, heedless of his clothes or his boots or the cold bite of the late March night air. He couldn't remember now how many buckets he'd filled and dumped. His arms grew tired with the effort long before the rest of him quit burning.

Afterward, he hadn't tried to sleep. Still dressed in his sodden clothes, heedless of a wintry wind that cut to the bone, he'd thrown himself into whatever hard, physical labor he could find that could be done by lamplight. He'd kept on throughout the following day, driving himself without rest until his body was too tired and sore and aching to torment him. And then he'd fallen into bed and dreamed of soft, female bodies pressed close against his, whispering secrets in the dark.

Since then, whenever the need and the loneliness hit harder than usual, he'd put the energy into the farm where it belonged. Someday—someday soon, he hoped—the farm would be doing well enough and he'd be far enough out of debt that he could think of taking a wife. But until that day came . . .

Zeke's grip on the rough wood pickets tightened until a sliver of rotten wood pricked his palm.

He breathed out hard and forced his hands to ease their grip, his muscles to relax.

Until that day came, he'd do well to stay away from temptation, no matter how it came dressed and primped to deceive him.

Through the leaf-heavy branches of the cottonwood he could see the two women standing on the rickety front stoop, the one lush and slatternly, the other tall and stiff and prim. One available, for a price; the other beyond his reach because a man who wasn't planning marriage didn't fool with decent women. Not ever.

In spite of the silent inner warnings, however, it was on Sophronia that his gaze fixed. Something in her proud carriage, in her determination, in the way he'd felt when he'd held her in his arms drew him to her, willy-nilly.

And that scared the hell out of him.

When Sophie came through the front gate, Zeke was standing in the dusty, weed-choked shade of the cottonwood, his hands shoved deep in his pockets, his shoulders hunched, his expression one of stoic misery.

She'd seen that look before. It was the expression all males above the age of five wore when they'd been told to wait while their wives or sisters or mothers engaged in some embarrassingly feminine activity, like discussing babies or having a corset fitted.

If Zeke had been standing under a sign marked "Ladies Underwear," he couldn't have looked more miserable.

"Thomas is out back," Sophie said, striving not to laugh. She didn't often have a man waiting for her, and she rather enjoyed the experience, no matter what his expression. "His mother says he might well run away if he sees me coming, so I thought maybe you could go around back and make sure he can't get out that way. If you wouldn't mind, that is?"

Zeke nodded assent and set off for the dirt track that led to the open prairie behind Mrs. Peabody's house.

Sophie found the boy in the long, narrow yard at the back of the house as promised, but he wasn't working. He was sitting on top of the stump he'd been using as a chopping block, morosely pitching bits of wood and bark at the sagging wire fence that ran down one side of the weed-infested lot and around the back of a dilapidated chicken pen at the far end. Tall, scraggly lilac bushes lined both sides of the property from front to back, providing a no-doubt useful aura of privacy.

The sound of the weeds brushing against her skirt made him look up. She could tell the instant he recognized her. His eyes widened and his mouth opened, as if he wanted to cuss but the words got stuck somewhere at the back of his tongue. An instant later, he was on his feet and sprinting for open country.

At the last possible moment, Zeke stepped out from behind the screen of lilac bushes, straight into the boy's path. Thomas dodged right. The minute Zeke followed suit, he dodged back and went zipping past his would-be captor, slick as greased lightning.

The only trouble was, the change in direction put him on a direct course for the run-down chicken pen, rather than the prairie. He didn't try to swerve. Instead, he yanked open the slatted door to the pen and darted inside, throwing the dozen or so residents into squawking, flapping confusion.

Even at a distance, Sophie could see the grin of

satisfaction on Zeke's face. Instead of trying to chase the boy all over kingdom come, all he had to do was corner him in the pen. Simple.

He hadn't reckoned with Thomas Peabody. The boy dashed into the falling-down coop and emerged an instant later with two hands full of fresh chicken droppings.

"You ain't gettin' me!" he shouted, and let fly.

Given his overlarge size and the restricted dimensions of the pen, Zeke didn't have a chance. He took one round on his ear, the other squarely in the chest.

The shock of it held him for a moment, stunned and gaping. Just enough time to give Thomas a chance to reload. Two more rounds connected, then another two, while the outraged hens flapped and squawked and careened into Zeke's legs and off again.

The next round of chicken droppings missed their target as Zeke ducked, then charged the bunker.

Thomas dived back inside, out of sight.

The chicken coop was small, far too small for Zeke to have a chance of going inside after the boy. He planted his shoulder against the side of the opening and, taking care to keep his face protected, groped inside in the dark, obviously on the assumption he could grab the boy, even if he couldn't see him.

He was wrong. While Zeke was blindly fumbling about, Thomas shoved up a back corner of the coop wall that was dangling by two bent, loosened nails, and scooted through. The minute he was out, he grabbed hold of the edge of the coop's roof and swung himself up, clearly bent on jumping through a gaping hole in the wire cover of the pen to the freedom beyond.

He almost made it.

Sophie cringed at a sudden, vivid vision of the boy's mangled, bleeding body caught on the wire. Instead, Zeke grabbed him in midair and dragged him down.

Zeke crowed in triumph.

The boy screeched, furious at the treacherous attack. "Put me down! Put me down, you stinking hunk of goat turd!"

He kicked and flailed and squirmed and squawked, but Zeke had a firm grip around his middle and a triumphant smirk on his face. Taking care not to bump his head on the low frame, he edged out of the pen, then settled Thomas under his arm like a sack of flour, head to the rear, and started in Sophie's direction.

"Bastard! Snot-nosed pile of pig swill!" Thomas shrieked. "I di'n't steal no basket and you can't say I did!"

All Sophie could see of him were his scrawny legs and two bare feet, soles black as crusted tar, thrashing wildly at the level of Zeke's waist. Judging from the loud thumps emanating from behind Zeke, the boy was pounding on his conqueror's broad back and rock-solid thighs with fury.

"I'll cut your heart out! I'll fry your liver and feed it to the chickens! I'll sic old man Clyde's dog on you and he'll tear you limb from fat, ugly limb. Just see if he don't!"

Zeke didn't pay any more attention to his captive's dire threats of vengeance than he did to his protests of innocence. Instead, he plowed through the weeds headed straight toward Sophie.

Sophie had to fight to keep from breaking out laughing.

Five minutes earlier, Zeke had been clean and neat in his worn work clothes. Now his shirt was smudged with black and white in four different spots, he had an ugly black streak across his cheek, black-and-white speckles adorned the arch of his ear, and he had a scratch on his chin that oozed blood. Despite the disaster of his appearance, however, Zeke looked disgustingly pleased with himself and with life in general.

In fact, Sophie had never seen him look quite so cheerful. Maybe she'd made a mistake in falling on him and bloodying his nose, instead of pitching chicken droppings at him, right off the bat. Perhaps if she suggested the idea to Delphi—

The enthralling vision of what Delphi would say if her daughter ever so much as mentioned chicken droppings to an eligible male was broken by a loud and anguished yelp. But this time the yelp came from Zeke, not Thomas.

"*Damn*! Why, you—! Here, now!"

For an instant, the battle was in doubt. Thomas managed to wriggle out of Zeke's flour-sack hold on him, but just before he broke free Zeke grabbed a thick handful of shirt at the back of the boy's neck and heaved him into the air.

Like a fighting fish on a hook, Thomas twisted and jerked and wriggled, but this time Zeke wasn't letting go.

"Quit squirming, you feisty little bantam," he snapped, glowering at him fiercely. "I'm not going to hurt you!"

Sophie couldn't tell if Thomas believed him or not. He certainly didn't obey him. As Zeke stomped over the last of the weeds, Thomas did his best to land a solid kick in his captor's rib cage, but without success. Zeke was more wary this time, and alert for his tricks.

He set the boy on his feet in front of Sophie and cautiously released his hold on his shirt. Like a jackrabbit released from a trap, Thomas instantly leapt over a stickery clump of weeds and bounded away.

Zeke charged after him. He was surprisingly fast for such a big man, but he lacked the boy's youthful agility and speed. Unless the boy stopped dead or tripped over something, he'd have no hope of catching him.

"Thomas! Wait!" Sophie called, dismayed. "I brought you something!"

Thomas stopped. With one wary eye on Zeke, he slowly turned to face her, curious and uncertain at the same time, poised for instant flight.

Sophie held the book up so he could see it. "It's the *A. B. C. of Electricity* that you were looking at," she said. "Remember?"

He remembered. She could see it in his face. She could also tell he was trying to figure out what kind of trick she might be playing on him. From the safety of the weed patch where he'd stopped, he studied the book, then Zeke, then her again, like a hungry mouse sniffing a suspicious hunk of cheese.

"Your mother said I could give it to you."

Mention of his mother didn't help matters. "Why'd you talk to her?" he demanded, suddenly sullen.

"Because she's the one who answered the door."

He cocked his thumb at Zeke. "Who's he? And why'd you come here, anyways? Ladies like you don't usually bother us 'ceptin' if they're plannin' to make trouble."

Sophie had an instant's vision of how her mother must have looked when she'd led the Ladies Missionary Society to the "rescue" of a fallen woman. She clamped down on the smile that threatened and said, "That's Mr. Jeffries. He's a . . . he's a friend who escorted me here. And I imagine your mother can take care of any unwanted ladies who come visiting, can't she?"

Thomas considered that for a moment, then thrust out his jaw defiantly. "Yeah. She throws empty whiskey bottles at 'em."

Sophie bit down hard. Her throat felt a little thick with the laughter choking it. "So I've heard. But she didn't throw any whiskey bottles at me, and I'm not here to make trouble. Of course," she added, casually tucking the book in the bag she carried and starting to turn away, "if you're not interested, I guess there's nothing more to say. I'll just take the book back to Mr. Hodgeson and see if he'll let me trade it for something els—"

"No!"

Sophie stopped and looked at him over her shoulder. "No?"

"I mean," Thomas added, fighting for just the right balance between casual and covetous, "you don't hafta take it back. Not 'nless you wanna."

"Oh," said Sophie, and made a show of giving the matter some thought. "Well, I don't think I want to." She pulled the book back out of her bag and carefully picked her way through the weeds to the stump he'd abandoned with such haste earlier. "Do you mind if I sit down?"

Thomas shook his head. "No'm."

The boy waited until she sat, then, still with one sharp eye on Zeke, strolled over with a great, and obviously assumed, air of casualness. He stopped in front of her, just out of reach, but close enough so he could grab the book and run if the opportunity presented itself.

Zeke edged closer, alert to any sudden break for freedom, but not so close he drove the boy off again. Thomas didn't budge.

Sophie placed the book in her lap and casually laid one hand on top of it. "I was wondering," she said, "if there was anyone who would help you with this. In case you wanted some help, that is."

Thomas's gaze had been hungrily fixed on the book, but he looked up at that, meeting her questioning gaze proudly. "I don't need no help. I'm plenty smart, you know."

"I'm sure you are. But where are you going to get all the things for the experiments the book talks about? You know, batteries and wires and switches and . . ." Her memory of what she'd read ran out at switches. "And whatnot," she finished lamely.

Thomas hadn't advanced far enough to consider that problem. He was still too excited at the prospect of having the book in the first place. "I'll find the stuff, don't you worry."

Sophie tightened her hold on the book. "You can't steal it like you stole my basket, you know."

All the eagerness went out of the boy's face, to be replaced by an angry scowl. "So you *did* come about that basket."

"No, I didn't. I don't care about the basket or the groceries that were in it. But I do care that you don't get into more trouble because I brought you this book."

The scowl lightened by a degree or two. "Mr. Sobeck'd help me."

"Are you sure about that?"

"Sure."

Sophie raised her eyebrows skeptically.

"Well," Thomas admitted reluctantly, "purty sure, anyways."

"If he doesn't, will you come talk to me? I know we can find someone else if we ask. But we have to ask," she added sternly, before he could object.

"Okay." A radiant smile lit Thomas's dirt-smudged face, making it glow. He eagerly reached to take the book, then hesitated and reluctantly drew back. "How'm I gonna find you if I need to? I don't even know your name."

"I'm sorry! Of course you don't." Sophie held out her hand. "I'm Sophie Carter."

Thomas swiped his hand down the side of his pants, then thrust back his shoulders and shook hands with all the dignity of a diplomat. "Pleased t'meetcha. I'm Tom Peabody."

"Tom? Not Thomas?" The question brought the scowl back.

"Tom," said Tom firmly. "Only Ma calls me Thomas. 'Cause of my father."

"Oh, I see." Sophie was afraid she did see, but it wasn't her place to venture into the boy's personal affairs. "Well, Tom. I'm pleased to meet you, too, and I hope you'll let me know how you're doing. Will you do that?"

Tom nodded shyly, and this time when she offered the book to him, he didn't hesitate. He grabbed it and held on tight, staring at it as if he'd just been handed the Crown Jewels of England.

Sophie wasn't sure he heard a word she said as she gave him the directions to her house and repeated her warning about asking for help. When she left him, he was once more seated on the stump, his head bent in rapture as he slowly turned the pages of the *A. B. C. of Electricity*.

Chapter 7

Once they were back on the road in front of Mrs. Peabody's house, Sophie pulled Zeke to a halt. While she and Tom had talked, Zeke had done his best to brush off the crud that had clung to his shirt, his cheek, and the top of his right ear, but he'd left a gray smudge on his cheek and missed a dot of white on his ear.

"Stand still a minute. There are some spots you missed of . . . of what Thomas threw at you." She fumbled for the handkerchief in her bag, uncomfortably aware of just how close they were. "I'm sorry you had to go through all that. I had no idea he'd be so . . . difficult!"

To her amazement, Zeke grinned. "Or so fast."

Relieved, Sophie smiled, too. "Or so fast. And ornery. I hope he didn't hurt you, kicking you and hitting you like that."

"No, ma'am."

Sophie thought she detected the faintest trace of discomfort in his reply. "When you shouted like that, I thought perhaps he'd kicked a little too hard."

Zeke shifted from one foot to the other uncomfortably. "It wasn't a kick. Exactly."

"No? Hit you, then." Her hand finally closed around the errant hanky. She pulled it out. Amazing how things could get lost in a bag.

"He didn't hit me," Zeke said. His voice had a definite note of strain in it.

"No?" Sophie frowned, puzzled. "Then what *did* he do?"

Zeke blushed more easily than any man she'd ever

known. He hesitated, then, as if afraid she might embarrass him further if he didn't respond, added flatly, "He bit me. On the . . . on the butt."

Sophie's hand froze halfway to his face. She gaped. Then she giggled. "He *bit* you?"

Zeke grinned in wry acknowledgment of the joke. "Hard. The little bugger's got good teeth."

Sophie burst out laughing. "Oh, my!"

"I don't believe that's quite what I said."

"No, you said 'damn you.' Very restrained, under the circumstances."

"Ermph," said Zeke, but he looked oddly pleased— and extraordinarily attractive, in a rough, boyish sort of way.

Just like the majority of the little boys in her Sunday school class who usually managed to get their faces dirty the minute her back was turned.

Without thinking, Sophie handled the matter of Zeke's dirty face exactly as she would have the boys in her class. She held the handkerchief to Zeke's mouth. "Spit on that."

He jerked as if she'd struck him, blinked, and then obediently did exactly as he was told.

Too late, Sophie realized just how far she'd gone beyond the bounds of propriety. What was acceptable in dealing with scruffy, five-year-old boys was *not* acceptable when dealing with a man like Zeke Jeffries.

Face flaming, she raised the hanky to his face and started to scrub. Her hand shook and her heart sounded as if it were thudding in her ears, but that didn't block her almost painful awareness of just how close his mouth was, of the warmth of his skin and the coarse rasp of his beard as she scrubbed at the smudge. Half an hour earlier, she'd wondered about that beard. Now she couldn't help brushing the butt of her hand, just once, along the line of his jaw.

The rough grate of stubble against her skin made her hand tingle and sent a jolt all the way up her arm. She flinched. He jumped. They both backed away a step. Then Zeke backed away another.

Sophie stared at him, dazed by the effect of that

brief, totally inappropriate touch. At least she'd gotten most of the gray off. There was a tiny trace on his cheek an inch west of the edge of his mouth. All she'd have to do—

Not a chance. She wasn't going to risk that again.

Besides, it was *right*, not west. And his mouth was flattening into a line so straight and disapproving she'd have to be mad even to consider it. He was staring fixedly over her shoulder at something in the distance, yet his eyes were unfocused, glazed into an ice-blue blindness, and the line of his shoulder and the cords of his neck had gone rigid.

Something dropped out of the bottom of Sophie's stomach. He was so embarrassed by her brassy behavior he didn't dare face her. Probably afraid his shock and disgust would show if he tried, and too much the gentleman to let it.

Sophie cringed. Her gaze fell. It slid down that solid column of throat, along his shoulder, down his chest, then stopped. She raised her head a fraction. There, right where his chest curved, was a lingering trace of Thomas's ammunition.

Sophie took a swipe at the black speck. She couldn't help herself. The speck didn't budge. She took a second swipe, harder this time, and suddenly found her hand engulfed in a huge, work-hardened male hand.

" 'S fine," Zeke said through clenched teeth. He tugged the hanky out of her hand and shoved it into his pocket, then flicked off the bit on his shirt she'd been aiming for. Only once there was no reason left for her to touch him did he release her hand and step away. "Thanks."

At least Sophie *thought* he said thanks. He was mumbling under his breath and refusing to face her, so it might have been a curse, instead.

When he offered her his arm, she reluctantly took it. She would have preferred to sink into the ground and out of his sight forever, but that, unfortunately, wasn't possible. She felt like a fool.

God knew what he thought, but whatever it was, it couldn't be good. All she had to do was glance at his face to know that. Every trace of his earlier good humor was gone, wiped out as if it had never been. The solid feel of his arm beneath her hand only emphasized the distance he was so carefully keeping between them.

Sophie burrowed deeper into the long, narrow closet that had been built in under the eves of her room. It was even harder to see inside when the only light in the room was the oil lamp that sat on the table at the side of her bed.

Way at the back, in the darkest, most inaccessible corner of the closet, she found the box of worn-out wool rags she was always promising to cut up for a braid rug. Now was a good time to start on the rug. She needed a distraction from the unsettling thoughts of Zeke Jeffries that had tormented her all afternoon and evening.

After all, she had more important things to do than think about a man who clearly wasn't interested in her.

She tugged the box free and began backing out of the closet on her hands and knees, dragging the box after her. Halfway out, with her head half buried under her heavy plaid wool skirt, she stopped.

What important things?

Sophie frowned at the skirt's taffeta lining, which was tickling her nose, and considered the problem.

After a moment's consideration, she backed up another foot or so to a point where the closet was actually tall enough for her to stand. She couldn't think of a single thing she needed to do, either now or tomorrow or in the next few weeks or months or years that was of any particular urgency, let alone importance. Not one.

It wasn't a pleasant thought.

Oh, there was plenty for her to *do*. There was shopping and cleaning and cooking and mending and laundry and ironing and sewing and gardening and social calls and . . .

The list went on and on and on. And when all those

things were done, she'd have to turn right around and do them over and over and over, all the way up until the day she died or went mad with boredom and frustration.

Not a very appealing thought.

Sophie leaned back against one of the bare wood studs of the wall and stared at nothing.

Dying of boredom never happened to heroines in books. They often came close to dying of abuse, or overwork, or starvation, or terrible danger, or the evil machinations of villains intent on gaining their inheritance, but they never, *ever* died of boredom. Never.

And why? Because, somewhere along the line, a tall, dark, handsome, and rich—well, usually rich— man came into their lives. Not that the men always realized the true worth of the heroines, of course. At least, not at first. But they always did eventually, and then they were willing to give up everything—wealth, position, power, even life itself—to protect and cherish the women they loved.

Look at Jane Eyre, for instance. Small and scrawny and unpretty, cast on fortune's pleasure to be a governess to wealthy Mr. Rochester, who, if not handsome, was at least *very* compelling. Jane endured all sorts of horror and suffering, but in the end, everything had worked out just fine, thank you very much.

And there was Elizabeth Bennett, who at least had the advantage of a little more secure social position and somewhat better looks than Jane, even though she hadn't had a hope of marrying well, either. But Mr. Darcy had fallen in love with her anyway. Against his own good judgment, too!

And there was Annabelle Lester, from *The Dangerous Duke,* the sweet, loving daughter of a drunkard father who had somehow charmed and won the heart of a rakish devil of a duke. And she shouldn't forget Dora Thorne, or Lucille, or Anna Belmont, or Jocelyn Salvandre.

Well, maybe not Jocelyn. After all, she'd already been married to poor Ardath when he, through the dastardly treachery of Simon LeGrange, had lost his business and his honor, then fallen to drink and despair. Jocelyn had pulled him out of that mess in the end, but it had been touch and go there for a while.

She could safely forget Jocelyn, Sophie decided, but not the rest. Jane and Elizabeth and Annabelle and Dora and their kind might have something to teach her, if she were clever enough to learn from their example.

With sudden resolution, Sophie fumbled around at the bottom of the closet until she found the footstool she used to reach the shelves above her. It took some time, but she finally found most of the books she'd tucked away up there in between old pillows and bundles of winter underwear. She put Jocelyn and a few of Jocelyn's similarly afflicted friends back on the shelf, but the rest she hauled out and stacked on the floor at the far side of her bed where her mother was unlikely to spot them.

She would, she vowed, read one every night until she'd read them all again. Somewhere in those thousands of pages were the answers she sought and she would find them, even if she ended up buying reading glasses to do it!

Zeke found the handkerchief when he was pulling the odd bits of whatever out of his pockets, getting ready for bed.

He turned it over in his hand, studying it in the dim light of the small oil lamp he'd set on the dresser. The handkerchief was made of some fine white material that seemed smooth as silk to his calloused fingers; the border of lace was almost indecently delicate, distinctly feminine.

Sophie wasn't delicate, but she *was* feminine. It wasn't the exaggerated femininity of somebody like her mother, who worked at it, or the mincing femininity of somebody like Miss Annie Talbot, who would always take care to look and act like the most proper of proper young ladies, no matter what. No, Sophie Carter's femininity was more instinctive, more a natu-

ral part of who she was than something she assumed
for the sake of convention.

Zeke knew, because he'd thought about it all the
way home from town, all through the afternoon's work
and the evening's chores, all through the solitary supper he'd fixed by the light of this same small oil lamp.
He'd tried not to think about it, but there were a
dozen little things that kept pestering him: things he
hadn't much noticed at the time but that his memory
insisted on dragging out later to torment him.

Like the way she moved, erect, yet graceful and
without any of the airs her mother so obviously
assumed.

Like the dignity with which she'd talked to Mrs.
Peabody there on that front stoop, for all the world
as if they were equals and Mrs. Peabody due the same
courtesy as any other lady around.

Like the soft, silky feel of her plain brown suit. That
suit looked plain, but it had fitted her better than any
glove had ever fit him, smooth and neat and the fabric
as slick and pleasant to the touch as silk.

That suit had fit almost as well as *she'd* fit against
him when he'd caught her and kept her from falling,
there in the street.

Zeke drew in a sharp breath at the memory of just
how well she'd fit. Every curve and angle and line of
her had seemed made to mesh with every curve and
angle and line of him. At least, that's the way it had
felt. He'd been more than a little bit rattled, so he
might have been mistaken about the odd angle or two.

He knew he wasn't mistaken about what her touch
could do to him.

At the thought of this afternoon and of Sophie's
hand brushing across his cheek and chest, Zeke
groaned. His hand clenched, crushing the soiled handkerchief, but nothing could stop the sudden, surging
heat in his veins . . . or the erection that sprang up,
eager as always for a party, even though the party
never came.

It might not have been so bad if he slept in his
drawers or a nightshirt, like most men did, but Zeke

preferred to sleep naked. And that meant there was
no way he could pretend that what was happening to
his body wasn't really happening. The visual proof was
right there, sticking out in front of him.

Zeke yanked open the top drawer of the battered
old dresser and shoved the handkerchief beneath the
small stack of worn shirts that lay there. Then he
slammed the drawer, turned down the lamp until the
flame died out, and threw himself down on the bed.
He didn't bother to pull the top sheet up; with the
heat that had hold of him now, he didn't need any
covers.

The night air coming in through the open window
was cool against his naked body, gentle as a lover's
touch ... or as gentle as he imagined a lover's touch
to be.

Zeke groaned and dragged the sheet up, then
flopped back on the pillow.

The sheet helped some, not much. It kept the
breeze off him, but it couldn't disguise the thick tent
pole that seemed to have arisen in the middle of it or
do anything about the fact that he was lying in a bed
made for two, not one.

His heart pounded, his erection pulsed, yet Zeke
tried to ignore the symptoms. He lay there under the
sheet, teeth clenched, and grimly stared up at the dark
above him.

He could count watermelons and the profits he
hoped to make from them. That helped sometimes.
Or he could work out his irrigation schedule for the
next two weeks. The schedule didn't do much, but
the thought of all that cold water pouring through the
ditches and into his fields was soothing.

Not as settling as a visit to the pump in the yard
would be, but he refused to let a spinster lady like
Miss Sophie, who was more inclined to get him into
trouble than not, disturb his sleep.

It must have been an hour later when he finally
admitted defeat.

With an anguished groan, Zeke threw off the sheet

covering him and rolled out of bed. Then he stomped out to the kitchen, grabbed up the three-gallon tin bucket, the largest one he had, slammed out the back door, and headed for the pump.

Friday, April 21, 1893

Over a week now since I bumped into Miss Sophie at Goveneur's Groceries and I haven't seen hide nor hair of her since. Or her mother or Mrs. Smith, even. Looks like I'm probably safe. Make a fool out of yourself once, folks laugh. Do it twice and the word gets around.

Once I get back to sleeping normal, things ought to sort out just fine.

She had to have a plan.

Sophie sat curled up in the middle of her bed, surrounded by a half-dozen tumbled stacks of books and the silence of a house at midnight, and thought about what to do next.

One thing her reading over the past week had shown—she lacked the one essential advantage that all her storybook heroines had possessed: access to the hero. Regular access, not just head-butting encounters in Goveneur's Groceries.

That fact had almost leaped off the page, it was so obvious. She wasn't governess to Zeke Jeffries' children, as Dora had been for Sir Reginald's motherless children . . . and Zeke didn't have children, in any case. She wasn't Zeke's ward and, unlike Annabelle Lester, she wasn't the beautiful, innocent daughter of the groundskeeper on his ancestral estate. Nor was she the sister of his very best friend, as Lucille had been the sister of George Devane's best friend, who had been killed in battle at Waterloo by taking the bullet that had been aimed straight at George's manly breast.

The important point was that everything had worked out for George and Lucille and every other pair of lovers Sophie had read about because fate had managed to throw them together in the first place.

So far, fate hadn't been doing too well on Sophie's behalf. It had certainly thrown her *on* Zeke, but that wasn't the same thing at all. In her romances, not one of the heroines had resorted to assault and battery in order to meet the hero. And those eminently feminine heroines certainly *never* humiliated the poor man in public or subjected him to a barrage of chicken droppings or treated him as if he were a five-year-old instead of a grown man.

Sophie, on the other hand, had managed all that—and more. All because fate hadn't done its job right the first time. Or the second. Or the third.

Which meant she would have to forget about fate and take matters into her own hands.

Tuesday, April 25, 1893

Some days, it just doesn't pay to get out of bed.

Delphi had her calf this morning about two o'clock. Got me out of a comfortable bed and the first good sleep I've had in days, mooing and kicking her stall and generally carrying on. Typical perversity of the female, if you ask me, since she dropped it easy and slick as a whistle. It's a bull calf, though. Fine, sturdy creature, but I'd wanted a she calf awfully bad. Now all I'll get out of him is some salt beef next year, or maybe a few dollars if I take him into the auction soon as he's old enough. And in the meantime he'll be taking milk I could be selling back to Mrs. Smith.

As if that weren't bad enough, a coyote got into the chicken coop and killed two of my best layers. By the time I'd got that cleaned up and had patched the wire where he'd broken through, I realized I was late opening the irrigation ditch. Must have lost a good half hour's worth of water, not to mention it reminded me I needed to be cleaning out a couple of ditches along the far field and repairing a couple of headgates, and I was already looking at enough work to keep me busy halfway into next week. And then I remembered

I'd forgotten to pick up those parts for the traction engine that were supposed to come in on Monday's train.

On top of that, I burned the bacon *and* the toast, cut myself shaving, and was just getting over those disasters when the pigs got out somehow and headed for the watermelon patch by way of the flower garden that old Mrs. Frellerhoff planted way back when and that keeps coming up, regardless.

I had a devil of a time getting them back in their pen—they liked getting out and kicking up their heels. Just for a minute there, I felt a tad envious and wished I could do the same, but I drove them back in, anyway.

And then Mrs. Smith drove up.

I would have hid in the hayloft if I'd had a chance, but she spotted me right off and waved and hallooed and smiled so wide I knew it was going to be bad.

By way of diversion, I showed her the mess the pigs had made and the slaughter in the chicken coop, then hauled her out to the barn to take a look at Delphi and the calf, all the time chattering away as hard as if I was sitting down to afternoon tea with the ladies.

In the end, all that effort didn't accomplish much except wear out my jaws. It certainly didn't head her off from what brought her. I knew it wouldn't, but a man has to try.

"Don't you worry about losing the milk," she said when she took a look at Delphi. "That cow has the biggest udder of any cow I've ever seen and she'll freshen up just fine. Always has. Her carrying on like that is just the way she is. She likes making a fuss and being the center of attention, especially if it's male attention. Why do you think I named her Delphi?"

Since I hadn't the slightest idea why and didn't think I wanted to find out, I just grunted a bit and tried to look like I already knew. A man can get away with that. Women don't bother. They just sail right through the conversation, regardless, and that's what Mrs. Smith did. Didn't even stop for breath, far as I could tell.

"But that's not what I came for," she said. "I'm here about Watermelon Day."

That didn't sound too bad. I told her I'd already promised Hiram all the melons he wanted. Seems Watermelon Day is a big to-do the folks here about put on every August when the watermelons are ready for market. It's like a county fair, I guess, only all the farmers donate melons so there's enough for all, and all of it free for the eating. That I could manage. But my stomach was twisting a bit, warning me worse was coming.

"Hiram takes care of that," Mrs. Smith said, flicking her hand to show she didn't waste her time on such details. "I told him to. No, what I was thinking was that you'd make a fine escort for the young lady who's going to cut the ribbon for the new racetrack. I'm sure I've mentioned her before. Miss Annie Talbot. Sweetest thing and *so* pretty. Took the prize for elocution . . ."

Mrs. Smith kept talking, but all of it sailed right past me. All I could think of was the ten dozen different kinds of fool I could make of myself if I tried to get up there in front of God and the people of Rocky Ford with Miss Annie Talbot beside me. I was already starting to sweat, just thinking of it.

"I don't think I can do that," I said.

Mrs. Smith stopped dead, right in the middle of whatever it was she was saying, and stared at me as if I'd suddenly grown an extra pair of ears.

"What do you mean you don't think you can do that?" she said, real calm, which should have warned me.

"Get up in front of folks and all. Not with Miss Annie."

"Of course you can!" Mrs. Smith said. I could see her feathers were starting to ruffle, but I didn't have any idea just how ruffled up she could get. Not then.

"I just can't," I said. "Look at the fool I made of myself at the social. If I—"

"The social!" said Mrs. Smith. "That was all Sophronia Carter's fault! Her and her mother's. I still can't imagine what got into her, making a spectacle of herself like that, right in front of everybody. Why, I don't think I've seen anything so disgraceful since Orville Stutter passed out dead drunk in church that time. And as if that weren't bad enough, I heard she attacked you, right in Goveneur's Groceries. Attacked you!"

Well, I tried to explain how it wasn't Miss Sophie's fault at the social and that we'd just sort of bumped heads at Goveneur's Groceries when I dropped my canned tomatoes, which is something that could happen to anybody, but Mrs. Smith wasn't having any of it. She must have gone on for a good quarter of an hour, saying how Miss Sophronia ought to be ashamed of herself, but maybe it wasn't all her fault since she'd been saddled with the kind of mother she had. And as for Mrs. Julius T. Nose In the Air Carter, said Mrs. Smith. Well!

If I tried till next Christmas, I don't think I could remember all that Mrs. Smith said. I doubt if she could, either, but that wouldn't be a problem because she'd easy come up with another dozen things to say about Mrs. Carter and her daughter Sophronia, and not one of them good.

I was almost grateful she'd got on to her soapbox because I figured she'd clean forgot about this knuckleheaded notion of hers that I should stand up with Miss Annie at the opening of the racetrack for Watermelon Day.

You'd have thought, after all this time, I'd have known better.

There she was, driving down the lane and still going on about Mrs. Carter, when she drew up all of a sudden and turned around and called, real clear, "I'll tell Annie you're agreed, then," and then she turned back around and drove off before I had a chance to say otherwise.

I swear, I'd have grabbed one of the mules and run after her, but right then the pigs got out again—guess they liked the watermelon too much to stay where they belonged—and I had to go roust them out of the field and rebuild the gate plus a few parts of the pen that were a bit shaky, just in case.

I got over to the Smith farm eventually, but by then Mrs. Smith had hightailed it into town to spread the good news.

Hiram wasn't any help, of course. "No sense in tryin' to catch her," he said. "She's long gone. By this time, I expect half the town knows you've agreed, whether you did or not."

He looked at me as gloomy as if his best sow had just dropped six runts and a rabbit. "Not a thing you can do about it, you know. She's got her rope around you good and tight, Zeke, and there's plenty of young ladies got the halter ready. If it ain't Miss Annie, it'll be Miss Marla May or maybe Miss Eliza. There's no help for it and you might as well make your mind to it. Save yourself the grief, if you know what I mean."

Well, I sure enough knew what he meant, but I didn't like it. I worried that thought all the way home and all the way through evening chores, but it wasn't until I crawled into bed about ten and tried to go to sleep that I realized I was wasting my time worrying about all the wrong things.

It's this foolish fancy for Miss Sophie that will get me in trouble long before anyone in Mrs. Smith's pack can corral me.

Here it is midnight and I still can't sleep any more than I've been able to sleep for the past week and then some. No matter how tired I am, the minute I get between those sheets I start to thinking about Miss Sophie and there I am again, hard as a fence post and not one whit more use in bed.

I'm beginning to wonder if that hanky of hers that I buried underneath my shirts isn't some sort of jinx or something. I can't think of any other explanation because I've known lots prettier ladies, but not one of them has ever given me so much trouble without even half trying.

And she's definitely troubling me. I haven't even *seen* her for over a week, yet there I am every night, staring into the dark and remembering how she laughed so sweet and how it felt with her pressed right against me and—

I don't imagine I have to go into details about that. I'm still having a hard enough time—

There I go, letting my mind get off track again.

No two ways about it. When it comes to Miss Sophie, I'm about six pennies short of a dime and losing cents all the time.

Chapter 8

Can't believe it's the end of April already, with May just around the corner. There's so much that needs doing, and I can't do the half of it alone, no matter how hard I try.

Like it or not, I'm going to have to get someone to help around here. Even if it's something as simple as slopping the hogs and milking the cow and feeding the chickens, it would be something. If I could ever get that traction engine going, it would help even more.

Went into town today. Those tractor parts I ordered weren't in and Patrick hadn't finished fixing the ones I gave him, either. Both Patrick and the clerk at the depot told me to come back Monday. Guess I'll have to, though I hate to waste another day fooling around.

Didn't see Miss Sophie, though I looked for her. Just being cautious, of course.

"Adelaide! Get off! Off, I say!" Delphi reached for Addy, but the cat was too quick for her. It leapt off the kitchen table to the floor and darted over to rub against Sophie's skirts, meowing indignantly.

"Yes, all right," Sophie said distractedly. "I'll feed you in a minute."

"Honestly, Sophie. If you keep feeding that cat like you do, you're likely to put us in the poorhouse. Canned salmon! Can you imagine! That cat eats better than we do."

"You don't like canned salmon, Mother," Sophie said, poking at the chicken in the roasting pan harder than she really needed to see if it was done. She was tired and cross and sweating from the heat of the stove, she still hadn't thought of a good excuse for spending more time with Zeke Jeffries, and Delphi had been difficult for days. Sophie wasn't sure which of the three afflictions irritated her the most.

"My dislike of salmon has nothing to do with the issue of feeding a cat food like that." Delphi frowned at the cat, who hissed back.

Sophie ignored both of them.

Delphi sniffed in disgust and abruptly changed the subject. "You know, Sophie, you should have listened to me when I told you you should drive out to that nice Mr. Jeffries' place and apologize."

Sophie scowled at the mashed potatoes, then gave them another quick lick for good measure. "Why?"

"Adelaide Smith got him to promise to escort Annie Talbot for the opening of the racetrack on Watermelon Day."

Sophie's head snapped up at that. "I didn't know that."

"Ella Bassett told me just this morning. And she heard it from Mrs. Purvis, who had it from Clara Randall, and *she'd* heard it straight from Thea Talbot herself, so it *has* to be true!"

"Clara didn't tell *me!*" Sophie protested.

"When are you ever home so she can?" Delphi demanded. She never wasted her opportunities. "Besides, what difference does it make now? Annie will have plenty of excuses to be seeing Mr. Jeffries every chance she gets . . ."

Sophie suddenly found herself intensely absorbed in draining the green beans.

". . . and you can be sure she'll make the best of every one of them. Once she's got him hooked, he won't stand a chance. And neither will you."

Delphi slumped in her chair, weighed down by the thought of Annie Talbot's advantages. "But do you ever listen to me? Of course not! Not a ruffle to your name, when I'm forever telling you that what gentlemen admire most is a well-rounded woman, and now Annie and that awful Adelaide—"

"The chicken's ready, Mother," Sophie interrupted, grateful for a diversion. The last thing she needed was for Delphi to guess how hard her news had hit. "Would you mind pouring the tea while I bring in the rest?"

Roast chicken and mashed potatoes were Delphi's favorite, so they made it halfway through supper before she picked up the broken refrain of her lament.

"This is a *delicious* meal, Sophie," she said, delicately dabbing at her lips with her napkin. "Really, you know, you're a *very* good cook. Any man would be pleased to have a wife who could fix a meal like this, and no matter how well she speaks, Annie Talbot is a *terrible* cook."

Sophie sighed. "From what I've seen, Mother, it isn't good cooking that lands a husband."

"Well, no, but it's certainly a help. Especially when a woman . . ." She hesitated, then plunged on, "well, when a woman lacks those other attributes which men find so appealing."

"Then perhaps you should suggest we have a pie-making contest for Watermelon Day this year, Mother," Sophie snapped. "Or maybe a bread-making contest. If I win a blue ribbon, I could wear it pinned to my chest as a sort of advertisement. Since I haven't anything else there to recommend me."

"Don't you get snippy with me, Sophronia Maye! I'm only thinking about what's best for you, after all!" Delphi angrily tossed her napkin down on the table and started to stand. Halfway up, she sucked in her breath with an odd little gasp, then plopped back down in her chair.

Sophie looked at her mother, startled. Delphi stared back.

"You know," Delphi said slowly, "that's not a bad idea. Not bad at all."

The crafty gleam in her mother's eyes made Sophie's stomach lurch uncomfortably. "Mother, I wasn't *serious*!"

Delphi wasn't listening. She was too wrapped up in the pleasures of her plot.

"The members of the Society would support a baking contest. I know they would." Delphi's perfect mouth curved upward in a wicked smile. "I might even get someone else to suggest it, just so Adelaide Smith won't get suspicious before we get the idea going. After all, Mrs. Purvis is inordinately proud of that devil's food cake she makes, and Cora Hodgeson gets terribly puffed up about her lemon squares, though *I* always thought they were a tad too bitter. Too much lemon for the sugar, you know."

"Mother, I wasn't *serious* about a baking contest. I was just—"

"Honey cinnamon bread. That's what you'll have to make, Sophie," Delphie declared, oblivious to her daughter's protests. "Then the only thing we have to worry about is how to keep Zeke Jeffries' attention on you and off Annie Talbot between now and then."

Like a surprise May Day basket, on Monday, the very first day of May, the perfect solution was literally dragged kicking and squirming to her front door.

"He says you're the one responsible, Miss Sophronia." Mr. Conner, the manager of the train station was frowning mightily. He didn't take lightly to trouble in his beloved train station, and trouble there had clearly been. "Now I'm bound to say, that didn't sound right to me, but—"

"He set off the burglar alarm I rigged for Mr. Conner's office!" Mr. Sobeck burst out. "I told him not to touch that switch, but that's precisely what he went and did! And then what does he do next but spill blue vitriol all over my desk and onto the floor. Bumped right into—"

"I din't mean to set it off!" Thomas Peabody wasn't about to take such accusations standing still. As usual, he wriggled like a fish on a hook. Two hooks, actually, since both men had a firm grip on him. "An' I din't mean to break the bottle an' spill that stuff, neither!

I was jus' tryin' to get outta your way when Mr. Conner there came stormin' in like—"

"—I felt we ought to talk to you first," Mr. Conner plowed on, regardless. "That alarm going off spooked the folks in the station, Miss Sophronia. Sent old Mr. Welks into heart palpitations, not to mention—"

"—the shelf where I keep it and—"

"—he was goin' to a fire an'—"

"Gentlemen, *please*!" Sophronia had to raise her voice to be heard above the hubbub. "If you'll all try not to talk at the same time, I may be able to help you sort this out." She forced a smile for the benefit of the two angry men and one hostile child who stood on her front porch and added, a little more uncertainly, "Eventually. I hope."

"I din't mean tuh do it." Tom's scowl was fierce enough to melt nails.

Sophie felt something in the vicinity of her heart twist in sudden pain. Obviously, neither of the men had looked at Tom closely enough to see the despair lurking beneath the surly bravado.

"Didn't mean it? Didn't *mean* it!" Mr. Sobeck's fat fingers dug so hard into the boy's shoulder that Tom winced and tried to pull away. "Do you have any idea the damage that vitriol will do? *Do* you?"

"I couldn't help it! You were flappin' around your office like a chicken with its head cut off, an' all on account of Mr. Conner here—"

"*Me*? Flapping like a—!" The telegraphist almost choked. "Why, you—"

"Sophie? Sophronia! What*ever* is going on out here? *What* are these gentlemen doing here and who in the world is this *filthy* boy?"

At Delphi's unexpected appearance on the scene, Mr. Conner immediately drew himself up to his most impressive height. He adjusted his tie and smoothed his hair and assumed an expression of the most respectful condescension Sophie had ever seen. Mr. Sobeck, on the other hand, sank his head down onto his shoulders like a snapping turtle drawing back into its shell and glared, clearly resenting the intrusion.

Thomas just scowled harder and squirmed to get free. Without success. Despite Delphi's distracting feminine presence, neither the stationmaster nor the telegraphist was about to let him off their hook.

"Missus Carter, ma'am," said Mr. Conner with great dignity. "I'm sorry to bother you, but we've come to talk to Miss Sophronia here about a little problem we've got."

"Really, Mr. Conner?" Delphi graced him with her most charming smile. "Now, whatever kind of problem can *you* have that my Sophie could possibly help you with?"

Sophie shifted uncomfortably. From where she stood, she could see the curtains lifted in the front parlors of three of their neighbors' houses, not to mention the two ladies out for a healthful stroll who had suddenly become fascinated by a clump of daisies poking out of the neighbor's wrought-iron fence.

"Perhaps we could go inside, Mother? Mr. Conner?"

After a moment's hesitation, Delphi graciously led the way into the parlor while Sophie brought up the rear. Sophie took the precaution of shutting the front door behind her, in case Tom suddenly decided to bolt. Mr. Conner was too taken with her mother to notice, and Mr. Sobeck was too angry with Tom to care.

"Now," said Delphi, gracefully settling onto the sofa. "Why don't you tell me what your little problem is that Sophie's supposed to fix."

Mr. Conner took charge of explaining.

The tale wasn't hard for Sophie to follow, but Delphi was so dazed by the idea of her daughter having bought a book on, of all things, *electricity,* for the son of that wretched female who had flung an empty whiskey bottle at her, that she had difficulty grasping the wider outlines of the plot.

Tom, evidently taking Sophie's strictures to heart, had somehow convinced grumpy Mr. Sobeck to let him help out in the telegraph office by sweeping floors and running errands in exchange for the chance to learn more about the mysteries of electricity. All had gone well for the first week or so until Tom's curiosity got the better of his judgment.

Entranced by Mr. Sobeck's thrilling recital of how he'd wired Mr. Connor's office with a newfangled electric burglar alarm, just in case anyone had evil designs on the two-ton steel safe that was kept there, Tom had dedicated himself to learning every detail about the system. Which was just fine, until he got the bright idea of improving one of the switches and ended up setting off the alarm just when the station was packed with people waiting for the afternoon train to Pueblo and parts west.

The sound of the alarm bell ringing had been everything a ten-year-old boy could wish for. The resulting commotion and consternation among the assembled populace had been everything a stationmaster like Mr. Conner dreaded. So far as Sophie could tell, the only thing that might have upset him more was if one of his beloved trains had decided to jump the tracks and plow through the station itself.

Tom's original transgression had been more than sufficient to bring down the combined wrath of his mentor and his mentor's boss. But then he had compounded his sins by somehow bumping the shelf where Mr. Sobeck had set a container of blue vitriol, which was used to renew the batteries that powered his beloved telegraph.

Clearly, Tom had erred by touching the alarm system, but judging by the two men's expressions and what *wasn't* said, Sophie guessed that Mr. Sobeck really had been charging about his office like a man demented, trying to cut off the alarm and dodge his employer's wrath and reassure the overexcited individuals who kept sticking their heads in his office, all at the same time. In the resulting chaos, Tom had bumped the shelf where the vitriol had been stored—against the rules, it seemed, because of its dangerously caustic nature—and thus heaped disaster on top of disaster.

And all of it was Sophie's fault.

It took a few minutes for her to realize that was the point of this visitation, to lay the blame where it belonged—squarely on her shoulders.

"It's not right to be filling a boy's head with big ideas, Miss Sophronia," Mr. Connor said gravely. "Especially a boy like Thomas here. I know you must've thought it was a good idea, but, there, you haven't any boys of your own, so I understand how it is you wouldn't know. About the trouble they can get into, I mean."

"But . . . but, *Sophie*," Delphi protested. "How in the world did you get involved with . . . with people like that? And without telling me! Oh, my. Oh, dear. Oh, dear, dear, dear."

"What I want to know is, who's going to pay for the damages?" Mr. Sobeck demanded, belligerent as a bulldog. "I was willing to help him out so long as he stayed out of trouble, but this here, this is going too far. You should see my desk!"

"I'm sure—" Sophie ventured, but was cut off by her mother.

"But *why* would you buy a book on *electricity*, Sophie? I don't understand."

"Well, I—"

"And however did you get involved in the first place?"

"It was—"

"She come out an' talked to my ma." Tom gave out that information in a tone that said he was begging for a fight with someone, and he didn't much care who.

"She— Oh, *Sophie*!"

"Miss Sophronia! You?"

"What about my desk?"

"Really, Mother! It's not as if I—"

"She wouldn'ta caught me if it hadn't been for that Mr. Jeffers she drugged along," Tom added sullenly.

"It was Mr. Jeffries, not Jeffers, and I didn't *drag* him along," Sophie snapped. Didn't *anyone* want to listen?

Delphi perked right up. "Mr. Jeffries escorted you? Sophronia! And you never said a word!"

"Zeke Jeffries took you to a place like that?" Mr. Conner demanded, clearly stunned. "How could he let a lady—"

"Jeffers. Jeffries. What difference does it make?" Tom demanded. "You still wouldn'ta caught me."

"Who cares what his name is?" Mr. Sobeck roared. "I want to know who's going to pay for the damages to my desk!"

"I just hope all that chicken shit I threw at him—"

"*What* did you say? Young man, there are ladies present!"

"You threw . . . At Mr. *Jeffries*? Oh, Sophie, what have you done?" Delphi sank back on the sofa, a broken woman.

"*I* didn't throw—"

"And don't you think I'm forgetting the time I'll have to spend fixing things up, either. The alarm's got to be reset and I'll have to get more vitriol for my batteries, and—"

"*I* threw that chicken shit," Tom announced, loud enough so there'd be no mistake who was speaking. "Caught him square between the eyes, purty near. You shoulda seen his face."

"Oh, my! Sophronia! How *could* you?" Delphi wailed, and fainted dead away.

It took some time to bring Delphi around, and even longer to convince Mr. Sobeck that she would pay for any damages for which Tom might be responsible, but Sophie finally succeeded in getting the two men out of the house and her mother calmed down enough that she could leave her alone while she took Tom home, despite his protests that he wasn't "no baby and didn't need no nanny."

Neither of them spoke for the first five blocks. Tom slouched sullenly at her side, outwardly unrepentant.

Sophie was too sunk in her own gloomy thoughts to pay much attention. Once again she'd inadvertently made Zeke Jeffries a target for gossip. If this kept up, the poor man wouldn't be able to hold his head up in public, and she'd be the one responsible. Which meant—

Tom broke into her grim reflections. "Are you gonna tell my ma? About . . . about Mr. Sobeck and all?" His casual tone implied he was inquiring out of curiosity, not concern, but the anxious little furrow between his eyebrows said otherwise.

Sophie resolutely set aside her own thoughts. "Should I?"

Tom considered that. "She din't know I was workin' at the depot. I don't see no reason to tell her now I ain't."

"Now you're not," Sophie corrected.

"Of course I ain't. I just said so, din't I?"

"It doesn't have anything to do with you working at the depot or not. 'Ain't' is not a proper word."

"Not proper?" Tom's frown deepened. "You mean it's like 'shit' an' 'damn' an'—"

"Not precisely like those words, no," Sophie hastily interjected. "But 'ain't' is ungrammatical. It is the sign of an uneducated person, or at least of someone who has not been taught how to speak properly. You should say, 'I'm not' instead of 'I ain't.' Does that make sense now?"

Tom mulled that over for a moment. "Nope, it don't."

Sophie blinked, thought about it, and decided he had a point. "Never mind. We can work on that later. We have to figure out what to do with you first."

Tom stopped, his eyes wide with sudden hope. "Does that . . ." He swallowed and tried again. "Does that mean I can keep on studyin' 'lectricity?"

"There's no one to stop you, now you have your own book," Sophie said, meeting his uncertain, questioning gaze squarely. "But I think it would be better if we found someone you could work with as you worked with Mr. Sobeck. Somewhere you won't get into so much trouble. What do you think?"

Tom blinked, as if she'd hit him. "You mean it? You ain't mad about what I done?"

"No, I'm not angry about what you did," Sophie gently laid the stress on the "did" and the "I'm not." "You were wrong to interfere with Mr. Sobeck's alarm system, but the rest of it sounds like an unfortunate accident to me. Unless you weren't being completely truthful," she added sternly, wondering if she was giving Tom rather more of the benefit of the doubt than he deserved.

"No way! Cross my heart an' hope to die."

The boy's eagerness was heartbreaking. He'd gotten into trouble, but it was intellectual curiosity, not vice, that had led him there. And no matter how disastrously his experience with Mr. Sobeck had ended, it obviously hadn't dampened his enthusiasm for learning.

"We'll have to tell your mother, of course," she added. "Get her permission."

"She won't care." There was a tiny, but unmistakable note of regret in his voice as he said it.

What was it Mrs. Peabody had said about her son? That he shouldn't waste time dreaming about what he couldn't have? Had that been resentment talking, Sophie wondered suddenly, or despair?

"She's still your mother, Tom, and she has to know. But don't worry, we'll work something out. You'll see."

Instead of resenting her bossiness, Tom grinned and gave a shout and a skip, then abruptly broke off a sturdy stalk of sunflowers and slashed at the weeds lining the road. "Hah!" he said. "Take that! An' that!"

Sophie watched him and wondered just what it was she'd gotten herself into.

They were almost past Patrick O'Boyle's blacksmith shop when an unmistakable voice called, "Sure, now, and were you really thinking you'd get by me like that? And you with no more man beside you than that bit of a boy you've got there?"

"Mr. O'Boyle!" Beside Sophie, Tom tensed as if preparing for flight.

"It's me, all right," the smith said, coming up to

them. "And who might this be, then? Not the boy as is interested in the electricity?"

Tom eyed Patrick suspiciously. "Who are *you*?"

"My name is Patrick Dwayne O'Boyle," Patrick said, "though I can't say my mother, may the Lord bless her soul, would think it proper for a youngster your size to be talkin' to his betters like that!" One dark brow swooped downward in a sort of half frown. "And what would your name be, then, lad? Or can't you say?"

When Tom didn't respond, Sophie nudged him.

He shrugged off her touch, but said reluctantly, "Tom. Tom Peabody."

Patrick nodded. "I thought it might well be, but there's never any telling now, is there?" He didn't seem to expect an answer. Instead, he eyed first Tom, then Sophie. Then he sighed like a man forced to a duty he didn't much relish, tugged the leather apron he wore over his head, dusted his work-grimed hands on his pants, and said, "I'll just keep the two of you company for a bit, shall I?"

"That isn't necessary," Sophie said stiffly.

"No more it's not," he said equably, "but there's no sense in arguin' since I'm goin' with you, all the same."

"But your shop—"

"Will do fine, I expect. It's not like to grow legs and walk off."

One look at Patrick's face told Sophie he was right, there wasn't any sense in arguing. He would go with them, no matter what she said.

"How the hell should *I* know if your stuff come in?" The harried clerk turned away from Zeke in answer to a stout and highly indignant lady's angry query.

"No, ma'am. Sorry. Didn't mean to cuss. It just slipped out . . . No, the telegraph's down for a bit . . . No, ma'am, I don't know when Mr. Sobeck'll have it workin' again . . . No, the stationmaster's not here, either . . . Yes, ma'am. I'll tell 'im. Thank you, ma'am."

The minute she was out of sight, the clerk added under his breath, "Danged fussbudgety old biddy. Why'd she have to pick today of all days to send a telegraph to that no-good son of hers?"

He turned back to Zeke. "Look, Mr. Jeffries, I'm sorry your package didn't come in last week like it was supposed to, and I'm sorry I can't help you now. Mr. Conner'd know about your shipment, or the baggage master. But the one's out with the boy what caused the commotion in the first place, and the other is tryin' to get things straightened out since everybody spread to heck and gone when the alarms went off, and some of 'em took their baggage with 'em, but he don't know who."

Zeke wasn't interested in the alarms, the baggage master's troubles, or the stout woman's complaints. He simply wanted the parts for his traction engine.

"Could I look for myself? I—"

"Absolutely not! It would mean my job if Mr. Conner was to hear of it!"

"Do you know when Mr. Conner will be back?" Zeke persisted. With all the work waiting for him at home, he didn't much like the idea of having to come back to the station later.

"No tellin'. That Peabody boy's a problem, and no mistake. Always has been." He tsk tsked in disgust, then shrugged. "Anyways, they were goin' to see Miss Sophronia Carter first, since the boy said she was the one got 'im into it. Though how Miss Sophie got mixed up in it, I do not know."

At the mention of the name Peabody, Zeke straightened. At the mention of Miss Sophronia, he sucked in his breath and felt a fire light in his belly.

He should go to her. After all, in a way he *was* responsible since he was the one who had grabbed the boy in the first place. If he showed up to help her out of this new trouble—why, who knew how grateful she might be? And if she were to—

The clerk broke into Zeke's thoughts, shattering a particularly appealing fantasy as to exactly what form Sophronia's gratitude might take.

"You plannin' on waitin' for Mr. Conner?" the
clerk inquired. "If so, I'd suggest you take a seat on
one of them benches over there. No tellin' how long
he'll be, like I said."

Which was, quite clearly, a politely worded request
that he move along and let the clerk get on with his
work.

Zeke moved off, thinking hard. He'd never been
one to butt in where he didn't belong, but Miss Sophie
might appreciate a little support.

On the other hand . . .

He sighed. On the other hand, she might not. Every
time he got close to her, she seemed to fall or trip or
do something equally embarrassing for both of them.
By now, she'd probably be grateful if he stayed away
from her for the rest of her life.

He had better things to do than worry about what
didn't concern him, after all. He needed some more
ten-penny nails and some tin sheeting and a roll of
chicken wire to replace the old, crumpled wire that
coyote had gotten through. O'Boyle would probably
have the other parts for the traction engine fixed by
now, too. By the time he'd taken care of those chores,
it was more than likely Mr. Conner would be back
and he could collect the parts he'd ordered. Assuming
they'd finally come in.

And then he could go home and get back to work
and forget all this Miss Sophie foolishness that seemed
to fill the space between his ears these days.

Chapter 9

It was a strangely uncomfortable trio they made—Patrick on one side of her, silent and oddly tense, Tom on the other side, suddenly hostile, his sunflower sword abandoned.

They found Tom's mother sitting on the sagging front porch of her little house, brushing out her just-washed, hip-length hair so it could dry in the sun.

She didn't see them at first, too absorbed in the almost hypnotic task to be aware of anything else. In one smooth, sensuous stroke, she brought the brush down from crown to waist and out, then let the strands fall back, only to repeat it over and over and over again. The heavy, golden-brown mass, untouched by gray, fell around her like silk spun from a magician's wand, shining in the sunlight.

Instead of the soiled and rumpled gown she'd worn the first time Sophie had seen her, she'd donned a simple white shirtwaist and a plain blue skirt. Simple and plain, that is, on anyone except her. The skirt flared out about her like a cape about a queen, emphasizing her narrow waist and the delicate line of her body from hip to thigh to ankle. She'd left the blouse open at throat and cuff, but the effect was strangely innocent, almost virginal.

Sophie halted at the front gate, stunned by the woman's unexpected transformation from slattern to storybook princess. It was only when Mrs. Peabody looked up, startled, that Sophie could see the traces left by hard drink and hard living in the unhealthy pallor of her skin and the puffiness about her eyes and jaw. Even then, the inborn beauty of delicately sculptured brow and cheek and chin shone through, as yet untouched by the life she'd led.

Patrick abruptly let his breath out in a loud whoosh that said, clearer than words, how much the sight of Mrs. Peabody affected him.

So much for his chivalric interest in protecting her, Sophie thought sourly, glancing at him. He'd forgotten she even existed. And yet . . .

Sophie frowned. The look on Patrick's face wasn't one of lewd fascination or animal lust. Or at least not what she imagined such expressions would be. There was an intensity about him, a . . . a yearning that surprised her.

Tom bristled. For an instant, Sophie thought he was going to attack the burly smith. Instead, he settled for kicking the gate open and storming through.

Mrs. Peabody cautiously rose to her feet. "Thomas! What . . . What's the matter?"

"Me an' Miss Sophronia wanta talk to you, Ma," Tom said, jaw pugnaciously set. "Right now."

"Right now?" She glanced from her son to Sophie to Patrick, as if seeking answers to this unprecedented invasion of her front yard.

Without the defenses of whiskey and shadow and a door she could slam shut in their faces, Mrs. Peabody was lost and, Sophie realized suddenly, frightened. Her shoulders were stiff with nervous tension. She held her brush in front of her like a talisman to ward off evil and her arms pressed so tight against her sides that her hair seemed to fall straight down in an unbroken curtain of sunlit silk.

She looked, Sophie thought, more like a timid schoolgirl among strangers than a hardened woman of the world on the front steps of her place of business. This close, it was easy to see that both the shirtwaist and the skirt were cast-offs, and that only heightened the impression of fragile vulnerability.

She gave Patrick a jerky nod of recognition. "Mr. O'Boyle."

"Ma'am." Patrick clasped his hands in front of himself and shuffled his feet, then thrust out his chin like a man whose collar has suddenly become too tight and deliberately looked away. He wasn't wearing a collar.

Sophie tried to ignore him. His reaction to being here reminded her unpleasantly of Zeke's. It was no concern of hers if Patrick—*or* Zeke, for that matter—had been one of Mrs. O'Boyle's customers. Absolutely no concern whatsoever.

How often, she wondered bleakly, was she going to have to remind herself of that? The thought of Zeke and Mrs. Peabody had cost her more than a few hours of sleep over the past days. Worse, that thought had led to other, less appropriate thoughts. Lascivious thoughts. Thoughts of *her* and Zeke and—

"I wondered if I could take a few minutes of your time, Mrs. Peabody," she said abruptly, and hoped no one would notice the sudden tightness in her voice. "I wanted to talk to you about Tom, er, Thomas."

Mrs. Peabody flinched and hunched her shoulder, as if to ward off a blow. She didn't look at her son standing beside her, didn't try to touch him. Instead, she glared at Sophie.

"He in some kinda trouble? Because of that book you give him? If he is, it's all your fault. It for sure ain't his, 'cause he wouldn'ta had that book, otherwise." The words were hard and aggressive, but without the whiskey to fuel her belligerence, Mrs. Peabody sounded more defensive than angry.

Tom glanced at Sophie, silently pleading for support.

"Thomas isn't in trouble," Sophie assured her. "At least, not much. And it really wasn't *all* his fault," she added hastily. "But that's not why I'm here. Or not what I want to talk about, anyway."

Mrs. Peabody stared at her doubtfully, then glanced down at her son.

"Please, Ma?" Tom said. "Please."

For an instant his mother wavered, then she hesitantly reached out and ruffled his hair. "All right. If that's what you want." She glanced back at Sophie. "You'd best come on in, then," she said, and led the way into the house.

Sophie followed her, conscious of a guilty little thrill at the prospect of seeing inside. She'd never been in a whorehouse. Not anywhere close to one, actually, if you discounted her first visit to Tom.

Would there be a painting of a nude woman? she wondered. Would the furniture be covered in wine-red velvet and tassels? Would there be pots of scent set about to perfume the air, and mirrors, *big* mirrors, to reflect what went on within those rooms?

What kind of setting did a woman need when she was gong to spend the night making love to a man?

No parcel.

No nails.

No Patrick.

Zeke glared at the empty smithy. The forge was cold, but Patrick wouldn't have left the shop open like this if he'd planned on being gone long.

Seemed like everything from the minute he got up was working this way, which was to say, not at all. The only consolation was, he hadn't been crazy enough to call on Miss Sophie to see if she needed any help.

He'd thought about it all the way from the train station to the hardware store to Patrick's smithy. He'd told himself he was a fool, then thought about it some more. In the end, he'd decided that, whatever the mess Tom Peabody had dragged her into, Miss Sophie was more than capable of finding her way out without his assistance.

Why that fact should bother him was something he'd think about later. *Much* later.

With a sigh, Zeke plopped down on the wide bench set at one side of the shop and leaned back against the wall. He hadn't stopped moving since Delphi's racket had dragged him out of bed at two this morning, and the long day was beginning to wear. Not to mention there were evening chores and still more work waiting for him when he got home.

He'd rest a bit and wait for Patrick. He might as well.

Things couldn't get any worse if all he did was sit here and wait.

To Sophie's disappointment, Mrs. Peabody's front parlor was small, drably commonplace, and surprisingly clean. Even the quilt-covered double bed visible in the small bedroom off the parlor looked unrepentantly normal. Not at all the sort of place she'd expected. Not at all what she'd hoped to see . . . whatever that might have been.

Perhaps sensing her prurient curiosity, Mrs. Peabody immediately crossed to the bedroom and pulled the door closed, then distractedly waved Sophie to a seat that faced the small front windows rather than the rest of the house.

Sophie took the seat, face flaming. She was acting just like Delphi at her worst, poking her nose into what didn't concern her in the hope of finding something shocking. If Mrs. Peabody chose to run her off now with a barrage of empty whiskey bottles, she'd have no right to complain. She'd pitch a few herself if their roles were reversed.

Patrick perched uncomfortably on the edge of a battered settee, straightened his back, and clamped his hands around his knees as if grateful for someplace to put them. He didn't so much as glance at Sophie, just stared at the faded pink roses climbing the wallpaper trellis on the opposite wall.

Mrs. Peabody chose a straight-back wood chair only slightly to the right of the roses Patrick found so fascinating. It took her a moment to settle. She adjusted her skirts, moved the chair to a more level spot on the uneven floor, nervously twisted her hair into a knot, then evidently realized she didn't have any hairpins handy and let it fall in a heavy rope down her back, instead.

Tom claimed right of place by standing next to her and glaring across the room at Patrick. The minute he was sure he had his mother's attention, he launched into a tangled explanation of the day's events complete with much hand waving and frequent protestations of innocence that only served to confuse his mother more.

As he spoke, Mrs. Peabody kept glancing surreptitiously at Patrick, as if she needed to convince herself he was really there, yet wasn't quite sure if she was pleased by that fact or not.

Every so often, Patrick would abandon the wallpaper roses and turn his head a fraction, just enough so he could get a better look at the woman on the straight chair opposite. The minute she caught him looking, however, he jerked his attention back to his floral studies.

The tension between the two was like an electric current Sophie had once seen generated at a Chautauqua that had come through town. The lecturer had worked some sort of magic with his metal rods and electric generators and suddenly a visible current had arced between two poles like lightning between earth and sky, crackling and flaring until the very air in the tent had seemed alive.

The air in the little parlor was like the air in that tent, charged with energy and an almost visible tension that set Sophie's senses on edge and made her jumpy, anxious, *hungry* . . . but for what, she didn't know.

None of her beloved books had ever mentioned anything like this. There Patrick and Mrs. Peabody sat, divided by the width of a room, without touching, without speaking, without even daring to look directly at each other, yet somehow they were as aware of each other as if they'd been sitting side by side, holding hands and gazing into each other's eyes like love-besotted fools.

If they could be like this now, what must it be like when they touched? When they kissed? When they took off their clothes and made love?

The thought made Sophie cringe with shame at the same time it made her bones go weak and that uncomfortable, secret place at the juncture of her legs grow hot and aching. She stiffened, willing her body not to respond, tightening her muscles against the ache and the heat in an instinctive response that had never yet managed to ease the wanting.

Was this what always happened between a man and a woman, and she'd just never noticed? Or was it something that only occurred in a place like this? Had the same electric energy snapped in the air whenever Zeke had "visited"?

Almost, she could picture him, sitting where Patrick sat now, his perfect features drawn taut and fine with tension as he looked across the room, not at Mrs. Peabody or wallpaper roses, but at *her*. Almost, she could imagine herself looking back at him, her own prim shirtwaist open at the throat and cuffs and her hair spilling unbound about her shoulders. She could see him rise and come to her and take her hand and lead her to that quilt-covered bed and—

Sophie viciously cut off the indecent fantasy. *It wasn't any of her business.*

But, oh! it might be! If only she could have what fate had denied her, a reason to be with him. A chance to show him she was worth loving, that she wasn't the silly, blushing, clumsy fool he'd seen so far. But that was just a silly fantasy. The sooner she admitted that—

"Miss *Sophronia*!" Tom was tugging on her sleeve, brow furrowed with irritation that she hadn't heard his question.

"What? Oh!" Sophie forced herself to focus on the boy. "I'm sorry, Tom. What were you saying?"

"Ma said nobody would teach me 'lectricity, not after I made Mr. Sobeck so mad. But I said that Mr. Jeffers, the one I hit with the chick—the one who caught me," he hastily amended, "knows something about machines and stuff. He was at the station last week lookin' for some kind of parts for a traction engine he's working on. I *heard* him! If he knows about that stuff, maybe he knows about 'lectricity, too, and then he could help me. Don't you think he'd help me? If I 'pologized?"

Sophie sucked in air until the buttons on her shirtwaist threatened to pop.

" 'An you'd take me out there, wouldn't you, Miss

Sophie? If I promise to behave? Huh? Wouldn't you? Please? If I promise?"

Patrick didn't say a word the entire time they were in the house, but as they were leaving, he took Mrs. Peabody's hand and held it, ignoring her nervous, almost frightened attempts to pull free. When he spoke, his voice was low, but so heavy with emotion it carried all the way to where Sophie waited by the gate.

"I've not changed my mind," he said, "nor will I. You've only to say the word and I'll come."

Mrs. Peabody jerked her hand free and backed away, head down. "*I* ain't changed my mind," she said, her voice low, yet fierce, almost desperate. "You ain't welcome here. I've said it before. I won't say it again."

He stood there a moment staring down at her, his expression set and grim, then he turned away and came to where Sophie was waiting at the gate. For a minute, Sophie thought he'd walk off without her, but at the last second, almost as an afterthought, he offered her his arm.

All the way back to his shop, Sophie turned his words over in her mind. Only one explanation offered itself. It was vulgar and prying and absolutely none of her business, but she couldn't help it. When they were still a good block from his shop, she dug in her heels. He stopped, startled, then swung around to face her, puzzlement clear on his face.

"Mr. O'Boyle?" Sophie said. "You didn't go with me just to make sure I'd be all right, did you? You wanted to see Mrs. Peabody and going with me gave you an excuse. Isn't that so?"

He flinched, then looked down at his massive hands. There was a smudge of black on the side of his right hand. He frowned as if surprised to find it, and rubbed at it with his thumb.

"I know it's none of my business," Sophie said, "but if I can help—"

"Her name's Sarah Jane," Patrick said, just as if she hadn't spoken. "Only she's not given me the privilege of callin' her that." He turned his hand over and studied the trace of black that now stained the callused pad of his thumb. "Fact is, she's told me not to visit, you see."

"Oh," said Sophie. "Yes, I think I see." She thought about it a minute longer. "No, I don't. Why doesn't she want you visiting?"

He met her questioning look squarely, as if challenging her to mock him. "I asked her to marry me."

"Marry—? But . . . that's wonderful!"

"It would be, if she'd say yes. But she won't. She told me not to come again. That she'd not have me botherin' her or . . . or drivin' away her customers."

"Oh," said Sophie, and this time she didn't even pretend to understand.

"She said she'd had enough of men's promises and she'd just as soon not waste her time listenin' to more. She said—"

Patrick cut off his words abruptly, as if just realizing what he was saying. "Well, no matter. It's not right for me to be talkin' of such things with a lady." He thrust back his shoulders and drew in a deep breath, then let it out slowly. "You'll be forgivin' me, miss, but I've work to do and I'd best be gettin' to it. Good day to you."

And then he stalked off without another word.

Zeke was leaning back against the wall, half asleep, adrift on thoughts that refused to take shape. He hadn't felt like forcing them, too content in the lazy afternoon heat to rest and not worry about all the work that was waiting for him, even if only for a few minutes. The instant Patrick's boots scrunched across the packed earth floor of the shop, the formless thoughts tore into shreds and disappeared. He jerked upright.

Patrick charged into the shop like an angry bull looking for someone to toss. The instant Zeke sat up, he jumped back a step and his hands came up, already making fists.

"What the—? Oh! it's you. What are you about,

man, to go scarin' me so?" He dropped his fists and forced his fingers to straighten, but the expression on his face gave no sign he was pleased to see a customer.

"I was waiting for you. The shop was open. I figured you'd be back soon enough." Zeke rolled a shoulder, easing some of the kinks from the awkward way he'd been slumped, and climbed to his feet. "I thought you might have those parts I left ready for me by now."

"Ah," said Patrick, and stared at the open door as if he'd never seen it before. "Yes. Parts. Well." He took a deep breath in through his nose, then forced it out in a long, slow whoosh of air. "Yes, they're ready. I'll get them for you, shall I?"

Without waiting for a reply, he stomped out of the shop and around to the back where he kept most of the work he'd finished.

Zeke couldn't help grinning. His mama always said, misery loves company, and he for sure had some company today. The clerk at the train station, the harassed man at the hardware store, and now Patrick O'Boyle, who was usually one of the best-natured men he knew. Maybe it was something in the air.

Zeke froze. Or maybe something else entirely was responsible. Unless his eyes were playing tricks, that was Miss Sophie headed this way, head high and chin set in a determined line.

Miss Sophie, who had played a starring role in his sleepless nights lately. Miss Sophie, whom the station-master had gone to see about his little disaster. Miss Sophie, who was following in the wake of an angry Patrick O'Boyle.

The clerk in the hardware store hadn't said anything about her having been around when he'd complained about his lack of tenpenny nails, but who knew? Maybe the poor fellow just hadn't made the connection yet.

As she came closer, Zeke felt his knees grow weak and something in his middle flop over.

This was what he got for spending so much time thinking about her. If he'd had the good sense God gave a goose, he'd have stayed home and tended to his own business. Now here he was, trapped and no way out unless he trampled her going out the door. Or hid under a workbench until she went away again.

And yet, trapped wasn't quite what he was feeling. Thinking, maybe, but not feeling. Interested might be a little closer to what he was feeling. Eager, even, though he didn't think that queasy sensation in his stomach necessarily went with eager.

And nervous. He was definitely nervous.

"Miss Sophronia," he said as she walked through the open shop door. He cleared his throat, twice, then added, "Nice to see you again."

Monday, May 1, 1893

I knew I should have hid under the workbench. But when did a man's brains ever work when his belly was in an uproar?

Just seeing Miss Sophie was enough to get my insides twisted around. I was scared spitless I'd make a fool of myself by suddenly standing to attention, whether I wanted to or not. After all, a man doesn't always have much say in the matter, even if it is attached to him, and what with her upsetting my sleep a good deal lately and me not expecting to see her, well . . .

Then I got a better look at the expression on her face.

All set and determined like it was, I stopped worrying about embarrassing myself and started worrying about the trouble I might be getting into.

Five minutes later, I knew what the trouble was, but by then I was hip-deep and sinking fast.

Now, I'd have sworn it would be easier to say "no" to Miss Sophie. After all, she's close to being as tall as I am, which puts us on more of an equal footing, so to speak.

It's not near so easy to argue with a woman like Mrs. Smith, who's so short that when she's talking to you, she's usually staring straight at a shirt button that's not two inches north of your belt buckle, which isn't exactly calculated to make a man comfortable. With Miss Sophie, on the other hand, you can pretty much look her in the eye instead of wondering if she's studying any spots on your shirt that might be leftover from breakfast.

But looking in her eyes turned out to be a big mistake. I kept thinking about how pretty they were, and how I liked those little flecks of gold I could see buried there in the brown, and how thick her lashes were, and before I knew it, I'd agreed to take on a shit-slinging hellion dressed up as a boy who will probably turn out to be a lot more trouble than he's worth.

All because, when it comes to Miss Sophie, my brains seem to have moved south to my pants.

It might have been better if she'd stared at a button.

Breakfast was finished, but Delphi's diatribe wasn't.

"And as if *that* weren't bad enough, what must you do but take that wretched boy back to his mother. My daughter! Consorting with . . . with loose women! Never did I think I'd see the day, but, there! What could I expect from you, as determined as you are to ruin whatever chance you might have to marry?"

When Sophie refused to respond, Delphi's tone softened, turned pleading.

"Oh, Sophie, I don't mean to be difficult, really I don't. But after the social and then you bumping Mr. Jeffries' head in Goveneur's Groceries . . ."

Sophie winced.

". . . well, you can just imagine how I felt when I heard what that awful little boy did to Mr. Jeffries! And he's such a *nice*-looking man, too!" she added on a soft, despairing wail.

"I . . . I just don't know if I can stand it, Sophie. Really I don't. There isn't a chance in the world he'll look twice at you now, especially not since Adelaide Smith got him to promise to escort Annie Talbot for the racetrack opening. Even you winning the baking contest won't do any good if you've already driven the poor man off."

Sophie sighed, and carefully aligned her fork and

knife across her empty plate. Given half a chance, Delphi would turn the whole thing into a horse race between her and Annie Talbot, even though Annie stood the best chance of winning. And not by a nose, either. Annie might be six inches shorter than she was, but she was almost as generously endowed as Delphi.

And pretty, Sophie reminded herself. She shouldn't forget that. Annie Talbot was definitely pretty.

"I suppose," said Delphi, her voice heavy with resignation, "we'll just have to forget about Mr. Jeffries for you and think of somebody else."

Delphi stared at Sophie. Sophie stared at her plate, but kept a wary watch on her mother out of the corner of her eye. She saw the change in her mother's expression the instant it appeared.

"You know, I'd never considered it before," Delphi said slowly, as if weighing every word, "but that nice Mr. Conner isn't married."

Sophie abruptly stopped staring at her plate. "Mr. Conner is old enough to be my father!"

"Oh, no! Not so old as that! Well, maybe. If he'd started *very* young. I'm almost sure he's younger than I am, and *I'm* certainly not old!"

"Not *much* younger!" Sophie tried to remember how he'd looked yesterday, there on their front porch, but all she could remember clearly was the way he'd straightened up and slicked back his hair the minute Delphi had appeared. Come to think of it . . .

"You know, Mother, I'm almost certain he has his eye on you!"

"On me!" Delphi's eyes widened. "That's ridiculous! Why, I've never so much as batted an eyelash at him!"

"Maybe not, but I'd swear he perked up when you came to the door!" The more she thought about it, the more convinced Sophie was that she was right. "Didn't you notice how he puffed out his chest and his voice got a little deeper all of a sudden?"

"Now, why would I notice a thing like that?" Despite her protests, Delphi was obviously pleased at the thought of Mr. Conner having "perked up" because of her. "Do you really think so?"

"I'm sure of it!"

"Well! Imagine that!" Delphi said, and automatically patted her neatly ordered curls. "Fancy!"

The thought that her mother might actually be interested in an eligible bachelor hit Sophie like . . . like a ton of bricks, for want of a better simile. She'd been so busy fending off her mother's matchmaking efforts on her behalf that she hadn't once thought that Delphi herself might be feeling lonely.

Yet it would be strange if her mother *wasn't* interested in marrying again. She was only forty-five, after all. Forty-six come November. And she'd been a widow for the last six of those years.

Sophie had no doubt that Delphi had truly loved her husband in her own fashion, but six years was more than enough time for her mother to have put her grief behind her and gotten on with the business of living. And living, to Delphi Carter, meant having a man around.

Just the thought that an eligible male might be interested in her had brought a glow to Delphi's cheeks and put a sparkle in her eyes. Sophie tried to imagine what Delphi would be like if she actually had a beau squiring her around town. Why, there was even the possibility she'd get so wrapped up in her own affairs that she'd forget to meddle in her daughter's!

The thought held her spellbound for all of a minute.

She should have known better.

"Well, you know, Sophie," Delphi said with the look in her eyes that indicated her mental wheels were spinning as fast as they could go, "if Mr. Conner really is taken with me—and I'm not saying you're right about that, mind!—then we'll just have to work harder on getting Mr. Jeffries to forget about Annie Talbot and think about you, instead."

"Mother!"

"But Mr. Jeffries is such a *nice*-looking man, Sophie! You don't want Annie Talbot to have him, do you? Think of it! We could have a joint wedding! Me and Mr. Conner, and you and Mr. Jeffries. Now wouldn't *that* be nice?"

Friday. Already.

Zeke's hands tightened around the heavy pottery mug of coffee. He'd had four days to get out of this mess he'd gotten into, but somehow he'd never quite worked up the nerve to drive into town and tell Miss Sophie that he could not, absolutely *would* not, take Tom Peabody.

And now they were coming. Today.

And he couldn't think of a single place to hide where they wouldn't find him if they tried.

Chapter 10

"How much farther, huh? Will it be much longer? He ain't—isn't—gonna change his mind, is he? You *sure* he said yes, Miss Sophie? For certain sure?"

The farther they'd gotten from town, the more insistent Tom Peabody's questions had become. He was sitting on the buggy seat beside Sophie, his small body taut with excitement and fear. His mother had scrubbed him and dressed him in clean clothes, but there was a patch on the left elbow of the faded shirt and the bottom of his pants legs hung a good two inches above the top of his overlarge boots. The scrubbed shabbiness made him seem touchingly vulnerable, not at all like the tough, defiant little boy who had pitched chicken droppings at Zeke.

"We ought to be there pretty soon," Sophie told him for the dozenth time in the past quarter hour. "Like I said, I've never been out here before, so I'm not sure. You'll know as soon as I do when we get there, all right?"

Tom tilted his head to look up at her anxiously. "You ain't mad I asked, are you?"

Sophie's heart squeezed. "No, of course not. Truth to tell, I'm a little nervous, too."

"You are?" Clearly the idea of an adult being nervous was a revelation.

Sophie nodded. "Umhum. I'm sort of responsible for you, too, you know. Especially now I've talked your mama into letting you stay out on the farm all summer. Until school starts again, anyway."

Tom squirmed on the seat, obviously troubled by

the weight of responsibility that suddenly rested on his small shoulders. "I'll be real good. I promise."

"You won't touch that traction engine without Mr. Jeffries' permission?"

"I swear."

"And you'll do what he tells you? You understand you're earning your way here by helping him out with the chores and some of the other work? Farming's not easy, you know."

"I'm tough," Tom said with just a touch of his old bravado. "Long as I get to learn about how that steam engine works, I don't mind. 'Course, it ain't—*isn't*—'lectricity, but I figure I gotta know about the other stuff, too. In case I need it when I start buildin' 'lectric systems and things."

Sophie didn't respond. The closer she got to Zeke Jeffries' farm, the less certain she was that this was a good idea.

Tough boys of ten don't cry, so Tom hadn't shed a tear when he'd said good-bye to his mother earlier. His eyes had gotten a little misty and his lower lip had trembled, just for an instant, but Sophie had known better than to comment on those telltale traces of youth. He'd thrown his small bundle of clothes into the back of the buggy, then climbed up beside Sophie and, after one brief wave to his mother, had bravely squared his shoulders and faced front. His mother had stood at her front gate anxiously watching them until they were out of sight, but Sophie didn't tell him that.

More than just worrying about Tom, however, she was worried for herself. That she'd gone too far. That she was being a fool and setting herself up to be a laughingstock. Again. Only this time it would be deliberate, not accidental.

"Getting desperate," they'd say. "Miss Sophie hasn't been able to catch herself a man so far, so now she's taken to running after them." "Poor Zeke Jeffries," they'd say. "Too nice to say 'no,' and now look at the mess he's gotten himself into."

Then again, maybe she was being a fool to worry about what anyone else would say. Jane Eyre and An-

nabelle Lester hadn't worried—or not too much, anyway—and everything had worked out just fine for
them. Maybe it would work out just fine for her, too.

She just wouldn't think about Annie Talbot and
Zeke's promise to escort her for the racetrack opening. Without even lifting one of her delicate fingers,
Annie had been handed the chance that Sophie had
been forced to find for herself. Not that there was
anything she could do about it, Sophie reminded herself. And besides, a lot could happen between now
and then.

Before Sophie could waste more energy thinking
about the terrible things that *might* happen, they
reached the rutted dirt turnoff onto Zeke's farm. A
wind-scoured sign on a tipsy fence post announced
"FRELLERHOF" in shaky, faded letters.

"We're here!" Sophie said, and wondered if her
face showed the same eagerness mixed with trepida-
tion that Tom's did.

The alfalfa fields on the east side of the track were
rich green and knee-high, almost ready for the first
cutting. On the west, rows of young corn marched
straight and even to the horizon.

Beyond the first fields were smaller fields of melons,
beans, and onions, and beyond those stretched land
that had clearly been productive farmland at one time
but had since been left to go to weeds and rank grass.
Farther still, Sophie could see the dense green line of
cottonwoods and willows that marked the course of
the Arkansas River.

Smack in the center of it all, a cluster of tall cottonwood trees sprang up suddenly out of the flat farmland, sheltering the single-story farmhouse that nestled
among them from the summer heat and the blasts of
cold that would roar in from the north come winter.
The farmhouse itself had once been painted white, but
the paint had yellowed and turned scabrous over the
years. The roof needed reshingling, the porch needed
propping up, and only three of the six shutters that
had once been attached to the front windows had survived. To one side, a weed-choked flower garden still

struggled valiantly to give a touch of color to the place.

A fair-sized barn in serious need of repair stood back from the house. A few of the pens and corrals near it had recently been rebuilt, but the rest had been left to weeds and rot.

Old man Frellerhof, Sophie knew, had been one of the original settlers in the Rocky Ford area. He'd built up a substantial and highly productive farm, but the death of his only son in a farm accident a few years earlier had destroyed his interest in farming. By the time he finally gave up and sold the property, the land had gone back to the wild and the buildings had fallen into serious disrepair.

Zeke had taken on a daunting task in trying to reclaim the place. That he'd accomplished as much as he had in the past few months, especially working on his own, was little short of a miracle. If he was lucky and wasn't hit by hail or flood or locust or sickness in his stock, in a few years he might be able to turn the place into a good-paying proposition with enough time and money leftover to repaint the house and rebuild the barn. But it wasn't going to be easy.

"I see him!" Tom pointed to the tall figure coming toward them from around the edge of the barn.

At the sight of Zeke—in those wonderful red suspenders, no less—Sophie felt something in the middle of her chest suddenly tighten. Her palms grew damp, her heart started racing, and her corset tightened around her rib cage. That's the way it felt, anyway. It might just have been that she was suddenly finding it difficult to breathe normally.

Too late now to turn and run.

Sophie guided the horse into the yard and under the shade of a cottonwood. By the time she'd drawn up, Zeke was standing by the buggy, ready to help her down. One glance at the expression on his face helped calm her fidgets. He looked just as nervous and uncertain as she felt.

Or maybe he was just worrying about the damage she could do if she fell on him while getting out of the carriage. When she politely refused his offer of help, Zeke readily backed up and let her climb down on her own. Too readily.

Sophie resolutely ignored the sting of embarrassment, but it wasn't so easy to ignore the thought that he might have been a little more insistent in offering his help if it had been Annie Talbot getting out of the buggy instead of her.

Tom clambered down the other side and came around the end of the buggy. He didn't venture an inch farther, however. With studied nonchalance, he dropped his bundle of clothes on the ground at his feet and leaned his shoulder against the buggy's frame. When Zeke beckoned him forward, he flinched, then reluctantly obeyed. The closer he got to Zeke, the slower his steps became until he stopped about three feet away.

He craned backward, shielding his eyes against the sun as he stared up at Zeke. "I didn't 'member you was so *big*," he said with clearly heartfelt misgivings.

Zeke grinned and squatted down on his heels, which brought him to eye level with the boy. "And I don't remember you were so clean. Mom get you scrubbed up, did she?"

Tom grimaced in disgust. "Yeah. She even scrubbed behind my ears. Said I was 'sposed to look respectable. I told her I was gonna be sloppin' hogs and workin on a traction engine, an' that hogs and engines don't care what a fella looks like, but she wouldn't listen tuh me."

Zeke nodded gravely. "Mothers do that sometimes, I've noticed. But around here, a man has to clean up pretty regular, even if there aren't any lady folk around. Working in the sun all day, you get to sweating something awful, you know. By the end of the day, you're so ripe you can't stand yourself any more than anyone else can. Not to mention what being around those pigs will do to you."

Tom's chest swelled. The threat of daily baths paled beside the glory of being called a man and told he'd stink at the end of the day. "I guess I can manage that. Long as you don't scrub behind my ears," he added after a moment's thought.

"I won't," Zeke assured him. "I have trouble enough with my own."

"Oh," said Tom. The idea that grown-ups might get dirt behind their ears, especially grown-ups as big as the man before him, had obviously never occurred to him.

He glanced at Sophie for reassurance. Sophie, amused, made a little shooing motion with her hands to encourage him to go on. They'd already discussed, a dozen times over, what he was supposed to say to his new "employer."

Tom reluctantly turned back to face Zeke. "I wanted to 'pologize for throwin' that chicken shi—" He stopped, blushed, and reconsidered his choice of words. "For throwin' the chicken poo—" He grunted in exasperation. "I wanted to 'pologize for throwing that stuff at you."

He looked at Sophie doubtfully.

"And . . .?" Sophie urged.

"Oh, yeah, and for bitin' you on the . . . for bitin' you. I'm very sorry, and I won't never do it again. So help me."

Zeke glanced up at Sophie, amused but fighting hard not to hurt the boy's feelings by showing it.

For a moment, Sophie hung suspended in that gentle blue gaze.

Forget Annie Talbot. Forget Annabelle Lester and Jane Eyre. Forget her own spinsterhood. Sophie was suddenly very, very glad she'd brought Tom here. For Tom's sake, not for her own. The boy would be in very good hands if he was with Zeke Jeffries.

Maybe that was why Sarah Jane Peabody had been so willing to let Tom try this experiment with Zeke. Maybe she, too, had seen that same compassion Sophie saw now in the handsome face and the aquamarine eyes.

Before Sophie could explore that rather astounding thought, Zeke turned back to Tom. "Apologies accepted. So long as you don't do it again," he added in a mock threatening voice that Tom saw through instantly.

"Sure thing, Mr. Jeffers!"

"Jeffries," Zeke corrected him. "But you can call me Zeke."

"All right." Tom rolled it around in his mouth a second, as if getting the feel of it. "Zeke."

"Good. Now, why don't you grab your things and take them in the house. The back bedroom off the kitchen'll be yours. You can't miss it. I already made up the bed."

Tom, obviously relieved at having survived the apology, grabbed his bundle and raced off to do as he was told.

Zeke watched him go, a faint smile on his face, then rose to his feet with an easy grace that somehow abandoned him the moment he turned to Sophie. He nervously dusted his hands on the sides of his pants.

"I . . . I thought you might want to stay for dinner. Before you had to drive back into town, I mean. I'm not much of a cook, but there's stew and—"

"I brought a few things," Sophie hastily interjected. "I thought it might be easier. Fried chicken. Some bread and pickles and corn relish. A dried apple pie." The words came out in little gasps. This close to Zeke, and without the presence of a ten-year-old boy to distract her, she somehow wasn't capable of thinking too clearly. She certainly wasn't capable of speaking in complete sentences.

It had been a lot easier in Patrick's blacksmith shop, where the shadowy interior softened things and gave her the sense that she wasn't quite as . . . exposed as she felt right now.

"Fried chicken? Dried apple pie?" A smile that angels might have envied suddenly spread across Zeke's face. "I haven't had much of that since Mama died last year. If taking on a terror like Tom means I can get both, I'll take a dozen just like him."

The thought of food evidently eased his nervousness because Zeke didn't even twitch when they bumped shoulders trying to reach for the picnic basket at the same time.

"Excuse me!" Sophie said, and backed up, blushing hard. Her upper arm tingled with the unexpected contact. Without thinking, she wrapped her other hand around the affected limb, just above the elbow.

Zeke immediately set the basket on the ground by the wheel and reached for her. "Did I hurt you? I'm sorry! I didn't mean—"

"No. No, it's all right," Sophie assured him, dropping her hand and turning so her other shoulder was to him. "I'm just clumsy. I didn't mean to bump *you*."

His fingers had grazed the back of her hand. Little more than a feather's touch, but enough to set her nerve ends singing. It was wonderful. It was exciting.

It was absolutely frightening. If a chance touch could unsettle her like this, she'd be mad to want more.

He frowned, as if uncertain whether or not to believe her, but before he could say anything, Tom exploded out the kitchen door. He was halfway across the yard before the screen door banged shut behind him.

"I found my room! Can I see the traction engine now? Can I? Is it in the barn? I can find it by myself if—"

"No!" Sophie and Zeke got it out in a perfect chorus, just as if they'd practiced beforehand. Sophie looked at Zeke, surprised. He looked at her. Then they both burst out laughing.

Tom scrunched up one side of his face in suspicious disapproval. "What's so funny? Was it somethin' I said?"

"No. It wasn't anything you said." Sophie took a steadying breath. She'd never realized laughter could be quite so . . . stimulating.

Zeke picked up the picnic basket, then waved it in front of Tom. "Miss Sophie brought fried chicken and apple pie. Don't you want some first?"

"No! I wanna see the—" Tom abruptly cut his vehement demand short, as if he'd only just remembered his promises to mind his manners. "That is," he said, dragging his words out reluctantly, "if you wanna eat first, I guess—"

"I'd like to see this traction engine, too," Sophie said, taking pity on him. "Maybe if we asked him nicely, Mr. Jeffries would give us a tour."

"Mr. Jeffries won't. I will, though, but only if you'll call me Zeke. And we can leave the picnic basket at the house first."

She was going to have to stop looking into his eyes, Sophie told herself sternly. Every time she did, she got dizzy and so flustered she could scarcely think. But for once, she didn't need to think.

"Zeke," she said, and happily took his arm when he offered to escort her and her picnic basket to the house.

The pigs were "nice." The melons were "nice." The corn was "nice." The onions and beans were "nice," as was the carefully maintained system of irrigation ditches that had turned prairie into productive farmland. Nothing, however, elicited more than a polite but unenthusiastic "nice" from Tom until Zeke threw open the doors at the far end of the barn to show him the magical traction engine.

That brought a whoop and a "Whooee!" Not even a quick reminder from Sophie that he'd promised not to touch the engine until Mr. Jeffries said he could was enough to slow Tom down.

"It's *grand*, Zeke! You 'bout done fixin' it? What's wrong with it? How fast's it go?" Tom danced around the engine, as eager as if it were a huge birthday cake all for him. "It's *big*, ain't it? Purty near as big as that one came through on that flatcar a few months back, huh? Did you see that one? An' you're gonna show me how to work on it, right? Can we start today? Right now? Can we, Zeke?"

Zeke laughed. He winked at Sophie, then crossed to the eager boy and began explaining how the monster machine worked and what the problems were that kept it from running.

Sophie was more than content to remain where she was. To her unappreciative eye, the machine which everyone swore would eventually replace the horse and ox teams that pulled the plows and worked the fields looked like nothing so much as a giant tin can set on wheels and decorated with bewildering array of valves and pipes and gears and levers. In shape, it rather resembled one of the antiquated steam engines she occasionally saw on the railroad except that instead of an engineer's cab, it had a seat at the rear, like on a riding plow but perched high up, and its back wheels were enormous, cleated iron hoops that were almost as tall as the machine itself.

She might not be impressed, but boy and man were obviously enthralled, whether it worked or not. Watching Tom's rapt expression as Zeke recounted the problems he was having in getting the beast to run, Sophie decided that much of the pleasure came from the fact that the thing *didn't* work. After all, where would the triumph be if all they had to do was turn it on and let it go?

When it became evident that neither Tom nor Zeke was likely to recover from the enchantment anytime soon, Sophie abandoned them to their pleasures and wandered farther into the barn.

It was a big place, built for big hopes that had come to nothing. At least, not for Mr. Frellerhof. Old, cracked leather harness hung from some of the supporting beams, and a row of empty stanchions along one wall testified to former plans for a dairy herd. Most of the floor on the north side of the barn had been swept clean, ready to receive the first cutting of hay. Or whatever part of it Zeke didn't sell to neighboring farmers with more stock to feed than his few head.

There was no overhead hayloft, just the beams and rafters and the roof . . . and the occasional hole in it.

When Zeke had let the livery horse into the pasture with the mules, he'd said he had plans for a dairy herd sometime in the future. The herd was still a distant dream, but the one milk cow he had at the moment

had wandered into the open stall at the far end of
the barn, obviously hoping she'd be offered something
more enticing than the grass in the open pasture outside. She poked her broad white head over the top
bar of the stall and mooed piteously.

Sophie picked up a few wisps of hay that had fallen
to the floor and gingerly offered them to the beast,
which immediately thrust out a huge, rough pink
tongue and took them out of her fingers. Sophie
squeaked and jerked her hand back, but the cow
merely stared at her and chewed on the hay, completely unimpressed.

When the cow had finished the hay, it mooed again,
demanding the next tidbit. Sophie dutifully bent to
gather some more hay, and for the first time spotted
the small roan calf standing close to its mother's side,
watching her from between the lower bars of the stall.

While the mother was intently chewing the second
bit of hay, Sophie gathered her courage and reached
through the bars to touch the calf. The calf edged off
a half step, just far enough to be out of Sophie's reach,
and regarded her with interest.

"He's a little over a week old," Zeke said, coming
up behind her unexpectedly.

"He's awfully . . . cute." Cute didn't sound like a
proper farm word, but it suited the calf.

"Would you like to pet him?"

Sophie eyed the calf, then the calf's mother. "Can
you get him that close to the bars without his mother
getting upset?"

As if in answer, the cow mooed, a low, sad moo,
and poked her nose at Sophie. Sophie backed up two
steps uncertainly.

"Don't worry about her," Zeke said. "She's like
that all the time. Likes to be the center of attention
and makes a big racket when she isn't. But she's a
good milker, I'll give her credit for that. Never known
one better."

The cow mooed again, this time more insistently,
and shoved against the bars, demanding her fair share
of the attention, and more.

"Oh, hush, Delphi. Mind your manners." Zeke shoved the cow back.

Sophie gaped. "*What* did you call her?"

"Delphi."

"Excuse me?" Sophie felt an odd pressure building up in her chest. It was the pressure that was affecting her hearing. It had to be. Zeke *couldn't* have called that cow what she thought he'd called her.

"I called her Delphi,' Zeke said patiently. "I haven't got a name for the calf, yet."

"That's what I thought you said."

"Mrs. Smith named her, and I couldn't think of any name better, so I just left it. And anyway, she doesn't seem to mind. Mrs. Smith says it suits her."

Sophie choked, then she exploded.

"Some more chicken?" Sophie extended the almost empty plate of fried chicken. "There's a wing left, a thigh, and the two pieces of the back."

Zeke rubbed his well-filled stomach and considered the matter. "I'll take the wing. I'm not sure I can even hold that, but it's so good I don't want to stop."

Sophie neatly speared the wing with a fork, then leaned forward to dump it on his plate. It was a simple action, nothing at all out of the ordinary, but Zeke found himself watching her every move, savoring the way she tilted her head and stretched out her hand.

They'd decided to celebrate Tom's arrival with a picnic in the shade of the cottonwoods. Zeke had dug up a couple of moth-eaten but not too musty horse blankets from the barn and spread them on the sparse grass that passed for a lawn, then rousted out an equally worn but notably cleaner damask tablecloth that had belonged to his mother and spread it on top of the horse blankets. They'd used the blue-and-white enamelware plates that were Zeke's everyday dishes, and enamel mugs for the lemonade Sophie had brought in a heavy pottery jug. The rest Sophie had pulled out of her seemingly bottomless basket.

The food had been . . . well, incredible. Even his Mama had never made fried chicken that good, nor

bread quite that soft and flavorful. Zeke couldn't comment on the dried apple pie. He hadn't tried it yet.
He was too full of chicken and bread and corn relish
and homemade pickles and . . .

"Mmmm." The wing was the infamous last straw.
The minute he polished off the last thin bone, Zeke
lay back, propped one arm under his head, and closed
his eyes in the exquisite agony that came from eating
too much good food. "That was wonderful."

"I'm . . . glad you liked it."

Zeke opened one eye and looked up at her. She
was sitting on the other side of the untidy mess of
plates and serving dishes they'd spread on the ground
between them, watching him, a small, rather hesitant
little smile on her lips. He closed his eye, satisfied,
and said, "Best cooking I've had in ages, and that's
counting the meals Mrs. Smith's served me, now and
again."

A moment of silence, then Sophie giggled.

Zeke opened the one eye again. A moment later,
understanding dawned. He jerked upright, then
groaned at the stress that put on his over-stuffed
middle.

"You won't tell her I said that, will you? It'd be as
much as my hide is worth for her to find out I preferred your fried chicken to hers."

Sophie shook her head, and even in the heavy shade
her golden brown eyes twinkled. "I won't tell. I
wouldn't dare."

She wasn't laughing, but her voice was so light it
sounded like laughter. Gentle, happy laughter. The
kind that made a man feel good all over.

Zeke grinned. He couldn't help it. "I don't know
anybody'd be foolish enough to try that!"

"Except my mother. Delphi would *enjoy* telling her,
you know! Especially if she ever finds out about
your cow!"

Zeke laughed, then gasped and grabbed his stomach. "If I'd had any idea . . . !"

Sophie gave him a conspiratorial wink. "That's all
right. We have a scrawny little alley cat that's always

getting in fights, even with cats that are three times
her size. Mother calls her Adelaide, the Cat, but I call
her Addy. Maybe you can call your cow Del and pretend you never knew about the rest."

"Del, huh? I guess I could manage that." He stared
at her, and as he stared he could feel his grin fading
and an odd, sort of lost, sort of hungry feeling take
hold of him.

He'd thought, from the way she'd tormented his
nights, that he'd remembered every detail of her. He'd
been wrong. Today she was different, more relaxed.
Softer somehow, with the sunlight slipping through the
leaves to cast a strip of gold across the crown of her
head and the point of her shoulder, bright yellow
against the shadowed curve of her throat and breast.

As he'd rummaged around in the house for the
plates and mugs and tablecloth, Zeke had found himself drawn to the window just to see what she was up
to. He couldn't help himself. It was as if something
grabbed him by his suspenders and pulled him there.

She'd been bent over the scraggly flower garden old
Mrs. Frellerhof had left, pushing the wild grasses back
so the bright spring blossoms could show through.

Until that moment, Zeke had never realized how
shabby the thin patch of grass and neglected garden
had looked. The farm had been the important thing.
Getting the first fields plowed and planted, fencing the
pasture and rebuilding the pens and corrals he needed
for the stock. He'd been working at building a farm,
but he hadn't given much thought to building a home.

Until now, he hadn't thought there was a difference.

"Zeke?" Sophie said, smiling at him, half puzzled,
half amused. "Are you all right?"

"Me?"

"You were laughing, then all of a sudden you were
looking so serious, as if you'd just remembered you'd
forgotten to feed the chickens or something."

"Naw." He forced himself to smile, then lay back
on the ground with a theatrical groan and covered his
eyes with one arm. "It's just I'm so stuffed, my belly's

pushing on my brain . . . which means neither one of 'em has room left to work!"'

She laughed. "You shouldn't have taken that last chicken wing. Or that fifth slice of bread and butter."

Zeke grinned and stretched. Gingerly, so it wouldn't put too much pull on his belly. It felt so *good* to relax like this. He hadn't realized just how much the last six months of hard work from sunup to long after sundown had worn on him . . . until now.

What he really wanted was to lay his head in Sophie's lap and go to sleep with the cottonwood leaves barely stirring above him and the air warm and lazy around him and that faint scent of lily of the valley that she wore tickling his nose like it was now, ever so gently.

Any other woman would be chattering away a hundred words to the minute and clattering the dishes and asking for his opinion or saying, "don't you agree?" or "isn't that so?" every so often, just to assure herself he was still listening.

But not Sophie. She was the first woman he'd ever met who seemed to understand what "restful" meant and didn't feel the need to yammer like a magpie every spare second she got. She was also the first woman he'd ever known who could sit still, even, instead of constantly jumping up to get something, or straighten something, or change something around until a man started to wonder when she'd be trying to change *him* around.

He couldn't remember *ever* feeling this comfortable around a woman. Not since the age of fourteen or fifteen, anyway, when he'd first realized there was something more to girls than pigtails and pinafores.

He'd have to get back to work in a few minutes. Sophie would be wanting to get back to town. He didn't want her to go, but since she couldn't stay—probably wouldn't *want* to stay—he'd settle for enjoying these last few minutes before she climbed to her feet and gathered up her things and drove off.

Leaving him, though he didn't want to think about it just yet, with a youngster who was probably going to be more trouble than he was worth and all the chores that hadn't got done today because he'd been too busy trying to get cleaned up and presentable.

And there were a *lot* of chores. There was that irrigation ditch to the bean field that needed cleaning out. Not to mention the old pigpens he was trying to rebuild so he could stock a couple more sows. And he needed to check the cultivator before he got into the corn next week, and there was the . . .

The endless list of chores spun off into warm, blank nothing as Zeke drifted into sleep.

Chapter 11

So much for her charm and conversational talents.

Sophie stared at the six feet four inches of slumber-ous male stretched out on the other side of the damask-covered horse blankets. The poor man *did* look tired, but she'd be willing to bet he wouldn't have fallen asleep if Annie Talbot had been chattering charmingly away in her place!

Ah, well, what had she expected? That he'd read love poems to her?

A fat, lazy fly swung over the remnants of the fried chicken, checking out possibilities. Sophie swatted at him, irritated. There wasn't anything else she could swing at. Or that she dared swing at, anyway.

She missed. The fly buzzed off over Zeke's nose. Neither Zeke nor his nose so much as twitched.

With a sigh, Sophie leaned back against the tree. In the abandoned field beyond the melons, Tom was poking at rabbit holes, but without any luck. Beside her, Zeke started to snore, very, very softly.

Elizabeth Bennett had never had any trouble keep-ing Mr. Darcy's attention. John Singer had never, ever fallen asleep on Lucile Maitland. Mr. Rochester might often have been rude to Jane, but he hadn't been inclined to doze, either. Except, of course, when his mad wife tried to burn him in his bed.

In any case, Zeke didn't have a wife, mad or other-wise, and she, Sophie, didn't sleep in a room down the hall from . . .

No, better she not think about bursting into his room in the dark of night, because what came to mind wasn't remotely like drenching him in cold water, as Jane had drenched Mr. Rochester.

Maybe Delphi—the *human* Delphi—had been right after all. If she was going to get Zeke's attention, maybe she *would* have to put more emphasis on her cooking. Fried chicken and fresh-baked bread were the only things that had worked so far. Short of physical assault, that is.

The only thing was, she'd have to be a little more conservative. After all, Delphi had said the way to a man's heart was through his stomach, but she *hadn't* said anything about feeding him so much he couldn't move for an hour after.

Sophie glanced over at Zeke. He looked so comfortable, stretched out there. If she wanted, all she'd have to do is lean across the almost empty platter of fried chicken and the jar of corn relish and touch him.

She couldn't think of a single good reason to touch him . . . except that she wanted to. Badly.

She managed to keep her hands to herself, but she couldn't help studying him as he lay there.

The long, powerful bulk of his body. The way the toe of his boot cocked up at the sky and his other leg bent at the knee just so. The way his hand lay across his belly, the fingers loose, relaxed, the swell of his chest, the strong, masculine curve of his throat, the hard line of his jaw that was softened by the gentler curve of his mouth, the straight ridge of cheek softened by the thick black lashes above them.

Especially, she studied his mouth—the carefully outlined top lip and the fuller, longer lower lip. The way they parted, ever so slightly, whenever he took a breath that was just a little deeper than the rest.

She found herself wondering what it would be like to feel his lips press against hers in a kiss.

And that thought led her gaze back down the length of him to that enticing trace of hidden secrets that his pants revealed. Unlike the too tight trousers he'd worn to the social, Zeke wore his work pants comfortably loose. In the normal course of things, there wasn't much to see at the front of his trousers except the placket for his trousers buttons. But asleep like this, with his long legs stretched out in front of him, Sophie could make out the intriguing outline of an object that was rather larger than she'd imagined such things to be.

Just the thought was enough to ignite a reaction in her.

Sophie stiffened, willing her body not to respond, tightening her muscles against the ache and the sudden heat in an instinctive response that only made matters worse.

Friday, May 5, 1893

I can't get to sleep, but at least tonight I'm not tail-dragging weary on top of it all. Must have slept a good hour this afternoon, maybe more. I suppose I should be ashamed, wasting daylight when I could have been working. I *know* I should have been ashamed to have been so rude to Miss Sophie. Sophie, I mean. She said she'd rather be called Sophie by her friends, which made me feel pretty good, taken all in all.

When I woke up, she was still sitting there beside me, propped up against the tree and staring out over the melon patch with this faraway look in her eye, as if she was dreaming about faraway places. China, maybe. Or Siam.

Now me, when I look at that melon patch, I think about how many melons I'll get and how much they'll bring if I ship them off to Kansas City, say, instead of sending them to Denver. I think about the bugs and the sun and the water, and will hail get them, or will the pigs trample half of them the next time they get out.

Sophie for sure wouldn't see the bugs or calculate the profit she might make. I doubt she's ever had to worry about things like bugs and hail and profits in her whole life. Young ladies that grow up in nice homes in town don't usually have to.

If I'd ever needed a reminder that I should be tending to my business and not letting thoughts of her get me in such a lather every night, that was it.

Still and all, it was mighty nice to wake up and see her sitting there, so prim and yet, somehow, not prim at all. It was even nicer to have her turn to me and smile. She didn't say a word, just smiled a little, then looked away to where Tom was coming up the road. Almost as if she was used to me sleeping beside her, then waking up and finding her still waiting.

Which is not at all a proper thought to be thinking.

While I'd been sleeping, she'd packed up the left-overs from lunch and sort of tidied up the place. Even picked a few flowers out of the garden, though by the time I opened my eyes, she'd pretty much shredded every one of them. Their petals were strewn all over her lap and that old damask tablecloth of Mama's like tiny bits of a rainbow.

Tom was coming up the lane. His pants were dusty and his hair was mussed and even from a distance he appeared to be pretty pleased with himself and life in general. He kept whistling like an out-of-tune black-bird and stopping every once in a while to take aim at a sunflower with his slingshot.

It was awful nice, lying there in the shade, still kind of lazy and heavy-eyed, with a pretty woman beside me, smiling so soft, and a little boy whistling and doing the sort of thing that little boys always do. It felt like family. Or at least how a family ought to feel, seems to me.

Not that I should be wasting time thinking about family. I can't afford a wife, much less a passel of kids. Though there's no denying I'd sure like to have them. Half a dozen would be about right, I think. Three of each, with the girls tall and proud and smiling like their mother.

Which is a thought that's getting so far ahead of possibilities, it might as well be off in Kansas, for all the sense it makes.

Of course, the minute she saw I was finally awake, Sophie got to her feet and brushed off all those flower petals like so much dust and said she'd best be getting back to town. I tried to apologize for falling asleep like that, but she said, all polite and formal, that I wasn't to worry. That I'd looked like I could use a little rest and she suspected that now I had Tom to keep an eye on, I probably wouldn't be getting much.

I wonder what she would have said if I'd told her that *she's* the one responsible for upsetting my sleep so often lately?

Anyway, I hitched up her horse for her while she washed the plates and mugs we'd used, even though I told her not to bother, and then she drove away down the road and left Tom and me to fend for ourselves.

We never did touch the pie, though she left that for us. Guess we'll have it tomorrow. Since it'll be me cooking, it's probably not such a bad idea to have a little touch of nice to go with whatever I manage to burn for supper.

I showed Tom all the evening chores. He's never milked a cow or slopped a hog, as he prefers to call it, but he's willing to learn so long as he gets to work on that traction engine, too.

Not that everything went perfectly smooth, of course. We had a couple of discussions about just what was what. Bound to have, even though it's plain he means to try. Part of it was being tired, I think. Most of it was he was missing his mama and not wanting to admit it.

You can see he's had a tough life, what with his mama in the trade and all. Which makes me plenty ashamed of myself. When I'd gone to Mrs. Peabody's that night, I'd never imagined she had a son. Knowing that she does, and that she loves him regardless of her drinking and her whoring puts the matter in a whole different light, for sure.

Though that isn't what's keeping me from sleeping tonight. And it isn't thinking about Miss Sophie. At least, not in any of the ways that have been sending me out to the pump in the middle of the night lately.

No, I keep thinking about her staying there beside

me while I slept and how she was there when I woke up.

She looked so pretty, sitting there with her high collar buttoned all the way up and her skirts spread out around her, covered with flower petals. Sort of half formal, half . . . free, I guess.

I lay in bed thinking about her, picturing the way she'd smiled and the way she'd looked and how all those flower petals had come spilling off her skirt when she stood. And the more I thought about it all, the more impossible it was for me to get to sleep.

Took me a while to figure out what it was that was bothering me. Then I realized. That double bed, the room—they all seemed so . . . empty.

Funny, even though Tom's here, the whole house seems emptier tonight than it ever has. A whole lot emptier.

As soon as she'd cleaned up the breakfast things, Sophie pulled on an enormous old linen duster she wore whenever she plunged into major cleaning.

Instead of cleaning, however, she traipsed out to the shed behind the house and began rooting around among the discarded screens and drain pipes and old rolls of tar paper that always seemed to collect in such places. She was looking for the bicycles she and Delphi had bought a couple of years ago when Mr. Hodgeson had received an unexpectedly large shipment at a ridiculously low price. Everyone who was anyone had bought one, and Delphi had insisted they be among the first.

Once Delphi had discovered that riding a bike was more likely to skin her nose than let her fine figure show to advantage, however, she'd abandoned the contraption and never looked at it again. Sophie had wobbled around on her bike for weeks—and skinned her hands and ruined a good walking skirt in the process—until she finally got the hang of it. And then she'd pretty much put it up in the shed with Delphi's and forgotten about it.

Until now. Last night, actually, when she was plan-

ning how to get out to Zeke Jeffries' farm regularly—
to check on Tom, of course—without rousing the curiosity of the town busybodies.

The farm was a little more than four miles out of
town. Not an impossible walk, but not one Sophie
cared to make if she were going to be carrying food
for three. Or more like four, if you considered how
much Zeke had managed to put away.

She didn't dare rent a horse and buggy from the
livery stable. Not on a regular basis. That *would* cause
talk! And she certainly couldn't count on being able
to hitch a ride out and back whenever she wanted
to go.

Which left the bicycle.

There'd be nothing to attract attention if she suddenly decided to go pedaling around on a bicycle, especially if she used it every day and not just on the
days she visited Zeke and Tom.

Fortunately, when she'd bought the bicycle she'd
also bought panniers to go with it. She'd never used
them, but they were already in place and more than
large enough to carry a loaf or two of fresh bread,
say, or a package of fried chicken without anyone
being the wiser.

Unfortunately, the panniers were in good shape, but
the bicycle they were attached to was not. Two years
of storage had rotted the tires and packed enough dust
into the gears and chain that major maintenance was
going to be required. Delphi's bike wasn't in much
better shape, though it did have fewer dents.

Sophie scowled at the two wretched vehicles. How
was she ever .. ?

The scowl slowly changed to a smile and the smile
to an indecently wide grin. She'd been looking for a
solution to another little problem that had been bothering her ever since she was dragged into Tom's troubles, and the dust-caked bikes, half hidden behind a
stack of torn screens and a barrel full of discarded
shingles, were it.

She dragged the screens away and tugged her bicycle out from behind the barrel, then pushed it out to

the pump to wash it off as best she could. That done, she hung the duster on a nail in the shed and slowly pushed the bike with its dirt-clogged, protesting gears into the alley. It was Saturday, so most of the businesses in town would be open until one o'clock or so. She just hoped the one she wanted was open as well.

Patrick O'Boyle was hard at work at his forge when she pushed the bike into his shop almost half an hour later. He looked up and his eyes widened. A moment later, his thick black brows crashed together in a ferocious frown.

"I'm sorry, miss," he said, though he didn't look the least bit sorry about anything, "but I'm busy."

Sophie smiled. "I'll wait."

She propped up the bike in the open shop doorway, then sat on the bench against the wall. She settled her skirts neatly about her, clasped her hands together and laid them demurely in her lap, then proceeded to stare.

At Patrick. At the forge and the workbenches and the stack of scrap iron in the corner and the tools hanging from pegs on the wall. But mostly she stared at Patrick.

He was worth staring at. He wasn't as good-looking as Zeke. His face was craggier and rougher, as if he'd been hammered by life as hard as he hammered the iron on his anvil. He was slightly shorter than Zeke, but far more massive. His work had developed his arm and chest muscles to almost intimidating proportions. If Sophie hadn't already known that he was an essentially gentle man, she might have been a tad nervous just at the sight of him.

None of the gentleness was showing today. Sophie couldn't be sure, of course, but she suspected that some of the violent energy he was expending on pounding that red-hot piece of iron was due to her presence.

When Patrick had told her that Sarah Jane Peabody had rejected his offer of marriage, he'd still been reeling from the emotional currents that had surged between him and Sarah Jane. He'd regretted his confession the minute he'd made it. He wouldn't have stomped off and left her in the street, otherwise.

Sophie didn't claim to know much about men, but one thing she did know, the creatures weren't fond of anyone knowing they weren't always as tough as they liked to pretend.

Sarah Jane had been almost as bad. It hadn't taken Sophie long to realize that Sarah Jane was just as unsettled by Patrick as Patrick was by her . . . and just as unwilling to admit it.

Sophie just hoped her little stratagem would help. Fortunately, Patrick was finding it increasingly difficult to ignore her presence. Eventually he gave up even trying. He slammed his hammer down on the anvil and turned to face her.

"*What,* then?"

Sophie beamed. "I have some work for you."

"I doubt I'll have time to get to it for . . . for weeks! Longer, maybe."

"I need you to fix my bicycle here." Sophie cocked her head to the side to indicate the bike in the doorway, but didn't take her eyes off Patrick. "It needs new tires, and the gears and chain and whatnot need to be cleaned and oiled."

"Greased."

"I beg your pardon?"

"They use grease, not oil. Rafe Fedder could probably do it for you. I can't. I'm a blacksmith, not a mechanic."

"And I need it by the first of next week. Mr. Hodgeson usually keeps a stock of tires, since he's the one who sold them in the first place."

"Talk to Rafe," Patrick said curtly, turning to pick up his hammer.

"I need it so I can get out to see Tom, you know."

With the tongs, Patrick picked up the piece of iron he'd been working, studied it a moment from all sides, then thrust it back into the fire and pumped the foot-powered bellows until the coals at the center glowed white-hot.

"Then once you've finished my bike, I figured you could work on Delphi's."

Patrick snorted and pumped the bellows harder.

Sophie was rather enjoying herself, even if it was cruel to tease the poor man so. "I thought Sarah Jane could use it to go out and visit Tom, too."

Patrick's shoulders stiffened. He didn't take his eye off the flames, but he did stop pumping the bellows.

"Of course, after the bike's fixed up, someone will have to help her learn to ride it."

Not a peep. The only sound in the smithy was the muted roar of the fire in the forge.

"That someone doesn't have to know how to ride a bike himself, of course," Sophie added slowly, as if she were just that moment considering the problem of teaching Sarah Jane to ride a bike.

Patrick poked at the strip of iron in the fire with his tongs, shifting it, pushing it deeper into the coals, then pulling it back out to inspect it.

"Just hold her on the seat when she starts off, and pick her up when she falls. Sort of cheer her on, you know."

Like a bull turning to face a tormentor, Patrick turned to face Sophie. "I think it'd be best if you just tended to your own business and let me tend to mine."

"You know, my mother does it all the time. It annoys the very dickens out of me, but there are times it needs doing, nonetheless."

Patrick stared at her from under lowered brows. "Am I supposed to know what it is you're rattlin' on about, then?"

"Sticking your nose into other people's business. Like I said, my mother does it all the time, and I believe I've inherited the tendency. Although to a slightly lesser degree," Sophie added, not wanting to claim credit where credit wasn't due.

"And you've come to stick your nose into my business?"

Sophie rewarded him with her widest smile. "That's it."

"Well, I thank you, and I'll be needin' none of it. Now if you'll excuse me . . ."

"I know. You have work to do." Sophie rose to her feet and delicately shook out her skirts. "I'll bring the other bike on Monday, when I come to pick up this one. All right?"

She didn't wait to hear whether it was all right or not.

She was halfway out the door when she stopped, then turned back to add, "Oh! I'll just stop at Mr. Hodgeson's on my way home and tell him to charge four bicycle tires to our account and that you'll be picking them up, all right?"

She didn't wait to hear if *that* was all right, either.

She was all the way out in the street and pointed toward Sarah Jane's when she heard a low roar from the interior of the smithy that sounded very much like "Aarrrggghhh!"

Zeke was in the melon field on the following Friday when Sophie suddenly appeared, pedaling past him up the lane like a demented steam engine, puffing and panting and so red in the face she looked ready to explode.

She didn't see him. She was hunched over the handlebars, staring at the road right in front of her as if she were afraid it might suddenly disappear. She didn't even try to avoid half the ruts in her way, just plunged into them and bounced up on the other side so hard she came halfway off the seat. Every time she did, Zeke could see the pink ribbons on her hat flip up like wings behind her.

Zeke threw down his hoe and gestured for Tom to follow. By the time he reached Sophie, she'd pulled to a halt in the shade of one of the big cottonwoods and was drooped over the handlebars, shoulders heaving with her effort to catch her breath and her feet planted flat on the ground on either side of the bicycle as if she were too tired even to crawl off the thing.

"Tom! Bring a dipper of water. Quick!" Zeke didn't wait for Sophie's permission. He wrapped his hands around her waist and lifted her free of the heavy bicycle, then swung her into his arms as the bike fell on its side with a heavy metallic crash

"There's a . . . jar of . . . jam . . . in there!" Sophie protested between gasps of air. She waved vaguely at the leather panniers mounted on the back of the bike, but Zeke ignored her.

He carried her over and set her down on the little grassy plot where they'd shared their picnic and carefully propped her against the tree's broad, rough trunk.

"Whatever were you thinking?" he demanded, then immediately added, "No, don't talk. Just catch your breath first."

Sophie obediently shut her eyes and tilted her head back against the trunk, mouth open to gulp down air.

Her face was scarlet. Sweat ran in rivulets off her brow and tendrils of hair were plastered to her temples and brow, dark brown with damp. Zeke pulled out his handkerchief—clean, thank heavens!—and dabbed at a trickle of sweat that threatened to plunge off her eyebrow and into her eye, then clumsily mopped her brow and cheek and chin, trying to wipe away the worst of it.

It didn't seem to help. She didn't even open her eyes to protest his awkward ministrations or attempt to take over the job herself.

Zeke tossed his handkerchief into her lap and reached for the buttons of her high-collared blouse. Her collar was too tight; she'd breathe much easier once it was loosened.

A fraction of an inch from the top button, his hand froze. How many times had he thought of doing exactly this? Imagined it in such excruciating detail that he'd ached? He'd gotten it wrong, obviously. Not once had he ever imagined that, once the moment arrived, Sophie's heavy breathing would be due to overexertion, not excitement.

"Beg your pardon," he said between gritted teeth, struggling with the small, round buttons that insisted on evading his callused fingers, "but you'll feel better when you can breathe free."

He managed to get about a dozen of the little buttons undone, just far enough to release the pressure around her throat, before she finally realized what he was doing.

"Oh!" she said, and her eyes snapped open. "Oh, my! I . . . I'm fine. Really," she said, and struggled to sit up.

"I brought a bucketful *and* the dipper," Tom announced, setting an overflowing bucket of water on the grass beside Zeke. The water slopped over the rim, splashing Zeke's pants and Sophie's skirt impartially.

Zeke snatched up the handkerchief in Sophie's lap and held it out to Tom. "Here. Pour some water over this, will you?"

Sophie took it from his hands and mopped at her face, squeezing it until the cool water trickled down her throat and under the edge of her open collar.

She sighed and leaned back against the tree, eyes closed. "Ahhh. That feels . . . good."

Zeke stared at the lingering droplets on her skin, the path the water had taken as it slid down that delicate arch of her neck. He could see the pulse at the side of her throat, just beneath the surface, and suddenly he wondered what it would feel like to rest the tip of a finger there, to *feel* the life flowing through her veins. One finger, very gently, and then he could trace—

"Could I have . . . a drink? Please?"

Her eyes were open and fixed on him. Zeke felt his own face flush. Had she read any of what he was thinking in his eyes? Had she sensed it from his touch?

Shame filled him, a shame oddly mixed with excitement and a touch of . . . could he call it awe? Or was that just his own blood pounding so hard through his veins that his ears rang and his thoughts spun like pinwheels?

He helped her sit up, grateful for an excuse to avoid her gaze. With her propped against his shoulder, he handed her the dipper Tom had filled from the bucket. Fat drops of water dripped onto her skirt, but she ignored them as she wrapped both her hands around the dipper and took a long, eager swig.

"Just a sip!" Zeke warned her. "No, a *sip*." He wrapped his free hand around the bowl of the dipper, covering hers. "You'll make yourself sick if you drink too much too quickly."

By the time she relinquished the dipper with a satisfied sigh, Zeke's muscles were trembling, and not just with the effort of maintaining his awkward position. He propped her up against the tree and rocked back on his heels. He hadn't felt this shaken and bewildered since old Mr. Gordon's bull had tossed him when he was twelve.

"Thank you." She blinked, then ran his handkerchief across the tip of her chin to catch an errant drop of water. "This is so . . . awkward."

"Is something wrong?" Zeke ventured hesitantly. "That you needed to get out here so fast, I mean."

Sophie gave him a wry, shy smile tinged with embarrassment and shook her head. "Nothing's wrong. I was afraid that if I stopped, that I'd just turn around and go home, so I just kept pedaling." She glanced up at Tom. "I promised your mother I'd come out and check on you, tell her how you were doing."

"I'm doin' okay," Tom said. He abandoned his post by the water bucket and cautiously squatted down beside Sophie, just out of reach. "Is Ma okay? Is she gonna come visitin' sometime?"

"She's just fine. She said I was to tell you that she'd come out for a visit, too, just as soon as she learns to ride the bike Patrick is fixing for her. If it's all right with Mr. Jeffries, that is," she added hastily, glancing up at Zeke.

Zeke jumped. His thoughts had been on other, more physically unsettling subjects. "Uh, sure. Why shouldn't she come visiting?"

Sophie glanced at Tom. "She was afraid it might not be good for your . . . reputation."

"Oh," said Zeke. He blushed. She had a point. Especially if Mrs. Smith were ever to get wind of it.

Tom tensed and his young face took on a hard, defiant cast. Before he could say anything or get to his feet and stomp away, Zeke said, more firmly this time, "I don't see why she shouldn't. But only if she doesn't arrive half dead like you just did!"

Tom grinned and let out a tiny, almost inaudible sigh of relief, but Zeke would almost swear that Sophie's face fell, just a little.

What had she done? Sophie watched, stunned, as Zeke walked away, leaving her and Tom to get "caught up." Not once had she thought that, by helping Sarah Jane, she was throwing away her own excuse to visit, the excuse she'd spent weeks trying to find.

It wasn't that she wanted to keep Tom from his mother, Sophie reminded herself, but if Sarah Jane could come all the way out here for a visit, what excuse would *she* have for coming herself?

"An' that ol' sow, she like to near bit my foot off, only I scrambled over the fence before she could catch me, see—"

Tom's account of his first week on the farm finally managed to drag Sophie back to an awareness of where she was.

"—An' Zeke showed me how to chase her back so she don't get so obstrep'rous, which is what he said she was. An' I've been workin' real hard in the truck garden, Miss Sophie. Honest I have!" Tom hesitated, then admitted, " 'Course he had to plant another row of radishes, an' half a row of carrots, but *I* didn't know they wasn't—weren't weeds, Miss Sophie! Honest I didn't! And Zeke, he didn't seem to mind too much that I hoed down some of his lettuce and stuff 'cause he says *everyone* hasta learn. Leastwise, he didn't beat me like he coulda. And I *am* learnin'. Honest I am!"

Tom was having a hard time sitting still, he was so excited. His eyes sparked and his eager smile stretched clear across his face.

"An' you should see what we're doin' with that old

traction engine! Got a bunch of parts all out on the barn floor an' I'm helpin' Zeke clean 'em and put 'em back together. Month or so, he says we might have the thing runnin'! An' he says I can learn to drive it an' everything! Ain't that grand?"

"Sounds pretty grand to me," Sophie agreed. The boy's enthusiasm was contagious. Without being sure exactly why, she felt a whole lot better already. "So you and Zeke are getting along all right, huh?"

"We get along purty good." Tom hesitated, then added reluctantly, "But I gotta say, he ain't—isn't much of a cook. Not like Ma. Or like you, Miss Sophie. And he's hell— er, he's awful strict about bathin'."

"Is he?"

"Yup. Makes me wash up *every* night! Even if I'm not real, real dirty! Can you imagine?"

"Fancy that!" Sophie said. Considering how dirty Tom had been that first time she'd seen him in Hodgeson's Emprorium, a daily washing wasn't a bad idea at all.

"*He* even washes up twice, some days!"

"Really?"

"Yup. Come midnight or so, seems like purty near every night he's trailing out to the pump."

"Really?" That came out a little weaker.

"Yup. He sleeps in the altogether, you know, so it ain't—*isn't*—much of a problem."

"Really?" That one was *definitely* shaky. the image of Zeke Jeffries in the altogether . . . Well, no real lady would be picturing the kinds of things that thought roused in her. "I .. didn't know."

"He just grabs a bucket and fills it straight from the pump, then he tips it over his head like he was sloppin' hogs or somethin'."

Sophie didn't even open her mouth.

"Does that three or four times. Sometimes more if he's 'specially dirty, I guess. Though it beats me how he could get that dirty when he always takes a good wash before bed."

Tom scrunched his eyebrows together and pooched

out his lower lip as he considered the problem. Evidently, it was beyond his powers of comprehension, because he shrugged and shook his head.

"Me, I'd think it'd be awful cold, middle of the night like that, but Zeke's powerful set on clean, Miss Sophie. Worse'n my Ma in one of her cleanin' moods. Thing is, Ma don't get those moods but every so often, when she ain't—*isn't* drinkin'. Zeke's got it bad every day. Sort of like that lady from that revival meetin' that came through town last year. She'd come out and stand in front of our house every day and start prayin' as loud and hard as she could go, even if she'd already prayed at the meetin'. Used to make Ma purty mad, but then the revival meetin' left town and so did the prayin' lady. But Zeke, he just about sleeps with that pump, seems like."

What man in his right mind would feel compelled to douse himself with buckets of cold water in the middle of the night?

Something her friend Clara Randall had told her when Clara was expecting their first child teased at Sophie. What had Clara said, exactly? Something about her husband Joe wanting his marital rights, but Clara hadn't been feeling well so she'd told him to go out to the pump and soak his head so he wouldn't be tempted to bother her.

Clara hadn't said if Joe had followed her advice or not, but Sophie thought the remedy sounded just like Zeke's midnight soakings. But was the original complaint the same? Was Zeke hoping for a bachelor's version of marital rights, but not having any luck? And if so, why?

Or rather, who?

Who was it that was getting Zeke so all-fired hot and bothered?

Chapter 12

Two months. Two whole months! Or almost, anyway.

Sophie gave the flour sifter a sharp slap to shake the last of the flour into the mixing bowl, then dumped in the lard for the morning's biscuits.

Two months now she'd been going out to Zeke's twice a week, regular as clockwork. She'd started tutoring Tom in math and reading, but that was just her excuse for chasing Zeke. She'd lost track of how many chickens and hogs had sacrificed their lives so she could make fried chicken and roast ham to add to all the other delectables she'd baked and pickled and boiled for those two ravenous males. Not that it had done her any good. Tom was progressing by leaps and bounds in his studies, but, so far as Zeke was concerned, Sophie's love life was stalled at the wishful stage, and it didn't show any promise of getting better.

Not that Zeke was unfriendly—far from it!—but friendship wasn't what she wanted, and it certainly wasn't enough to pacify Delphi's increasingly insistent prying. By dint of a little misdirection and a couple of outright lies, Sophie had managed to keep her visits a secret, but that couldn't last much longer. Especially not now that Adelaide Smith had started escorting Annie Talbot out for a "friendly" visit every now and then.

Annie's visits, and Adelaide's pleasure in telling Delphi of them, had exacerbated Delphi's growing irritation with her, Sophie's, continued lack of a beau. If Mr. Conner hadn't started asking Delphi to walk out with him in the evenings, Sophie knew life at home would have been as close to unbearable as might be. Having a gentleman caller didn't quite set Delphi's cup to running over, but it helped. The knowledge that Adelaide thought Mr. Conner ought to be paying court to the widowed Mrs. James almost filled it to the brim.

"You can't *imagine* the nerve of that woman!"

Delphi's unexpected appearance in the kitchen doorway made Sophie jump. Delphi had attended a ladies-only supper last night and Sophie, unwilling to hear the gossip her mother would inevitably bring home, had gone to bed early. She should have known she couldn't escape for long.

"What woman, Mother?"

"That Adelaide Smith, of course! There isn't another soul in a hundred miles that can rile me like that woman can, and you know what a peaceable woman I am, Sophronia!"

Sophie's fingers convulsively squeezed the lard-and-flour mix. When her mother started talking about how "peaceable" she was, there was a fight brewing and no mistake. The animosity between her mother and Adelaide Smith had grown until the two of them were, as Zeke would have said, prickly as cockleburs on a dog's back.

"What's Adelaide done now, Mother?"

"Done! She's meddled, that's what! Stuck that pointy little nose of hers in where it doesn't concern her, and now look!"

Delphi waved her hands in the air as if she were conjuring whatever it was Sophie was supposed to look at, then abruptly pulled out the chair at the opposite end of the kitchen table and sat down.

"I had it all arranged, you know," said Delphi. "I talked to Mrs. Bassett and Mrs. Bassett suggested it to Milly Purvis and Ida Duncan, who told Dora Stevens that she'd be a shoo-in with her angel food cake, which she won't, but there! What can you say? So Dora told Mrs. Bassett they really *ought* to consider a bake contest—"

Ah! thought Sophie. It wasn't always so easy to identify the subject of Delphi's diatribes.

". . . because Watermelon Day is getting so big, and they're showing off fruit from the farms, and it would certainly be appropriate to have a bake contest, you know, and what with the new racetrack opening there'll probably be hundreds more people than usual, but then Adelaide said—"

"So now there isn't going to be a baking contest?" Sophie asked, trying to bring her mother to the point before Delphi got lost in her own verbiage.

"Not be a contest?" Delphi ruffled indignantly. "Whatever gave you that notion? Did I say anything about there not being a contest?"

"No, of course you didn't."

"I didn't think so! However . . ." Delphi frowned. "Where was I?"

"Adelaide said . . ."

"Oh, yes! Well, Adelaide said a baking contest was all well and good but why were we worrying about Watermelon Day when Fourth of July was coming up? Shouldn't we try to think of something new for that? she said. Something a little more 'sophisticated.'" Delphi pronounced the word with a supercilious sniff that indicated Adelaide Smith had no more notion of what "sophisticated" meant than a frog. "Can you imagine?"

Sophie shook her head and mumbled something her mother didn't bother deciphering, then dumped the biscuit dough onto the mound of flour in the middle of the breadboard and began rolling it out.

"She wants to have a 'cultural' program. She couldn't very well argue against the baking contest because Eliza Neumann is known for her pies, you know. And there's Dora, of course, and Thea Talbot. Not to mention that Adelaide prides herself on her breads, though why she should has *always* been a puzzle to me!"

Sophie sighed. "Do you want one egg or two for breakfast?" There was a slight chance breakfast might distract Delphi, though Sophie wasn't over hopeful.

"Two. No, one. Anyway, it's not bad enough that Adelaide managed to trap poor Mr. Jeffries into escorting Annie Talbot for the race track opening. Oh, no! Now she wants Annie—better make that two—to declaim something 'serious' for the Fourth! I suppose she means something grim, like 'Thanatopsis,' that we've all heard a hundred times, at *least*. We wouldn't be lucky enough to get the Gettysburg Address. *That* would be too short! And, she said, Marla May has such a lovely voice she could sing if Mrs. James—you know she's been trying to get a husband for Mrs. James since a week after they put the poor man in the ground!—would play the piano. And Annie and Marla May could sing a couple of songs together, she said, completely ignoring the fact that *you* have a much nicer singing voice than either of *them*! No, make that one. And of course Eliza's mama, who hasn't any more sense than to let that poor girl wear pink, said— One *egg*, Sophie! Whatever did you *think* I meant?"

Tuesday, June 27, 1893

The melons are growing fine. I hope Mr. Swink's right about there being a good market for them in Kansas City and St. Louis and parts east. I was calculating up matters, and if prices hold come harvest, my fields ought to bring in $3000! At least! Add to that the onions and the beans and the hay, and in five or six years I ought to have the debts on this place paid off and some money in the bank, to boot. Sooner, if that traction engine works as well as I hope.

If Mama weren't already there, she'd be thinking she'd died and gone to heaven. She didn't know much but debts and taxes all her life. That and hard work. But she always said the hard work would pay off, and it's beginning to look like she was right. In just one year, too!

Hiram, of course, he's a bit more doubtful, but that's just his way, I think. Especially when Mrs. Smith gets to lecturing him a little more vehement than usual. She's not too pleased with me these days and she's been taking it out on him.

Seems I haven't quite come up to expectations. She's hauled Miss Annie over here few times—thankfully, never when Sophie's come visiting—and they both make a point of bringing me something or other that they're "experimenting" with. A pie or a fancy cake or something like that. Just a neighborly visit, Mrs. Smith always says, but it seems to me that Miss Annie is always a tad more gussied up than ladies usually are when they go off for neighborly visits.

Thing is, all their pies and cakes and neighborly visits haven't gotten me in for another church social, or a bake sale, or convinced me to buy any of those crocheted pot holders Miss Annie was hawking to raise funds for something or other. I suspect Mrs. Smith had figured I'd be courting her by now—Miss Annie, that is—but she was far off on her figuring if that was the case. Miss Annie's a fine lady, and I suspect I won't die if I really do end up escorting her to that racetrack opening come August, but that's as far as it goes. Those pretty, determined little women scare the living daylights out of me, and there's no doubt Miss Annie is on the hunt for a husband, with Mrs. Smith aiding and abetting just as hard and fast as she can.

The worst was this afternoon, when Mrs. Smith wanted me to hear Miss Annie recite. Seems she was having a hard time choosing between some godawful gloomy thing called "Thanatopsis" and President Washington's first inaugural address for the Fourth of July festivities.

They'd been to the Ladies Missionary Society meeting earlier, but there'd been so much debate among the ladies over which of the two Miss Annie should recite that they decided *I* should choose, since I represented the masculine point of view, so to speak.

It was a choice between culture and patriotism, Miss Annie said, and that's why she couldn't decide. As if it made any difference. They're *both* an affliction on the rest of us by the time the ladies get done with them.

What beats me is that Mrs. Smith and Miss Annie

even thought I *wanted* to listen to a poem about dying *and* a speech by a man who's been dead and buried going on a hundred years—and all in one chunk, too!

Now, I'll admit that Miss Annie does have a mighty powerful way about her when she goes to speak, even if she is a little thing. It's that big, deep chest she's got, I guess. Lots of lung space despite her runty size. But there I was with irrigation water running and the onions to weed, so I just wasn't in the mood for recitations.

It didn't help any that I was wearing the same work clothes I'd worn for the past four days because I forgot to take the laundry in to Gee Ging last week and I wanted to save my last clean ones for when Sophie comes tomorrow. A man feels mighty uncomfortable when the ladies are all tidied up and he's stinking like . . . well, like a man who's wearing his dirty laundry and has been sweating hard on top of it.

No help for it. There I sat, polite as can be, trying to look like I was listening and not fidgeting or staring at the flower garden that Sophie's got cleaned up and blooming to beat the band. I especially didn't want Mrs. Smith, who was sitting right beside me on a kitchen chair I'd brought out for her, to start wondering why that ratty old garden had suddenly spruced up so. And she'd have been bound to notice if I stared, because when she wasn't smiling and nodding encouragingly at Miss Annie, she was keeping a mighty sharp eye on me to be sure I was paying attention and enjoying the show.

Anyway, I was doing pretty well and Miss Annie was swinging right along with that "Thanatopsis" thing when pure Bedlam suddenly broke out on the far side of the barn.

I jumped to my feet right in the middle of some impressive lines about winding sheets—or maybe it was gauzy gowns or some such nonsense—and was starting to apologize to Miss Annie that I had to go see what was going on, when around the corner of the barn galloped that old spotted sow of mine with a whole herd of piglets right behind.

Behind *them* came Tom, dripping brown muck and eyes wide and showing white behind the brown. I'd told him before he wasn't supposed to ride that pig because he could get hurt and the sow wouldn't much like it, either, yet that was obviously what he'd gone and done. And this was the third time he'd done it, too.

That pretty much broke up the party. Turns out Miss Annie doesn't think much of pigs, piglets, or boys, and all three came zipping past her hell-bent for the highway. Or the nearest watermelon patch, anyway.

Miss Annie shrieked. Mrs. Smith started shouting at me and Tom and the pigs, pretty much share and share alike. Tom was yelling at the sow to come back and at me that he hadn't meant to do it. And the pig and her piglets were just squealing and having a gay old good time.

We managed to keep the pigs out of the fields, but it was a close-run thing. Must have taken us a good hour to get them all herded back to the pen, even with Mrs. Smith helping. Miss Annie couldn't help because she'd right away climbed up in the buggy and started having palpitations, even when there wasn't anybody left to notice. On top of it all, I had to patch the gate to the pen again, because when the sow threw Tom, he hit the gate and broke the latch, which is how the pigs got out in the first place.

In the end, the weeding didn't get done, the irrigation water didn't get shifted into the field I'd planned, and I got another notation in Mrs. Smith's black books, which are probably getting pretty full of notations lately.

Miss Annie did decide on President Washington's address, however. It came to her as she watched the pigs run past, I guess, though I can't quite make the connection, myself. Maybe she figured we couldn't quite cope with culture and would just have to settle for patriotism as being less demanding, so to speak.

Anyway, once the ladies were gone and the pigs were settled down, I dragged Tom off to the pump

and half drowned him trying to rinse off all that muck.
I sort of enjoyed seeing somebody besides me get a
dunking, though Tom didn't think much of the
process.

When I was dousing Tom down, I noticed for the
first time that there's a hole beginning to develop
where the water gets sloshed. If I keep going as strong
as I have lately, I reckon I'll have my own swimming
hole by Thanksgiving.

I suppose I'll have to drive by Miss Annie's house
next time I'm in town and apologize. Even if she
wasn't invited, it's not proper to upset a lady like Tom
and those pigs upset her.

All the same, I can't help thinking that Sophie
would have been watching the uproar and laughing
that laugh of hers that always digs down and grabs
something right in the middle of me, and she'd be
thinking the disaster was pretty good entertainment,
for the price. That is, if she wasn't chasing after those
pigs herself and seeing who could catch more piglets,
her or Tom.

Sophie swept into the farm lane almost half an
hour late.

If he hadn't spotted her first, Zeke would have
heard her coming. The rough road made the frame of
her bike shudder and rattle like a tin can filled with
rocks. She'd learned to pace herself since that first
visit and become more adept at avoiding the ruts, but
some of that original determination to make it all the
way to the house showed in the firm set of her shoulders and the way she kept her eyes focused on the
road five feet in front of her instead of looking around
at the scenery.

Tom spotted her from the onion patch and sent up
a hallo that chased the blackbirds from the trees. Sophie took one hand off the handlebars long enough to
wave in response, then grabbed hold again and steered
through the last set of ruts and into the shade.

By the time Zeke had finished the side of the pigpen

he'd been working on, Tom had dragged Sophie across to the main barn doors.

"And we fired her up yesterday!" Tom was saying, eyes alight. He danced around her, too eager and anxious to merely walk. "Only for a bit, but Zeke says we'll give her a real run today. An you can ride her if you want to!"

"I don't know about— Zeke!" Sophie stopped short, then smiled across at him.

For a moment, Zeke had the crazy urge to dance around her, too. Or, better yet, pull her into his arms and dance with her. Swing her around, then draw her close against him and whirl her about again until they were so dizzy they collapsed on the hay that now filled half the barn. And then they would—

Zeke forcibly cut that thought short.

"Tom says you have the traction engine running!"

Zeke wasn't sure how, but Sophie's smiles always made him think of sunshine. He shrugged and abruptly turned to stare at the engine. "Maybe." From one minute to the next, the temperature in the barn seemed to have shot up a good ten degrees.

"We do! You know we do, Zeke!" Tom wasn't going to settle for adult reservations, not when it came to his beloved steam engine. "And *I* get to ride it!"

The behemoth looked better than it had when half its innards were spread across the barn floor, but it still didn't look nearly as impressive as one of the newer, bigger, more powerful models. It *had* run yesterday, though, and if it worked half as well as similar machines Zeke had seen in the past, it would make his life ten times easier when it came to plowing and harvesting and the heavy work of breaking ground for new fields.

If it worked, he reminded himself sternly, trying to concentrate, to think about anything except what he always thought about whenever he looked at Sophie.

"You really do have it running?" Sophie was almost breathless, as excited as Tom and more than willing to share in their enthusiasm.

Zeke nodded. He couldn't think of a thing to say that wouldn't sound half-witted.

Tom didn't hesitate to fill in the conversational gap. He launched right into a confusing, eager recitation of their first venture in getting the thing going.

While he pretended to study the traction engine, Zeke watched her out of the corner of his eye, desperately wishing he possessed the gift of gab so she'd tilt her head like that to show she was listening to him and not Tom, so she'd lean toward him as he pointed out the work they'd done, like Tom was doing now.

This was what he waited for each week, he thought. For the chance to see her smile and catch the sparkle in her eye. For the chance to be near her, even for a little while, to smell the scent of lily of the valley she wore and to listen to her soft, sweetly modulated voice. She didn't have the clear, carrying kind of voice Miss Annie had, but he could listen to her all day and half the night—if she'd ever rattled on that long, which she'd never yet shown any sign of doing. She was the least gossipy female he'd ever met in his life.

He'd probably even enjoy listening to her if she'd decided to recite "Thanatopsis," and that was saying something after what he'd endured the day before.

He'd be better off not thinking about any of it.

"Do you want to see it run?" he asked, grasping at the most obvious diversion at hand, not caring if he interrupted Tom's fervid explanation of how the drive train worked.

"Yes!" Tom shouted.

"Of course," Sophie said, smiling and making Zeke melt in his boots without even trying.

Clean shirt and all, Zeke started to sweat.

Sophie watched from a prudent distance as Zeke got the metal monster started. Even in the big, drafty barn it sounded as if a dozen trains had suddenly come roaring through. Tom made sure the doors were swung wide and the wire fence to the abandoned fields open and out of the way, then he scrambled up beside Zeke and the two were off in a cloud of steam. The great gray beast easily rolled right over the piles of last year's tumbleweeds, which had blown up against the fence line. The cleats on its massive iron wheels dug into the compacted prairie soil and spat out chunks of dirt and prairie turf.

Zeke sat atop the thing like a knight atop his gallant steed, his expression set hard as he concentrated on steering it down the field and watching the dials and gauges of the machine, all at the same time. Tom perched beside him, king of all he surveyed and twice as happy if that grin was anything to go by.

They reached the bottom of the field, then swept around in a wide circle and headed back toward Sophie, leaving a trail of churned dirt and crushed weeds in their wake. Zeke almost wouldn't need to plow. He could tear up and down the field on his steam-driven beast and simply grind the earth under his wheels. With a belch and a roar, Zeke brought the thing to a halt at the gate. Even from this far away, Sophie could see the excitement and the pride in his face.

Tom reluctantly clambered down and darted across to Sophie. "Zeke says he'll give you a ride if you want!" he shouted over the noise.

"That's all right—" Sophie tried to say, but Tom wasn't going to let her wriggle out of it.

"Come *on*, Miss Sophie. It's fun! Honest!" He grabbed her hand and dragged her to the back of the steam engine.

Zeke twisted around on his seat and grinned down at her with a grin that was even wider than Tom's, if that were possible. "Come on! You'll like it! Just put your foot there and grab hold of this and you can climb up." He glanced at his controls to make sure the monster wouldn't run away without him, then leaned down and extended his hand toward her.

Sophie's breath caught somewhere right in the center of her throat. This was how she'd always imagined one of the heroes from her books must look when he was with the woman of his dreams—alive and vital and heart-stoppingly virile. Too bad it needed a steam traction engine to generate that kind of enthusiasm.

About the only thing that had come close since she'd known him was her deep-dish apple pie.

The iron monster was chugging and snorting and altogether terrifying, but Sophie screwed up her courage and reached for the handhold Zeke indicated.

The first step wasn't too bad, but her skirts hampered her reach for the second. Without a word, Zeke bent and wrapped an arm around her and half dragged, half lifted her up beside him.

Sophie squeaked and sucked in her breath at the contact, then hastily grabbed his shoulder to keep her balance. Suddenly, she was short of breath and unreasonably warm. Under her clothes, the skin over her ribs and across her back burned where his arm had pressed.

"Watch it!" Zeke warned, and placed his hand at her waist to steady her. "You sit on this ridge of metal behind you and hang on here."

Sophie shakily propped her fanny on the ridge he'd indicated, then grabbed hold.

"And watch your skirts! You don't want them getting caught on the wheels!"

What had looked easy for a boy Tom's size was not, Sophie discovered, at all easy for a woman her size. They hadn't even started yet and already she was wobbling and the muscles in her legs were trembling from the strain of keeping her balance . . . and keeping out of Zeke's way.

His touching her had nothing to do with it. Absolutely nothing at all.

Zeke frowned, studying the problem. "Guess you'd better grab hold of my shoulder."

Maybe she'd better just get down and leave the riding to Tom.

Coward! Sophie told herself sternly. Tentatively, as if he were a bug that might bite, Sophie rested her hand on his shoulder.

"No. grab hold! Dig your fingers in!" Zeke told her.

Not an easy thing to do with shoulders that broad and heavily muscled, but Sophie did her best. Her hand tingled with the contact, with the solid feel and heat of him.

They set off with a jerk and a roar. They hadn't even reached the gate when Sophie transferred her grip to his opposite shoulder and leaned against him for balance. If she'd had the nerve, she would have wrapped both arms around his neck and pressed herself tight against his back—not out of any desire for seduction, but out of sheer terror.

The steam tractor snorted and belched and shook so hard her teeth rattled inside her head. Impossible to talk unless the conversation was conducted in shouts. Impossible to think because her head was being shaken off its pins. Impossible to do anything but lean against Zeke and hold tight to his shoulder with her left hand while her right maintained its death grip on the handhold.

It wasn't that they were going so fast—a good horse could have trotted faster than the traction engine's lumbering pace—but that they were making such an unholy racket and seemed, to Sophie's rattled senses, on the verge of exploding in a cloud of steam at any moment.

Zeke tilted his head so he could glance back at her. "Isn't this great?"

"Great?"

It came out as a shriek, but Zeke evidently took it for assent. "Watch this!"

He fiddled with the controls, then spun the steering wheel to the right. With a roaring clattery-clack, the beast came about faster than a horse at the end of the furrow and headed for home, then charged off, back the way they'd come but twice as fast. Dirt kicked out in great chunks from the wheels and the red needles on the gauges tilted around to the right as they raced down the field at what must have been close to fifteen miles an hour. They got to the end of the field and Zeke once more yanked the monster around in a careening turn.

Sophie abandoned all pretense of courage. She threw her arms around Zeke and hung on for dear

life. Her breasts pressed against his shoulder blade.
She could feel every move he made, the way his
weight shifted on the seat and the powerful interplay
of bone and muscle as he stretched to adjust something or other. Intimate as lovers, but even that
thought couldn't counter the sheer terror of being
atop this great, hulking, steam-spouting Goliath.

As the far fence came racing up to them, Sophie
shut her eyes, pressing her forehead to his shoulder
while the roar and clatter of the traction engine filled
her ears, and prayed.

Once they were around again, Zeke leaned forward,
pulling her even closer against him, and adjusted
something. Immediately, the engine slowed until it was
barely crawling forward and the noise died down to
what seemed, in comparison, a muted mumble.

Cautiously, without releasing her hold on Zeke, Sophie opened her eyes and peered over his shoulder.
The world was still there, and Tom was still standing
by the open gate, one hand shading his eyes as he
watched them chug back.

Zeke turned his head. She could see his grin, the
faint dimple in his cheek, the clean, patrician line of
his nose. For the first time Sophie became aware of
the scent of bay rum and man.

"Was that really so bad?" he asked, his grin widening. His long lashes lowered, as if he wanted to hide
his laughter from her, but there was a subtle, unconsciously erotic flavor to it that made Sophie catch
her breath.

Slowly, she forced herself to loosen her grip around
his neck and to sit back. "Terrible," she said at last,
and realized her voice was shaking.

Zeke twisted even farther around on the seat. His
grin vanished. "Really? I . . . I'm sorry. I didn't mean
to frighten you."

"You didn't frighten me," Sophie corrected him
shakily. "This thing did. There's a difference." She
hesitated a moment, then added, "I'm sorry I hung on
you like that. I didn't mean to, really."

That was a lie, Sophie realized suddenly. She *had*

meant to, even though she hadn't realized it at the time. And she'd enjoyed it, in spite of the terror. Her nipples hardened suddenly at the memory of how warm and hard and comfortingly solid he'd felt.

She didn't have a chance to say more, because Zeke was guiding the monster past an exuberant Tom, then into the barn.

Zeke shut the monster off. It jerked, gave a belch of protest, then an odd clank or two before settling into silence with a long, wheezing sigh of escaping steam.

For a moment, Zeke just sat there on the seat, his hands clenched around the driving wheel while he stared straight ahead. Sophie couldn't tell if he was listening to the machinery, or trying to come back to earth after the excitement of actually getting the beast to run.

After a minute, he shook himself and swung away from her, out of the seat and off the traction engine.

Marooned atop the metal monster, Sophie suddenly wondered if she'd imagined the excitement of those last noisy minutes, the energy that had hovered in the air between them, amplified by the belching beast they'd ridden.

An absurd thought. Just as Zeke had, she shook herself back to reality and swung off her uncomfortable perch.

It was harder getting down than climbing up. She couldn't see where to place her feet, her skirts were in the way, and mud and dirt covered so much of the metal frame that some of the former handholds were now mere lumps of dark brown sand and loam. Sophie leaned to the side, craning for a better view, when Zeke abruptly claimed her. His strong hands wrapped around her waist, pulling her free of the machine, swinging her around and to the ground.

The closer she got to the ground, the higher up her sides his hands slid, as if he were balancing her weight against the downward pull of the earth beneath them. From waist to ribs, from ribs on up until his hands

pressed just under her arms and his fingers brushed
at the sides of her unbound breasts.

And then she was on the ground, dazed by the
shock of the unexpected, intimate contact, her breasts
suddenly aching and her breath trapped in her lungs
so that for one mad moment she thought she might
burst from the pressure of it.

Zeke hadn't let her go. His palms still pressed
against her side, his fingers against the curve of her
breasts. She could feel the warmth of his breath
against the tip of her ear, as though he hung above
her, caught in the same sharp awareness she was.

He was warm. Sophie could feel the warmth of him
through the light cotton of her blouse and under vest.
Or maybe it was her own temperature that had risen.
All she knew was that she wanted to lean back against
him, wanted him to reach forward and cup her breasts
in his hands, to hold her tight and safe within his
embrace and kiss the curve of her ear and her
throat and . . .

"Hey, Zeke! That was great! Looked like you was—
were really goin' out there! You shoulda seen it!"
Tom's eager words cut through the dazed heat of the
moment, startling them both.

With a sharp hiss, Zeke let her go and backed away.

Chapter 13

"Two months! Two *months* that girl has been trailing out to Zeke Jeffries' farm, bringing him cakes and homemade bread and whatnot until I'm surprised the man hasn't burst!" Mrs. Granger was whispering loud enough that half the ladies in the kitchen and everyone in the parlor must have heard her.

Sophie had been drafted to help with laying out the luncheon for the Ladies Missionary Society, but at Mrs. Granger's denunciation, she hastily set down the platter she was carrying and pretended to rearrange its burden of finger sandwiches. She only hoped no one noticed the hot blush spreading across her cheeks. Behind her, someone in the kitchen tittered, then was peremptorily hushed.

"Not that it's done her the least bit of good, mind you," Mrs. Granger added with satisfaction. "Not the least! He hasn't so much as shown his face at another social, and he didn't ask her to that subscription dance, no matter what kind of airs her mother put on that he would. I don't know what the younger generation is coming to, but it can't be to much good when young ladies of good family are allowed to go gallivanting about the countryside in pursuit of a man. Mother would have been scandalized if she'd lived to see such goings on. Positively scandalized!"

"I know just how you feel, Mrs. Granger," Mrs. Purvis said in an equally carrying whisper. "I could hardly believe my ears when Mrs. Joerring told me. I never thought it of her, but there, what can you expect, being egged on like she is."

Sophie's fingers trembled so she almost dropped

one of the sandwiches. What a fool she'd been, thinking people wouldn't notice just because they never noticed much else she did.

Marla May suddenly giggled beside her, making Sophie jump. "I didn't have any idea, you know. Not the faintest!"

Sophie stared at her, appalled.

"Egged on or no," Mrs. Granger whispered back to Mrs. Purvis, "I *never* thought Annie Talbot would stoop to such unladylike behavior. Not even with her mother and Adelaide Smith both trying to help her catch a husband. I feel sorry for that poor Zeke Jeffries, indeed I do!"

They were talking about Annie Talbot, not her!

Relief swept through Sophie, immediately followed by shame that she was glad it was Annie being ridiculed when she was guilty of the same crimes. If you could call helping a troubled boy and making friends with a lonely man "crimes."

A small little voice in the back of her mind hissed that "making friends" didn't include clinging to a man as she'd clung to Zeke on that wild tractor ride yesterday. The memory of his hands at her side, his fingers just touching the swell of her breasts, was enough to make her blush all over again.

"Did you ever guess Annie would chase after him like that?" Marla May demanded in a whisper that was only slightly less carrying than her mother's. "Even if he *is* the best-looking man in the county and just as nice as they come. *I* certainly never thought she would!"

Sophie mumbled something, she wasn't quite sure what, and carried the platter into the dining room where the ladies' luncheon was laid out. Neither Adelaide Smith nor the Talbot ladies, mother and daughter, had arrived yet, which explained the eager gossip. Sophie felt a sick little twinge in the pit of her stomach. She should have known no one would be so outspoken if they'd been talking about her. Not while she was there to hear, at any rate.

All gossip about Annie's affairs came to an abrupt

halt when she and her mother walked in a few minutes later. As they made the round of the group, shaking hands and exchanging greetings, nothing was said but much was conveyed in expressively lifted eyebrows or delicate smiles that followed them around the room.

Sophie couldn't bear to watch. There was nothing really malicious in the gossip. Everyone in the room sincerely liked Annie and her mother, and most were good friends with Adelaide Smith—but that didn't make it any more comfortable.

The fascination lay in the eternal, and eternally changing mating dance that unmarried young men and women were forced to endure, even if they never quite mastered the intricacies of the steps. That Annie was beautiful and Zeke strikingly handsome simply added to the observers' enjoyment.

But if beautiful, talented Annie could be a source of gossip, Sophie thought despondently, how much more entertaining would her own romantic failures be?

"Really, Sophie! How long are you going to stand there staring at the aspic like a half-wit?"

Sophie jumped and almost knocked over a bowl of butter curls. She glanced at her mother nervously.

Delphi suffered from a burning desire to be acclaimed the most gracious and elegant hostess in town, and she spared none of Sophie's pains in the process of competing for the coveted accolade. This time, however, Mrs. Granger's eager gossip had clearly exacerbated the stress of entertaining. Only the knowledge that there were plenty of eager ears around prevented her from venting her frustration at the unfair advantage she thought Annie Talbot had gained.

Since she couldn't say what she really thought, Delphi settled for complaining. "You shouldn't have put the pickled onions in that silver dish, Sophie. Don't you know the acid will pit the silver? And those finger sandwiches shouldn't be stacked like that. This isn't a re-creation of the pyramids, you know!"

"Of course, Mother. You're quite right. I'll redo them immediately." Sophie picked up the platter she'd set on the table only a few moments before.

"Really, Sophie! Whatever were you thinking?"

For an instant, Sophie considered telling her—but only for an instant.

Monday, July 3, 1893

Tom talked me into driving the traction engine into town for the big doings tomorrow. A couple of the other farmers are going to be showing theirs in the parade through town and Tom felt we ought to get a little of the glory ourselves. . . though he didn't put it quite that way.

"Zeke," he said, serious as a preacher on Sunday, "we gotta go. We owe it to ourselves."

"That so?" I said, not sure exactly what he meant.

"Yup," he said. "Most folks thought we couldn't do it. Drivin' that old engine in there would just show them they was wrong. Right?"

I couldn't argue with him there, but I could see it wasn't the engine Tom wanted to show off so much as that he *had* done it, no matter how many folks stood by and shook their heads and said he couldn't and that he'd never amount to much of anything. No way I'd keep him from his bit of glory, so of course I said we'd take the traction engine.

I just hope we don't break down getting there. I bought a new shirt and a new pair of work pants just for the occasion and I'd hate to get them dirty right off. It wouldn't do to show up looking like I was planning to plow the back forty when all the town gents Sophie's used to will be there with their sweet-smelling hair oil and their good suits and high collars and fancy ties.

I thought about buying a suit, but decided that was going a mite too far. A man doesn't have to have a new suit just to ask a lady if he can buy her a lemonade and slice of pie from the church booth in the park.

Besides, I'd feel like a fool and I'm nervous enough already. I've never bought a lady a lemonade or a slice of pie before and I'm not entirely sure how a fellow goes about doing it. Just says it right out, I suppose, and hopes the lady won't turn him down. At least, not in front of God and everybody.

Not that I expect Sophie to say no. She's too soft-hearted and she knows I'm not exactly at my best when I'm out in public. Besides, I've been practicing, though I can't say my Delphi or the spotted sow have been too impressed with my polite inquiries as to whether or not they'd prefer the cherry pie or the angel food cake. I tried again this afternoon, but the sow just grunted and turned over on her side and went to sleep.

Fortunately, Sophie doesn't grunt. At least, not that I've ever noticed. And she's for sure not going to roll over in a mud hole—always assuming I don't knock her into one in the first place.

I'm determined not to make a fool of myself if I can help it. I even stopped at the barber's and got a regular haircut last time I was in town. Have to admit it looks some better than my usual job with the shears, though Mr. Mandel couldn't do anything with my cowlick, either. It's still waving in the wind like tassels on top of a cornstalk.

What worries me is her mamma is going to be there, and Mrs. Smith and Miss Annie, and all of them will be keeping a pretty sharp eye on me, fancy haircut, new work shirt, and all. That's not an ~~exager exxajerr~~ It's not bragging to say so. I *know* those ladies.

I try to tell myself there's no sense worrying about it because I probably won't get up enough courage to ask Sophie about the lemonade, anyway. No matter how many times I practice with that old sow.

It makes more sense to worry about getting all those melons picked and shipped come the end of July. Timing's everything according to Mr. Swink and I've never grown so many melons in my life, even totted up altogether.

Makes me nervous, thinking how much can go wrong and how much I'm counting on that crop. After all these years of farming, you'd think I'd be used to worrying about will it rain during harvest, or will locust hit my crops, or will there be enough water, or

whatever, but I'm not. I still fret about things as much
as an old maid frets about men.

Well, best stop worrying and get to bed. I suspect
there'll be plenty enough to keep my mind occupied
come tomorrow, regardless if I screw up the courage
to ask Sophie about that lemonade or no.

"You sure there's enough for Mr. Conner, too?"
Delphi demanded for the fourth time that morning,
peering into the heavily laden picnic basket Sophie
had prepared.

"Absolutely sure, Mother," Sophie said. She'd gotten used to cooking for Zeke and Tom. Mr. Conner
couldn't come close to their consumption levels, even
if he ate two times more than he normally did.

"And you *are* going to wear that pretty green muslin dress I made you buy last week, aren't you?"

"Yes, Mother. I've already laid it out."

"You promise you'll wear your white straw hat and
not that awful old brown one?"

"Cross my heart."

"Sophie?" Delphi dragged her name out, the threat
implicit in her tone.

"Yes, I promise I'll wear the white straw." And
carry a ton of patience if she could find it, Sophie
added silently.

She'd been thinking about the annual Fourth of July
celebrations for weeks, and she still couldn't decide if
she was excited—or terrified.

Zeke had said he was coming—for Tom's sake, if
nothing else, because Patrick had finally talked Sarah
Jane into letting him escort her for the day. Sarah
Jane, growing bolder in the protection of the big Irishman's friendship, had announced she would prepare a
picnic lunch for the four of them. Like family, she'd
told Sophie shyly, clearly excited by the prospect.

Sophie supposed she ought to be worrying what
Delphi would say if she caught her talking to Sarah
Jane as she had every intention of doing, but she had
other, more immediate concerns.

Would Zeke speak to her? *Really* speak to her, not

mumble and blush as he was prone to do whenever he encountered her in public? She wasn't sure she could bear it if he behaved like a nervous fool in front of everyone, or, worse yet, ignored her entirely. Not when Annie Talbot was sure to make a point of seeking him out.

That wasn't Sophie's major concern, however.

Her big problem was, what was *she* going to say to Zeke? Especially with her mother and the rest of the world looking on?

The festivities began with a parade through town.

Mr. Conner had taken charge of the picnic basket and an umbrella and folding chair for Delphi, then made sure they got a good spot in front of Hodgeson's Emporium, where there was a sliver of shade left. His job was to fuss and fidget making sure Delphi was comfortable while Delphi preened and fluttered and cooed. Both were delighted with their allotted responsibilities and did their best to live up to expectations.

Sophie, attired to Delphi's satisfaction in the new green muslin and white straw hat, tried to spot Zeke and his crew in the milling crowd.

If any of the four were here for the parade, they'd picked another spot from which to watch it. Before Sophie could start worrying about whether Sarah Jane had backed out at the last minute, a flourish of trumpets, only slightly off-key, announced the start of the parade.

First came the three trumpeters—the butcher, the baker, and old Jem Collings, who spent most of his time in the local saloon but liked to toot his horn every chance he got. In the position of honor behind the trumpeters were the mayor and the state representative in a big, fancy carriage brought in especially for the occasion. The mayor's sixteen-year-old son was driving the matched bays and looking proud enough to explode like the firecrackers that numerous small boys were setting off all along the parade route.

Right behind the mayor came a string of carriages the various clubs had decorated with streamers and ribbons and colored paper woven through the spokes of the wheels. Club members and their wives and children packed the carriages and perched on the frames, happily waving to the friends and family who had assembled to watch them go past.

Two enterprising souls had hitched their horses four abreast to mock Roman chariots, donned tin helmets, and wound themselves up in sheets draped to look like togas. The children behind them leading pet dogs, goats, and one small pony were too intent on keeping their charges under control in the midst of the rumpus to pay much attention to anything but their families' delighted cheering from the sidelines.

The proprietor of the town's largest saloon had loaded a hay wagon with bales of hay, barrels of beer, and some of the players who would be in the afternoon's baseball game. Since the players had already broached one keg and were now eyeing a second with enthusiasm, Sophie made a mental note to avoid the baseball field unless she was assured of a sober escort.

The town band marched past with well-drilled precision, belting out "Yankee Doodle" loud enough to almost cover the roar and rumble of the steam traction engines that brought up the rear of the parade, right after a flock of bicyclists, another half-dozen decorated carriages, and a flag-flying wagon from the cannery.

Usually Sophie cheered and shouted right along with the crowd, but today she spent most of her time craning for a glimpse of Zeke. He had to be *somewhere* in the crowd—but where?

It wasn't until the third traction engine had passed in a belching cloud of smoke that she spotted him, proudly seated atop his metal monster with an ecstatic Tom perched on the frame beside him, waving as hard as a politician stumping for reelection.

The minute Tom spotted her, he jumped to his feet. He would have toppled off if Zeke hadn't grabbed him by the back of the pants.

"Hey, Miss Sophie!" he bellowed. "Don't she look *grand*?!"

Sophie, forgetting herself in the excitement of the

moment, cupped her hands around her mouth and bellowed back, "She sure does!"

"Sophie!" Delphi swung about on her folding chair, aghast. "Have you forgotten your manners?"

The bystanders on either side looked around, clearly startled by her appalling lapse.

Mr. Conner gaped. "Miss Sophie! Do you mean to say you're still consorting with that little devil?"

"Ma made fried chicken!" Tom shouted, oblivious. "You gonna join us?"

Cheeks burning but head held high, Sophie settled for waving in response.

"Zeke says he's gonna buy me a lemonade! He said he'd buy you one, too, if you want!"

Fortunately for Zeke, the parade inexorably dragged them forward, safely out of range of Delphi's suddenly roused curiosity. There wasn't a chance in the world Tom could shout over the noise of the monster traction engine that brought up the rear of the procession with a cheering rabble of machine-mad boys in its wake.

Sophie didn't know whether to cheer along with the boys, or take advantage of the rapidly thinning crowds to slink around the side of Hodgeson's Emporium and scurry home through the alleys.

On the one hand, there was the satisfaction of knowing that Zeke Jeffries was going to buy her a lemonade . . . and that half the town would know about it before he got close enough to say, "May I?"

On the other . . .

"Since when have you gotten to know Zeke Jeffries well enough for him to buy you a lemonade?" Delphi demanded, eagerly rising to her feet. She was so anxious to hear the answer, she didn't even notice Mr. Conner's startled attempt to help her up. "You didn't tell me—"

"Gracious!" Sophie exclaimed. "Just look how fast everyone's disappeared. Don't you think we should get on over to the park?"

She bent to check the picnic basket, which saved her from having to face her mother's avid look. "I want to be sure and get a good spot. After all, there are the speeches and the band concert—"

"But what about—"

"—and Annie's going to recite President Washington's first inaugural speech, you know." Sophie stood, the picnic basket firmly in hand. "I really don't want to miss that."

"Here, let me get that, Miss Sophie!" Mr. Conner protested.

"Sophronia! I want to know—"

"I'll see you there, all right?" Sophie bestowed a conspiratorial wink on Mr. Conner. "You two just come along whenever you like. No rush."

"But—!"

Delphi's protests couldn't compete against Mr. Conner eagerness to rid himself of the double encumbrance of Sophie and her picnic basket. He beamed.

"You go right ahead, Miss Sophie," he said. "We'll be along eventually. Won't we, Delphinea?"

Sophie beamed back approvingly. "I'll save you a spot," she promised as she hurried off in the wake of the crowd that was headed to the park.

Delphinea, was it? The only other person who had ever been allowed to call Delphi by her given name was Sophie's father.

Sophie shifted her grip on the picnic basket and walked faster. It looked like her mother was going to do just fine.

Now, if she could just turn the invitation for lemonade to good account . . .

Zeke pulled the traction engine into line with the others at the far side of the park. He'd let Tom off at the end of the parade so he could join his mother and Patrick, but even after the last of the steam had vented and he could safely leave the machine, he didn't move. His hands were still tightly wrapped around the steering wheel, his palms so damp they slipped over the metal if he didn't hold on tight.

What insanity had possessed him to tell Tom about his plans for a lemonade? He should have known the boy would blurt it out the first chance he got. It was just his bad luck that Tom's first chance had been at the top of his lungs when half the town was watching.

Now there was no way out of it . . .and what if she said no? What if she was so embarrassed that she never even showed up?

Annie Talbot wouldn't have minded everyone in town knowing he'd invited her for a lemonade—that is, assuming he'd had any intention of inviting her, which he hadn't—but Sophie wasn't like that. Despite her friendliness and her comfortable ways, she hadn't even shown any particular interest in him. Not as a beau, anyway. He'd hate to ruin a comfortable friendship by being too precipitate.

Precipitate. Now there was a nice, big, four-dollar word. If he used a peck of them, maybe he could fool someone into thinking he had some sense.

With a sigh, Zeke let go of his death grip on the wheel and reached under the seat. Much to Tom's displeasure, he'd held up their departure that morning to cut a couple of flowers form Sophie's garden. He wasn't sure what the things were called—buttons something-or-other, or maybe it was something-or-other buttons—but they seemed to be Sophie's favorites. He'd picked three: a white, a bright blue, and a dark purple, then punched a hole in the lid of a jar so he could keep them fresh without fear of the water sloshing out on the way to town.

It wasn't easy shoving them through a buttonhole when he didn't have a mirror, but he finally got them arranged to his satisfaction. He smoothed his hair, tucked in the tail of his shirt, then climbed down, taking care not to get any dirt or grease on his clean clothes. No telling when he might run into Sophie and he wanted to look his best.

He almost ran into Adelaide Smith and Miss Annie and her mama, instead. The three of them were standing in a cluster of ladies, their backs turned toward him and chattering like magpies. If it hadn't been for Hiram and Mr. Talbot standing at their side with the other gents and looking forlorn, he might have walked right past them and been snagged for sure.

Hiram spotted him right off, but he understood. Didn't so much as blink to give the game away. Mr. Talbot just stared at the back of his wife's hat and looked like he wanted to be anyplace but where he was.

Zeke edged away, careful to keep as many trees and bushes between him and Mrs. Smith as he could.

He found Sarah Jane and Patrick before he had much of a chance to look for Sophie. They'd spread a blanket on the ground under the shade of a sturdy elm, far enough back to be away from the crush of picnickers, but close enough they'd be able to hear all the speeches.

Patrick lumbered to his feet as Zeke approached. "Ah, you made a fine show, my friend, you and young Tom," he said, grinning and offering his hand. "I thought sure and the lad would fall off the way he was dancing around up there."

"He looked so . . . happy!" Sarah Jane added, smiling up at him.

"Well, so do you!" Zeke said. "And pretty as a picture to boot." The simple flattery came surprisingly easy. Perhaps because it was true.

Sarah Jane was sitting at the edge of the blanket in a neat little straw hat and a primly starched white shirtwaist with her skirt neatly tucked under her. The past two months had wrought an enormous change in her. Or rather, Patrick's faithful and undemanding attentions had. It was because of him that Sarah Jane had given up drinking, and at his insistence that she'd ventured out today. Patrick hadn't yet convinced her to renounce her deplorable profession, but Zeke didn't think it would be long before he did. From there, it would be a short trip to the altar.

Zeke sat down cross-legged across from Patrick and Sarah. "Where'd Tom get to?"

"Off tellin' some boys that are as machine-mad as he is how he fixed that traction engine." Patrick grinned and winked at Zeke. "With your help, of course."

Zeke laughed. "Is he? I'm glad I could help."

At the mention of her son, Sarah Jane's smile faded into an aching earnestness. "You have. More than you can ever know." Her hands curled into white-knuckled fists in her lap. "More than I ever did."

"Ah . . ." Zeke said, squirming in sudden embarrassment.

"Here, now! We'll none of that," Patrick protested. "You've done the best you could."

Sarah Jane gave him a hesitant smile, then leaned across to affectionately pat his knee. "Which wasn't much good at all. But I'm doin' better . . . thanks to you."

Zeke caught the look that passed between the two. It was going to be a *very* short trip to the altar.

The thought brought a odd, empty sensation in its wake. Before he had a chance to wonder why, Tom swaggered up.

"Zeke! I was just tellin' the fellows about how we fixed that old traction engine."

"Were you?" Behind him, Patrick's cough covered a laugh.

"Yup. Told 'em all about it. They're some jealous, I can tell you!"

Sarah Jane laughed. "Are they as hungry as you?"

"Whatcha got?" Tom demanded, eyeing the enormous picnic basket with interest.

"Fried chicken and corn bread and potato salad."

"Great! Your fried chicken's almost as good as Miss Sophie's! I could easy eat a ton." Tom plopped down on the one remaining corner of the blanket. "Can I have a drumstick?"

"Of course." Sarah Jane hastily busied herself with pulling neatly wrapped plates of food out of the basket, a task which gave her the perfect excuse for keeping her head down so they couldn't see her face.

Patrick passed around tin plates and cutlery, then filled four heavy mugs with buttermilk from a stoneware crock and passed those around, too. Zeke, deprived of any useful task to hide his own embarrassment, kept Tom chattering about the boys and how impressed they'd been. Clearly, the chance to preen in front of boys who had mocked him in the past had been balm for his young soul. Only a fat drumstick and a heaping plateful of food diverted him from his recital.

In the confused ritual of a picnic lunch, Sarah Jane gradually regained some of her previous cheerfulness, but Zeke sensed a wariness that hadn't been there earlier.

Although the spot Patrick had chosen was out of the way, they weren't invisible. More than a few of the ladies who passed tilted their noses in the air when they spotted Sarah Jane and carefully kept their distance. The men were even worse. Some gawked, a few pointedly ignored them, and several, safely unobserved by the womenfolk, openly leered.

Blissfully unaware of the public reaction to their presence, Tom rattled on, talking around mouthfuls of food that made his cheeks bulge. Patrick and Zeke tried to fill in the gaps with light chatter, but in spite of their best efforts, Sarah Jane slowly began to wilt under the public disapproval.

"I shouldn'ta come," she whispered to Patrick forlornly after one particularly disdainful sniff from a beak-nosed lady Zeke didn't recognize.

"Whist, now," Patrick said soothingly. He moved the empty plate of chicken out of his way and scooted closer. Not too close, since they were in public, but close enough to take her hand in his and pat it comfortingly. "We've nothing to do with such hoity-toity folks, nor they with us. I'll not let them bother you, and that I promise."

Sarah Jane smiled up at him gratefully, but the light had gone out of her face and she sat, stiff and uncomfortable, holding on to Patrick's broad hand as if it were the only thing in the world that kept her from going under.

Eventually his mother's distress broke through even Tom's satisfied self-preoccupation. He glanced at

Sarah Jane, frowning, then looked around just as a nattily dressed young man stopped to goggle at them.

Tom's eyes grew glitteringly hard. He tensed and his shoulders hunched until he looked like an angry turtle that couldn't decide whether to retreat into its shell, or snap at the first thing that came in range.

The young man must have sensed his animosity even at that distance for he abruptly scuttled off.

With careful deliberation, Tom placed his half-gnawed chicken leg on his plate, then shoved his plate away. "I'm full," he mumbled, climbing to his feet.

"Thomas?" Sarah Jane stretched to touch her son's arm, but Tom swung out of reach.

He shoved his hands into his pocket and glared at the trampled grass beneath his feet. "I'll be around."

An instant later he was gone.

Zeke got his feet under him, ready to rise and go after the boy, but Sarah Jane stopped him.

"Leave him be," she said. "Ain't nothin' you can say that'll change things, anyways." Her eyes were awash with tears, but there was a proud, angry tilt to her head that said more clearly than words she didn't want his pity, or anyone else's.

"Besides," she added, "the mayor and whatnot are about to start, and we come here to listen to 'em, didn't we?"

"That's right," Patrick chimed in with false heartiness. "You can't go till you've had some pie, Zeke. Especially since Sarah Jane said I'd be taking me life in me own hands if I tried to eat it all meself."

Zeke sat. "In that case," he said, "I'll have to take an extra big piece. For your sake, Patrick." He grinned at Sarah Jane. "And so I don't get dyspeptic from too many speeches on an empty stomach."

Since Sophie had staked out a prime spot under one of the big cottonwoods, several members of the Missionary Society had gathered their chairs around Delphi's during a break in the speech making. The men had long ago retired to discuss politics and sample the more potent potations available from the brewer's wagon behind the bandstand, leaving the women to their own urgent issues.

It had taken a full twenty minutes for the conversation to veer around to the scandal of Sarah Jane Peabody appearing at a function like this.

"Can you imagine the gall of that woman, mixing with decent folk? And Patrick O'Boyle right along with her! I *never* thought I'd see the day!" Dora Purvis pursed her lips, clasped her hands in her lap, and looked scandalized.

"And that nice Mr. Jeffries right there with them!" Mrs. Granger happily added. "I must say, I was shocked when I saw him. Shocked!"

Since Annie was safely out of the way, chatting with friends, Thea Talbot didn't hesitate to look shocked right along with her and the rest of the ladies. Even Delphi frowned.

Rather than say something she knew she'd regret, Sophie refilled her glass of tea, grabbed the ice pick, and stabbed the chunk of ice they'd laid on a copy of last week's newspaper. The violence of the act was strangely satisfying.

She'd been in the middle of packing up the luncheon things when the ladies arrived. Delphi had immediately drafted her to help arrange chairs and pour tea so she hadn't managed to slip away as she'd intended. Now she wished she'd abandoned her mother and fled first thing.

Adelaide Smith took immediate exception to Mrs. Granger's report of Zeke Jeffries' whereabouts. "Just what was the poor man supposed to do?" she demanded indignantly. "Considering he was kindhearted enough to take in that woman's son when the boy got into such trouble at the depot, he didn't have much choice now, did he? Not if he was going to do right by that child. And it was Sophie got him into the mess in first place!"

"Well, bad enough he should have taken in a fancy woman's thieving son, but—"

Sophie didn't give Mrs. Granger a chance to finish. She rose to her feet, ice pick still menacingly in hand.

"Tom Peabody is a good boy, Mrs. Granger." She had to fight to keep her voice low so no one outside the circle of ladies would hear. "And his mother isn't a bad woman, no matter what you all say!"

"And what would *you* know about a fallen woman like that Mrs. Peabody, Miss Sophie?" Adelaide burst out. "Just because you got her son out of trouble—"

"I know that he doesn't deserve to be treated like a pariah, no matter what!"

Sophie could have set off a dozen firecrackers right in the middle of the circle and the ladies wouldn't have looked more astounded. She hesitated, knowing she was inviting trouble by saying more, but she couldn't bear to stand silently by while her friends were verbally abused. Especially knowing how hard it had been for Sarah Jane to venture out with Patrick in the first place.

She took a deep breath and plunged. "I know that Sarah Jane Peabody is a kind woman who must have had a hard life to do what she's done. A lot harder than any of us have ever known. I know she loves her son, who is one of the smartest little boys I've ever met. I know—"

"Sophronia Mae! How *can* you?" Delphi was on her feet, bosom swelling with emotion.

"Are you saying you actually *know* this woman?" Dora Purvis demanded, thrilled to the core.

"Now, Sophie," Thea Talbot chided gently. "Surely you don't mean—"

"Oh, but I *do* mean, Mrs. Talbot! And, yes, Mrs. Purvis, I know the lady."

Twenty-six years of being a lady and doing as she was told and always minding her manners—up in smoke in an instant. Suddenly, Sophie didn't care.

Yesterday she'd listened to Mrs. Granger and Mrs. Purvis gossip about Annie Talbot's visit to Zeke's farm and she'd been afraid they were gossiping about her. Well, let them have something to gossip about. At least it wouldn't be behind her back!

No matter what, she wouldn't—*couldn't*—stand by while they tore at Tom and Sarah Jane and Zeke. Not shy, gentle Zeke, who'd only gotten involved because he was too kind to say "no" when someone needed his help.

"I've been visiting Mrs. Peabody twice a week every week for months," Sophie announced, exaggerating only slightly. "She's had her problems, but she's trying hard to overcome them and I hope I'm helping. And I've been tutoring Tom with his arithmetic and reading, and if he doesn't trounce every child in fifth grade this year when it comes to studying, I . . . I'll eat my hat!"

For once, Delphi was too shaken to say anything. She sank down on her chair with the stunned look of an ox that had just been whacked between the eyes with an ax handle.

No one moved. Not one person spoke. Mouths open, they all stared at Sophie as if at a madwoman suddenly gone amok.

"Well," Sophie said. She took a deep breath and suddenly realized she was still holding the ice pick. Her grip on it tightened. "Anybody want any more ice before I go say hello to Sarah Jane and Tom? I'll be *more* than happy to chop up the rest of that block for you, if you like!"

Chapter 14

Sarah Jane spotted her first. "Oh, my! There's Sophie! And she's comin' this way!"

Zeke spun around—not an easy thing to do when a man his size had been sitting on the ground for the better part of an hour.

Sophie *was* coming their way . . . and she looked like she was dragging a thunderstorm with her. Zeke had never seen her angry before. He sincerely hoped he wouldn't have to see her that way often—on a woman her size, it was mighty intimidating. Zeke climbed to his feet on the theory it might be safer than being seated. Good manners were a secondary consideration. Patrick immediately followed suit, then helped Sarah Jane to stand.

By the time Sophie reached them, however, she'd gotten most of her temper under control. The only traces that still showed were an unaccustomed tightness about her eyes and mouth and an awkward stiffness to her shoulders.

"Sophie!" Sarah Jane's greeting was obviously heartfelt, and colored with a substantial dose of relief at seeing a friendly face in the disapproving crowd.

"I'm sorry it's taken me so long to get over to say 'hello,'" Sophie said, forcing her mouth to ease into a smile. She clasped Sarah Jane's outstretched hand, then leaned forward and gave her a quick kiss on the cheek. "Seems like everyone in town is out today. Beautiful day, isn't it?"

"Beautiful!" Sarah Jane said.

Zeke mumbled agreement right along with Patrick, but it wasn't the day's beauty that teased him, it was

Sophie's. Angry or not, she looked like an angel in bright green with that white hat reflecting light all around her face. Good thing she'd always stuck to her starched white shirtwaists and practical brown straw hat whenever she'd come visiting. She looked good in those, but the way she looked now . . . It was enough to tempt a blind man, and he for sure wasn't blind.

"Hot, too," Sophie added, fanning her face with her hand.

Zeke hadn't noticed before, but now that she mentioned it, he thought he could detect a distinct—and unexpectedly sudden—increase in the temperature.

"Always hot for the Fourth," Patrick said.

"Wonderful parade. Didn't Tom and Zeke look grand up there on that monster?" Sarah Jane beamed, the painful slights of the past hour forgotten in the pleasure of having seen her son in the parade.

"*Very* impressive."

"Good parade," Patrick said. "Good speeches, too."

"And not over yet," Sophie added brightly. "The band's going to play again later, and there's the baseball game, of course, and some folks giving recitations, too. Annie Talbot, for one."

Zeke fidgeted under the burden of polite conversation. Sophie was trying hard not to look at him, and all he wanted to do was sit and stare at her. For starters, anyway.

He didn't get a chance. As if summoned, Annie Talbot sailed up, arms linked with Marla May Purvis and Eliza Neumann.

"There you are, Sophie!" Miss Annie called out. "Your mama didn't know where you'd gone! And . . . Mr. Jeffries, too! Why, fancy meeting you here! And Mr. O'Boyle, isn't it? What fun!"

Not one of the three even nodded to Sarah Jane.

His mama would have been shocked, but Zeke suddenly felt a strong urge to cuss.

Beside him, Sophie grew still and tense. Zeke could almost feel her drawing herself up to her full height, which put her a good head above Miss Annie and the rest. Some men might have found that intimidating, but he found it awfully comforting to have her at his side.

"I don't believe any of you know Sarah Jane Peabody, do you?" she said, cool as you please. "*Mrs.* Peabody, I *should* say!"

Miss Marla May tittered. Miss Eliza at least smiled and nodded. Only Miss Annie, after a moment's hesitation, stepped forward to offer a hand. "How do you do? I'm Annie Talbot."

Sarah Jane nervously shook hands, then immediately snatched hers back. She locked her fingers together in front of her, hunched her shoulders, and stared at the ground. She looked, Zeke thought, like a frightened child unexpectedly called upon to perform for disapproving and very frightening strangers.

When Tom had first come to him, Mrs. Smith had tried hard to convince him of the folly of having anything to do with the likes of "that boy." As proof, she'd recited a gruesome detail some of Sarah Jane's activities while under the influence of strong drink, including her rout of the Ladies Missionary Society.

Watching Sarah Jane now, Zeke thought he finally understood why she'd resorted to drink—it created an unbreachable wall between her and a hostile world that was far more ready to condemn than to understand.

"Well, we certainly didn't mean to barge in on your little get-together," Miss Annie was saying, "but we thought Sophie might want to join us. I'm going to be reciting President Washington's First Inaugural Speech, you know, and I wanted my friends to have a good spot. Of course, you're welcome to join us, Mr. Jeffries." She smiled up at him sweetly, but had the good sense not to flutter her lashes. "That is, if you'd like to."

"Why, thank you, Miss Annie," Zeke said smoothly, "but I'm afraid Miss Sophie and I were just going to fetch some lemonade for the four of us." Anger made the words roll off his tongue as easily as cream out of a pitcher.

He didn't even look at Sophie. He was absolutely certain she'd back him, regardless. "You ladies are welcome to stay. We only have the four glasses, but I'd be happy to buy you all a glass at the stand, if you like."

Miss Annie glanced at Sophie, then back at him, clearly startled by his smooth response. Usually he tripped over every second word—and that was on a good day.

"Oh," she said. Her gaze dropped, then fixed on the flowers he'd plucked from Sophie's garden and stuck in his buttonhole. She laughed, but her laugh had a touch of brittleness. She surprised him by touching the flowers with the tip of her finger. "Well, you do put out fair enough warning, I suppose."

Zeke blinked. Out of the corner of his eye he could see Sophie staring at Annie, then at him. "I do?"

"The flowers, Mr. Jeffries," Miss Annie said with an awkward attempt at lightness. "That's pretty plain notice to all us poor spinsters, I guess."

"Ma'am?"

"Surely you knew? They're bachelor buttons, Mr. Jeffries. A man can't get much plainer than that."

Patrick said he'd get the lemonade, Sarah Jane swore she didn't want any, and Sophie insisted it really wasn't necessary, that no one would be watching to see if he'd been lying.

Zeke was adamant. He hadn't really planned on including Patrick or Sarah Jane, but he wasn't about to back down now. He also wasn't about to give up his advantage—Sophie *couldn't* turn him down. She wouldn't want to embarrass him, and she couldn't leave him to carry back four filled glasses all by himself.

Sophie refused to look at him. She'd refused to look at him ever since Miss Annie had informed him of the significance of the bachelor buttons. He wasn't even going to try to explain that it had been ignorance, not guile, that had led him to pluck those particular flow-

ers. Ignorance and the thought that they were pretty
and Sophie liked them.

Zeke picked up the glasses. So long as they were
empty, he could carry all four if he kept them pinned
between his forearm and his chest. That left his right
hand free.

In a burst of bravado, he grabbed Sophie's hand
and pulled her with him. To his amazement, she didn't
try to pull free, even once they were well away from
Patrick and Sarah Jane.

They were halfway across the park before Zeke got
up the courage to say shyly, "I really was going to
invite you for a lemonade, you know. And a piece of
pie at the church booth later, if you were willing."

"Really?" There was a hint of breathlessness in her
voice, as if he were dragging her along at breakneck
speed, rather than proceeding at a properly decorous
pace.

Zeke nodded, then added hesitantly, "But I hadn't
exactly planned on getting Sarah Jane and Patrick in
on the invitation."

He wasn't sure, but he thought the glint in her eye
might be satisfaction and, maybe, just a touch of excitement. He hoped so. He could feel his own heart
racing—he'd never held hands with a girl before. Or
a lady, for that matter. Emma Jean Shropmire didn't
count because he'd only been six at the time, even if
Emma Jean had been a good five months older and
therefore a more experienced woman of the world.

"But what about . . . Annie?" Sophie asked, as if
the words were forced from her.

"Miss Annie?" Zeke couldn't help it. His grip on
Sophie's hand tightened. "I wasn't going to ask her."

"Oh!" said Sophie, and smiled.

Behind them, Zeke could hear the mayor booming
out his introduction for Annie, but he didn't bother
to look. Neither did Sophie.

They found the lemonade stand all too soon. It had
been set up in a fair-sized tent with a couple of rickety
tables and a scattering of chairs provided for the comfort of the patrons, but the patrons had all chosen to

bring their own glasses rather than use the stand's and endure the heat trapped under the heavy canvas.

Zeke reluctantly released Sophie's hand so he could put the glasses down on the makeshift counter of two wide, rough planks laid on top of sawhorses. "Four lemonades, please. Lots of ice."

The heavy-set man behind the counter swiped at his brow. "Outa ice. My boy's bringing some. He oughta be back in a bit."

"How long is a bit?" Zeke didn't really care; he wasn't in any hurry to get back to Sarah Jane and Patrick.

The man frowned, then reluctantly admitted, "I figured he'd be back afore now. Guess I could go find out what's held him up."

"There's no rush." Sophie glanced at Zeke and smiled. "We can wait."

"No trouble." The man was halfway out of the tent when the sound of a steam engine starting up got his attention. He glanced at Zeke and shrugged apologetically. "If someone's fiddlin' around with one of them things, I guess I *know* what's kept him. I won't be but a few minutes."

He disappeared, leaving Zeke and Sophie alone in the tent.

Zeke, suddenly nervous, glanced at Sophie. Outside were hundreds of people, but here in the heat and the canvas-filtered light there was just the two of them.

Two had never before seemed quite so intriguing a number.

Not that a gentleman would take unfair advantage of the situation, Zeke unhappily reminded himself. "Would you . . . ?" The words seemed to stick halfway up his throat. He tried again. "Would you rather . . . wait outside?"

Sophie looked at him, then at the entrance, then at the shabby chairs and tables. "I think I would prefer to sit down," she said, pronouncing each word with care. "That is, if *you* don't mind."

Did he *mind*? Zeke took a deep breath, and wondered if he looked quite as silly or giddy as he suddenly felt. Of course, it could have been the rumble and clatter of the traction engine coming closer that was rattling his brains.

He pulled out a chair. "No, I don't mind. I don't mind at all."

Sophie took a half step toward the chair when a woman screamed. An instant later, pandemonium exploded outside the tent, almost overwhelmed by the noise of the approaching engine.

"Runaway!" someone screamed.

"Get the boy. Get the *boy*!"

"The tent!"

"It's headed for the tent!"

"Run!"

Zeke grabbed Sophie's hand, but before they moved a step, the front corner of the tent crumpled under the onslaught of the roaring metal monster. Canvas billowed as the beast caught the tent's guy ropes, ripping them off the stakes that anchored them. Before the ropes stopped snapping, the monster was raging off in search of new prey while the tent's ridgepole tilted drunkenly downward toward an entrance that no longer existed.

Zeke grabbed Sophie and pulled her to the ground and under him just as the tent came down on top of them.

A gust of hot air swished past Sophie's face as the canvas slowly settled on top of Zeke, who had settled on top of her.

Very much on top of her.

His broad chest pressed against hers, crushing her breasts. His hipbone ground into her hipbone; his legs sprawled atop her legs, pinning her to the ground wherever the heavy canvas of the tent didn't.

Sophie was dimly conscious of the shouting, screeching crowd that raced off in pursuit of the runaway traction engine, but it didn't seem like anything to be concerned about. She and Zeke were caught in a bubble of heat and filtered light that cut them off from the rest of the world as effectively as if they'd suddenly landed on another planet. A proper, well brought up young lady would be expected to fall into hysterics right about now, but given the unexpected advantages of the situation, she decided she didn't really mind at all.

Zeke propped his elbows on the ground on either side of her and levered himself up off her chest. The change forced his belly more firmly against hers—and deprived her of what little breath she had left after he'd knocked it out of her.

"My!" Sophie gasped, blinking up at Zeke. The light traced the strong lines of his brow and nose and chin, softening them and casting them in a golden bronze. His lips were parted, revealing the edges of white teeth and the shadowy depth of his mouth. He was panting, ever so slightly, and his breath brushed against her face, warm and infinitely unsettling.

Sophie licked lips suddenly gone dry. "We seem to be attracted to things that collapse."

"Yes?" Zeke's blue eyes had turned a soft, glazed black, as if he couldn't quiet focus on her face.

"Yes," he breathed, so softly Sophie almost didn't catch it. His eyelids with their thick, black fringe of eyelashes slid downward, hiding the remaining trace of blue. He lowered his head and gently, almost tentatively, pressed his lips to hers.

Yes! Sophie wanted to say, and *yes!* again.

She strained upward eagerly, hungry for this sweet unknown, and bumped her nose against his.

He flinched and drew back a fraction of an inch, blinking at the pain. For an instant their gazes locked, then they both burst into laughter.

The laughter quickly faded into intense awareness. Once more Zeke lowered his head. Their lips met.

As if of their own volition, Sophie's arms wrapped around his broad back, pulling him down on her, holding him tight against her. Her hands slid upward, across the hard landscape of his back, up into the thick shock of coarse black hair, pressing him closer still. Claiming him.

Was it one long, hungrily changing kiss? Or hundreds that merged, one into another with the melting, urgent heat the contact roused?

He murmured something—Sophie couldn't tell what—and moved against her, his body pressing tighter, more demandingly against hers. His mouth slid from hers as he trailed kisses across her cheek, over the corner of her eye, down to her jaw and the spot just beneath it where her skin was soft and her pulse beat.

Had her flesh always been this sensitive, or was it Zeke's touch, and his touch alonge that could rouse this mind-numbing, unsettling heat? Was it really possible to feel such exquisite, aching need at the same instant she could be so intensely aware of his hands, his weight, his mouth against her burning skin?

Answers, if answers there were, would have to wait. A small flock of worried picnickers suddenly came flapping back from their pursuit of the traction engine and began tugging at the corners of the tent until it shook and shivered around them like a wild beast roused from its sleep.

"Jeffries? Miss Sophie? You under there?" one man called.

"Anybody hurt?" another demanded in a panicked tenor.

"Grab this end!"

"No, that!"

"Pull!"

"Easy! That's it!"

"Jeffries?"

"I'm here!" Zeke croaked. "Miss Sophie, too! We're all right!"

For an instant his face, eyes wide with regret, seemed to hang suspended above Sophie while the canvas flapped around them, then he rolled off her and climbed to his knees. Head bent, shoulders bowed against the dragging weight of the tent, he held the canvas off her as she pulled her feet free of the entangling folds and sat up.

"Watch it!" Zeke called as the rescuers' efforts threatened to drag the broken ridgepole over them.

A moment later they were free and eager hands were helping Sophie climb to her feet, though it was Zeke who held her when she swayed dizzily at the sudden rush of air and light.

"That's your engine run over the tent, Jeffries!" an excitable gentleman shouted, "and that damn brat, Tom Peabody, atop it. You'd best go after 'im afore he ends up in Kansas . . . or in someone's front parlor!"

For a moment, Zeke hovered, indecisive.

"Go!" Sophie croaked, shaking her head to clear it. "Go on! You have to get Tom!"

Zeke was gone in an instant with all their rescuers after him, leaving Sophie standing in the wreckage of the lemonade stand, her hat crushed, her dress rumpled, and her heart pumping faster than Zeke's runaway traction engine.

Tuesday, July 4, 1893

. . . If it weren't for Patrick, jumping on the back of the engine, then climbing up to take Tom's place, the thing really *might* have ended up in Kansas.

At least the boy had the good sense to steer it straight down Main Street, even if he couldn't stop it. Nobody got hurt except a lady on the other side of the park who tripped over a tree root running to see what all the excitement was about, and she was nice enough to admit she should have paid more attention to where she was going and less to all the commotion around her.

All I had to pay for was the tent and a couple broken chairs and the Miller family's torn-up picnic basket and plates. Of course, Patrick and Sarah Jane argued about it with me for an hour after, but it was my engine, and me who taught Tom how to start it, but forgot to point out that he wasn't quite big enough yet to reach all the controls to stop it.

To my mind, the worst of it was all the folks whispering and saying what could you expect of a boy with a mother like that. Sarah Jane heard them. She couldn't help not. She bore up pretty well until we got her home, then she broke down into tears.

Sophie wasn't there—her mama had dragged her off first thing—so there was just Patrick, Tom, and me, all standing there like fools, not knowing what to do or say, and that made matters worse. Eventually she blew up and started shouting and cussing at herself and us and told us all to get out of her sight.

We all got, but I'm worried about what she might have gotten into once we left. Folks who drink as heavily as Sarah Jane tend to have a considerable stock laid by, even if they do stop drinking for a while. Just in case.

Goes without saying that Tom and I didn't stay for the fireworks after. There were the animals to tend to, for one thing, and Tom didn't have the heart for it for another. He'd just wanted to show off for all those boys who made fun of him before, and I guess I can understand that. I gave him a lecture about thinking about the risks before he jumped into something, but I left it at that. I figured having half the town running after him like they did, and knowing they'll be talking about him for a good long time to come is more than enough punishment. A boy doesn't need to get his pride stomped into the dirt to learn from his mistakes, no matter what some folks say.

Only comfort for him in this mess is that Sophie's coming out tomorrow. She promised, and she won't break a promise, no matter what.

I almost wish she would. Break her promise, that is. I'm not sure what to say to her, and I'm afraid of what she'll say to me. After what I did—

Zeke studied the words he'd written. The yellow light of the lamp made the ink seem softer, more like brown than black and somehow less permanent than ink on paper should be.

Irritated, he set the pen down and dragged his fingers through his hair. The cowlick on top of his head waved defiantly, despite the professional barbering. Zeke scowled. The only one who'd ever managed to

get it to lie down even halfway decent was Sophie.
He'd let her give him a haircut once, and the memory
of how it had felt with her hands in his hair and her
belly brushing against his back and shoulder had kept
him out at the pump for a week straight. He hadn't
had the courage to ask her again.

Zeke stared at his reflection in the dusty kitchen
window, remembering.

He had a lot more to remember since he'd gotten
so carried away under what was left of the lemonade stand.

Sophie probably wouldn't come within shouting
range now, let alone trim his hair for him or . . . or
kiss him.

If ever a man had taken unfair advantage of a lady,
his name was Zeke Jeffries. The tent hadn't even settled around them and there he'd been, without so
much as a by-your-leave, kissing her for all he was
worth.

The fact that she'd kissed him right back once she
got past that nose of his didn't change things any. His
mama had brought him up to mind his manners, and
the only thing he'd been minding there under that
canvas was the blood-pumping excitement of doing
what he'd been dreaming of for months.

Well, some of what he'd been dreaming of, anyway.
He hoped he'd have had the sense to stop before he'd
gone *that* far, disaster or no disaster.

He blinked, and turned away from the unsettling
reflection in the window. The change of scenery didn't
help much. The rest of the kitchen wasn't much better-
looking than he was. He managed to keep up with the
dishes, but the floor needed mopping, the stove
needed blacking, and he hadn't dusted in days.

It wasn't the dust that made the room so unappeal-
ing, though—or the rest of the house, for that matter.
It was the stark emptiness of the place. The lack of
any feminine touch to soften the bare outlines of walls
and windows and floors.

Strange. He'd never really noticed such things until
Sophie started visiting.

Maybe he ought to get a cat. If he had a cat to talk to, maybe he could forget about all the other things that had been plaguing him.

Zeke stared at his journal, at the pen and the bottle of ink and the pool of light they lay in. After a moment's thought, he picked up the pen, dipped it in the ink, and started writing at the point where he'd left off.

It's been a good eight hours since I last saw Sophie. Another couple since I kissed her. You'd think I'd have managed to get my thoughts up out of my pants by now, but no such luck.

All I have to do is think of her. I think about her laugh. It's the kind that tickles a man's insides and plain makes him feel good, just to hear it. And I keep thinking about her smile and her soft voice and her eyes and the graceful way she walks—like a queen, you know, all proud and straight—and that tiny waist and the hint of red in her hair when the sun shines on it and . . .

Zeke threw down his pen in disgust. It left a trail of ink spots across the page, then bounced and left a great, round blot of ink on the table before it rolled off on the floor to leave who knew what kind of ink stains there. He didn't care.

He was a liar and a coward who was so afraid to face the truth that he'd waste good paper pretending, rather than square up to it like a man.

Sophie's laughter stuck in his mind, but that wasn't really what bothered him. He liked watching her move and listening to her talk, and he liked her peaceful silences. He liked the way she kissed, all eager and sweet and warm, but that wasn't what bothered him, either.

No, what made him keep thinking about tall, slender, bright-eyed Sophronia Carter was that he wanted to make love to her. Again and again and again. And then again, just for good measure.

He wanted to make love to her at night before he

went to sleep and in the morning after he woke up
and in the afternoon, lying out under the cottonwoods
on those cloth-covered horse blankets they'd taken to
using for their picnics. He wanted to make love to her
in the barn and the kitchen and the parlor and out in
the flower garden and down by the river with the
water running past as smooth and slow as time itself.

But it was more than some desperate sexual frenzy
that had claimed him. Much more . . . and much
worse.

He wanted to see her across the breakfast table in
the morning and sit by the fire with her in the evening
when the work was done. He wanted to go to sleep
at night with her by his side, knowing that he'd wake
up to see her smile. He wanted it for tonight and
tomorrow night and for every other night for the rest
of his life.

He'd been thinking of it and dreaming of it for
weeks. Months!

Which was crazy, because he'd never even worked
up the courage to kiss her until the disaster this afternoon. Not once, despite all the thousands of times
he'd thought of it.

Writing about it didn't do a damned thing except
make him want to cover up the truth, at the same
time it made him hot and hurting and hungry for what
he couldn't have and shouldn't want in the first place.
And when she came tomorrow, he'd end up wanting
it all more than he already did.

With a curse that would have sent his mama flying
for the soap if she'd heard it, Zeke kicked back his
chair and stomped out of the house, headed for the
pump and the bucket he'd taken to leaving beside it.

Sophie deliberately sat up late with the household
accounts. Since Delphi considered it unfeminine for a
woman to worry about anything more than her pin
money and the grocery bill, when it came time to do
the accounts she always left Sophie in peace. It was
one of the reasons Sophie had slowly but surely been
able to add to the funds her father had left them.

Tonight, however, the neat columns of numbers in her ledger refused to add up the same way twice. She'd erased one sum so often she'd almost worn a hole in the paper.

She ought to concede defeat. She simply wasn't capable of dealing with numbers or notations on the cost of a box of blueing or three dozen pearl buttons and a yard of twilled silesia for a dress her mother was having made. Her head was too filled with the events of this afternoon.

Sophie capped the ink bottle and cleaned the nib of her pen, then bundled up all the receipts and scraps of paper and put them back in their cubbyhole in the big oak rolltop desk that had been her father's. The oil lamp cast a rich yellow light on the desk and the leather-bound journal, but the far corners of the room were dark. The heavy upholstered furniture that Delphi favored looked like ugly, lumpish monsters that had hunkered down in the parlor by chance, then forgotten to leave. The only sound in the little parlor was the ponderous tick-tocking of the clock on the mantel.

Only tonight, the parlor didn't seem so small. It seemed, in fact, very large and empty and echoing. Most of all, despite all the furniture and the knick-nacks that filled it, it seemed empty.

When her father was still alive and strong enough to get around, he'd sat there in the big patent rocker in the corner. He'd be reading while she labored with the accounts she was learning to manage. His glasses would slide down his nose and his thinning hair, cut long to cover his growing baldness, would fall forward to wave gently up and down as he rocked. He'd been oblivious to everything, including her, too lost in Walter Scott or Gibbons or Shakespeare to heed anything else. Yet as distant as he was, he'd been company in the silence.

Sophie suddenly wished she had some company now.

She wished that Zeke were sitting where her father had once sat. She wished she could look up and find

him watching her with a look in his eyes that said he
was glad she was there and that he was thinking about
her and about what they would share when she eventually finished the accounts and turned down the lamp
and he led her to bed.

How many times had she wondered what it would
be like to lie with a man? How many nights had she
lain alone in her tall, narrow bed and tried to imagine
how a lover, a husband, might touch her, how his body
would feel pressed against hers?

The fantasies had tormented her ever since she'd
grown to womanhood, but they'd become more urgent, more insistent with each passing year until some
nights she wondered if she would suddenly shatter into
a thousand pieces with the longing.

Sophie knew her fantasies were shameful, that no
decent woman would indulge in them. Once or twice
she'd tried to ask her closest friends if they ever experienced such illicit cravings, but it wasn't the sort of
thing you could ask straight out, and no matter how
carefully she edged around the subject, her friends
never seemed to know what she was talking about.

Or never let on that they did, at any rate.

And still Sophie wondered, and ached, and worried.

There wasn't much in life she was afraid of, but one
of them was dying a spinster and never knowing what
it was like to make love to a man, or to have a man
make love to her.

That kiss this afternoon had been a good start. A
very good start.

But while it had comforted her to know that Zeke
had invited her for a lemonade and not Annie Talbot,
that wasn't anywhere near the same as knowing he
was in love with her and wanted to marry her.

If Tom hadn't run that traction engine over the tent,
they probably wouldn't have gotten any farther than
holding hands . . . and they wouldn't have gotten even
that far if she hadn't been chasing Zeke for the past
two months.

She hadn't had the skills *or* the nerve to try and flirt
like Annie Talbot could, but what she had managed—

feeding him good cooking and hanging around so he couldn't help but think of her was starting to pay off.

Maybe what she needed to do was take the pursuit one notch higher.

But how did she go about doing that? And what came after a kiss potent enough to make her heart sing, even now?

Chapter 15

The milk spurted into the bucket in a thick stream, heavy with cream. As he always did, the calf was standing in the corral outside making an unholy fuss about being separated from his mother. Delphi didn't seem to care. She was just glad someone had finally gotten around to the milking.

Zeke had taken such care to dress and shave and comb his hair this morning that he'd gotten behind on everything. It hadn't helped that he'd wasted close to half an hour looking for the red suspenders he'd mislaid the night before. Sophie had said once she liked the bright red color on him, and he'd made a point ever since of wearing them whenever she came calling.

Red suspenders and clean clothes didn't go far to solving the questions plaguing him this morning, however.

Tom didn't seem to be doing much better. He was perched on the top bar of Delphi's open stall, silent and glum.

Maybe it was the weather. Hiram had said yesterday they'd be getting rain today, possibly hail. Zeke hadn't seen any trace of storm clouds in the brilliant blue arc of morning sky, but he'd learned early on that didn't mean much.

For several minutes the only sound in the stall was that of Delphi's chewing and the milk splashing into the pail. Then Tom asked, almost too casually, "You gonna marry Miss Sophie?"

Zeke jerked upright, knocking over the milking stool and slopping the milk. "What?"

"I said, you gonna marry Miss Sophie?" Tom enunciated each word carefully, as if he were dealing with a half-wit.

"No!" His startled protest came out too loud. A moment later, he added, more calmly this time, "Why do you ask?"

"I think you oughta."

Zeke finished his task, then climbed to his feet. He swung the pail of milk onto a bench where it would be safely out of the way and let Delphi out with her calf. By the time he turned back to Tom, he had himself a little more under control. "*Why* do you think I oughta?"

"You're sweet on her. I can tell. And she's awful sweet on you."

"Ahh." He didn't dare risk saying anything more.

"I been watchin', you know. An' I seen the way you two was—*were*—last time she was here. She was lookin' up at you like she was almighty happy to be here, and you was lookin' down at her with this silly expression on your face, just like that spotted sow when she got into the garden. Like she was about to bust, she was so pleased with herself."

Tom scrunched up his forehead, thrust out his lower lip, and assumed the air of a judge considering evidence against the accused. "I seen that look afore. Whenever a man like you gets it, it means pretty much for sure he's a goner. And Miss Sophie's been awful nice to me—nicer'n anybody else's ever been—but she don't—*doesn't* cook all that good food and come all the way out here just so's she can say 'hi!' to me."

Zeke shut the stall gate and carefully latched it, then just as carefully collected the pail of milk. He *couldn't* have been that transparent. Heck, he hadn't even realized just how bad it was until last night! How could Tom possibly have known?

"So, are you gonna ask her?" Tom wasn't going to let him get off easy.

"I—" Zeke stopped short in the open barn door as a disconcerting thought struck him. He set the pail down and sank onto his haunches so he'd be closer to eye level with the boy. "Are you asking me because you want to know, or because you've really got something else that's bothering you?"

Tom's eyes widened in an expression of utter innocence. "Why're you askin' me that?"

For only being ten, the kid had an unnerving ability to slide out from under whenever you tried to pin him down on something. "Because I think maybe you're wondering about your ma and Mr. O'Boyle more than you're wondering about me and Miss Sophie. Am I right?"

"Well . . ." Tom frowned down at the toe of his boot, then scuffed it through the dirt.

"Tom?"

"If he was gonna ask her to marry him," Tom said reluctantly, as if the thought hurt, "wouldn't he have done it already?"

"Maybe. Maybe not. Does he look as silly as you say I look about Miss Sophie?"

Tom considered the question, then nodded. "Yeah." After a moment, he added, "I di'n't like it at first, 'cause he used to come visitin'. *You* know."

Zeke nodded.

"Yeah. Well, see, at first I thought maybe he was jus' tryin' to get on Ma's good side so he wouldn't hafta pay her, even though she says it's the only way she can make a livin'. An' that made me purty mad."

"But you don't think that now?"

Once more Tom considered the question. "Nah. I think he's purty much for sure gone sweet on her. He wouldn't have taken her to the picnic yesterday or brung her all the way out here to visit if he wasn't, would he?"

"So what's the problem?"

"He hasn't asked Ma to marry him."

"Are you sure?"

"Purty sure." The tone of his voice said clearly he wasn't at all sure. "Ma ain't told me—*hasn't* told me he did, and she would've, wouldn't she? If he had?"

This conversation was a lot like walking through a sticker patch in your bare feet—you couldn't help but get stuck, no matter where you stepped. "Maybe Patrick hasn't asked her yet."

"Or maybe"—Tom brought the words out with almost painful slowness—"he ain't gonna ask her."

Zeke felt a little queasy as he realized what really lay at the heart of Tom's questions. "Are you afraid he won't ask her to marry him, even if he *has* gone sweet on her, because of . . . of what she does?"

Tom let out his breath in a sudden gasp of relief. "Yeah. You think he'd do that? Not ask her, I mean?"

"I . . . don't know. Do you . . .?" Zeke hesitated. "Do you want her to marry him?"

"Yeah." Tom frowned, as if considering his answer, then added more firmly, "Yeah. I want her to marry 'im. I wanna have a family. A *real* family, like most folks've got. I want her to stop workin' and just be a ma because I . . . I *hate* what she does."

The last burst out with explosive force, as if it had been bottled up inside him for so long he couldn't contain it a minute more.

"I want her to get married and be like the other ladies. Like Miss Sophie, you know? Where the church ladies don't cross to the other side of the street every time she goes shoppin' and the men don't . . . don't *look* at her like that. Where she's always clean and smells good and she don't ever drink. An' she ain't been—*hasn't* been drinkin' since Mr. O'Boyle started teachin' her to ride that bike. An' if she ain't—*isn't* drinkin', that must mean she likes him some, dontcha think? Huh?"

The spate of words stopped as abruptly as if a cork had suddenly been shoved back in that bottle. He shrugged, clearly embarrassed by his confession, then scowled at the scuff mark he'd left in the dirt.

"It certainly sounds to me as if your ma likes Patrick. And if Patrick likes your ma that much . . ." Zeke's words trailed off. He hated to lie to the boy, but he didn't have any nice, comfortable truths to tell him, and he hated that even more.

"Well, that's what I wanna know," Tom said, his chin set hard in determination. "Is Mr. O'Boyle gonna

ask my ma to marry him? An' what makes a man ask
a lady to marry him, anyway? Since *I* know it can't
possibly be just the . . . the kissin' an' . . . an' stuff,
there's gotta be more to it than that, right?"

Zeke slowly pushed to his feet. His legs were feeling
uncomfortably wobbly, but it wasn't from having been
hunkered down in front of Tom for so long.

Tom Peabody might be only ten years old, but he
had an uncanny knack for seeing straight through to
the heart of a question. The trouble was, Zeke didn't
have any answers, from the heart or otherwise.

"I guess that's right," he said at last, picking up the
neglected pail of milk. "There's gotta be more to getting married than just the kissing and the . . . There's
gotta be more to it than that."

"Yeah," Tom said. "So?"

"So . . . what?" Zeke glanced down at the boy
beside him. He was getting lost in this troublesome
conversation, even if Tom was not.

"So is Patrick gonna ask my ma to marry him? And
are you gonna ask Miss Sophie to marry you?"

The sound of a wagon coming up the lane diverted
Zeke before he could think of an answer.

Tom was first out of the barn. "It's Ma! An' Patrick!" He darted away, his doubts forgotten in the
excitement of his mother's unexpected visit, leaving
Zeke to take the milk to the springhouse.

Zeke tugged open the heavy plank door of the
springhouse and stepped down into the cool darkness.
The big, wide-mouthed glass jars that he'd cleaned
with such care the night before were lined up on the
bench at one side waiting for him. He unscrewed the
metal tops, then lifted the pail to transfer the milk.

His hands were shaking. The milk poured out in a
jerky stream, first hitting the lip of the jars, then slopping inside, then dribbling down the outside to puddle
on the top of the bench.

Was he going to ask Sophie to marry him?

Last night he'd been sure of it. Today . . .

Tom was right. Marriage was about more than kissing and sex, about more than having someone to laugh with.

He ought to know. He'd watched his father avoid most of it . . . and all of the hard part.

Was that why Sarah Jane kept refusing Patrick's offer of marriage? Because she'd rather continue as she was than face the responsibilities and demands of being married?

Patrick *had* asked, more than once, and Sarah Jane had turned him down every time. It wasn't something Zeke could have explained to Tom. He didn't understand it himself.

Zeke tipped the last of the milk into a jar, then screwed down the lids and stuck the jars in the stone-lined trough where the springwater would keep them cold until Mrs. Smith picked them up tomorrow. Instead of taking the milk pail back to the house for a thorough wash, he rinsed it with the runoff from the spring, then threw the slops out the door and hung the pail on a protruding nail. He'd pick it up later, when he had time to do things right.

Patrick was still stiffly perched on the seat of his wagon when Zeke strolled around to the front of the house. Sarah Jane had climbed down to talk to her son, but Tom, head down and arms defiantly folded across his chest, clearly didn't want to listen to whatever she had to say.

"I won't!" he said fiercely. "I *won't* go. You said I could stay all summer if Zeke would have me." He spotted Zeke and immediately darted over and grabbed his sleeve. "You'll let me stay, won't you, Zeke? Tell her I can stay and help you work on the engine. I *promise* I won't try to drive it, not ever again. No, nor pester that old sow, neither. *Honest!*"

"I—"

"We have to go, Thomas," Sarah Jane said. Her voice was pitched high, strung tight with suppressed emotion. "We can't stay here. Not no more."

"But I don't wanna—"

"I don't want to, neither, but—"

"Sarah Jane? Tom?" Neither paid Zeke the slightest heed. "Mrs. Peabody!" This time he spoke loud enough to cut through their self-absorption. "What's going on?"

Sarah Jane stared up at him, clearly uncertain what to say.

"Ma wants to go away!" Tom interjected. "Pueblo, maybe, or way off to Denver. An' I don' wanna go!"

"We gots—we *have* to, Thomas. What have I been tellin' you?"

"But—"

"We're not welcome here. You saw it, there at the picnic. It's 'cause of me, not you, but we gotta go. Try someplace new where don't nobody know me."

She brought the words out hard and unadorned, but there was pain in her eyes, as fresh and sharp as yesterday's humiliations. There was also the faint bite of whiskey on her breath. It was the first time Zeke had ever smelled it on her.

"Surely you don't— Wouldn't Patrick—?" Zeke glanced up at his friend.

The angry tension in the big Irishman gave him all the answer he needed. Patrick had tried to talk her out of it, tried once again to get her to marry him, but Sarah Jane had been adamant.

"But where will you go?" Zeke asked, bewildered. "What will you do?"

"Don't know," Sarah Jane said. Her jaw was set as stubbornly as her son's. "Not what I been doin'. Not if I can help it. Miss Sophie said I could maybe work as a cook in a restaurant. There ain't—There *isn't* much else I can do, but I can cook. If folks don't know me, maybe—"

"So why can't you cook *here*?" Tom demanded, unwilling to concede defeat. His mother just looked at him, and his thin shoulders slumped.

"I'll get my things," he said. Halfway across the hard-packed yard, he kicked a stone with such force it sailed over the flower garden and ricocheted off one of the cottonwoods.

None of the three adults spoke until they heard the kitchen screen door slam behind him.

"You're leaving right away?" Zeke asked at last. He found it surprisingly difficult to get the words out. In the past two months Tom had come to seem like a son to him. He'd been prepared for September, when Tom went back to school, but this leave-taking . . .

"This afternoon," Sarah Jane said. "Not for good. Not yet. Thought I'd take a couple, three weeks, see if I could find me a job. A real job, you know?"

Zeke nodded. He tried to imagine some of the ladies he knew venturing out into a disapproving world with a son and a disreputable past to hold them back and no education to help them along. Only Sophie would have had the guts and determination to make a go of it, he thought. Sophie and Mrs. Smith. He wasn't at all sure Sarah Jane did. It would be so easy to fall back into the old ways.

"Patrick said he'd keep an eye on the house for me." Sarah Jane glanced up at the big man sitting on the wagon behind her.

"You'll remember what I said?" Patrick demanded gruffly.

She nodded. Her lips thinned into a straight, hard line. Zeke thought he saw the sparkle of tears in the corners of her eye, but she resolutely blinked them back.

"I'll not take back my offer, Sarah Jane Peabody," Patrick said. "You've a home with me anytime you want it. A decent, honorable home. All you have to do is say the word."

Sarah Jane's lower lip trembled. "I can't, Patrick. I told you that. I just . . . can't."

The words were barely a whisper, but Patrick flinched as if they stung like scorpions. The sound of the kitchen screen door slamming cut off anything he might have said in reply.

Tom emerged lugging an awkward bundle of his clothes, wadded into a ball and wrapped around with a length of coarse rope. The torn sleeve of a shirt trailed from one corner of the bundle and dragged on the ground behind him, but he ignored it.

Without speaking, Zeke took the bundle from him and tossed it into the back of the wagon. Tom climbed up the wheel and over the low wood sides.

"Tell Miss Sophie I took the books," he said. He was fighting hard not to cry.

"I'll do that." Zeke extended his hand.

Tom took it eagerly, pleased at being treated like a man. His hand almost disappeared in Zeke's. "I'm sorry about tryin' to drive the traction engine." He hesitated, then added, "But it sure was fun!"

The corner of Zeke's mouth twitched. "I expect you'll do better next time."

"Next time?"

"I'm hoping you'll come back and help me keep it running."

Tom's eyes lit up. "You mean it? You'd take me back?"

"If your mama let's you," Zeke added hastily. He didn't want to encourage Tom to run away.

Tom's jaw set. He squared his shoulders. "I'll be back. *Soon.* An' that's a promise!"

The news of Sarah Jane's imminent departure hit Sophie hard. She'd dismounted from her bike and wheeled it into the shade. But as Zeke told her what had happened and what had been said, she let it fall, forgotten.

"It's my fault," she exclaimed, dismayed. "I was the one who encouraged her to go to the picnic with Patrick. If I hadn't—"

"She wasn't blaming you," Zeke said, picking up the bike and propping it against a tree. His matter-of-fact tone couldn't quite disguise his own doubts. "Though why she refuses to marry Patrick . . ."

He shook his head, then abruptly turned to stare into the arching branches of the cottonwood as if he expected to find an answer hidden there. Sophie could have sworn he blushed, but it was probably just a trick of the light.

Only then did the full significance of his news hit her. Without Tom to serve as chaperon . . .

Much the same thought must have been going through Zeke's mind because he suddenly moved away, casually circling around her to peer in the bike's panniers as if lunch was the only thing on his mind.

"Ham!" he exclaimed. "And little chocolate cakes! Do I get Tom's share, too?"

Sophie laughed. She couldn't help it. "Even *you* can't eat that much, Zeke Jeffries! Not on top of what you usually put away!"

He grinned and something in Sophie's middle did a back flip. All her vows to behave as if nothing had happened vaporized in the charged awareness that suddenly arced between them like lightning from the dark clouds that glowered on the horizon.

Sophie tensed, caught in the sparking energy, unable to move or look away.

Only once had she felt anything like it—in the energy that had crackled through the air between Patrick and Sarah Jane all those long weeks ago. She'd thought then it was a product of the place itself, but she'd been wrong.

Zeke felt it, too. His head came up and his eyes fixed on her. His chest rose and fell with his suddenly unsteady breathing. He licked his lips, then swallowed nervously. Even at this distance, Sophie could see the faint sheen of moisture his tongue left behind.

Whatever it was inside her that had done the back flip suddenly lit a firecracker and sent sparks sizzling through her veins.

Sophie made herself look away. Anywhere, so long as it wasn't at Zeke. She fumbled for something to say, something to divert her thoughts.

"Do you think it will rain?" she asked. She had to force the words past the constriction in her throat.

"Maybe."

Sophie glanced at him from the corner of her eye. He was staring at the clouds on the horizon as if he were afraid to look at anything else.

"Hope it doesn't hail," he added after a moment's consideration.

"Yes."

Above them, a faint breeze from the distant thunderclouds stirred the cottonwood leaves, making them rustle.

"You hungry?" Zeke asked, after what seemed like eternity had ticked past.

"Yes!" The word burst out too eagerly. "That is, if you are," Sophie added awkwardly.

"I'm always hungry." He cleared his throat. "I— That is, Tom and I thought maybe we could have our picnic out under that big cottonwood at the far side of the melon patch. For a change, you know."

Sophie eyed the tree in question. How much trouble could she possibly get into sitting at the edge of a watermelon patch?

"That would be nice," she said, and shivered. Whether from excitement or nerves, she didn't know.

Zeke stuffed the food she'd brought into a big, fraying basket, then threw the worn damask tablecloth in on top. Since that first picnic under the cottonwoods, the cloth had become a part of their luncheon ritual. This afternoon it looked freshly washed and ironed, as if Zeke had just brought it back from Gee Ging's laundry.

He led the way across the field, moving easily despite the lopsided weight of the basket. Every so often he'd stop to peer under the broad, coarse leaves of the melon vines.

"I know it's here someplace," he muttered, as if talking to himself. He moved a little farther down the row. "Ah, here it is!"

He set the basket down and pulled out a pocketknife. Sophie heard a rustle and a snap, then he stood with a small but perfect watermelon in his hands. It was dark green, with a slightly lighter band of green where it had lain on the ground. A fine sprinkling of sand and dirt clung to the smooth surface.

"It's an early one, a little small, but perfect." He smiled shyly. "I thought you might like to share the first one of the year with me. That's assuming you like watermelon, of course."

"Hah! I'll have you know, I won the ladies seed-spitting contest at Watermelon Day last year." A giggle snuck out. "But don't you tell Delphi I said so! It took her weeks to get over the humiliation!"

Zeke laughed as he settled the melon under one arm like a trussed pig, then picked up the basket and led the way to the end of the field. Before he set his burdens down, he cast a speculative glance at the distant storm clouds.

"I think we'll be all right. I still haven't quite got the hang of this Colorado weather. In Ohio, you can go for days and not see the sky. Here, the sun can shine and it will *still* be raining."

He waved to the patch of tall grass around the base of the cottonwood. "Will this do?"

"It will do," Sophie said, suddenly feeling breathless. Her legs trembled as she gathered her skirts and sank onto the tummock of grass. For the very first time, she was truly alone with Zeke. She hadn't really realized what that might mean . . . until now.

Her heart beat a hard, unsteady tattoo against her ribs as she watched Zeke set down the basket and the melon, then settle on the grass beside her.

Zeke took a big bite of his sandwich—the third Sophie had made for him so far this afternoon—and leaned back, savoring the salty ham and tangy mustard and Sophie's soft white bread, which was so much tastier than his usual dry biscuits.

Sophie sat at the far edge of the old tablecloth tossing crumbs to a couple of audacious magpies. The birds watched her every move with their bright black eyes, then squabbled over each bite she tossed them.

Watching her was like chewing on his sandwich, Zeke decided. There was the soft, sweet pleasure and her laughter and the light in her eyes and the way she moved. But there was also the sharp, almost bitter tang of knowing she wouldn't be visiting now that Tom was gone.

Without Tom to serve as chaperon, Zeke had al-

most sent her home right off. He was glad now he
hadn't.

It had been awkward at first, sitting at opposite sides
of that old tablecloth pretending they were more interested in the meal than they were in each other, but the
awkwardness had soon eased back into the comfort of
friendly familiarity. Now he simply wanted to savor
these last couple of hours while he still had her all
to himself.

Which just went to prove he couldn't possibly be in
his right mind. This morning he'd been shaking at the
mere thought of asking her to marry him, yet here he
was acting as if he'd never see her again. For one mad
moment just there in the yard, he'd even thought she
was suffering from the same heated awareness that
was afflicting him.

He couldn't have come up with a more addlepated
notion if he'd tried. Ladies didn't feel the same kinds
of stirrings as men did. Not real ladies like Sophie,
anyway. Ladies like Sarah Jane were a different matter entirely. At least, that's what he'd been told and
had believed—until yesterday. Now he wasn't so sure.

Zeke thoughtfully took another bite out of his sandwich. He couldn't help glancing over at Sophie. She
was leaning forward, trying to convince one of the
magpies to take a hunk of bread from her fingers. The
motion emphasized the graceful, slender lines of her
body and dragged his thoughts in dangerous
directions.

"You're as bad as Muriel," she scolded the bird.
"Never take a handout from anybody, no matter
what."

Zeke sat up, curious and in need of something to
distract his thoughts. "Who's Muriel?"

"Muriel?" For an instant Sophie looked confused,
then a delicate blush stole across her cheeks. "Oh!
Muriel."

"Is she a lady from town?" Zeke prodded when she
didn't offer anything more.

"Muriel's a heroine in a book," Sophie said at last,

reluctantly. Her voice sounded muffled, as if she were having a hard time getting the words out.

"What kind of book?"

"A novel." He must have looked blank because she added, even more reluctantly, "A romance novel, actually."

"Ah." Zeke searched for something more intelligent to say. "My mama always liked romance novels."

"*Did* she?"

If he'd known that bit of trivia would make her eyes light up like that, he would have told her months ago. "Said she liked to read about people who ended up happy, no matter what kind of troubles they might have had beforehand."

"Which ones did she like?" Sophie unconsciously edged closer. "Do you remember?"

"Which ones?" Zeke scooched over a mite, as well. Deliberately. "Er, umm, there was a Miss Austen. I know that for sure. She was always talking about some family named the Bennetts. And a Mrs. Southword, I think."

"Southworth. Yes! And . . . ?"

"And . . . Hmmm, and a Jane somebody or other. Or maybe that was the title, I don't exactly remember."

"*Jane Eyre*! One of my very favorites. What else?"

"That's all I can remember, I guess," Zeke reluctantly admitted. He hated to let go such a promising topic too soon. "Though seems to me there were some more. I've still got a few of her favorites if you'd like to read 'em. I couldn't bear to give 'em away, Mama enjoyed them so."

"I'd like that. Thank you!' A heartbeat's hesitation. "Did you . . . Did you ever read any?"

It was his turn to hesitate. "A couple."

"Did you like them?"

Now there he'd gone and done it. Things were going so smooth, but he couldn't shut his trap and now he was going to land himself in trouble if he told the truth. He edged around the answer delicately. "Well, it's been a while since I read one."

The light went out of her eyes suddenly. He'd swear
her shoulders drooped, just a tad. "You didn't like
them."

"Well, no, not much." He *knew* he should have
shut up.

"Why not?"

Zeke sighed. It wasn't very sporting of her to slam
a fellow up against a conversational wall like that, but
he supposed he *was* the one who'd started it.

"No fellow I ever knew acted like the fellows in
those books," he said, drawing each word out with
care. "It seemed to me . . ."

"Yes?" she prompted when he didn't continue.

Her "yes" wasn't so much an invitation as a warning, but Zeke couldn't see any way out of this mess
he'd made except straight ahead. He gulped and
plunged onward.

"It seemed to me that the lady writers were writing
a story for the lady readers, I guess, not the gentlemen. Seemed the heroes in those books were just sort
of doing things the way the ladies'd want a fellow to
do 'em, not the way a fellow really does 'em. If you
see what I mean," he finished lamely.

"Is that so?" The words came out so precise and
cool they might have had ice around the edges.
"How interesting."

Oh, Lordy! He'd done it now. The frost was thick
enough to wilt his vines for a quarter mile 'round.

"Not that I'm an expert, you know. Never claimed
to be." Zeke gave her his most ingratiating smile. "I
expect you know better about those sorts of things, so
you needn't pay any attention to me. My stomach's
so full, it's probably stopped my brain from working."

She stared at him for a moment, then she blinked
and swallowed hard, as if something she didn't want
to swallow insisted on going down anyway.

"I imagine you're right," she said in a small, tight
little voice. All the fight had gone out of her, just
like that.

Zeke wasn't sure what he'd said to upset her so,
but it didn't take two eyes to see he'd made a big

mistake somewhere along the line. Probably the minute he'd opened his mouth for anything except eating.

"How about some of that watermelon?" he said. He
surely couldn't get in much trouble with a watermelon.

Chapter 16

Sophie watched as Zeke delicately brushed the sand off the watermelon he'd picked. Its smooth, green surface shone in the sun. When he set it down on the grass again, it gave a solid, echoing *thunk*!

Much like the sound her head would make if it were thumped, she supposed, since it had to be as thick as that melon. Nothing else explained her madness in thinking she could seduce Zeke. Especially since he scorned the very notion of romantic heroes. *Especially* when she could so easily be upstaged by three ham sandwiches and a watermelon!

What did she have to do to get Zeke to kiss her again? Throw herself in his arms? Rope and hog-tie him?

If the only thing that worked was burying him under a collapsed tent, she was in bigger trouble than she'd thought.

Zeke paid not the slightest attention to her or the curious magpies, who had ventured closer in hopes of more handouts. He pulled out his large pocketknife, unfolded it with due care, and delicately polished the blade on his pants leg.

Sophie watched, resigned. There was something about a watermelon that affected the brains of ordinarily reasonable males. She'd yet to see a man who didn't approach the carving of a melon with the same intense concentration he brought to a debate on politics or a discussion of farm prices.

Women, always the more practical of the two sexes, just stuck the knife in and got on with the business. She wished Zeke would do the same. Instead, he

balanced the watermelon in his hands, gravely studying it first from one side, then the other. Then he
squinted down the length of it. At last, after due consideration and with the focused concentration of a
master carver, he plunged his knife into one end of
the watermelon and carefully sawed a line to the other
end. Juice oozed from the wound. He frowned, evidently displeased, but it was too late to turn back.
With exquisite care, he made a second cut, then gently
tugged the quarter of melon free and held it up for
her inspection.

"What do you think?" From the glint in his eye,
applause wouldn't be out of place.

The corner of Sophie's mouth quirked upward. She
couldn't help it. He looked more like a boy who had
conquered the world than a grown man who'd managed to take one slice out of a melon. "It looks delicious. Nice and juicy."

"And just the right shade of pink, don't you think?"
Zeke held the quarter out at arm's length so she could
get the full benefit of its pinkness.

"Just right," Sophie agreed solemnly.

Zeke frowned and turned the quarter so he could
study it from another angle. "Of course, it's the taste
that counts."

"Of course."

"That's what sells to the fancy hotels back East,
you know."

"Absolutely."

"If they don't taste good—"

Sophie leaned forward and plucked the quarter slice
out of his hand. She got a good hold on each end—
the only approved grip for eating melon if you were
brave enough to dispense with a fork—made sure she
was angled so the juice wouldn't dribble down her
clothes, and took a bite. A big bite.

The sweet, firm flesh gave a faint snap as she bit
through it. Juice flooded her mouth, rich with flavor.
Her nose filled with the smell of summer.

Zeke watched her anxiously as she chewed.

Sophie was tempted to keep him in suspense, but

that would have been cruel. The poor man was already close to exploding.

"Wonderful!" she said, and took another bite.

Zeke's smile spread across his face like sunshine. He hacked off another quarter slice and took a giant bite in the center. Juice dribbled from the corner of his mouth as he chewed.

Sophie watched, entranced, at the sensual transformation of his face. His eyelids lowered, his lips pressed tight together, moving as his jaw worked, puckering, then opening as his tongue flicked out to catch an errant dab of juice.

"Mmmmm."

"Good?" Sophie teased, knowing it was.

"Mmnnnn." Zeke nodded, still chewing. Before the first bite was gone, he took a second. His teeth carved neat half-moons into the ridge of pink. His fingers curled around the ends of the slice protectively, lovingly. He swallowed, then gasped for air. "Wonderful!" It was a benediction . . . and a prayer of thanksgiving.

It was the prayer of every farmer—a good crop, and a high-paying market to sell it in. He had the crop, or would have in a few weeks when the rest of the melons ripened. The market was already there. All Zeke had to worry about now was getting his watermelons to it on time and in good shape.

Sophie took another bite. This one came with a seed. She chewed around it, devouring the sweet flesh, then spat out the seed.

Zeke eyed the results critically. "Not very good for the ladies seed-spitting champ," he said, grinning.

Sophie sniffed and tilted her nose upward. "I'm out of practice, that's all."

"Hah!" The grin widened. Zeke chomped down on the melon. He chewed energetically for a moment, then spat a seed out in a long, arcing trajectory. A moment later he spat a second, then a third seed. Each one sailed farther than the last. "Let's see you top *that!*"

"You're on!"

They plowed their way through the slices of melon, laughing and choking and spitting seeds in all directions. When the first slices were nothing but hard green rind and a few sad traces of pink, they tossed them away and split the remaining half of the watermelon.

Sophie conceded defeat before she was halfway through the second slice. "I can't!" she protested. "And don't make me laugh by wiggling your eyebrows and looking smug! I'm so full, I'll pop if I even think about moving!"

Zeke laughed and looked wicked. He set his own unfinished slice to one side, then leaned forward to take hers out of her hands.

"Did you know you have watermelon juice on your nose?" he asked, teasing.

Before Sophie had a chance to reply, he leaned closer still and brushed the tip of her nose with his finger.

Sophie froze. Her breath caught somewhere in the middle of her chest as she stared into his eyes. So close . . . and so very, very blue. She could see his pupils dilate an instant before those indecently thick, dark lashes slid down. His gaze dropped to her mouth.

"And there," he said, delicately flicking the corner of her mouth with another fingertip. His voice had suddenly grown lower and slower and slightly raspy, as though he found it hard to speak.

"And there." This time there was no quick touch but a slow, tender stroke over the crest of her upper lip, then down to the curve of her chin. The callus on his fingertip scraped at her skin; the melon juice slipped like tears beneath his finger.

"And there," Zeke said. He was barely breathing, his words no more than a sensual whisper, as soft and tantalizing as his touch. This time he didn't try to brush away the lingering sweetness. Instead he slowly, delicately traced the swell of her lower lip.

It must have been instinct that made her open her mouth, and instinct that led her to lick at the tip of his finger with her tongue.

The juice he'd brushed from her lips was sweet, with the faintest trace of salt. From his skin . . . or hers, perhaps.

Something between her legs suddenly tightened, aching with unexpected need. She shifted her position, caught between the competing poles of her body's response. Her eyes widened. Her vision filled with Zeke.

Why had none of her books ever spoken of the tumult a simple touch could produce? He hadn't even kissed her, yet—

"Sophie?"

Sophie's heart stopped beating. "Yes?"

"I . . ." Zeke swallowed, licked his lips, and tried again. "I'd like . . . to kiss you. If you don't mind, that is."

Time hung, unmoving. Sophie's lungs stopped working. Her mouth went dry and whatever it was that resided right in the middle of her stomach gave another ecstatic leap.

"May I?" Zeke was having trouble managing a whisper. He breathed in deep—Sophie could see his nostrils flare and his chest swell. At least *his* lungs were working. "Kiss you, I mean?" he added.

It came out more a croak than a whisper, but Sophie got the message.

"Oh, yes!" she whispered back. She took one deep, shaky breath, closed her eyes, and leaned forward expectantly.

He'd never been more frightened in his life.

What if he'd fooled himself yesterday and didn't really know how to kiss? What if he bumped her nose or hit her head or rammed her lips against her teeth in his excitement?

What if, God forbid, he slobbered?

Zeke felt like a tightly strung fence wire. Only his fingertip had touched her, yet every muscle in his body vibrated from the contact. He had to brace one hand on the ground to keep his trembling limbs from betraying him.

He leaned toward her. Their lips touched, ever so gently.

Sophie's lips were soft and warm against his, tantalizing in their unspoken promise of wonders yet to be discovered.

A moment, no more, then Zeke slowly pulled back, dazed. There was a tight, hot pressure in the middle of his chest. His pulse hammered in his ears like the eager pounding of a steam locomotive roaring downhill. The demanding creature between his legs had already roused into tormenting life. It strained against the seven securely fastened buttons of his pants, clamoring for release.

A release he couldn't claim.

He'd had his kiss. He wasn't supposed to ask for anything more, no matter how much he wanted . . . everything.

Zeke dug his fingers into the ground, fighting for balance, but the worn damask cloth divided him from the solid earth, leaving him nothing but crumpled cloth to anchor himself to. The muscles in his arms and across his back trembled with the struggle. He forced his eyes shut, willing himself not to look, not to want . . .

His lips burned and his erection suddenly flexed against the restraining cloth, reminding him just how very much he wanted.

Zeke sucked in his breath and prayed—for what, he wasn't quite sure.

". . . again?" Sophie's soft plea was almost lost in the confusion of his senses.

Zeke forced his eyes open. She was watching him, amber eyes wide, lips parted.

The muscles of his belly suddenly contracted, making the ache in his groin even more tormenting. So much for good intentions.

He stared at her, unable to speak.

How many times in the lonely, restless hours of the night had he imagined her looking at him like this? How often had the longing to touch her, to claim her for his own driven him to the cold relief of icy water

and chill night air? He didn't know. He wasn't sure
he could count that high.

Here he was with Sophie only inches from him, face
flushed with heat and confusion and need, just as he'd
imagined her . . . and suddenly he was afraid. Afraid
and hungry and so damned uncertain about his own
lack of experience that he couldn't move or think,
could scarcely breathe.

"Zeke?" she said, nervous now.

Someone, somewhere groaned. Zeke heard, but he
didn't care. He lowered his head to Sophie's. His
mouth claimed hers . . . or maybe she claimed his. He
wasn't sure of anything except the need for her that
shot through him like a firecracker on the Fourth.

His doubts faded as instinct grabbed hold. His lips
parted over hers and his tongue flicked out to taste
and explore.

Her lips were sweet, warm, and welcoming. Her
mouth opened, her tongue touched his, teasing him,
tempting him farther into the unknown.

Zeke stopped breathing, gasped, and plunged
ahead. Sensation flooded him . . . and wonder.

The kisses deepened, expanded, but they weren't
enough. He wanted to hold her, to feel her body warm
and firm and tempting against his.

He shifted. Too far.

Off balance, he tried to brace himself without losing
Sophie. Sophie jerked, started by the awkward movement. Their noses collided. His shoulder bumped hers,
throwing her off balance, too.

"Zeke!"

Zeke cussed, tried to sit up, and clobbered the picnic basket instead.

Sophie stared at him, wide-eyed. Zeke stared back,
uncomfortably conscious of the rapid, uneven rise and
fall of her breast as she tried to catch her breath. His
own breathing was none too steady.

They both burst out laughing at the same time.

"Oh, dear." Sophie giggled, then blushed. "It was
never like this in the books."

"I figured I had it there for a minute," Zeke admitted, embarrassed. He could feel his face turning red as he shoved upright.

Sophie's gaze fixed on him. Then she drew a deep breath and let it out very, very slowly. "You did," she said. There was an odd little catch in her voice as she said it.

Zeke blinked. For a minute, he wasn't quite sure he'd heard her right. He gulped, squirmed, and, somehow, dredged up the courage to ask, "Want to try again?"

Sophie nodded.

Zeke's mind went blank. What was he supposed to do now?

Sophie was no help whatsoever. She stared at him expectantly, waiting for him to make the next move.

"Mind if I . . . ?" Embarrassed, Zeke made a vague gesture with his hands to indicate he wanted to move closer.

Sophie just smiled and looked hopeful.

Zeke awkwardly scooted over. He felt more like a schoolboy than a man who'd just kissed a beautiful woman, but he decided he'd worry about that later. If Sophie was willing to overlook his lack of polish, who was he to argue?

From somewhere behind him, thunder rumbled. Zeke ignored that, too.

It took a bit of experimentation to find the right way to take Sophie in his arms. Zeke could have sworn there were a couple extra elbows somewhere in the tangle, and the question of where to put his hands wasn't exactly easy since he wanted to put them . . . well . . . everywhere.

"This all right?"

Sophie snuggled closer. "Better."

Her left breast pressed soft and tantalizing against his ribs. Zeke tried not to breathe as he pulled her closer still. "Better?"

She tilted her head back against his shoulder. Her smile sent sparks shooting through his veins. She ran her fingers along the line of his jaw, over the faint roughness of his beard. Her touch was light, like a whisper of wind brushing past, and it made him tremble with its power. She pulled his head down to hers.

"*Much* better," she whispered an instant before their lips touched.

Zeke kissed her mouth, exploring the richness, then her chin, her cheek, her temple. She kissed his jaw, trailed kisses down his throat and back again. He played copycat and traced his own hot kisses over her soft throat, down to her crisp, starched collar and around the front to the other side and up.

He kissed the warm skin at the angle of her jaw where her lifeblood pulsed, and, because he couldn't help himself, nibbled the soft lobe of her ear, then caught his breath in startled wonder as she moaned and arched against him and twisted so he could kiss her there again.

Her fingers threaded through his hair, tugging at the heavy strands, holding him captive. She ran her palm down the back of his neck, across his shoulder and over the bunching muscles of his arm. Twice her fingers dug into the muscle, digging deep in an involuntary spasm until he could feel the bite of her nails through the heavy cloth of his shirt. Zeke hissed at the pain, then moaned at the responsive throb and ache in his groin.

Tentatively, yet with an urgency that made his fingers tremble, Zeke drew his hand up from her waist, over the curve of her ribs to the delicate swell of her breast.

A grumbling rumble shook the air as if some guardian beast were angered at his presumption and warning him to go no farther. Wind whipped past him, clattering through the leaves overhead until they'd sounded like a rattlesnake's warning rattle.

Zeke's hand slid away from Sophie's breast, his fingers trailing over the smooth curve of flesh beneath the starched linen of her blouse. There was a roaring in his ears and a fiery protest in his veins and belly, but still Zeke pulled away.

"Zeke?" Sophie shifted in his arms. Her mouth was

swollen, her expression dazed, like a sleeper just roused from her dreams.

"Storm's coming." It wasn't a lie, even if it wasn't the reason for his withdrawal. "Best get back to the house before it breaks."

Too late he remembered there would be no one there but the two of them.

The rain caught them before they'd gone a hundred yards, pelting out of the sky in needle-fine drops that stung when they hit.

Rather than plow through the heavy soil of the melon field, Sophie followed Zeke at a lurching trot along the irrigation ditch, head ducked against the storm. The picnic basket dangled from Zeke's hand. In their haste, they'd thrown everything in any old how. A forgotten corner of the old tablecloth stuck out from under the basket lid like a small boy's shirt-tail stuck out of his pants, disreputable-looking and unheeded.

The ditch bank should have been easier going, but after the bone-melting heat of Zeke's kisses, Sophie's muscles simply refused to work right. She stumbled and staggered after Zeke like a drunk on a Saturday–night binge. Forget the thunder and the lightning and the driving rain—their mind-numbing power couldn't begin to compare with the effect even one of Zeke's kisses had on her.

"We'll head for the barn," Zeke yelled over his shoulder. "It's closer!"

By the time they swung the broad double doors shut against the storm, Sophie was out of breath, soaking wet, and cold. Chest heaving, she slumped against the solid door frame and wiped the water from her face. Long strands of hair clung to her cheeks and neck like dank water weed. Her shirtwaist was soaked through to the skin and her heavy gabardine skirt hung like a limp, dead-weight around her legs. Her legs trembled with the effort of holding her upright, but their trembling owed little to her mad dash across the fields.

"Sophie?" Zeke eyed her uncertainly. "You all right?"

All right? Sophie wasn't sure she'd ever be "all right" again. How did you recover from kisses like the ones she'd shared with Zeke—was it only a few minutes ago?

She tried to laugh. "I'm wet. In case you hadn't noticed." She nervously pulled at her sodden shirt-waist, trying to get it away from her skin. "I must look a wreck."

"Nooo," Zeke said, drawing the word out slowly. His gaze slid from her face to her throat to her breasts that were perfectly outlined by the rain-soaked linen.

Sophie's hand froze in the act of tugging at the cloth. The heel of her hand grazed her cold-tautened nipple, but her body reacted as if it were his hand that touched her, his fingers that brushed against the top of her breast.

Zeke didn't look a wreck. He looked . . . raw and elemental and heart-stoppingly male. Water rolled out of his hair and down his face, dripping off his nose and chin and the arch of his ears as from some perfect, living sculpture. His work shirt was plastered to his body. She could see the faint outline of the ribbing of his undershirt, but even two layers of cloth couldn't disguise muscles honed and shaped by years of hard labor. His pants clung to his legs, revealing the tanta-lizing outline of powerful calves and thighs and . . .

Sophie abruptly fixed her gaze on the packed dirt floor as an aching heat blossomed within her. What madness was this? Her skin pricked at the cold and wet, yet inside she was ablaze and so exquisitely aware of Zeke that she knew the instant he lifted his hand to gently touch her shoulder.

"Sophie? I . . . I'm sorry. I shouldn't have—"

Sophie's head snapped up. *"No!"*

Not sorry! *Never* that he was sorry he had kissed her!

"I *wanted* you to kiss me," she said, so fiercely he flinched and drew back. "And I wanted to kiss *you*."

She took a step toward him, but this time he didn't

retreat. Her voice dropped, turned rough with desire, trembled with emotion and the need suddenly welling up within her.

"I wanted to kiss you, just as I wanted to touch you," she said just as fiercely, laying her right hand on his broad breast, "and I wanted you"—Sophie claimed his right hand and drew it toward her—"to touch . . . me." Her gaze fixed on his face as she pulled his hand to her breast.

He gasped, then groaned like a man tortured, but his hand readily curved over her breast, enfolding the soft, intimate roundness. The tip of each finger and the edge of his thumb marked a ring of fire across the crest as the heel of his hand pressed against the soft curve beneath, gathering her into his grasp, claiming her. His palm rubbed against her nipple, dragging the layers of wet linen and cotton that divided them over the sensitive tip.

Sophie's eyes slid shut at his exquisite, unsettling touch. She pressed her hand more firmly over his, sliding her fingers between his long, strong ones, holding him against her, tightening even as his hold on her tightened. The hair on the back of his hand rubbed against her palm, coarse and wet with rain, teasing her senses. She took a deep, involuntary breath, then another deliberately, dizzily trying to sort through the myriad unfamiliar sensations coursing through her.

"Yes," she said. Her head fell back as she arched into Zeke's hand. "Oh, yes." The word hissed out on a long exhalation as the fingers of her right hand dug into the hard muscles of his chest.

She scarcely noticed when he covered her hand with his, weaving his fingers between hers. She was blind, dazed, deaf to the thudding roar of the rain against the old barn. Her world had narrowed until it consisted of his hand on her breast and her hand on his, of heat and need and a hundred physical clamorings for which she had no name.

"Sophie! Don't!"

Her eyes snapped open. Her mind spun, unable to grasp his meaning. "Don't . . . ?"

"Don't torment me, Sophie," he pleaded. "Not like this."

"Torment you?" Sophie blinked, dazed. He wasn't making sense. *He* was the one tormenting *her*. It was his touch, his nearness, his kisses that had brought her to this.

"*Please,* Sophie."

The agony in his voice broke through the turmoil of her senses. Sophie tried to pull free, but couldn't. Zeke wouldn't let her.

"You don't want me to touch you? You . . ." Sophie fought against the fear. "You don't want to touch me?"

"Not want—?" His words cut short in an explosive sound halfway between mad laughter and a curse. "Not *want* to touch you!"

Suddenly he grabbed her arms and pulled her close, almost shaking her in his anguished fury. "Do you know how many nights I've *dreamed* of touching you? Of holding you and making love and—"

He shoved her away so abruptly she staggered, his eyes wild. "Not *want* to touch you? It's almost driven me mad that I can't! That I shouldn't. That you . . . !"

As abruptly as he'd pushed her away, he snatched her back, dragging her into his arms and crushing her against his chest as he lowered his head to hers, claiming her mouth in a kiss that not even the cold rainwater still streaming over his skin could quench.

Sophie's last coherent thought as she gave herself up to the sweet heat and flaring need was that she wasn't sorry. That she would never, ever allow herself to regret what lay ahead.

The promise beat through her fading conscious in time with her racing heart.

Never sorry. Never, never, never sorry.

Chapter 17

Sophie had unbuttoned the first six buttons on Zeke's shirt before he realized what she was doing. From somewhere deep inside him he dredged up the last, lingering drop of self-control and pulled away.

"Sophie." It came out as a groaning protest. "Think of—"

"I don't want to think," she shot back. There was a mad, bright light in her eyes as she leaned into him, throwing him off balance. "I've done enough thinking in my life."

Her breasts pressed against his chest, her thigh against his. His hand burned where it had touched her.

Zeke couldn't let go. The feel and taste and heat of her tormented him past bearing. He wanted to make love to her so badly he was afraid he might explode, yet he couldn't do it.

No—he *shouldn't* do it. Not here. Not now. Not like this.

The words spun in his head like wooden horses on a carousel, up and down, around and around until his head threatened to spin off with them.

Last night he'd ached for this. Now, when she was so blatantly, temptingly within his grasp, a few thin shreds of sense fluttered at the back of his mind, reminding him he had no business taking a wife, let alone claiming a lover.

Too late. Sophie undid the buttons on his undershirt and slid her hands in against his cold, wet skin. Where her fingers touched, fire burned.

She pulled her hands free and impatiently tugged the braces over his shoulder. He'd pulled his braces

off countless thousands of times. Not once had the
simple act sent such hungry fire shooting through his
belly. When she turned to to unbuttoning more buttons,
Zeke became an eager accomplice.

Their fingers tangled together, fumbling with the
buttons, tugging impatiently at the shirt and undershirt
to pull them free. They forgot one cuff. It caught when
Zeke peeled his shirt away. He tugged, swore, then
simply ripped the shirt off, shredding cuff and sleeve.
He tossed the mangled shirt aside, then pulled the
undershirt over his head and flung it after.

He reached to perform the same office for Sophie,
but froze with his hands in midair, caught in her startled, hungry gaze.

She stood before him, head high, eyes dark and avid
as she studied him. Her mouth worked, but no sound
came out. She took a deep, shuddering breath and
tried again.

"I never knew . . . a man could be . . . so . . .
beautiful."

Like a sleepwalker, or a dreamer in a trance, Sophie
raised one hand and slowly traced the ridge of his
collarbone to the boney V at the base of his throat.
She lingered there, one fingertip lightly pressed against
his skin. A touch as light as a breath of wind, yet
Zeke suddenly found it difficult to breathe.

Like a trickle of rainwater tracing a path across his
skin, she dragged her finger down his breastbone and
into the whorls of black hair, parting them, curving
around them, trailing downward. Her gaze followed
her finger as though bound to it . . . and to him.

Zeke watched her, as shaken by her unabashed fascination with his body as by her exploration.

She paused to press her hand over his heart, fingers
spread like sensitive antennae, then slowly trailed her
splayed fingers over his ribs and down his belly. He
sucked in a sharp breath at the fire she left in her
wake. His erection suddenly strained against the seam
of his pants like a wild beast raging to be let out.

He couldn't hide his reaction—he was past wanting
to—but when Sophie's hand dropped below his waist,

Zeke gritted his teeth and hastily pulled her away. "No! Not . . . not yet."

The startled look on her face slowly changed to one of triumph as she caught the frantic need that drove him to such roughness.

Wildly, he looked about the barn. The hay was sweet and fresh and mounded deep as a dream, but they needed a blanket. Something besides the heavy old horse blankets that hung on the wall . . . but what?

Outside, the storm raged and crashed, throwing its might against the old barn in an angry thrash of wind and rain and what might be the first rounds of hail. Impossible to run to the house and there was nothing . . .

A tail of white stuck out of the discarded basket like a flag. The tablecloth! With a growl of triumph, Zeke released Sophie and bent to pull out the cloth. The damask was old and worn, but soft as silk to the touch and more than large enough for their needs.

As he stood, the cloth mounded in his hands, Sophie gave a slight, faintly breathless laugh, and took it out of his hands.

"The hay?" she said, and laughed again when he nodded, too shaken at the thought of what lay ahead to speak.

It wasn't the tidy wedding bed with fine linen sheets that she'd always imagined, but it would serve.

Sophie stared down at the waist-high mound of hay they'd pulled out of the larger stack to make a thick, fragrant cushion beneath the old blankets. The white-on-white pattern of the damask cloth they'd laid on top shown faintly gray in the storm-darkened barn, oddly elegant against the dusty green of the hay.

Zeke stood at the far side of their makeshift bed, watching her, wary and uncertain now their intentions were so clearly laid out between them.

He wanted her. *Her!* Sophie was sure of it. As sure as she was that just the sight of him standing there, half naked and glorious, was enough to set the blood singing through her veins.

Nothing in her books had prepared her for this. None of the eager speculation she'd indulged in with her friends had taught her what she needed to know, and the world outside would be all too quick to condemn her for what she was about to do.

None of it mattered. *This* was what she wanted. Zeke. This moment and nothing else.

Staid, plain, practical Sophie had washed away in the storm, leaving behind the fiery heart of her she'd thought existed only in her fantasies. This wasn't romance. Not the kind she'd read about in her books, anyway. It was far more elemental . . . and far more consuming.

Whatever came after, this moment was hers and Sophie intended to make the most of it. She would simply have to trust instinct to guide her where knowledge failed.

Almost breathless at her temerity, Sophie slowly and with calculated deliberation began to unbutton her shirtwaist.

Four tiny, pearl-white buttons on each cuff. Three at her high collar. Five down to the point of her breasts.

Eyes wide and dark, Zeke watched with unblinking fascination as she released each one, like a cat mesmerized by the fire.

Her fingers were on the sixth when he moved.

Zeke unbuttoned the seventh and the eighth. By the eleventh button, Sophie was incapable of counting. He pulled her shirtwaist free and slid it from her shoulders.

He didn't touch the camisole. Instead, he reached behind her and, one by one, removed the hairpins from the tangled wreck of her hair. His arms encircled her, strong and solid and safe.

Sophie wrapped her arms around him and laid her head against his breast. The thudding of her heart mingled with the beat of his, drowning out the storm. His skin was warm against hers, dry now from the heat of him. His dark man scent teased her as his fingers sifted through her hair, freeing it to tumble over his hands and down her back.

Beneath the curtain of her hair, his hands moved to her camisole, her skirt, her underskirt.

Clumsily, eagerly, like children unwrapping longed-for presents, they undressed each other.

Neither spoke, the only sounds between them a swift intake of breath, a sigh of pleasure, the unsteady rasp of lungs struggling for air.

As the last damp piece of clothing slid away, Sophie stepped back one faltering step. Her bones were melting, her muscles turning to water at the heat and need rippling through her. She was dizzy and excited and . . .

And suddenly she was afraid.

She'd been right. Zeke *was* beautiful. But she wasn't—never had been—and now there was nothing left to hide her own long, lanky, unfeminine body.

Zeke's gaze fixed on her. Sophie nervously tried to cover her breasts, then the dark thatch of curls between her legs. His gaze followed her hand down, fixed on that intimate, secret part of her. Something inside her tightened, making her ache in a way that was surely as indecent as it was irresistible.

"This—" Zeke was having a hard time getting his mouth to work. "This is how an angel looks."

He threw a nervous glance over his shoulder at the makeshift bed, then turned back to her. His eyes were dark, unfathomable wells. "You're . . . sure?"

Something in that darkness, in his reverent admiration and his own uncertainty stilled the doubts. Sophie nodded, once.

It was enough. Without a word, Zeke picked her up and carried her the few steps to the bed of hay they'd made while the rain, softer now, drummed on the roof high above their heads, whispering in their heated silence.

Not once in all his hungry imaginings had Zeke imagined it could be like this. The ache and heat in his groin were the same. The trembling of his muscles was the same. The urgent fire in his belly was the same—and yet it was all different, transformed by the magic of Sophie, by the sheer wonder of her beside him.

They were clumsy, uncertain, yet instinct and the insistent demands of their bodies carried them through the first fumbling attempt at union until they discovered how easily he fit between her parted thighs, how surely their bodies meshed.

At his first rough plunge, Sophie cried out and arched against him. Zeke froze, frightened by her pain and the barrier he could feel within her. Boyhood whisperings behind the schoolhouse had never prepared him for the tension that clamped her body beneath his or the desperate need that urged him on, regardless.

Sophie whimpered and twisted beneath him. Her nails dug into the muscles of his back, sharp as talons. In spite of his need, Zeke tried to pull out. He couldn't. His muscles trembled at the effort to hold his body off her, yet something inside him drove him on. He plunged deeper, harder, until suddenly the invisible barrier parted and he buried himself within her.

Sophie drew her legs up. The silken skin of her inner thighs brushed against his thighs, his hips. Her hips shifted, somehow accommodating him more comfortably even as muscles deep within her clenched around him in a mind-numbing torment.

When it began, Zeke couldn't tell, but somehow he was moving, thrusting in and out in an increasingly urgent rhythm. And Sophie was moving with him—not in fear this time, but in a hesitant rhythm to match his own. Retreating, meeting, arching to take him deeper. With each thrust, each welcoming response, Zeke spun inward until his world narrowed to pure sensation and a desperate, pounding need for completion.

The end, like the storm outside, came in a rush and a roar, drowning him in its power. From far away, Zeke heard a shout and a groan and knew that both had been torn from him. Every muscle in his body clenched as he curled into the spurting heat at his center.

Like the storm, the passion slowly ebbed, grumbling and rumbling away with an occasional burst of lightning to catch him by surprise. Zeke slumped over Sophie, wet with sweat. His lungs heaved, trying to drag in air.

Only very slowly did he become aware of her trembling beneath him, of her hands moving over him like butterflies dashing themselves against a barrier, as if she were seeking some point to anchor herself, but found none.

His eyes opened, focused. Slowly, Zeke levered himself up off her chest without breaking their physical union.

She lay, hair spilled across the patterned damask, eyes wide and hollow. Her breathing was as erratic as his. To his amazement, Zeke realized suddenly that she was still squeezing him . . . *there*.

Gently, fingers trembling, he smoothed an errant lock of hair away from her face. Her skin was hot and damp.

"Sophie?" She blinked and slowly seemed to focus on his face. "Are you all right?"

Her tongue flicked out. She shifted restlessly under him. The cushion of hay rustled and shifted with them. "I . . . I don't know.'

"I didn't mean . . . to hurt you." Another squeeze, so powerful it made him flinch and drove him out of her.

Sophie made a little mewling sound of protest. Her hands dug into his back.

"Sophie? What is it?" Zeke demanded, frightened now.

"It hurt and then . . . it was over so . . . suddenly," she whispered. "I feel like I . . . like I'm hanging from a precipice. As if I want to go over the edge, but I can't. I don't know how."

Zeke gaped at her, too dazed from his own completion to even begin to understand what she meant.

"Kiss me, Zeke," she said, and dragged his head down to hers.

One kiss became two, then three, then three became

a dozen as Zeke found himself launched on a sensual exploration that was slower and sweeter, but no less urgent than the first.

To his delight, he discovered secret, sensitive places where a kiss or a flick of his tongue roused unexpectedly eager responses in her—just beneath her jaw, her throat where her pulse beat, the soft skin where arm and chest were joined.

His little triumphs made him bolder. He showered kisses over her breast, then, after one hesitant glance to see if he had ventured too far, took her nipple in his mouth and sucked. Sophie gasped and arched into him as a bolt of fire shot between his legs, rousing him back to life.

Within moments he was achingly ready, yet the pleasures of this slow voyage of discovery were too sweet to abandon hastily. He claimed the other breast with his mouth even as he kept possession of the first, kneading it, tugging at the nipple until Sophie writhed and whimpered and begged for more. Willingly, Zeke gave it, and in the giving got back far more than he gave. Sophie melted under his touch, molding her body to his with untutored ease as the fire within him flared bright and hot and urgent.

This time there was no barrier to their joining.

This time Sophie moved with him, urging him on, dragging him with her as she climbed and climbed until, with a choked cry of wonder and exultation, she tumbled over the edge of her precipice, pulling Zeke over after.

The storm had passed by the time Zeke roused. Beside him, still asleep, Sophie lay wrapped in his arms and her glorious hair and nothing else.

Carefully, so as not to disturb her, Zeke propped himself up on one elbow. There were so many details he'd missed—the faint shadow her eyelashes cast on her cheek, the glint of red and gold in the tangled strands of her hair, the mole at the base of her right breast.

His palm tingled at the thought of her breast cupped

in his hand, of his mouth on that small, soft, tempting mound.

If they were married, he could wake like this every morning with her warm and soft beside him. And then, when she awoke . . .

As though summoned from her dreams, Sophie stirred, blinked, curled into his warmth, then stretched like a lazy cat. A tentative beam of sunlight slipped through a gap in the wall to caress her shoulder with gold. Dust motes drifted in the light and Zeke smelled damp earth and dry hay and the lily-of-the-valley scent in her hair. Beneath it all, faint and musky and infinitely tantalizing, lay the mingled scent of their bodies.

Sophie shifted so that she faced him. As she raised herself up on her elbow, her hair fell over her shoulder, hiding her breasts. She made no effort to cover herself and met his questioning gaze with a quizzical smile. "I don't think I'll ever eat watermelon again without . . . remembering."

Zeke had thought it impossible for his body to rouse again. He'd been wrong. As her gaze slid downward, he sprang to attention.

She flushed, then touched him gently, hesitantly. "I've heard it's called a cock," she said in an awed whisper tinged with amusement. "I never dreamt it was because it stood so proud and haughty like this."

Zeke gasped at her touch, then laughed. "Just like a rooster. Crowing and claiming *it* was the one brought the day."

Sophie snorted and grinned and ran her fingers teasingly over the silky surface. "The cock 'o the walk. Chief boss in the henhouse."

The object of her attention jerked beneath her hand as if objecting to not being taken seriously.

For one horrible moment, Zeke thought he might shame himself. He grabbed her wrist, pulling her away from him.

"Do you . . . do you think this cock 'o mine might . . ." It wasn't easy to get the words out against the hunger once more surging through him. Sweat beaded on his brow. ". . . might take another walk?

Before . . ." He gulped down the eagerness. "Before it walks off all by itself?"

Afterward, Zeke rolled over to lie on his back. He drew Sophie with him so that she lay on top of him, her head pillowed on his breast. Gradually his breathing slowed and his heartbeat returned to normal. Neither of them spoke.

He stared up into the shadowed rafters above him and listened to the soft sound of her breathing. Her fingers brushed against the damp, curling black hair of his chest as he gently stroked her back under the mass of her hair, tracing the line of her spine. Her skin was warm and damp with her sweat.

"Sophie?"

"Mmmm?" She lifted her head. Her hair tumbled about her in a wild disorder. Her mouth was swollen and the skin of her cheek and throat spotted red where his beard had rubbed.

Zeke thought he had never seen anyone more beautiful in all his life . . . and still he couldn't bring himself to say the words that kept ringing in the back of his mind.

Will you marry me? So simple, and yet . . .

Tom had been right. Marriage wasn't about sex and kissing, no matter how much you enjoyed them both. It certainly wasn't about having someone around to keep the loneliness at bay, though that had to be a part of it, too.

It was about responsibility and commitment and . . .

He didn't know what it was about. Not for sure. Not enough to say what he ought to say.

Instead . . . "You're so . . . beautiful." It was a whisper, a rasping croak. It was the truth.

She smiled, then she pressed a warning finger across his mouth. "Shhh. Not now."

"But—"

"Not now," she said, and silenced him completely by covering his mouth with hers.

When Zeke awoke again, the angle of the light told him the afternoon was far advanced. The air in the barn was still and warm, as if there had never been a storm. He lay still, trying to remember what it was that had awakened him.

Beside him, fast asleep, Sophie lay on her side with her head pillowed on her arm. The old tablecloth was twisted and crumpled beneath her, stained with sweat and, lower down, slight traces of blood.

Suddenly, the old barn was flooded with light as someone shoved one half of the big double door open.

"Yoo-hoo! Zeke?" Adelaide Smith's voice cut through the still air like a dull, rusty knife. "Are you there?"

"Mr. Jeffries?" Annie Talbot's more melodious voice grated just as harshly. "I brought you a little surprise."

Chapter 18

Sophie pushed her bike all the way home—most of it in the dark with nothing but a pale half-moon to light her way. She couldn't bear to sit on the hard seat, not on that rutted road.

Zeke had begged, pleaded, argued, and, finally, angrily demanded she let him take her home in the wagon, but she'd been adamant. She needed time to think, time to sort through the confusion of the past few hours.

Even a four-mile walk wasn't near long enough for the job. The light in the kitchen window gave fair warning she wouldn't be able to avoid awkward questions, and even more awkward explanations.

Just as well, perhaps. Delphi had to be told. It wasn't the sort of thing a mother was supposed to hear third hand through gossip over a cup of tea.

The details of their discovery were still hazy in Sophie's mind. She remembered hearing Adelaide's and Annie's cheerful calls. At first, she hadn't even been sure where she was, but one look at Zeke, naked beside her, had brought her brutally awake.

Zeke managed to climb to his feet. He snatched up Sophie's skirt to cover himself while Sophie hastily wrapped herself in the crumpled tablecloth—just in time, too.

Despite Zeke's shouted assurances that he'd be right out, Adelaide blithely charged into the barn and around the haystack, Annie firmly in tow. At the sight of them, Adelaide gasped, turned crimson, then fled, gabbling like a duck.

Annie simply stood there staring at them as if they'd

both suddenly grown an extra head. They'd stared stupidly back. After what seemed an eternity, Annie had mumbled something that must have been an apology before fleeing in the wake of her preceptress.

Sophie wearily leaned her bike against the shed. All she wanted right now was to hide in her room for the rest of her life. She couldn't bear to face Delphi—but she couldn't stay outside all night, either. Resolutely, she ran her hands over her shirt and skirt, trying to make sure everything was buttoned and fastened and tugged primly into place.

It hadn't been easy getting dressed. Her clothes, badly crumpled and still unpleasantly damp, had been strewn across the barn's dirt floor. She'd only found half her hairpins, and had to make do without a comb or a mirror.

All of it bad enough. Listening to the sounds of Zeke getting dressed had been worse by far. Every scrape and rustle and snap had been like fire to her senses, reminding her of what they'd done. What *she'd* done.

Delphi was waiting for her, just as Sophie had feared. She was decorating a new hat she'd bought the week before, determinedly piling on ribbons and dried flowers and more ribbons and bows until the hat itself was almost invisible.

"You're later than I expected," Delphi said primly, setting down her creation. Her voice carried the same chill disapproval it had since Sophie had defied the ladies at the Fourth of July picnic the day before.

"The storm . . ." Sophie couldn't carry it off. She couldn't lie, no matter how much she would have preferred it to the truth.

Without bothering to take off her own sadly wilted hat, Sophie pulled out the chair opposite Delphi and sat down. "There's something I have to tell you, Mother."

Delphi's mouth pursed. "I suppose you want to share the details of your edifying session with that . . . that woman's son. Well, I'm not interested, Sophie. If you want to ruin—"

"It's not that, Mother!"

Before Delphi had a chance to say more, Sophie poured out her story. Her discreet pursuit of Zeke over the past months, the picnics, the kisses, the storm. Everything . . . including Adelaide's and Annie Talbot's discovery of them in the barn.

Even after her tale dragged to its pitiful close, Delphi remained silent. Her face had grown pinched and drained of color. The pupils of her eyes were mere pinpoints from shock.

The kitchen was silent except for the dim ticktock of the parlor clock. Just when Sophie thought she could bear the silence no longer, Delphi forced a weak smile.

"The wedding will have to be very small, of course," she said, gamely trying to suppress the quaver in her voice. "I guess it's just as well you grew too tall for my wedding dress since you can't possibly wear white, but I have a piece of silk set aside—"

"I'm not marrying him, Mother." There, it was out.

"Not— Of course you're marrying him!" Delphi snapped, suddenly stirred to life. "He *has* to marry you! You *know* he has to! If he won't ask—"

"He's already asked, Mother." When Delphi merely gaped at her in disbelief, Sophie added tiredly, "He asked me any number of times—once Adelaide left. But not before then. Not until he had to."

"If he asked you, then—"

"I said no."

"You said— But . . . why?"

"Because he doesn't love me."

"What does that have to do with anything?" Delphi demanded. "Oh, Sophie! You don't understand! Your reputation's ruined! You can't just—"

"I can . . . and I will! I won't marry anyone if I don't want to!" Sophie jumped up, ready to march out of the room.

Without the brightly lit lamp between them, half blinding her, she got her first really good look at the strained, frightened expression on her mother's face.

Sophie closed her eyes, willing herself not to see,

and slowly sat back down. "I . . . I know what you think, Mother, how you must feel, but . . . I *can't* marry Zeke Jeffries just because the world thinks I should. Not when I'm the one responsible. I *won't*. I . . . I'll just have to find some other way to make things right."

Delphi opened her mouth to protest, but no sound came out. Her gaze dropped. She picked up the hat she'd been working on and blindly stared at it as if it were some grotesquerie unexpectedly dropped on her table. With a sharp, inarticulate protest she angrily tossed it aside and lurched up out of her chair. For a moment she stood there, hands propped on the table as if to keep her from falling over, and stared at Sophie without speaking. Tears welled up, then spilled over to course down her cheeks unheeded. Her mouth crumpled.

"Oh, Sophie." They were barely a whisper, yet the two words vibrated under the weight of a hundred crushed dreams and expectations. Without another word, Delphi turned and tottered from the room.

Sophie didn't move. Her hands curled into fists in her lap. A sharp pain cut into her chest, like tears that refused to be shed.

Because of her, Delphi would become an object of speculation, gossip, pity, and contempt. Delphi, to whom social position meant everything, would be laughed at and she, Sophie Carter, would be the one responsible.

What price would Zeke pay for their lovemaking?

Granted, he'd been as willing and eager as she. If they hadn't been discovered, something wonderful might have developed between them.

But they *had* been discovered, and Adelaide wasn't one to keep her mouth closed when there was as delectable a morsel of gossip as this to chew on.

Since men were expected to "have their fling," no one would be as quick to point the finger in Zeke's direction as they would be to point it in hers. Still, the upright folk in the community would expect him to make an honest woman of her. It wouldn't do him any good if she refused him, because everyone would think he'd never asked. It simply wouldn't occur to anyone that plain, too tall Sophie Carter might reject his offer. Not under the circumstances.

They wouldn't believe Sophie would reject his offer under *any* circumstances, no matter what.

Zeke caught his distorted reflection in the beveled glass of Sophie's front door the minute he stepped onto the porch. He stooped to get a better view, then carefully smoothed down his recalcitrant cowlick. His tie looked sadly lopsided and a mite crumpled after his five attempts to knot it properly, but he didn't have the heart to try again. As nervous as he was, he'd likely make a greater botch of the job than he already had.

He'd dragged through his morning chores. He hadn't slept at all, so tightly strung between remembered shame and an even more sharply remembered lust that sleep was impossible. He didn't feel too good now. His palms were sweating, his stomach threatened to turn topsy-turvy at any moment, and his knees displayed a disconcerting tendency to wobble.

His knock on the door echoed in the silent, shrouded interior. He knocked a second time before he caught the sound of footsteps coming toward him.

Delphi opened the door. She looked as stiff and disapproving as if she'd been dipped in the same starch as her high white collar, and she eyed him with a scorching disfavor that made Zeke melt in his boots.

"Is So— Is Miss Sophie here?" Zeke hoped his voice really wasn't as high and tight as it sounded.

Delphi frowned, considering the question—and him. "You'd best come in," she said at last, reluctantly stepping aside to let him pass.

Zeke edged around her carefully.

Something in her inspection must have satisfied her because she waved him to a chair in the parlor. "Please have a seat, Mr. Jeffries," she said primly. "I'll go fetch Sophie."

Zeke studied the prospect doubtfully. The crowded

parlor with its heavy, carved furniture and its spindly tables covered with bric-a-brac was the stuff of nightmares. There were too many things a man his size could bump, knock, shatter, or break. Zeke took the first chair that looked sturdy enough to hold him and sat down to wait.

Sophie didn't keep him waiting long. The creaking of the floor announced her approach. Zeke was on his feet by the time she walked into the room. To his immense relief, her mama was nowhere in sight.

She stopped in the doorway, too far away even to shake hands. Her face was pale, the skin drawn taut across her cheekbones. Dark shadows under her eyes betrayed her—she'd gotten as little sleep last night as he had.

"You . . . didn't have to come, you know." Her voice, at least, was steady.

"I wanted to." Zeke couldn't think of anything to say beyond that and neither, evidently, could Sophie. She stared at him and he stared right back, drinking in the sight of her.

The sound of Delphi rather obviously banging pans in the kitchen brought them both out of their strained mutual inspection. Sophie threw a nervous glance in the direction of the kitchen, then, even more nervously, gestured to the chair in which he'd been sitting.

"Please. Won't you sit down?"

Zeke sat.

After a moment's hesitation, Sophie chose a stiff, straight-backed chair across from him. She clasped her hands in her lap and studied the cabbage roses in the carpet. Zeke frowned at the roses. So far as he could see, they didn't have much to recommend them, but then, he'd never been partial to roses, on the floor or otherwise.

When the silence threatened to stretch into forever, he cleared his throat and ventured, "You got home all right."

"Yes."

That wasn't much help. "Delphi—your mama—knows?"

"Yes."

Definitely no help. Zeke scowled at the roses. They weren't any help, either. "What'd she say?"

"She said . . ." Sophie's mouth twisted in a mocking smile. "She said it didn't matter that I got too big to wear her wedding dress, after all."

Zeke flinched. "You could have one made, couldn't you?"

The silence stretched. Then, "I could, if I were getting married."

"Sophie—"

"Don't, Zeke!" Anger splashed red across her cheeks. Her eyes sparked fire. "I didn't . . . do *that* just to force you to marry me. No matter *what* anybody says."

"*I* know that, so why—" The sick expression on her face stopped him cold. "Sophie?"

Sophie's throat worked as though she were trying to swallow a huge and particularly nasty pill. The red receded from her cheeks as fast as it had come.

"I lied," she said. It was barely a whisper. "I *did* try to seduce you."

The confession broke her. Like the lemonade stand with its guy ropes torn away, she seemed to fold in on herself, become smaller, limp, broken. Zeke, himself bereft of speech, had to strain to catch her words.

"You're the kindest, most decent man I know. I've wanted you, and wanted you to want me, since the first time I saw you, there at the social." Her gaze dropped. "Trouble was, I knew a man like you would never notice someone like me. Not with Annie Talbot around. That's why I . . . chased you. Tried to get your attention. That's why I—"

He couldn't stand any more of this. Not one word of it. Zeke sprang out of his chair, but Sophie was on her feet before he could reach her, hands up to fend him off.

"No! Don't touch me! Just listen. Please? Zeke?"

Confused, Zeke backed off. The floor seemed to

rock beneath his feet, throwing him off balance, shifting so there as no firm footing anyplace.

Sophie drew a long, shuddering breath, then slowly straightened—like a condemned man suddenly confronted with the gallows who is determined to be brave, in spite of everything.

"You need to know that . . . that I don't blame you. For any of this," Sophie said. "I don't expect you to pay the price for what I've done."

Zeke bit back the angry protest that threatened to burst out. She wanted him to listen, but her words didn't make much sense. He wasn't supposed to pay for what *she'd* done? What about what *he'd* done? Surely she hadn't forgotten that he'd had a part in creating this mess, too.

"I wanted you to fall in love with me," Sophie said. "Just like in the books. I figured all I'd have to do was give you the chance to get to know me and . . . and it would all work out. I . . ."

She sucked in air as if it hurt to breathe. Her mouth twisted in self-mockery. "Seems like you were right and I was wrong, after all. About the books, I mean. About . . . the way things really work."

"So this is all your fault, is it?" The words exploded out of him. "And I'm just a brainless fool who thinks with his—" Zeke choked, flushed, and tried again. "Who doesn't think? Who just . . . charges in? Is that it?"

"No!"

"No? Funny. Listening to you, it sure sounded like I was. Yet I'd swear *I* was the one who kissed you, right at the start. Did I get that wrong?"

"No." Sophie shook her head dazedly, stunned by his vehemence.

"I didn't think so. I seem to remember, in fact, that it went sort of like this . . ." Zeke pulled her into his arms.

"And this . . ." He bent his head. His heart was hammering so hard he could hear it driving the blood through his veins.

"And this . . ." he muttered an instant before his

mouth claimed hers. The warmth and taste and scent of her swamped his senses, dragging him under.

"So sweet, Sophie. So sweet." It was a moan, a prayer, a plea, yet he didn't want to be rescued. What had they been arguing about, anyway?

Zeke shifted his hold on her, drawing her closer as her mouth opened to him and—

With a sharp, almost frightened cry, Sophie wrenched free of his embrace. "Don't! Don't lie!"

Zeke gaped at her, too dizzied to think straight. "Lie? About what?"

"About the way you feel. About me." Sophie panted with the violence of her feelings. "You may have kissed me. You may even have *wanted* to kiss me. You certainly seemed to enjoy making love to me. But you didn't want to marry me, did you?"

"But I asked—"

"Not until after! Not until you realized the whole town would know that we—that I—" Sophie broke off, fighting for control. "Tell me—honestly!—that you would have asked me to marry you, otherwise," she ordered.

"Well . . . I—"

"Honestly!"

Zeke gulped and felt the world fall out from under his feet. Honestly? He was damned if he knew *what* he'd wanted. All he could be sure of was that right here and right now he wanted to kiss Sophie again. In spite of the fact that kissing her was what had gotten him into trouble in the first place.

"Well?" Sophie demanded. "Would you have asked?"

"I'd thought about it," he admitted at last, reluctantly. That, at least, was honest. He'd sure as hell thought about it.

"You'd thought about it?"

"I'd been crazy with wanting you for . . . weeks! Longer than that!"

"But . . . ?" Sophie's tone revealed she knew there was a "but" in the whole mess.

This, Zeke thought wildly, was how a bull felt when

the cattle dogs were nipping at his heels, driving him in a direction he didn't want to go—baffled, resentful, crazed.

And maybe, just maybe, a little bit afraid.

"But . . . ?" Sophie said again with foot-tapping impatience.

Zeke sighed. "But I hadn't planned on getting married. Not until the farm was going good. Not—"

"You see?" Sophie said triumphantly. The look on her face said she didn't think she'd won.

Zeke tried to pull her back in his arms, but she dodged out of reach behind her chair. He tried to follow. Two spindly tables with their load of bric-a-brac blocked his way. Sophie could get through, but if he tried, he'd break something for sure.

He let out his breath in explosive exasperation. "Do you know how hard farming is, Sophie? I mean really *know*?" he demanded.

She didn't answer. Her hands curled over the carved top of the chair as if she needed to make sure of the barrier between them.

"It's hell is what it is," Zeke snapped. "Hard work and long hours and no guarantee you won't lose everything at the end of it. That's what my mama had all her life. Killing work and days that never ended and not much else but grief—all because my daddy couldn't provide for her proper. He didn't really try, if you want the downright, ugly truth."

His breathing came fast and hard, as if he'd been running. He glared at her. She glared right back.

"That's not what I wanted for my wife! Especially not for someone like you, who's used to a nice home and pretty things instead of sixteen-hour days spent washing and cooking and milking and canning and working in the fields."

"But—"

"That's all I can offer you, Sophie! Did you think I'd be low enough to ask you to give up . . . this"—he gestured at the fashionable, over-furnished parlor around them—"in exchange for . . . me?"

Sophie's head came up. "And you didn't care

enough to ask me which *I* thought was more
important."

"Are you saying that you fell in love with me?"
Zeke demanded, angry now, though he wasn't sure
why.

"Yes!" It was more defiant than honest.

"You sure? Or was it maybe some storybook hero
you took out of a book and pretended was me?"

She flinched.

Zeke waited. She didn't move, didn't utter a word.
The unpleasant suspicion grew to a bitter certainty.
"That's why you won't have me, isn't it? I can't measure up to some hero in a book. I'm just a farmer
with mud on his boots, not a—"

"That's not true!"

"You know what they're going to say about you,
don't you? About both of us?"

"I know *exactly* what they're going to say!"

"And you'd rather face that than marry me?"

Sophie's jaw set in a line that would have made his
mule proud.

Zeke threw up his hands. He'd said more in the
past half hour than he'd said in weeks, and it had
gotten him nowhere but confused. He'd come here
determined to do the right and honorable thing and
convince Sophie to marry him, even though he didn't
want a wife, and now here he was, hot under the collar
because she didn't want to have anything to do with
him.

A particularly loud clatter of pans from the kitchen,
immediately followed by an indignant yowl from a cat
and an indignant screech from Delphi clinched the
matter.

Zeke drew himself up the way a vanquished hero
was supposed to, all stern dignity and noble pride. If
he remembered his mama's romances right, there was
supposed to be a treasured ribbon or a handkerchief
or some small token of remembrance safely stored in
his pocket over his heart. But Sophie wasn't wearing
ribbons and he'd burned the handkerchief and that
lumpy, simpering china shepherdess on the table

would poke him something awful, assuming it fit, which it wouldn't.

"I guess there's nothing more to be said, then.'

Sophie let out her breath in one long, loud sigh and cautiously let go of the chair back. "No. Absolutely nothing."

"Well, then . . ."

"Yes, well . . ."

They stared at each other, unspeaking, for what seemed an age. Zeke broke away first.

He cleared his throat rather too loudly. "Guess I'd best get going." Under the circumstances, good manners seemed a little beside the point, but he didn't feel he could quite march out the door without a word, no matter what a proper hero would have done.

"Yes. Yes, of course." Sophie shook herself as if she were shaking off an irritating fly and cautiously edged out from behind the chair. "I'll show you to the door."

Zeke was out the door and halfway across the porch when he stopped, then turned back. One last try . . .

"Sophie? I . . . I really am sorry I—"

"No!" Sophie snapped back to indignant life. "Don't say you're sorry!" For an eternity she stood there in the open door staring at him, head high and proud. "Don't *ever* say you're sorry, Zeke Jeffries, because *I'm* not. Not for any of it."

She'd shut and locked the door and disappeared into the shadowed depths of the hall before Zeke got his wits back in sufficient working order to stagger off the porch and out the gate.

Chapter 19

Sophie was sitting at the kitchen table, hunched over a cold cup of coffee and blindly trying to see her future in its murky depths, when a knock at the back porch door startled her from her grim reverie.

She frowned and shoved the cup aside. It was long past nine, and regular callers would have come to the front door, not the back. Delphi, indignant and near tears at her daughter's obstinacy, had retreated to her room long ago. The only person Sophie could think of who might be at the door was Zeke, and she wasn't sure she wanted to see him.

Or, rather, she wasn't sure she had the strength of will to hold fast against his appeal. She'd almost given in this afternoon when he'd taken her in his arms and kissed her. Thank heavens he was too honest to lie. If he'd said he really *had* meant to ask her to marry him, she'd have given in, doubt, guilt, and insecurities notwithstanding.

The knock sounded again, louder and more insistent this time. Adelaide, the Cat poked her head out of her basket by the stove and meowed in disgust at this interruption of her slumbers. She yawned, stretched, then hopped out of the basket and strolled over to the door, loudly demanding to be let out.

Sophie sighed. No help for it. She'd have to answer the door. If the persistent knocking didn't rouse Delphi to more complaints and recriminations, the cat's noisy demands would.

She tugged the back door open and peered out uncertainly. The dim, bulky outline of a man showed against the dark on the other side of the screened porch. "Zeke?"

"No, ma'am. It's Patrick."

"Oh. Oh, yes. Patrick." Foolish to feel such a sharp stab of disappointment. She crossed to unlatch the screen door.

The minute she pushed it open, Adelaide zipped past her and disappeared into the night. Patrick backed off the steps as she swung the door wide. In the dim light from the kitchen, he looked intimidatingly hard and threatening.

"Please. Come in."

"Beggin' your pardon, but I was hopin' you'd come with me, Miss Sophie. It's Sarah Jane. She's back and . . . and she's beat up pretty bad and cryin'. She won't talk to me, but I thought maybe she'd talk to you . . . if you'd come."

Sophie had once seen a man who'd been beaten. That had been bad enough. Facing a woman who'd been abused made her sick to her stomach.

Sarah Jane had carefully combed her hair, then left it loose so it hung about her face like a curtain, hiding at least part of the damage. She'd tried to cover up the bruises, but even a heavy coating of powder had its limitations, and there was no disguising her swollen lip or blackened eye. She was battered, drawn with pain and exhaustion, and clearly frightened. She sat huddled beside Sophie on the sofa, shivering despite the July heat that lingered in the little frame house.

Tom, angry and withdrawn, had slipped away as soon as they'd arrived, but Patrick stood in front of the door, massive arms crossed over his broad chest. He looked like a large black bulldog determined to guard against all trespassers. If whoever was responsible for Sarah Jane's injuries were to show up right now, Sophie had no doubt Patrick would tear the man limb from brutal limb, then stomp on the pieces that were left.

"I didn't even see him, at first," Sarah Jane said shakily. "He knew me . . . from before. He was drunk, and he wanted to . . . to hire me. I tried to tell him I wasn't workin' no more, not like that, but he didn't believe me. Said he figured if I'd come to Pueblo, it had t'be 'cause I was lookin' for more . . ."

Sarah Jane sniffed. Her lower lip trembled, but she forced herself to finish. ". . . for more customers, and I could just as well start with . . . with him. And then he . . . he . . ."

Patrick growled, low in his throat, but didn't budge from his place in front of the door.

Sophie patted Sarah Jane's knee soothingly. "Don't think about that. Not right now. You'll be all right and Tom wasn't hurt, was he?"

"No." Without thinking, Sarah Jane started to chew on her battered lower lip. She flinched, then ducked her head to hide her tears. "Thomas went after him. When he . . . when he heard me screaming."

Sarah Jane stared at her hands, so tightly knotted together in her lap that the bones and tendons stood out white and sharp under the skin. "He'd been lookin' in the windows of a store as was showin' some books and I left him there, just for a minute, never thinkin' . . ." Sarah Jane crumpled.

"I never meant it to be this way," she wailed. "His father promised me. We'd be married, soon as he got back. He was just going to the city, to Chicago, he said. He'd find work, a house, then he'd come back. We'd be married, so it . . . what we done . . . it was all right. That's what he said. Because he was for sure going to marry me. He *swore* he was!"

Sophie awkwardly wrapped her arms around Sarah Jane's shoulders, but nothing could comfort the woman. The years of accumulated guilt and loss and pain flooded out in a torrent of words.

"I didn't have no choice in the end. You gotta understand. My family, the minute they knew I was increasin', they kicked me out. What was I to do? There weren't no place for me to go. I can't read nor write, and no decent woman would hire me as a maid, not with a baby on the way."

She stabbed at her flowing tears with the handkerchief Sophie gave her, heedless of her damaged eye and cheek. "A farmer took me in. An old man whose wife had died. He didn't want another wife, but if I was willin' to do all the things a wife would do, he'd be sure Thomas was taken care of, he said. Leave us the farm and all."

The memory made her rear back, angry now, as well as hurt. She glared at Sophie, but the rage in her, Sophie knew, was for the second man in her life to betray her. No, the third, Sophie angrily amended, for what kind of father would put his daughter out in the streets like that, no matter what the circumstances?

"He made lots of promises, too, just like Thomas's daddy," Sarah Jane said fiercely, "and he didn't keep 'em no more'n Thomas Peabody did. There weren't no will. When he died, his cousin got it all—the farm, what money there was in the bank, everything—and you can be darned sure that cousin didn't share any with us.'

The anger did far more good than any of Sophie's efforts at comfort for Sarah Jane straightened in her chair, tossed back her hair, and glared at the wall opposite, as if defying everyone in the world beyond those walls to blame her for the choices she'd been forced to make. The choices she'd never had, beyond that first, disastrous choice that had been made out of love.

Patrick, head bent, stared at the unwaxed floor beneath his feet as if he expected to find answers written in the rough grain of the wood. His big, work-toughened hands curled into intimidating fists and the muscles in his arms grew taut, as if he were forcibly holding himself back from hitting something.

"I didn't have no choice then," Sarah Jane was saying. "I . . . I took Thomas and we went to Chicago. It didn't take long to find a place, a little house in a part of town where men would be looking for . . . for a woman. Thomas was six by then, old enough to know that what his mamma got into wasn't right, but there wasn't nothin' he could do about it. I tried to explain, but he already knew, I guess."

She met Sophie's gaze, but her eyes were bleak and empty. "I thought of leavin' him at an orphanage when I decided to come out here. Maybe it would have been better for him if I would've, but I couldn't do it. He was all I had left and he loved me, no matter did I deserve it or not. I think . . ."

She choked, stopped, trying to regain control of her voice, her throat working. After a moment, she continued, her voice low and rough, little more than a whisper, "I think he's the only one who *ever* really loved me."

"I'm sure he understands. And he knows you love him," Sophie said, her own voice scarcely more than a whisper. "That counts for a lot. An awful lot."

Patrick muttered something and shuffled his feet unhappily.

If Sarah Jane heard either of them, she gave no sign of it. She shrugged. Her face twisted in bitter self-mockery. "I'd started drinkin' back there, you know. Just a little, at first, but it helped me forget . . . and I wanted to forget so bad it hurt. I was purty much broke by the time I got here, but somehow I always found enough for a bottle, then another, and another . . ."

In his corner, Patrick had gone as still as if he'd been carved of raw rock, not human flesh. Finally, he could restrain himself no longer. "Why didn't ye *say* something?" he demanded, his brogue heavier than Sophie had ever heard it. "Why didn't ye ask for help? There're those—"

"Who'd be more than willin' to give me a dried crumb of bread for an hour or two's preaching," Sarah Jane broke in angrily. "But those kind don't never let you forget. Not ever. I saw it back there, and I saw it here, with them fine ladies who were always willin' to tell me how I *ought* to live, but never willin' to help me find a way to *do* it. Miss Sophie's the only one who's helped me without all the preachin' thrown in."

She stopped, her gaze unflinchingly fixed on Patrick. The hard glitter in her eyes slowly softened into a gentle glow. "And you," she said, so low the words were almost inaudible.

For the first time, Sarah Jane smiled. A very faint, sad smile that was twisted by the swollen lip and cheek. "I always appreciated that you didn't just . . . that you'd talk to me. As if it was more a . . . a social call than . . . business. And you were always so . . . gentle. Like you was afraid to hurt me. I . . . I liked that."

Patrick's head snapped up. His big body almost hummed with the angry tension holding him. His dark eyes fixed on the battered woman in the chair, suddenly alight with hope.

"Ye've only to ask," he said, his voice thick and low with emotion. "I . . . I said I'd be here when you got back and . . ." He couldn't finish it.

Sarah Jane's smile slipped. Her lips trembled and the tears she'd refused to shed earlier suddenly slipped over to trace a course through the powder on her cheeks.

"I thought, if I went away, if I could start over, I could . . . could make myself good enough for you. I didn't even . . ." She hiccuped, gulping down the sobs that choked her. Her words poured out with the tears in a bitter, anguished rush. "I didn't even get started 'fore my sins caught up with me. Not even that far, and I wanted so bad—"

Patrick was across the room before she could finish. Whatever else she meant to say was lost as he awkwardly gathered her into his arms, cradling her head against his broad chest as he murmured incomprehensible words of love.

Sophie didn't think he really noticed when she got up from the sofa, but he readily shifted to take her place. As she quietly slipped out the door, he was holding the woman he loved close against him and smoothing his hand over her hair and rocking her as she cried.

The streets were almost empty. Here and there Sophie encountered someone hurrying home, or an occa-

sional couple strolling past, but otherwise it felt like
she had the town to herself. As they had the night
before, the half-moon cast its dim, silvery-white light
at her feet and a faint breeze stirred the lingering heat,
making the leaves of the cottonwoods and elms rustle
as she passed. From front steps and open windows,
Sophie caught the low murmur of voices, the creak of
a porch swing. Oil lamps turned the rectangles of windows a soft, welcoming gold, as if inviting her in out
of the dark.

How many of the people on those porches and in
those lamp-lit rooms would invite Sarah Jane in if they
knew about her past? All anyone ever discussed was
her disreputable present, with an occasional animad-
version on the lack of morals that had led her, so
everyone supposed, to drink and prostitution in the
first place.

How many knew what she herself had done? Sophie
wondered. How many more would learn of it tomorrow, or the next day, or the day after that?

She hadn't had the courage to venture out today,
but she couldn't stay buried in her room forever. What
was she going to say to her friends and acquaintances?
What would they say to her? Worse, what would remain unspoken because she'd stepped beyond the
boundaries they and all the rest of the world had established for her?

She could just picture them shaking their heads as
they talked about it. "My, my, my," they'd say.
"Who'd ever have thought Sophronia Carter would
land a man like Zeke Jeffries? Of course, she had to
seduce him to do it, and Lord knows how hard *that*
must have been, considering. But then, Sophie always
did have brains even if she couldn't lay claim to much
else. You can't help but feel sorry for poor old Jeffries, though. Probably never knew what was coming
before it was way too late."

They'd be right, of course, much as it hurt to
admit it.

Sophie's back stiffened and she drew herself up

straight and tall, even though there was no one to
see her.

Let them say what they liked. She wasn't going to
force Zeke into marrying her jut because they'd been
caught, literally, in the hay. Nor was she going to run
away, or hide—well, not forever, anyway—or let herself be trapped as Sarah Jane had been trapped.

She'd known it would be difficult, but after listening
to Sarah Jane's heartbreaking story, she almost felt
like shouting the news from the housetops just so
there'd be no mistake that she, Sophronia Maye Carter, spinster, had made love to a man and had absolutely no regrets.

Well, none except that he hadn't fallen in love with
her, no matter how hard she'd tried to tempt him.

Thursday, July 6, 1893

Mama used to say, when times were roughest and
Daddy was off chasing his dreams, that no woman
who had any pretensions to good sense ever expected
a man to act totally reasonable. According to her,
soon as a man started talking about being reasonable,
he'd for sure up and do something that wasn't reasonable at all.

Seeing how Daddy was, I never really blamed her
for thinking that way. On the other hand, I never
really believed her, either. Especially not when the
womenfolk I know seem to get their feathers fluffed
over the darned silliest things, things that no man in
his right mind would think twice about—even Mama,
and she was the most sensible woman I ever knew,
barring the foolishness of marrying Daddy in the first
place, and putting up with him all those years in the
second.

Anyway, that's all by way of saying I guess she was
right after all. Had to be, or I wouldn't be sitting here
past midnight, thinking about Sophie.

When I drove into town this afternoon, I pretty
much figured it was a done deal. I didn't see how it

could be otherwise, considering. I sure didn't plan on Sophie being so obliging as to turn me down.

A man in his right mind would just thank his lucky stars or kiss his rabbit's foot or whatever and light out for safety.

All the way home, and all this afternoon and evening, all *I* can think of is the way Sophie looked in that doorway, all tall and proud and . . . fierce, almost, when she said she didn't regret having made love, even if we *had* been caught. That and how empty the house is going to feel, knowing she isn't ever coming back, let alone moving in.

For as long as Sophie could remember, she'd devoted Friday afternoons to shopping. This Friday she would happily have foregone the pleasure, even if it meant starvation, but Delphi wouldn't let her.

Delphi had spent the morning immured in her room, wailing whenever she was sure Sophie was listening, nervously pacing when she wasn't. She emerged at last, beautifully coifed and dressed and with her face artfully powdered to disguise her swollen eyelids.

"Are you ready, Sophronia?" She didn't bother to wait for an answer. "We'll stop at the bank first, shall we? Then Goveneur's Groceries, the baker's, the butcher's, Mather's dry goods, and Hodgeson's Emporium, just like we always do. Have I forgotten anything?"

Sophie's grip on the shopping basket tightened. "Nothing, Mother." *Except a parade through town.*

They got a parade, anyway.

To Sophie's intense mortification, their progress along Main Street was avidly noted by any number of saunterers, shoppers, and storekeeps, each more willing than the last to pass the word. Heads popped out of doorways to verify the news, then popped back in. At each shop window, Sophie could feel people watching them as they passed. Delphi made matters worse by nodding and smiling and waving at everyone with whom she had a speaking acquaintance, and a few she'd probably never seen before, just for the practice.

Sophie gritted her teeth and forced a smile and a nod, as well. She drew the line at waving, mostly because she was afraid if she took even one finger off her basket, she'd simply toss it away and run like a panicked goose. For one mad moment, she even considered hiding in an alley on the off chance she could sneak home after dark unobserved, but common sense reasserted itself at the last minute. Someone was bound to notice if she tried to climb in an empty barrel or cower behind a pile of empty crates. Someone *always* noticed, no matter what a body did.

Amabelle Marlen, who had been married in early spring and was just beginning to show with her first child, was the only customer in the bank when Sophie and her mother entered.

"Why, Sophie!" she cried, loud enough for the back walls to hear. "Fancy seeing you here! And Mrs. Carter. How *do* you do? And what's this I hear about—"

Sophie smiled and left Delphi to fend off the gossip while she made the necessary withdrawal.

Old Mr. Thorn looked up from the bills he was counting to frown and say, "Miss Sophie," with a rather terrifying iciness.

Mr. Finley, whose second son's wife was no doubt responsible for spreading the news in these exalted regions, didn't exactly frown, but his mustache bristled and twitched and pulled down at the corners alarmingly. "Mornin', Miss Sophie."

"Good morning, Mr. Finley." Sophie slid her withdrawal slip under the ornate iron grill of the teller's cage.

He solemnly studied the slip, then just as solemnly counted out the usual combination of bills and coins. As he slid the money under the grill, he said, "My John's Bessie tells me there's to be a wedding soon." It wasn't a question.

Sophie's hand froze on top of the change. At least she'd gotten the source right. "Why, no, Mr. Finley, there's not. I'm afraid Bessie's mistaken."

Mr. Finley's eyebrows shot up toward his hairline. His mustache quivered. "No wedding?"

The top of Mr. Thorn's head appeared over the polished oak dividing the two tellers' cages. His eyes bulged with the effort of standing on tiptoe. "Miss Sophie?"

"I'm not getting married, Mr. Finley," Sophie said, unreasonably pleased with how calm she sounded. "What ever made you think I was?"

"Why, Bessie said . . . er . . . that is . . ." Mr. Finley loudly cleared his throat. "Must have misunderstood," he muttered into his mustache.

Mr. Thorn wasn't so easily cowed. "Did I hear that right, Miss Sophie? You're not getting married?"

"That's right, Mr. Thorn. I am *not* getting married." She gave him her sweetest smile. "You might want to tell Mrs. Thorn that. I know how much she enjoys such things."

Since Mrs. Thorn's doom-and-gloom perspective on life made even her gloomy husband seem like a cheerful cherub, Sophie knew the shot struck home. Mr. Thorn blushed and harumphed and mumbled, "I'll do that," as he sank back into his cage.

"Give my best to Bessie, won't you, Mr. Finley?" Sophie graced him with her brightest smile as she tucked the money in her purse.

"I'll do that, Miss Sophie. I'll certainly do that." Mr. Finley suddenly found a possible discrepancy in his tallies that required all his attention.

Delphi put an unpleasant damper on Sophie's satisfaction with the exchange the minute the bank's doors closed behind them.

"Amabelle wanted to know when the wedding was," she said with forced cheerfulness. "I told her you hadn't set a date yet, but—"

"You what?" Sophie swung around to glare at her mother. "I just told Mr. Finley and Mr. Thorn that I'm not getting married. How . . . how *dare* you tell Amabelle I was?"

Delphi drew herself up haughtily and glared right

back. "You can *not* go on like this, Sophie! Think of *my* reputation, even if you won't think of yours!"

Before Sophie could respond, Dora Stevens chugged around the corner and into hearing range. With her sharp ears always tuned to gossip, she'd have heard if Sophie so much as whispered.

Delphi pasted a smile on her face. "Why, Dora! Fancy seeing you here!"

Dora eagerly stumped up the steps to them. "Delphi. Sophie."

Sophie grimaced. "Mrs. Stevens."

"I hear you're getting married." Dora tittered and tried not to gawk. "So unexpectedly, too!"

"Sophie—"

"I'm afraid you're mistaken, Mrs. Stevens," Sophie said, cutting Delphi off without a qualm. "I have absolutely *no* plans to get married. None," she added even more firmly as Dora Stevens' jaw dropped in disbelief.

"So nice to see you. Shall we go, Mother?" With a cheerful little wave, Sophie sailed down the steps and up the street, leaving Delphi no choice but to follow.

The respite was all too short. Mrs. Purvis pounced the instant they walked in Goveneur's Groceries. "Why, Delphi! How nice to see you! And Sophie! My dear, I am so excited about the news! Fancy! You and Zeke Jeffries! Whoever would have thought—?"

"Evidently everyone, Mrs. Purvis," Sophie interrupted. This time she took her cue from Amabelle and made sure her voice carried to the farthest corners of the store. No sense in repeating herself if she didn't have to. "Unfortunately, everyone has it wrong. I am *not* getting married to Mr. Jeffries . . . or anyone else, for that matter."

Delphi gave a faint little gasp and tottered back to the canned beans. Mr. Goveneur instantly busied himself ringing up Mrs. Purvis's purchases. Old Roger Makepiece, as usual securely ensconced in a chair midway between the cracker barrel and the cheese board, cackled in delight and lifted a cracker in salute.

Mrs. Purvis at least had the good taste to blush. "Oh!" she said, very faintly. "I'd heard—"

"I'm sure you did." Sophie gave her a smile calculated to freeze her to the tips of her toes. "And now you can be the first to spread the news that the common gossip was wrong. That is, if Amabelle Marlen and Dora Stevens don't beat you to it."

Mrs. Purvis choked. Only Mr. Goveneur's announcement that her bill came to $1.13 saved her from even greater indignities. She mumbled an excuse and hastily turned away to fumble for her coin purse, but not before Sophie had the satisfaction of seeing the red in her face extend all the way down to her collar.

Old Mr. Makepiece snorted and grinned and gave her a thumbs-up, then popped another bit of cheese in his mouth and gummed it enthusiastically. Sophie flushed, then grinned and gave him a thumbs-up in return when Mrs. Purvis rushed from the store, letting the screen door bang shut behind her. She ignored the groan of dismay, hastily stifled, that issued from somewhere around the canned beans.

Emboldened by her confrontation with Mrs. Purvis, Sophie marched through the next stops on their itinerary, head high and tongue sharpened. By the time she led the way to Hodgeson's Emporium an hour later, Delphi was a broken woman. Twice she implored Sophie in faltering tones to abandon the rest of their shopping expedition. Sophie insisted.

"Just a little longer, Mother," she said firmly. "Besides, didn't Mrs. Hodgeson say they were expecting a new shipment of perfumes and toilet waters? You can't possibly let Adelaide Smith take the best before you even get a chance to sample them, you know."

"Oh, Sophie, how *can* you?" Delphi protested plaintively.

"Quite easily. In fact, I'm rather beginning to enjoy myself."

To her surprise, Sophie realized she really *was* beginning to enjoy herself. The hot, tight little knot of pain and guilt that had lodged in the middle of her chest two days earlier was beginning to ease, little by little. After a lifetime spent being dull and dutiful, there was a certain satisfaction in being so abruptly elevated to the interesting position of an unrepentant fallen woman.

Everyone around had expected her to creep into public as abject and cringing as a twice-kicked dog begging for forgiveness. The bold front she'd adopted instead had proved the perfect armor against their smug, pitying condescension. Besides, she wouldn't have to keep it up forever. Eventually other scandals would come along to dull folks' memory of hers.

It would be easier if Zeke Jeffries hadn't settled here, of course. A fling with a traveling salesman would be far easier to put behind her than one with the county's most eligible bachelor, but she *would* put it behind her. She had to if she was going to be able to continue living here.

Someday, maybe, a man would come along who really did love her and want to marry her. That no man could ever live up to Zeke Jeffries was beside the point. It had to be. After the glories of those few brief hours in the barn with Zeke, she didn't want to spend the rest of her life as a spinster.

The thought took all the enjoyment out of her recent triumphs over the gossips. When Mrs. Hodgeson greeted them with a startled, "Why, Sophie! I didn't expect to see *you*!" Sophie snapped back, "Some people's expectations frequently prove unfounded, Mrs. Hodgeson. Didn't you know that?"

"Well!" Mrs. Hodgeson gasped, slapping her hand over her heart against the shock. "I never!"

"No, I don't imagine you did," Sophie muttered, but this time she said it low enough that only Delphi caught it. Mr. Hodgeson, who'd been stocking shelves farther down the counter, abruptly abandoned his inventory and moved toward them, frowning mightily.

Delphi tossed her a warning glance and quickly stepped between them. "Good afternoon, Mrs. Hodgeson! Mr. Hodgeson!" she said in an impressive imitation of careless good cheer. "I thought I'd stop by to see if you received that new order of perfumes you were telling me about. Just this morning I said to Sophronia, 'Sophie!' I said. 'I simply *can't* wait any longer. Hodgeson's *always* has such lovely toiletries, you know, and I couldn't bear it if I missed something new!' That's what I said!''

Mrs. Hodgeson unthawed only slightly under Delphi's flattery. "Indeed, Mrs. Carter? Well, I'm sure *some* people appreciate our efforts!" She cast Sophie a resentful look, then ostentatiously pulled out her key chain and unlocked the curved glass display case where the more expensive toiletries were stored.

Footsteps sounded from nearby, startling Sophie. She'd been so intent on her own troubles, she hadn't noticed there were others in the store. A second later, Thea Talbot emerged from behind a tall display of brooms and kitchen mops that filled the center of the floor. Annie was three paces right behind her.

Chapter 20

From the strained expressions on their faces, it was clear Thea and Annie Talbot had caught the exchange with Mrs. Hodgeson. Sophie's stomach twisted painfully. It was one thing to face down Mrs. Purvis, quite another to confront Annie and her mother, especially in front of witnesses.

"Sophie!" Thea exclaimed, just as if she were surprised to see them. "Fancy seeing you here! And Delphi! You're looking lovely, as always." She beamed at Mrs. Hodgeson. "Did I hear you were going to show them some perfumes? That new scent you showed me would be perfect for Sophie, don't you think, Mrs. Hodgeson? What was it? 'New Mown Hay?' So fresh and natural after 'Sweet Pea' or 'Jasmine,' don't you think?"

Annie and Sophie both turned red. Annie's face crumpled around the edges as if she were on the verge of tears, but she gave Sophie a brave little smile. She looked so shattered that Sophie could almost feel sorry for her. Almost. She had too many troubles of her own to spend too much time worrying about Annie.

"It sounds wonderful, Mrs. Talbot," she said, mustering up her reserves of defiance. "Unfortunately, it's Mother who's interested in perfumes, not me. I was going to check on the books. There was a volume on parlor games that intrigued me the last time I was here." She smiled, daring the woman to comment. "If you'll excuse me?"

At the back of the store, the sounds of the strained conversation being conducted at the front mercifully faded to an indistinguishable murmur. The familiar glass case stood waiting for her, filled with new books. Sophie stared at them, unseeing.

What insanity had possessed her? She'd never been intentionally rude in her whole life, yet she'd spent the past hour insulting half the people she knew. If the other half had come in her way, she'd probably have insulted them, too. She couldn't ignore them. They wouldn't let her, as was all too evident in their eagerness for all the scandalous details. She refused to apologize, and she certainly wouldn't cringe and cower. That only invited more gossip and scandal. A dignified silence would be more . . . well, dignified, but it went against the grain to stand by and do nothing. So what was left?

Her troubled thoughts were interrupted by a softly whispered, "Sophie?"

Sophie turned to find Annie watching her.

"If you'd rather, I'll go away," Annie said, clearly troubled.

"No. It's all right."

It wasn't, but Annie had never deliberately done or said anything to hurt her. She couldn't help it if she'd been born with all the feminine charms that Sophie so conspicuously lacked. It had to be one of fate's crueler jests that Sophie should be the one plunged into scandal.

"I . . . I wanted to say how sorry I was. About yesterday, I mean," Annie said. She edged closer, as cautious as if she were afraid of being bitten. "And I wanted you to know that I didn't . . . say anything. To anyone."

"No?"

"Adelaide brought me home and . . . She'd been so determined to hitch me up with Zeke that, well, I guess she got a little carried away."

"She would," Sophie said dryly. Adelaide would have gotten carried away no matter whom she'd found with Zeke. That she'd caught Sophie and not one of her own favorites simply made it all that much more interesting.

Annie flinched. When Sophie didn't say anything more, she edged even closer. "I didn't know that you . . . that you and Zeke . . ." The color in her cheeks darkened, but on Annie, the blush only added to her beauty. "If I'd had any idea that the two of you were . . . friends . . . I wouldn't have let Adelaide, um, you know . . ."

Sophie couldn't help smiling at that. "I know."

"Yes. Well." Annie's gaze dropped. She fiddled nervously with the small gold ring on her right hand as she worked up the courage to go on.

"I ran into Dora Stevens before we came here," she ventured at last. "Did you *really* turn Zeke down? When he asked you to marry him, I mean," she added hastily, then blushed even rosier as she realized the question implied Sophie hadn't turned Zeke down on everything. "That's what she said, but it seemed so . . . farfetched. I didn't tell Mother."

"I really turned Zeke down," Sophie said flatly. The truth sounded unbearably final. "I refuse to get married just because everyone thinks I should."

That seemed a little weak, yet she could not—absolutely would *not*—admit to Annie that Zeke didn't love her, that he'd only asked her to marry him out of a sense of responsibility tinged with guilt.

If she was going to be a scandal, Sophie decided suddenly, she would claim full credit. It was the only satisfaction she was likely to get out of the whole mess.

"I don't think a woman should be forced into marriage just because she . . . wants to explore life a bit," she said with what she hoped was properly sophisticated daring.

The shock and awe on Annie's face were strangely satisfying.

Annie's eyes grew round as saucers. "Was it . . . Was it as wonderful as they say?" she demanded, almost breathless with excitement and curiosity. "The making love, I mean?"

"Better!" That much, at least, was true.

"Ooooh!" Annie's eyes grew wider still. She gulped. "I wish *I* had your courage, Sophie!"

It was Sophie's turn to gape. "You do?"

"Oh, yes!" Annie hesitated, then plunged on, "I've always admired you, you know. You're so . . . independent. So sure of yourself. You've never been like the rest of us, desperate to get married because we don't know what else to do with ourselves."

Fortunately for Sophie, Annie's admiration was cut short.

"Annie?" Thea Talbot called. "Where *have* you gotten to?"

"Coming, Mother." Annie threw an anxious glance over her shoulder, then turned back to Sophie, leaned close, and said, "If you really don't want Zeke Jeffries, Sophie, would you mind awfully if I . . . if *I* kept visiting him?"

Any pleasure Sophie might have gotten out of Annie's unexpected homage vanished in an instant. She wanted desperately to shout, *Don't you dare touch him!* but that would have been foolish as well as irrational.

She forced a smile on her face and tried to ignore the sick feeling in the pit of her stomach. It wasn't easy. "Of course not. Zeke's a free man, you know. He can do anything he likes, including ask you to marry him."

Annie's expressive eyes lit up. "Really? You really mean that?"

Of course I don't! He's mine and you can't have him!

"Of course I do."

That's where lies got you, Sophie thought bleakly as she watched Annie walk away, in trouble from beginning to end.

Her gaze dropped to the bookcase. She stared at it blindly, wondering what she was going to do. The title of one volume in particular caught her eye—*Her Only Sin,* by Bertha M. Clay. She would have laughed if it hadn't been so horribly ironic. She never had liked Mrs. Clay's books much.

Sophie scanned the rest of the titles. There were a number of new ones that sounded appealing—or would have a few days ago. Right now nothing really appealed to her except hiding in her room for the rest of her life.

At least she'd have books to keep her company in her solitary old age. It wasn't much comfort, but it was all she had.

To Sophie's dismay, Thea and Annie Talbot were still there when she walked back to the front counter. Five heads turned to stare at her as she approached, which set Sophie's back up all over again. Even her mother seemed to have arrayed herself with the Talbots and Hodgesons during her absence.

"So you're going to be marrying Zeke Jeffries, are you?" Mr. Hodgeson asked disapprovingly the minute she reappeared. "Mrs. Hodgeson was telling me about it last night, and Mrs. Talbot filled us in on the details. Must say, I wasn't expecting that kind of news from *you*, Miss Sophie! Thought you were above those kinds of shenanigans."

Annie squeaked and edged back behind the brooms. Thea Talbot assumed an expression of righteousness that was echoed by Mrs. Hodgeson. Delphi was too shaken to do more than moan softly and lean against the counter for support.

Sophie smiled. "It's wonderful how quickly news gets around, isn't it, Mr. Hodgeson. Too bad they don't always get it right. I am *not* marrying Mr. Jeffries, no matter what some folks say."

"But, Sophie," Delphi protested faintly. "He was so insistent yesterday. And he's such a *nice* man."

"Yes, he is," Sophie agreed, goaded. "He is a *very* nice man. Very nice indeed. But that doesn't mean I'm going to marry him, regardless of what any busybodies might say."

Mr. Hodgeson turned an indignant red. "Miss Sophie! You watch yourself. I don't permit anyone to talk like that in front of Mrs. Hodgeson. And there's your mama and Mrs. Talbot and Miss Annie, too!"

"Yes?" Sophie gritted her teeth and feigned inno-

cence. "Since you all seemed so eager to discuss my
personal life, I thought you'd want to know the facts.
Just goes to show how mistaken one can be, doesn't
it?"

Before anyone could respond, she added brightly,
"Well, I really do need to get going. So many things
to do, you know!" She eyed the items on the counter.
"I believe Mother already has everything she wanted,
but I would like to get a bottle of that new perfume
Mrs. Talbot so kindly recommended. The 'New Mown
Hay,' you know."

"Really, Sophie!" Thea Talbot's expression was a
perfect blend of indignation and embarrassment at
having her insult so blatantly thrown back in her face.

Sophie ignored her protests and Mr. Hodgeson's
sputtering.

"Oh! And please add *Gaskell's Penmanship* and
Electricity Simplified to that order, Mr. Hodgeson.
You knew I've been tutoring Mrs. Peabody and her
son, Thomas, didn't you? For several months now,
in fact."

Sophie smiled at him encouragingly. Even though it
was quite beyond the pale, she couldn't help herself.
"You know Mrs. Peabody, don't you, Mr.
Hodgeson?"

Mr. Hodgeson's flush turned a brighter crimson. His
throat worked as if there was something blocking it.

Sophie ignored both his blushes and Mrs. Hodgeson's indignant hiss as she added, "Oh! and Miss Mu-
lock's *Plain Speaking*. I couldn't possibly forget that,
now, could I?"

Annie tittered, Thea Talbot stiffened in outrage,
and Mrs. Hodgeson's mouth pinched shut so tight it
virtually disappeared.

Delphi groaned and looked suddenly faint. "As long
as you're adding things to our order, Mr. Hodgeson,"
she said in failing tones, "would you please add a
bottle of Bromo Vichy and one of Peptonic Stomach
Bitters?"

She closed her eyes and delicately pressed her fingertips to her temples. "The extra-large size," she added in a pained whisper. "For both of them."

Sunday, July 9, 1893

At least I suppose it's still Sunday. Might be Monday, but I'm too tired to go get Daddy's pocket watch to see.

Can't sleep and I can't bear to go out to the pump for a dunking. It would be like washing off Sophie, and that's not what I want. Now that I know about . . . well, about what's possible between a man and a woman—really *know*, I mean—it isn't quite as easy to wash away the wanting.

Did my accounts earlier this evening. It wasn't until I'd totted everything up that I realized I was trying to see if I'd been wrong about being able to support a wife and family. Like I want to, that is. Figured it up three ways, but the numbers came out the same, regardless. Even with a good sale on the melons and a good harvest with the rest, I can't pay off all the debts. Not this year, and probably not next year, either. I for sure can't be thinking about fixing up the house or having any extra to buy a woman the nice things in life. And if anything goes wrong between now and the harvest . . .

Best not to think of that.

Best not to think of everything else I've been thinking about, either. Especially not Sophie.

Might not be so hard if Tom were here. With him gone, the house seems as empty as . . . as I don't know what. I can't imagine anything that big and empty and echoing.

Tuesday, July 11, 1893

Mrs. Smith and Miss Annie showed up today. Said they both wanted to apologize for barging in on Sophie and me like that.

Miss Annie did quite a job of it. She blushed pink as a rose and wouldn't look at me. She even dug the toe of her shoe in the dirt and hunched her shoulders and twisted her hands together, just like a schoolgirl caught kissing the boys.

Mrs. Smith said she was sorry, too, but you can tell she didn't mean it. I doubt if she'd have said it if she hadn't figured the saying it would give her a good excuse to drag Miss Annie over for a visit.

Don't know how, but they both knew that Sophie turned me down flat, in spite of everything. They didn't say anything about me and Miss Annie, of course, but I could tell the two of them have decided that my being in disgrace isn't enough reason to quit plotting how to get me hitched—preferably to Miss Annie.

Fortunately, they'd come just before I had to open the irrigation ditches so I had a good excuse to run off before they could say too much. Judging from the straight-backed way Mrs. Smith drove off, she wasn't any too pleased with my getting away from them like that.

Can't believe Sophie won't be coming out for a visit. No matter how hard I try to tell myself it's so, I just can't believe I won't be seeing her come rattling down the lane on that bike of hers, or digging in that old flower garden, or laying out a meal on that old tablecloth . . .

Best not think of that tablecloth.

Wednesday, July 12, 1893

Went into town today. Couldn't stand it any longer.

It didn't do me any good. Sophie refused to talk to me.

You'd think I'd be relieved, knowing I've done what I can to convince her to let me make an honest woman out of her, but I'm not. Not even a little bit.

Other than an ugly, greenish-yellow bruise on her cheek and another, smaller one on her throat, the marks of Sarah Jane's battering had disappeared. Even those tell-tale traces were easily forgotten in the light of her radiant happiness.

"Most of my old customers who've come around have been real nice about it," she told Sophie, blushing prettily. "One gent, he even brought me flowers and said he hoped I'd be happy."

They were sitting side by side on Sarah Jane's parlor sofa, so it was easy for Sophie to reach over and squeeze her friend's hand encouragingly. It wasn't as easy to push down the sharp regret that she wasn't looking forward to being a blushing bride, too.

"Sophie?" Sarah Jane timidly broke into Sophie's unpleasant thoughts.

"Umm?" said Sophie, forcing an encouraging smile.

Sarah Jane hesitated, chewing the edge of her lip, then shyly ventured, "Patrick told me about . . . you. An' Zeke. About what . . . happened. An' that you won't even talk to him. Zeke, I mean."

She frowned, obviously uncomfortable. On her, the expression was oddly appealing, almost innocent. "Is that true, what Patrick told me?"

Sophie released her friend's hand and sat back. "Yes, it's true."

Sarah Jane blinked and her throat worked as if she were trying to swallow something unpalatable. When Sophie remained silent, she said nervously, "Lord knows, I ain't one to be castin' stones, but do you . . . do you think that's wise, Sophie? To be turnin' him down like that?"

Sophie didn't say anything. There wasn't anything she *could* say. Wisdom didn't have anything to do with it, anyway.

When Sarah Jane continued to stare at her, waiting for an answer, Sophie said reluctantly, "I won't marry a man who doesn't love me, Sarah Jane. No matter what *anybody* thinks. It wouldn't be right to marry without love." That came out fiercely, as if impelled by an unshakable conviction. A moment later Sophie added more doubtfully, "Would it?"

"I . . . I don't know, Sophie. I don't know much about love. Lots about makin' love, but not much of nothin' about real stick-in-your-heart love."

"Don't you love Patrick?" Sophie asked, surprised.

Sarah Jane hesitated. Her eyes grew blank and vacant, as if she were looking inward for an answer to that question.

"I . . . don't know," she admitted at last. "But I . . . I'm happy with him. You know? An' I know he loves me. Got to, or he wouldn't go throwin' himself away on a woman like me. Not a good, decent man like him."

Sophie winced. "That's the difference between us. Patrick loves you." She drew a deep breath, then reluctantly added, "Zeke doesn't love me."

"You sure about that, Sophie? *Real* sure?"

Was she sure? What did she really know about love, after all? Everything she thought she knew, she'd gotten from novels, not real life. She'd never had a chance to find out the answers for herself. Not until it was too late.

"As sure as I can be," Sophie said at last, thinking of the way he'd looked yesterday afternoon, standing on her front porch. He hadn't spotted her where she'd cowered behind the curtains, unable to resist looking at him, and even more incapable of facing him. There'd been nothing in his manner or in his wide-shouldered stance to indicate he was suffering from unrequited love. When Delphi had conveyed the message that she, Sophie, didn't care to see him, he hadn't looked in the least bit heartbroken. He'd simply nodded and politely said thank you, then turned around and walked away, just like that.

Sarah Jane remained silent.

"Wouldn't he have *said* something if he was in love with me?" Sophie demanded. The words hurt as much as if they'd been torn from her by red-hot pincers. "*Before* we made love, I mean? Wouldn't he?"

Sarah Jane hesitated, considering the question. "I don't know, Sophie," she said at last. "What if he didn't *know* he was in love until after? And what's so terrible about him askin' after, anyways? Did *you* know you was in love with him before? I mean, really know for sure? After all, didn't neither one of you *plan* on makin' love in that old barn, did you?"

When Sophie's only response was a reluctant shake of her head, Sarah Jane continued, "An' he told you he didn't think he could take care of a wife proper. What's so terrible about him wantin' to be sure he could afore he said somethin'? Lotsa men don't worry none about it until it's too late. Women, neither. But they sure enough end up regrettin' it, and they got years to do it, too. Years and years. All the rest of their lives. I *know*, Sophie. *Believe* me."

"I believe you." The words were little more than a whisper. Tears stung Sophie's eyes.

"It's harder than I thought," she admitted, fighting against the need to cry. "Lots harder. Everywhere I go, I can feel folks staring at me. I can almost hear them thinking, and I don't even have to guess at what it is they're thinking."

She swiped at the tears that threatened to spill over, then sniffed and hiccuped and, after a moment, added, "I've lived here most of my life. This is my home. These are the people I know, and they know me. But now suddenly I . . . I don't belong. I don't fit anymore."

Sarah Jane simply nodded. Her silence carried a world of understanding.

"I don't want to spend the rest of my life like this, but I *refuse* to live it according to someone else's ideas of what I *ought* to do." Sophie stared down at her lap, then carefully, angrily smoothed her plain brown skirt over her knees. "When I marry—*if* I marry!—I want it to be for love, not . . . not *shame!*"

Sarah Jane's hand curled tight in her lap, but she didn't look away, didn't flinch. "Shame ain't too comfortable, that's for sure. But pride ain't much of nothing special, neither. Not if you let it get in the way of your bein' happy."

Sophie's head snapped up. "What do you mean?"

"I mean," said Sarah Jane firmly, "that pride won't keep you warm on a cold night. An' it sure ain't worth much if you ain't happy. My Pa, he was stuffed full of pride. That's why he kicked me out, you know. Not 'cause of what *I* did, but 'cause of how it made *him* look. He's probably still proud to bustin', but he ain't never met his only grandson because of it, an' he never will. That's a mighty high price to pay for bein' proud and proper, seems to me."

There was more sorrow than anger in Sarah Jane's words. Sophie could hear all the lost, lonely years reverberating in them.

"But I'm not—I don't want—It's not like that!"

"No?" Sarah Jane's eyebrow arched in doubt. "Seems to me it's pride that's standing between you and Zeke right now. Pride and not much else. You're too proud to marry just 'cause other folks think you oughta, even though marryin' Zeke is what you want more'n anything else in the world. An' Zeke was too proud to ask you to marry him 'cause he ain't got much money, an' you do."

Sophie stared at her, stunned by the simplicity of Sarah Jane's argument.

Sarah Jane evidently took her silence for disbelief. "Don't neither reason have much to do with bein' happy, far as I can see," she said, the warning clear in her voice.

"But he doesn't *love* me!" The protest broke from Sophie before she could stop it.

"Does he?" she plaintively added a moment later, when Sarah Jane didn't respond.

The silence stretched between them, heavy with the uncertainties for which neither had an answer.

"I don't know, Sophie," Sarah Jane admitted at last, reluctantly. "I just don't know."

Thursday, July 13, 1893

I'm headed into town tomorrow morning to pick up Tom. I wasn't planning on going back in, but Sarah Jane sent Patrick out this evening to ask if I would.

Seems Sarah Jane's pretty much recovered from her beating and Tom's getting restless and wanting to work on the traction engine. Patrick wants him out from under his feet, too. Now that Sarah Jane's finally agreed to marry him, Patrick's started fixing up that house of hers and adding another room off to the side. He's hoping to get everything done by the wedding in September, but with Tom helping him, he swore he'd be lucky to have it finished by Christmas. I could see his point. Tom's a wizard with mechanical and electrical gadgets, but he's downright dangerous with a hammer and nail. His pestering Patrick to install an electrical generator so they could have electrical lights didn't go down all that well. Patrick figures giving him another chance to work on the traction engine will keep him from coming up with even more harebrained ideas.

Besides, I miss him. I told Patrick I'd be glad to have his company, not to mention his help. We set it up between us that I'd come in tomorrow, even though I was just in town.

What I didn't tell Patrick was that I got so flustered at Sophie's refusing to see me yesterday that I plumb forgot to pick up the boards and nails to make the crates I'll need for the watermelons come harvest. Just zipped right out of my head because I was thinking about Sophie and our troubles, and that didn't leave any room for worrying about practical things like melon crates.

Might as well stop at the depot and see if Mr. Conner will be a little more reasonable than he was a few days ago. Now that he's walking out with Sophie's mama, he's pretty much taken Sophie's troubles to heart. He holds me responsible, which is only right and proper. I can't blame him for that. Trouble is, he's for sure making life difficult. I was trying to make sure there'd be enough freight cars available for when my melons are ready to ship, but when I asked him to put my name down on the schedule, he just glared at me and said he'd see, that it was too soon to be worrying about it. Which isn't true. Most everybody I know has already got some sort of confirmation that the cars will be there. Everybody except me, that is.

Well, sufficient unto the day, as Mama always said.

Which reminds me. I'll need to get a few things at Goveneur's Grocery, too. For all his runty size, Tom can put away almost as much food as I can, so I want to be prepared.

Life wasn't fair, Sophie decided sourly as she followed Delphi into Goveneur's Grocery. Whenever she'd visited Zeke it had always felt like a year between visits, even though she'd gone out there at least twice, and occasionally three times a week. On the other hand, she'd gone shopping with Delphi last Friday, a whole week ago, yet it felt like only yesterday that she'd run the gauntlet of curious stares and undisguised interest from everyone they met.

She'd hoped some of the excitement over her fall from grace would have died down by now, but it hadn't. If anything, interest in her affairs was running stronger than ever. Folks weren't used to a well-bred young lady flaunting her depravity by charging around town as if absolutely nothing had happened, and they were making the most of the spectacle.

Her mother wasn't any happier about matters than she was, but Delphi covered her discomfort by assuming a fluttery, gushing manner that was far more effective than Sophie's cool-eyed haughtiness in keeping the inquisitive at a distance.

Neither Mr. Goveneur nor stout Mrs. Bassett had a chance to get a word in edgewise as Delphi sailed straight from "Good morning!" to "Goodness gracious, this heat is enough to prostrate a body, don't you agree, Mrs. Bassett? Why only yesterday . . ."

Sophie gave a small, wry smile and let her mother's monologue fade into a background murmur. She'd already heard the same litany of trivia and complaints three times this morning. Most folks would have worn down by now, but Delphi simply grew more fluent with every recital.

As always, Roger Makepiece was comfortably ensconced between the cheese and the cracker barrel. He tilted back in his chair, stuck his thumbs under his suspenders, and gave her his best toothless grin. "Mornin', Miss Sophie."

She returned his greeting, but without enthusiasm.

The old man could be a trial on the best of days. She didn't relish having to deal with his teasing today, on top of everything else.

He cocked his head to one side and eyed her speculatively. "Folks givin' you a hard time, is they?"

To Sophie's surprise, there was more compassion than curiosity in his manner. She couldn't help it. She nodded and gave him a wavery smile in return. "A little," she acknowledged.

"Not surprised." He scrunched up his mouth as if he were chewing on something. Rather like a frog trying to decide whether the fly he'd just caught was tasty enough to swallow. Sophie giggled, very faintly.

"That's the ticket," Roger Makepiece said approvingly. His little eyes glittered. "Don't you let 'em get you down, you hear? If they take to tormentin' you, you just torment 'em right back. Works a wonder, every time."

"Does it?"

"Yup. *I* know," he said with satisfaction.

Before Sophie could ask him what he'd done to make folks want to torment him, the cowbell over the front door rang to indicate a new customer had arrived. The old man craned his neck to peer around her, then brought his chair back to earth with a thump. "Hot damn! This oughta be interestin'!"

"Why, Delphi Carter! Fancy meeting you here!" Adelaide Smith's sharp voice was unmistakable.

Sophie closed her eyes, fighting against panic. Should she try to slip out the back door and risk attracting Adelaide's attention, or would she be better off just standing still and hoping she blended in with the woodwork?

"Mrs. Smith." Delphi's tones were precisely calculated to depress the pretensions of a social upstart like Adelaide Smith, but Adelaide wasn't one to be easily depressed.

"How *are* you getting on these days? You and Miss Sophie, I mean," she inquired with mock solicitude. "I've been so . . . *worried* about you, you know. And I never did have a chance to apologi—"

"No apologies necessary, I assure you!" Delphi sniffed.

Sophie flinched and tried to make herself smaller.

"Of course, I never *dreamed* that—well, *you* know! I didn't stop blushing for days!"

"What a shame you seem incapable of blushing for all your *other* . . . faux pas!" Public disgrace or not, Delphi wasn't about to let Adelaide Smith get the best of her!

Sophie started edging toward the back of the store.

"I feel for that poor Mr. Jeffries," Delphi added with heartfelt passion. "Never knowing when his neighbor's going to come charging in, and without so much as a by-your-leave, too! Enough to make a body turn over in her grave, I'm sure!"

"Really? Well, let me tell you—!"

Whatever Adelaide Smith was going to say was interrupted by the cowbell jangling as another customer walked in.

Sophie's heart fell into her boots. Zeke Jeffries. Here. Now. And walking smack dab into the middle of a quarrel between Delphi and Adelaide.

At the sight of him, the two women fell silent. Delphi thrust her shoulders back and patted her perfect curls. Adelaide scowled.

"Can't run, you know, and you shore can't hide," old Roger whispered gleefully in Sophie's ear. "Things'll only get worse if they have to roust you out of the potato bin."

Before Sophie could protest that she had absolutely no intention of hiding in the potato bin, the cowbell jangled yet again and Annie and Thea Talbot walked in.

Sophie squeezed her eyes shut and tried not to scream. The potato bin might not be such a bad idea after all.

"Why, Zeke!" said Annie. She stopped, blushing prettily.

Her mamma pushed her farther into the room . . . and closer to Zeke. "Good morning, everyone," she said, for all the world as if she didn't know that disaster was brewing. "Good morning, Mr. Jeffries."

"Ma'am." Zeke sounded as if someone had their hands wrapped around his throat and was squeezing hard.

"And Sophie, too!" Mrs. Talbot added gaily. "I almost didn't see you, standing there in the dark like that."

Sophie didn't even try to acknowledge the greeting. She was afraid to move so much as a little finger for fear of making an even greater fool of herself than she already had and thereby adding to the town gossips' pleasure.

Delphi, Adelaide, and Thea were smiling and sizing each other up, preparing for the next round of shots. Their opening comments had been nothing more than a way to test their range and the wind conditions.

Behind the front counter, Mr. Goveneur's face had assumed the sick, fascinated expression of a rat caught between a hungry cat and a juicy hunk of cheese.

Once more the cowbell jangled. Sophie groaned. Town Hall on election day had never been this popular.

Stout Mrs. Bassett stumped in, closely followed by Dora Stevens. At the sight of the assembled crowd, the two stopped short, clearly uncertain about venturing farther.

Delphi decided the matter by saying brightly, "Mrs. Bassett! Dora! Why, get a few more members and we can have a meeting of the Missionary Society right here! It's good to see you both!"

Mrs. Bassett reluctantly stepped forward. Dora wasn't so hesitant. The possibility of fireworks had already made her eyes light up. It could have been the press of people in the small open space at the front of the store, or it could have been another reason entirely that made Annie Talbot sidle closer to Zeke.

If Zeke noticed, he gave no sign. His gaze was desperately fixed on a calendar that hung on the wall behind Mr. Goveneur as Mrs. Bassett drew the other ladies' attention by some comment that Sophie couldn't catch.

It was only her imagination, Sophie told herself sternly, that made her think he threw a nervous, covert glance her way every now and then. Imagination and a totally unreasonable hope that he wasn't totally oblivious to her presence.

Old Mr. Makepiece, clearly disappointed, popped a cracker into his mouth and chewed it morosely.

Spotting her chance, Sophie cautiously worked her way around to the far side of the cracker barrel . . . and closer to the back door.

"Let me cut you some cheese, Mr. Makepiece," she said, low enough so no one else could hear her. "Would you like another cracker?" If his mouth was full, there was less chance he could alert anyone to her escape.

She had the third hunk of cheese lined up on its cracker when Zeke suddenly appeared in front of the cracker barrel.

"Sophie," he said in an urgent whisper, "we gotta talk."

Sophie jumped and dropped the cracker. "Not now," she whispered back, even more urgently. She threw a nervous glance over her shoulder and found, to her dismay, that all conversation had stopped and that six pairs of feminine eyes were firmly fixed on the two of them.

Zeke twisted around to see what had caught her attention, and froze. It might have been a curse he muttered under his breath, but Sophie couldn't be sure. Her heart was beating so hard it seemed to be pounding in her ears, drowning out everything else.

Almost everything. "You two make such a *nice* looking couple," Mrs. Bassett said. "You're both so . . . *tall*."

Sophie forced a small, sickly smile on her lips. Zeke took a half step away from Sophie, obviously uncertain what to say.

"Have you set the date, yet?" Mrs. Bassett asked. "For the wedding, I mean?"

A dead silence fell. Sophie would have sworn she could hear the dust motes as they fell.

Delphi cleared her throat nervously. "I haven't . . . That is, they haven't really discussed it yet," she said. The warning look she shot Sophie would have stopped a bear in its tracks.

Sophie grabbed the edge of the cracker barrel. Her knees were suddenly so wobbly she was afraid she might fall if she didn't. What should she say? What *could* she say? She'd already announced she wasn't marrying Zeke. That she didn't want to.

The thought of repeating that lie made her stomach churn. There'd be no backing down if she publicly refused him. Not ever. She wouldn't have the courage to make such a fool of herself.

Pride won't keep you warm on a cold night. An' it sure ain't worth much if you ain't happy.

Sarah Jane's words rang in Sophie's ears. Were they premonition? Or warning?

Suddenly, Zeke's hand closed around hers, big and warm and comforting. Strong, like the man himself. For an instant, his gaze held hers, but Sophie couldn't read anything in his eyes except concern and an uncertainty to match her own. She couldn't see love there. Not even a hint of it.

He straightened slightly, her hand still firmly clasped in his, and turned to face the crowd at the front of the store. "We haven't had a chance to—"

I won't marry a man who doesn't love me, Sarah Jane. No matter what anybody thinks. It wouldn't be right to marry without love.

Sophie tugged her hand free of his grasp. "We aren't getting married, Mrs. Bassett," she announced, loudly enough so that everyone could hear.

The cowbell broke the stunned silence with its metallic clanging as Tom Peabody strolled into the store. He hesitated for a moment, clearly surprised at the number of people crowding the entrance. Then he spotted Zeke.

"Hey, Zeke," he called, blithely unaware of the frozen shock of every adult around him. "I know you said to wait in the wagon, but I forgot to ask if you could maybe get some sugar cubes. Delphi and that spotted sow really like 'em an'—"

"*What* did you say?" Delphi Carter demanded in terrible tones.

"I said—" Tom broke off his explanation. "Say, ain't you Miss Sophie's ma? The one with the same name as Zeke's cow?"

This time, Sophie didn't wait for the fireworks. She knocked over a small pyramid of tinned marmalade in her rush to get to the back door before all hell broke loose.

Chapter 21

To Sophie, the heat of August seemed even more oppressive than the heat of July. The dust in the streets puffed up beneath her feet, coating the hem of her skirt with a pale, gray-brown grit that weighed her down almost as much as her leaden spirits. Each step forward took an effort of will, but no one, she had decided long ago, was going to be privileged to see Miss Sophronia Maye Carter cry or cringe or creep along like a lizard with its belly to the dirt. No one.

The trouble was, good intentions couldn't keep her from feeling even lower than that nonexistent lizard's nonexistent belly. A month of facing her friends' and acquaintances' eager, disapproving curiosity had been horrible.

A month of thinking about a lifetime without Zeke Jeffries had been even worse.

Sarah Jane had been right. Pride wasn't worth much. It was, however, all she had left. After the debacle in Goveneur's Grocery, Zeke had given up asking her to marry him. No man appreciates being publicly rejected, and she couldn't have been much more public if she'd shouted it from the top of the church steeple.

Sophie clutched the small book she carried tighter against her chest. It was for Tom, a more advanced text on modern electrical equipment than any he'd yet had. She'd bought it on impulse, spurred by the thought that it would provide an excuse to bicycle out to see Zeke. The minute she'd plunked down a dollar forty for it, she'd known she would never have the courage to see Zeke again. Not deliberately. She simply couldn't bear the pain of knowing she'd had a chance, and she'd thrown it away with both hands.

At least her friendship with Sarah Jane gave her the opportunity to learn what he was up to, even though the information came in frustrating bits and pieces as Sarah Jane chattered away about Tom and his doings. Sophie didn't dare ask for more.

No sense dwelling on it, she chided herself, not for the first time. She'd made her bed and now she'd have to lie in it, no matter how hard and lumpy and uncomfortable it was.

If she'd hoped for any sympathy from Sarah Jane, she was destined for disappointment. Sophie found her friend perched on a wobbly step ladder, trying to hang wallpaper in her little parlor. Sarah Jane's hair was pinned up in an untidy bun, she was wearing a torn and paint-spattered old cotton dress with a rip in the sleeve, and Sophie thought she had never looked more beautiful.

Patrick had finished the most urgent patching and repairs on the house and now was spending most of his free hours working on a new addition that would give them a bigger kitchen and a larger, more comfortable bedroom once they were married. Despite Sarah Jane's protests that it didn't make much difference if he moved in right away, considering, Patrick had steadfastly insisted on treating his bride-to-be with all the respect and concern he would have shown a virginal girl of eighteen. His restraint had been the final proof Sarah Jane had needed that he really did love her as much as he said he did.

Sober now and radiantly happy, she'd thrown herself into the job of painting and wallpapering and sewing new curtains with an energetic enthusiasm that left Sophie gasping for breath . . . and more than a little envious of her happiness.

The enthusiasm was slightly tarnished at the moment, however.

"Darned paste makes a mess, and the paper won't hang straight, an' I cut the first roll wrong. Didn't realize afore I'd hung it, neither," she grumbled as she struggled to keep the present roll from tangling around her head before she got it in place. "If I get crazy enough to try this again, you gotta promise to shoot me."

Sophie laughed. "I imagine Patrick would have something to say about that!"

Sarah Jane grinned down at her. "Yeah. He'd prob'ly shoot me first. I had so much glue in my hair yesterday he said he'd prob'ly get the rheumatiz just tryin' to brush it out.'

"I can imagine." Sophie's good humor disappeared as quickly as it had come. What she could imagine was Zeke combing out *her* hair, his fingers sifting through the heavy strands, his touch—

Better not to think about that. *Much* better not!

She tucked Tom's book safely away on a shelf in the kitchen and was in the process of rolling up her sleeves to help Sarah Jane when Tom burst through the kitchen door.

"Miss Sophie! You're here!" An expression of unutterable relief spread across his face. "Your ma wouldn't tell me where you'd gone and I was gettin' real worried I wouldn't find you!"

Sophie froze, stunned by a sudden, almost overwhelming fear. "What's wrong? Is Zeke all right? Does he need me? Where is he?"

Sarah Jane instantly abandoned her roll of wallpaper only half-hung. She clattered down the ladder and came into the kitchen, wiping her hands on her glue-spotted apron. "You in some kind of trouble?" she demanded anxiously. "Is Patrick all right?"

"It's Mr. Conner. He won't let Zeke load his melons. Says he's gotta wait till some other farmers load theirs, but they ain't ready yet an' Zeke, he's down there now with a ton o'melons, all crated an' ready t'go. He's some mad. An' worried, too, 'cause he can't afford t'pay the fellers he hired to help him again, an' he can't leave his melons in the sun, not for days, like Mr. Conner says he might have to, an' he don't know *what* to do!"

Tom stopped abruptly, gasping for breath. His whole body quivered with tension.

"Did Zeke ask for me?" Sophie asked. A faint, hot ember of hope suddenly glowed in the middle of her chest. She rolled down the sleeve she'd just finished rolling up and refastened each button.

"Tom? Did Zeke ask for Miss Sophie?" Sarah Jane demanded when her son remained silent.

Tom shifted nervously. "Not exactly."

"What do you mean, 'not exactly,' " his mother pressed.

Sophie fumbled with the last button on her cuff as the small, faint ember of hope faded to dull gray. Zeke hadn't asked for her after all. He didn't need her. He didn't *want* her.

"Well," said Tom reluctantly, "I *know* he needs Miss Sophie, but he din't exactly *say* so."

"Well, what *did* he say?" Sarah Jane demanded in sudden exasperation.

"He . . . he told Mr. Conner he wouldn't let 'im drag Miss Sophie into it, an' then Mr. Conner said somethin' about *he* was the boss of the station an' what he says, goes, an' then Zeke says that he din't have no business playin' games like that, an' then Mr. Conner, he says he don't play games 'cause they can get folks in trouble, 'specially if they don't wanna finish the game proper, and then *Zeke* says—"

"That's all right. I think I understand what's going on," Sophie said, cutting Tom's litany short. She willfully ignored Sarah Jane's worried frown as she considered what she ought to do.

Because of the commotion generated by his innocently informing Delphi that she had a milk cow named after her, they'd managed to keep Tom in ignorance of what had happened between her and Zeke. He'd been puzzled by the abrupt cessation of her visits, but he was so caught up in helping Zeke with the traction engine and the excitement of his mother's coming nuptials that he hadn't thought to press for details.

Sophie didn't care to enlighten him now, but she

couldn't ignore his plea for help, either. She was no expert on farming, but she knew that if Zeke couldn't get his melons to the big-paying markets back East before the rest of the farmers shipped theirs, he risked losing the profit he was counting on to pay his debts on the farm. Worse, if he was too late, his melons would be so far past their prime that he wouldn't be able to sell them at all, which meant he'd lose not only any hope of profit, but everything he'd invested into growing, crating, and shipping the melons in the first place. The losses would be hard for even a prosperous, well-established farmer to swallow. For someone just starting out, they could be devastating. Mr. Conner's stern determination to save his future stepdaughter's good name could destroy Zeke and everything he'd worked for.

She couldn't let that happen. She wouldn't let it.

As if sensing her determination, the recalcitrant button on her cuff meekly slipped through the buttonhole and neatly into place.

"I'll go see what I can do, shall I?" Sophie said to Tom, forcing a calm she didn't feel. "You stay here and help your momma get up the rest of the wallpaper, all right?"

Sarah Jane opened her mouth to protest, then shut it with a snap. When Tom glanced at her, clearly unwilling to believe he might be forced to deal with wallpaper rather than share in the brewing fight at the station, she smiled encouragingly.

"I need you to help me figger out how to cut that paper. With all you been learnin' about numbers an' such, I figgered you'd be a whiz at it, an' it's for sure that I ain't. I'm not, I mean."

Sophie gave her a grateful, encouraging nod and was relieved to see that the appeal to his mathematical talents had been more than enough to convince Tom to stay. Just as well. She'd like to have one friend left who didn't know how far she'd fallen off the pedestal he'd set her on.

* * *

The heavy freight car door slid slowly open with a heavy, metallic protest. Zeke shoved harder, grateful for some physical outlet for his anger. A month of frustration and doubt had done nothing for his temper. It had taken every ounce of self-restraint he possessed to keep from slamming his fist in Conner's face, though with what he was about to do, there was still a good chance he'd end up in a fistfight before the day was over.

For the first time in his life, he welcomed the thought.

He grabbed a handhold and swung up into the freight car, then turned in the now-open doorway to gesture to Patrick, who sat at the controls of the idling steam traction engine, waiting for Zeke's signal. The burly blacksmith waved acknowledgment, then set the engine into motion. The three long farm wagons hitched, one after another, behind the engine jerked and shuddered at the sudden tug, then obediently followed after, their head-high loads of crated watermelons jiggling.

"You sure you want to do this?" Zeke shouted over the roar of the engine as Patrick carefully maneuvered the behemoth up to the open door.

"Hell, yes!" Patrick's face split in a wide grin. His teeth gleamed brilliant white in the sun. "Are you sure *you* want to do this?"

Zeke gave him a ferocious grin. "Hell, yes! These are *my* freight cars and I'm damned if I'll let my melons rot while Conner waits for some other farmer to fill 'em!"

Patrick laughed, then carefully moved forward until the last wagon came even with the open freight car door. The instant Patrick cut the engine back to idle, Zeke grabbed the nearest crate. The two men he'd hired for the harvest had fled as soon as they realized what he intended, but Patrick was still here. Between the two of them, they'd be able to fill at least two freight cars with the three wagon-loads of melons.

If he had to park the traction engine in the middle of the tracks to do it, he'd make sure those two freight cars were hitched to the next east-bound train, no matter what Conner said. He'd already paid for a minimum of forty cars to carry his harvest and he intended to fill every one before anyone else got their crops out.

He'd unloaded enough crates to make a space for Patrick to stand on the wagon bed by the time the station clerk finally figured out what he was up to. Elbows flying, he came charging across the tracks to them.

"Here now!" he screeched. "You can't do that! Mr. Conner said you'd have to wait till he had cars free. You can't just take 'em like this! What do you think you're doing?"

Zeke ignored him. He grabbed one of the crates he'd stacked inside the open door and carried it to the front of the car. Then he returned and picked up the second crate and carried it over to stack on top of the first.

Without the two hired hands, it was going to take a whole lot longer to unload the wagons, but he didn't have any choice. If he had to do it alone, he'd ship those forty carloads of melons east and no one, not the clerk, not Conner, not the President of the United States himself was going to stop him.

By the time Zeke returned for the third crate, the clerk was staggering back across the tracks in search of reinforcements. With his long, scrawny legs and clumsy gait, he reminded Zeke of a flustered stork whose nest had just been invaded.

"Sure, now, and the fellow's likely to give himself apoplexy, flappin' and wailin' like that," said Patrick, grinning broadly. He easily swung a crate off the wagon and into the car, then turned to pick up another. "It's likely we'll have company in a bit."

"No doubt," said Zeke, watching the clerk lock the station door, then scuttle off in the direction his boss had gone not twenty minutes before.

Patrick hesitated, then carefully set the crate he held in the railroad car. "Conner's set on seein' you wed to Miss Sophie," he said in a bland, noncommittal tone.

"Yes." Zeke stared across the rows of tracks and

up the street where the clerk had disappeared. Sophie's house was over that way. Two blocks? No, three. Just three blocks away.

"I doubt he's a man as will give in easily," Patrick said. There was an unmistakable note of warning beneath the calm tone.

"No, he's not." Zeke frowned, then dropped his gaze to meet Patrick's. "But I don't intend to give in at all."

Patrick's black brows rose. "Not on anything?"

Zeke didn't intend to answer, but the words slipped out anyway. "I tried, Patrick. It's not me who said 'no.' "

"Indeed?" said Patrick politely.

Zeke caught himself an instant before he struck his friend. With a sharp oath, he bent and picked up the crate at his feet.

"We'd best get moving before company arrives," he snapped, then stomped off to the front of the car to set the crate on top of the small pile of crates rising in the corner.

He'd gone mad. That was the only explanation for it. And all because a tall, golden-eyed angel had refused to become his wife, the wife he'd been convinced he didn't want in the first place.

Countless times in the days and weeks since the disaster in Goveneur's Grocery he'd tried to figure out what he could have done—what he *should* have done—to stop her from publicly announcing that she wouldn't marry him. With half a dozen interested witnesses looking on, once she'd spoken out, there was no way she'd back down after. Not his proud Sophie.

His Sophie. Zeke shoved the crate into place with more force than was strictly necessary.

Not his any longer.

A thousand times since, he'd told himself it didn't matter, that he was sorry he'd had any part in damaging her reputation, but that he'd done everything he could to rectify the matter. If she wanted no part of *him,* that was *her* choice.

Her choice . . . and she'd chosen not to have him.

Zeke stomped back to snatch up another of the crates Patrick was stacking for him with such easy efficiency.

Patrick glanced up at him and grinned, clearly amused by his sour temper . . . and just as clearly aware of the reason for it. The only effect Zeke's angry scowl had on the man was to make him laugh.

"You'll get it straight in your head one day, my friend," Patrick said. "I did. Just takes a while for the notion to settle, so to speak."

"Humpf," said Zeke, and hauled the crate off to put it with the others. By the time he got back to the open freight car door, trouble had arrived. Conner, the station clerk, and another man whom Zeke took to be an employee of the railroad were headed their way. The third man looked just the type to enjoy a fight if it was offered, no matter who was offering.

Patrick set down the crate he held, dusted off his hands, and propped his fists on his hips. The expression on his face was as mild as milk, but Zeke was grateful the big Irishman was on his side and not Conner's.

"Jeffries!" Conner called. His voice cracked across the empty tracks. "I told you—!"

"And I told *you*," Zeke snapped back. "I paid for the cars, I intend to fill them and see them hauled east. I don't want a fuss about it, but if you're fixing to give me one . . ." He let the threat hang, wondering if the stationmaster was going to pick it up.

He did. "*I'm* master here, and if you think—"

A strong, clear feminine voice cut short his incipient tirade.

"Zeke! Patrick! Why didn't you wait for me?" Head high, Sophie picked her way across the tracks toward them.

Zeke jumped, startled. He'd been so intent on Conner and his men he hadn't seen her approach. "Sophie! What—"

"I got held up, but here I am!" she said brightly— too brightly. "Ready to help, just like I said I would."

Conner spun around, as astonished as Zeke at her arrival. "Miss Sophie! What are you—"

"I'm here to help Zeke," she said.

Her smile was wide and bright and guaranteed to catch a man's eye, but beneath the cheerful mask Zeke sensed a determination that didn't bode well for him *or* the stationmaster. That didn't stop his own mouth from curving into a welcoming smile. He couldn't help it. Just the sight of her was enough to roust his gloom.

Conner frowned. "Now, Miss Sophie—"

"I know. Those crates are heavy, but Zeke needs all the help he can get. I'd just hate to think he had any troubles on *my* account, you know!"

Mr. Conner's face grew red. "That's not the problem!" he huffed. "Mr. Jeffries is loading cars without my authorization. There are other farmers with melons to load, too, you know."

"There are?" Sophie's eyes widened ingenuously. She tilted to one side to peer around the end of the wagon, then tilted the other way to look down the tracks in the opposite direction. "I don't see any farmers. Except Zeke."

Conner's face reddened. Sophie gave him her best and brightest smile again, then stepped over to the wagon and held her hands up to Patrick. "Help me up, Patrick, will you please? I'd just as soon not climb over the wheels if I don't have to."

Patrick beamed in approval. "Sure, now, and it'll be a pleasure, Miss Sophie." He bent to wrap his own broad hands around her wrists, then lifted her up to stand beside him.

"Thank you. It's always nice to see a smiling face."

She was speaking to Patrick, Zeke knew, but she looked at him. A sudden tightness grabbed hold of his chest. He could feel his heart racing and a fire starting at the bottom of his belly and for a moment, for one dizzying moment, he thought she felt the same response.

Her smile dimmed and grew more distant. "Zeke."

Polite, but cool. If she felt any of the heat he did,

she didn't show it. Zeke could feel his own smile fade. "Sophie," he said, and wondered if she could hear all the unspoken longing that was bumping around inside him.

"Well," she said, straightening and looking around her briskly, "how about if I unload the crates from the wagon while you two stack them in the car?"

"Sophie . . ." Zeke's protest died unspoken. He couldn't bear to send her away. Not now. Not when he'd had to endure so many endless days without her.

"Now, Miss Sophie, you just come down from there." The stationmaster's voice had a distinct note of strain in it.

Zeke glanced down at him, torn between irritation at the man's insistence and sympathy for his predicament. Conner's face was growing redder by the minute, but it was clear he didn't have any more idea how to deal with the situation than anyone else.

The clerk settled for glaring at Sophie while the third man edged closer to the wagon and tried to peek up her skirt. Zeke's hands instantly curled into fists, but Sophie stepped away from the edge of the wagon and the man backed off, disappointed.

"I'm thinkin' it'd be best if you worked in there with Zeke," said Patrick, unperturbed. "Even with the two of you haulin' and stackin', you'll be hard put to keep up with me."

"Braggart," Sophie said, and grinned. She eyed the gap between the bed of the wagon and the floor of the freight car, then looked at Zeke.

He ought to send her away. The crates were too heavy for a woman to lift and there wasn't a chance in the world he'd be able to keep his mind on his work if she were there in the car with him, working or not.

He ought to say thanks, but no thanks, and deal with Conner on his own terms. He ought to scold her for risking more gossip by showing up in the first place. He ought—

Zeke extended his hand. "Watch that metal lip at

the edge of the car. It will catch your heel if you're not careful."

Without hesitation, Sophie placed her hand in his and stepped into the car beside him.

Seven cars loaded. Seven! Zeke swiped a bedraggled, sweat-stained handkerchief across his forehead and grinned across the open freight car doorway at the equally sweat-stained and bedraggled Sophie. She was leaning against the door frame, tugging off the heavy work gloves he'd given her and smiling at him like a cat that had just lapped a whole bowl of cream.

For a long, infinitely sweet moment their gazes met and held in comfortable mutual accord, then the sound of Tom's tired laughter coming from somewhere around the traction engine broke the spell. Her cheeks flushed, even under their thick coating of dust and grime. Her gaze dropped. With forced casualness, she stared over at the station platform where travelers were beginning to gather in expectation of the evening train. The train that would take his seven carloads of melons to those all-important markets back East.

"Only seven cars," she said. She gave a wry little laugh and shook her head. "If you'd asked me, I'd have sworn we loaded seven hundred."

"We wouldn't have loaded any if it hadn't been for you." Zeke forced his voice to take a casual tone. She glanced at him, then as quickly looked away, but Zeke thought he caught a glint of—was it pleasure? satisfaction?—in her eyes.

"Looked to me like you had a pretty good start when I arrived." She shrugged, then flinched. With a little moan, she pressed her fists against the small of her back and arched backward. "Mmmpf. I hurt in muscles I didn't even know I had."

Zeke was beside her in three longs steps. "I told you not to keep going like that," he scolded even as his hands curved over her shoulders. She tensed, but only for a moment. Then she relaxed into his touch as his fingers probed the tight, overworked muscles.

"Ahh, that feels good," she murmured. She lifted

her shoulder in a half shrug. "There. No, a little lower. Yes, that's it. Harder! Ohh!"

It *was* good. She felt wonderful under his hands. Warm and vital and *alive,* even beneath the dirt. The fire in the pit of his belly that he'd kept so carefully banked all day roared up, fierce at the sudden release from restraint.

"You must be exhausted," she said, twisting slightly so he could dig into the sore muscles at the base of her shoulder. "At least I could rest for a couple of hours every time you and Patrick went back for more melons. You two have been going all day."

"We're used to it," Zeke said softly, "you're not."

"No," she admitted wryly, "I'm not." She tossed aside the gloves she still held and turned her hands over.

Zeke gasped. The soft, delicate flesh of both hands was raw and blistered. Several of the blisters had broken. One oozed blood as well as fluid. A sliver of wood had been driven into the fleshy base of one thumb and a rough scrape, crusted with dried blood, adorned the other.

"Sophie! Why didn't you say something?" Appalled, Zeke spun her around to face him. Fighting against the self-disgust choking him, he gently cradled her abused hands in his as he inspected the damage. Nothing that time wouldn't heal, but her hands would be sore and sensitive for several days to come—and all because of him.

With the tip of one finger Zeke probed the sliver. Sophie winced and tried to pull free. His grasp automatically tightened.

"I told you to stop! Why didn't you listen to me? Why did you let it get this bad?" His anger was for himself, but Sophie's cheeks flushed an angry red as she jerked free.

"I wanted to help!" she snapped. "Wanting to help doesn't mean that I'm trying to chase you, Zeke Jeffries! It doesn't mean I'm trying to trap you into marriage, no matter *what* people say! It doesn't mean—"

Zeke grabbed her and pulled her against him before

she could back away. "*I* know that! That wasn't what
I meant!"

"Then what—?"

Zeke stopped her angry questions with a kiss. He
couldn't help it. He was only human and he'd been
fighting against the urge—no! the *need* to touch her
ever since she walked across those tracks toward him
this morning.

He couldn't fight any longer.

An instant's tension, a fleeting resistance, then her
lips parted and she relaxed into his arms, opening herself to him.

Zeke groaned and drew her closer. She tasted of
salt and dust and . . . Sophie. She tasted of heaven.

Dimly, he heard laughter, then a shrill whistle of
approval. Sophie gasped and shoved him away,
cheeks flaming.

"Atsa boy, Zeke! Go for it!" someone on the station platform yelled. "Kiss 'er again!"

"You got him hooked this time, Miss Sophie!"
someone else yelled. "Don't let him get away a second time!"

Before Zeke could think, Sophie grabbed the handhold beside the open car door and swung herself to
the ground. For a second she stood there looking up
at him, eyes wide and bright with sudden tears.

"Good-bye, Zeke," she said, so low he almost didn't
hear her. "Good luck!"

That was all, and then she darted into the lengthen-
ing shadows cast by the neighboring railroad cars and
was gone.

"Zeke?"

"Hmm?" Zeke looked up from his journal, then
reluctantly set his pen aside. Tom was sitting at the
far end of the kitchen table, hunched over the new
book Sophie had given him. The boy was too exhausted to read, yet he'd refused to go to bed when
Zeke had told him to.

"I . . . I heard about you an' Miss Sophie." In the
lamplight, Tom looked older, sadder somehow, and a

good deal wiser than was proper for a boy his age. "At the station. A couple of the fellows there were talkin' about it. I couldn't help overhear. I didn't mean to listen, you know."

Zeke flinched. "What'd they say?"

"That . . . that you an' Miss Sophie were caught in the barn. Naked. And that now you have to get married, but Miss Sophie's refusin' to marry you, no matter what folks say." The distress on the boy's face was clear.

"That's right." What else *could* he say?

"That's why she ain't been out here for any visits, isn't it?"

"That's right."

"*You* said it was 'cause it was too hot. That she didn't like to get all sweaty pedaling out here in the afternoons. *You* said she was busy."

The accusations hung in the air between them. Zeke didn't say anything.

"You lied to me, din't you, Zeke?"

Zeke sighed. "That's right." When Tom simply stared at him reproachfully, he added, "I couldn't hardly tell you the truth, now, could I?"

Tom frowned, considering the matter. "So . . . you gonna marry her?"

"I've asked her. Those fellows at the station were right, though. She doesn't want to marry me." He stared down at the journal on the table in front of him. The admission hurt.

"But she helped you toda—"

"Because she didn't like what Mr. Conner was doing."

"That's it?"

A muscle in Zeke's jaw jumped. Reluctantly, he nodded. "That's it."

Tom's eyes grew round. "You got a problem."

That was one way of putting it.

"Sorta like my ma an' Patrick had, I guess."

"But they finally got things straightened out."

"Yup, but I don't know as they would've if that bast—er that fellow hadn't tried to beat her up." Tom frowned down at the book he was holding, then carefully closed it and set it aside. "What I finally figured out was, she was afraid of gettin' married."

"Afraid—? Why would she be afraid of marrying Patrick?"

Tom scratched his head in a way that Patrick often did and scrunched up his face to show he was giving the question careful consideration. "Well, I think it's because she don't know nothin' about gettin' married, but she *did* know what she had. Even if she din't like it, she at least knew what it was, an' if she got married, it would be somethin' different. You see what I mean?"

Zeke turned the idea over. It made sense in a crazy kind of womenfolk way. "I think so."

"Don't— It doesn't make much sense to me, but then I've heard tell that no man can understand a woman." His left eyebrow shot up like a question mark. "You think that's true, Zeke?"

"*I* don't understand them, but I don't think that counts for much. I don't know much about them."

"But you know Miss Sophie."

"Yeah." Why did that sound so sad and lost?

"So . . . why don't she wanna marry you if . . . if she was willin' to sleep with you?"

"I think it's me, Tom. I think I . . . well, I should have said something sooner, I guess. Now she doesn't believe me when I say I wanted to marry her before . . . uh . . . before it happened."

"Didja? Didja really?"

Zeke thought about it. He knew the answer to Tom's question, but he couldn't see that it helped any. "Yeah, I did. But I didn't *know* I did, if that makes any sense. Not until after."

Tom mulled it over. "Yeah, I guess it makes sense. About as much sense as any of this kissin' an' fallin' in love stuff."

He folded his hands on top of the table and frowned across it at Zeke. "So, whatcha gonna do about it? If Miss Sophie won't speak to you, and she sure as heck isn't—" For an instant his face lit up at the sheer wonder of having gotten his verb right the first time without trying. "If she *isn't* gonna come out here anymore for visits, what're you gonna do?"

"I don't know. What do *you* think I ought to do?"

"Me? Hmmm." Tom's frown deepened. He "hmmmed" some more, then said, "Well, I guess if I was you, I'd get myself gussied up and go a'courtin'. Once the melons are gone, that is," he added hastily. "You don't wanna be flat broke when you ask her to marry you!"

Friday, August 18, 1893

Finally got all the melons shipped yesterday, late. Forty-three cars and every one of them stacked to the roof. The last of them rolled out of town at the end of the evening train headed East. I feel like I've been kicked, stomped, and abused, but if I were a drinking man, I'd be out on a tear tonight to celebrate. Those cars are some of the first to leave, which pretty much guarantees me good prices and a better profit.

I took Tom's advice today and went into town to buy a suit. Even the biggest one that Mr. Hodgeson had in stock wasn't big enough, but he swore Mrs. Hodgeson knew all there was to know about tailoring and that she'd have it fixed up in no time. She's even going to pick out a shirt and tie to go with it.

I've been trying to figure out how a fellow goes courting when he's in the kind of mess I am, but I haven't made much progress. Then Mrs. Smith and Miss Annie showed up this afternoon and solved my problem for me.

Mrs. Smith was right upfront about it. "Zeke," she said, "I heard about your troubles down at the station and how Sophie showed up to help." She frowned. "I even heard you were spotted kissing, right there in front of God and everybody."

I didn't bother to ask her how she heard. Given the way things get around, she probably knew about it almost as soon as Sophie and I did.

"Now I won't deny," said Mrs. Smith, "that I'm

seriously disappointed you latched on to Sophie and
not Annie, here. But I can see a cow when it's staring
me straight in the face and you have obviously got
your mind set on having Sophie, so there's no use
repining."

Miss Annie blushed at that, but she piped up in that
sweet voice of hers and said, "I'm *sure* she loves you,
Zeke, in spite of what she says."

Well, that perked me up some, but I didn't stay
perked up for long because her explanation just
doesn't make any sense. Seems she asked Sophie right
off if she had any objections to her—Miss Annie, that
is—visiting me, and Sophie said no, she didn't, that
she didn't care because she didn't have any intention
of marrying me, regardless, so of course Miss Annie
could go right ahead.

"Which all goes to show," Miss Annie said, "that
Sophie's head over heels in love with you and is just
dying inside because of it."

Now that's female logic if ever there was. Logical
or not, I'm desperate enough I agreed to go along
with the plan Mrs. Smith and Miss Annie cooked up
between them for Watermelon Day. They swore all
the other ladies are agreed. It's a pretty silly plan, but
I'm willing to give it a go if for no other reason than
because that water hole I've been scooping out by the
pump, a bucket at a time, is getting large enough it's
likely to be a danger to man and beast alike come
winter.

Chapter 22

Watermelon Day dawned bright, hot, and on time. Unfortunately. Sophie had been praying that somehow the week would skip from Friday directly to Sunday and forget about Saturday altogether, but it didn't.

She delivered her neatly wrapped loaf of honey-cinnamon bread to the judging area at nine o'clock, just as she'd been told. The long trestle tables had been set up for the competition under the rows of Mr. Swink's trees. Come midday, the shade would be more than welcome. Pies, cakes, breads, jams, and jellies crowded the tables set aside for the women's cooking contests, while even more tables sagged where the local farmers had laid out the best of their crops in a fiercely contested challenge to see whose would be named the best of the best.

It wasn't the agricultural or cooking contests that were the main points of interest, however. So far, those honors seemed to be equally divided between the head-high stacks of watermelons that filled two long rows between the trees, and the horses and horsemen that were beginning to gather at the new racetrack's barns for the day's races.

Sophie picked her way between the eager boys ogling the towering mountains of watermelon and the farmers inspecting their competitors' entries to the table where Dora Stevens and Mrs. Purvis were tagging the baked goods.

"Here's Sophie!" Dora called gaily. "We've been looking for you!"

"Looking for me?" Sophie frowned, then set her

bread on the table to reach for her small pocket watch. "It can't be past nine already, can it?"

"No, no. We just wanted to be sure you'd be here, you know."

"But—"

"Can't have a baking competition without your bread, now can we?" Mrs. Purvis hastily interjected, snatching up the bread. "Everyone knows about that bread, you know!"

"Absolutely!" Dora added with a smile bright enough to blind. "Why, we even have your number all written out. See?" She held up a square of paper with the number "seven" boldly printed in heavy black ink. "We just *couldn't* have this contest without you."

"Wouldn't think of it!" Mrs. Purvis added, taking the number from Dora and attaching it to the bread with a long bit of red yarn. "Everyone will be delighted to know you're here."

"Will they?" Sophie said faintly. This enthusiasm at her appearance was rather unnerving. "That's nice."

To her relief, a shouted query from someone working at another table drew Dora and Mrs. Purvis away before she was tempted to ask the reason for it. Only one explanation presented itself, and she'd just as soon not hear it confirmed before she had to.

Zeke must have finally come to his senses and decided to take an interest in Annie Talbot. After all, too tall Sophie Carter, who had spent the last month ignoring him, couldn't possibly hope to compete against pretty Annie, who had spent the last month shamelessly pursuing him. And today was the day Zeke was escorting Annie Talbot to the racetrack opening.

"Hey, Sophie!" Tom's shouted greeting broke into her grim ruminations. Sophie looked up to see him come galloping toward her like an eager colt, happily dodging around anything and anyone who happened to get in his way.

He pulled up in front of her, grinning like a fool. "Ma said you'd be here!"

"And here I am!" Sophie said with forced gaiety.

"I been here all morning! Zeke and me, we unloaded the melons early. He went off to Patrick's to get slicked up in that new suit of his since he's s'posed to escort Miss Annie, but *I* been with Mr. Sobeck. He's talkin' to the folks with the racetrack about is there maybe a way to use 'lectricity to figure out which horse wins a race in case it's real, real close."

"Mr. Sobeck let you go with him?"

"Yeah!" Tom was almost dancing on his toes beside her, he was so excited. "Him an' me, we're good friends again 'cause when we was at the station all the time with those watermelons, I told him about that 'lectric kit Patrick got me last time he went to Pueblo. I told him about me helpin' Zeke on the traction engine, too. Mr. Sobeck, he was real interested and said maybe I could come back and work with him after school this winter. And I promised—cross my heart!—I wouldn't fiddle with the alarm system without them sayin' I can. Ain't that grand?"

"Grand!" Sophie agreed, and wished she could look forward to the months ahead with the same enthusiasm. Right now, even the thought of trying to get through them without Zeke was frightening. She didn't even want to think about Zeke coming into town early just so he'd have time to get dressed up for Annie.

"Where's your mother and Patrick?" she asked to divert the conversation. "I'm going to sit with you since Mr. Conner got Mother a special box seat for the races."

"They're over there somewheres," Tom said, waving dismissively toward the crowd that was slowly making its way through the gates to the track. "*I'm* gonna go with Mr. Sobeck 'cause he knows the photographer an' *he* said he'd let me watch him work. Ma said I could!"

Sophie watched him race off, then reluctantly began making her way toward the track with everyone else. Despite the crowds and the numerous greetings from friends and acquaintances, she suddenly felt more alone than she ever had in her life. Everyone seemed to be with someone—except her. Tom was off with Mr. Sobeck. Delphi was with Mr. Conner. Patrick and Sarah Jane were inseparable these days, and Sarah Jane was slowly beginning to make friends in the community as word spread of her transformation into a radiantly happy, and happily unemployed, bride-to-be. Milly Purvis was on the arm of a solid-looking young man from La Junta, and a laughing Eliza Neumann was being escorted by her brother-in-law's cousin who happened to be visiting and who seemed quite taken by her charms.

Worst of all, Annie Talbot had Zeke Jeffries while she, Sophronia Maye Carter, had absolutely no one at all.

Sweat pooled under Zeke's arms and slid down his chest under his shirt. His stiff, high linen collar was in serious danger of melting and he could feel rivulets of sweat working their way out from under his hat. Another hour in the sun and folks would think he'd taken a bath in his clothes, rather than having everything specially brushed and cleaned and pressed and starched, just for the occasion.

Fortunately, nobody was really interested in him, which was just as well. He was afraid to look, but he had a sneaking suspicion even his fancy socks with their uncomfortable elastic garters were trying their damnedest to slide off his feet and into the toes of the pinch-toe shoes Mrs. Hodgeson had insisted he buy.

At least he'd held out for the white Canton straw hat instead of the black French pocket hat she'd thought he ought to get. It was the only thing preventing him from keeling over.

Zeke glanced over the crowd assembled around the observing stand, but it was hard to make out anyone specific in the crush of people. If Sophie was among them, he couldn't see her. Mrs. Smith and Miss Annie and half a dozen other ladies had already assured him she'd be here, but that didn't stop him from worrying. He'd done everything they'd told him to, just like they'd told him, and he couldn't see that any of it had done any good.

Sarah Jane had been keeping a pretty sharp eye on developments, too, but when she'd shown up at Patrick's this morning to fasten his tie just right and give a last brush to his jacket, she'd reluctantly admitted that she couldn't see any change in Sophie's attitude, one way or the other.

If Mrs. Smith's plan worked, it wouldn't matter. If it didn't . . .

Zeke shut his eyes against the dazzling light. He refused to think about it. He had to keep believing that Sophie really did love him, in spite of the muddle he'd made of things. He had to. He couldn't bear to think of the alternatives.

They were almost through the opening ceremonies before Zeke finally spotted her at the far edge of the crowd. Over where there were trees and some shade against the baking heat around the track.

Actually, he spotted Patrick first, but once he'd found Patrick, who was standing with his arm around a smiling Sarah Jane, it wasn't hard to find Sophie.

Tall, elegant, beautiful Sophie. How could he possibly have missed her? Zeke craned to get a better look.

She was standing a few feet away from Sarah Jane and Patrick, head high and with her hands clasped in front of her, just as if she weren't surrounded by heat and dust and commotion. She was too far away for him to be sure, but Zeke thought she looked a little tired and not at all happy.

For the first time in days, hope stirred in Zeke's breast. Maybe Mrs. Smith had been right after all. Maybe, just maybe, this crazy plan of hers would really work.

Sophie had arrived just after the opening ceremonies began. She was dimly aware of the noise and the press of people as each race was run, and she was pretty sure she'd made all the right responses to everything Sarah Jane or Patrick might have said to her. But her attention was focused on one spot, and one spot only—the chair on the observation stand where Zeke sat.

Well, that and the chair beside it where Annie Talbot sat, dressed in blue and white and looking like every man's dream of feminine perfection.

Just the sight of the two of them, side by side, was enough to make Sophie's stomach churn and her shoulders hurt from tension. It was worse watching the way Annie touched Zeke's arm to get his attention, or the way he bent toward her whenever she spoke to him, as if he enjoyed the intimacy of the gesture in the midst of so many people.

The very worst was just after the first round of races had finished and the crowd began streaming toward the shady grove of trees and the mountains of sweet, juicy watermelons that awaited them. Just thinking about watermelons and Zeke was unsettling, but thinking about watermelons while she watched Zeke solicitously help Annie down from the observation stand was enough to upset her entire system.

"Sophie? Sophie!"

Reluctantly, Sophie pulled her attention back to her immediate surroundings.

Sarah Jane stood three feet away, clinging to Patrick's arm with a proud and happy possessiveness that made her whole face light up. She smiled and said teasingly, "Did you see somebody that interested you?"

"Me?" Sophie forced a weak laugh, but it didn't sound very convincing, even to her. "Of course not!"

The effort of keeping up the pretense was simply too great. She could feel the smile sliding off her face, in spite of her best efforts to keep it in place. From the corner of her eye she spotted Zeke, head bent to catch something Annie was saying, working his way toward the tables where the cooking contest was set up.

The last trace of her smile vanished. She'd forgotten he'd been selected to serve as judge for the contest. Or maybe she'd chosen to forget. After all, it had been Annie who'd airily informed her that making him the judge seemed only right, since he was serving as her escort for the racetrack opening.

"Sophie?" Patrick's deep voice, sharp with sudden concern, cut through her thoughts. "Are you all right?"

Sophie forced herself to move so she couldn't see Zeke or Annie. "Not really." She grimaced and pressed her fingers to her temples. "I have a terrible headache, I'm afraid. With all this sun and the noise . . ."

It wasn't quite a lie. If she were forced to see any more of Zeke and Annie smiling at each other like little lovebirds, she really *would* have a headache.

"I . . . I think I'll just go home and lie down," she said, waving aside her friends' expressions of concern. "You two go on. Really. In fact, have a slice of watermelon for me. Delphi will tell me all about the cooking contest when she comes home."

Sarah Jane's eyes widened. She started to protest, but Sophie had slipped away into the crowd before she got a word out.

"Now remember," Annie said, "Mrs. Bassett doesn't know anything about this. We always choose her to run any cooking contests because she's the worst cook in town, but she always plays fair. You don't want to tip her off to the fact that we're *not* playing fair this time."

Zeke had to stoop to catch what Annie was saying. The eager crowd, stirred by the excitement of the races and thirsty for watermelons, surged around them, drowning out even Annie's clear voice since she couldn't risk speaking louder and being overheard.

"Sophie's entry is marked with the number 'seven' and tied with bright red yarn," Annie said. "The numbers for all the other entries are tied on with plain brown string so you can't mistake it."

Zeke nodded. "Brown string."

Annie pulled him to a halt, then stretched on tiptoe so she could reach his ear. "No, *red yarn*! Sophie's is marked with red yarn."

"Right." He could manage red yarn, even as nervous as he was now. For the fifteenth time that morning, he mopped his brow with the handkerchief Sarah Jane had swiped from Patrick because he'd forgotten his own. "You *sure* the other ladies agreed to this?"

Annie grinned at him, then stretched up to resettle his hat squarely on his head. "I'm sure. Adelaide and I asked everyone who'd signed up. They all agreed. In fact, a couple of them are already talking about what they ought to give you two for a wedding present. Sophie's the only one who doesn't now what we've planned. Sophie and Delphi. We didn't think it was safe to let Delphi in on the secret, either."

Zeke groaned.

Annie laughed.

Zeke stared down at her. She had a mighty pleasant laugh. In fact, she was a mighty attractive woman. But somehow her laugh didn't make him want to laugh, too, like Sophie's did, and five minutes after seeing her, he couldn't for the life of him remember anything much about the way she looked, while Sophie's face haunted him, waking or sleeping.

Like his mama always said, there was just no accounting for why folks fell in love, but they kept doing it, regular as clockwork.

Well, he'd fallen, and fallen hard. But if clocks were to run as badly as his love life had so far, mankind would have to go back to telling time by the sun and no mistake.

"Now don't forget," Annie warned him, "you have to try a bit of everything Mrs. Bassett hands you. We don't want anybody to guess what's going on. Fortunately, everybody knows Sophie's one of the best cooks around, so they're not likely to suspect anything, even when she wins."

"Right." Zeke wished he were as confident as Annie. It would make things a whole lot easier.

"Okay. Let's go over it again, just to be sure. What are you supposed to look for?"

"Red yarn and the number seven."

Annie beamed and patted him on the arm, just as

if he were a schoolboy who'd finally gotten his lessons right. "Lucky number seven. I picked it myself," she said.

Escape was a good idea. Unfortunately, it just wasn't possible. Sophie was so intent on getting away without even one more glimpse, however brief, of Zeke and Annie Talbot, that she didn't spot Delphi and Mr. Conner until it was too late.

"Just where do you think *you're* going?"

Delphi's sharp query easily cut through the racket of the crowd. Startled, Sophie pulled up short. To her dismay, Delphi, arms linked with Mr. Conner, stood squarely in her path, effectively blocking her escape route.

"I have a headache and I thought I'd—" Sophie didn't get any further.

"You can't leave!" Delphi said, a martial light in her eyes. "What will everyone say? I'll tell you what they'll say!" she snapped before Sophie had a chance to respond. "They'll say you were afraid to face Zeke Jeffries and that Talbot trollop, that's what they'll say!"

"Mother! Annie Talbot is *not* a trollop!"

Delphi snorted in irritation. "Maybe not, but she's sure enough got her claws in Zeke Jeffries, and if you don't show up for that bake contest, she'll *never* get them out of him!"

Sophie might still have escaped if Delphi hadn't abandoned Mr. Conner's arm and immediately grabbed Sophie's, instead. There was no way Sophie could get free without making a scene that would embarrass them all.

Whether she liked it or not, she was going to the bake contest, Zeke Jeffries or no Zeke Jeffries.

The races had drawn a lot more people than usual, half of whom seemed to know either Delphi, or Mr. Conner, or both. That is, if they didn't know Sophie, instead.

By the time the three of them finally worked their

way through the crowds to a spot in front of the tables, Sophie was a nervous wreck and Zeke had eaten his way through three slices of pie, a half dozen cookies, four slices of cake, and six slices of sweet breads and rolls.

All of the servings were small, of course, but he was still looking awfully unhappy. After every couple of bites, he'd mop his brow or run a finger around the inside of his collar, as if it had grown uncomfortably tight.

The assembled crowd watched him with unfeigned interest. The food had even drawn a couple of hungry dogs that slunk around the outside of the gathering on the off chance some crumbs and crusts might fall their way.

A stout gentleman near Mr. Conner leaned closer to say, "Had some problems at the start, I hear. Some boys got into the food and put things in a bit of confusion, but I guess they got it all back in order. Mizzus Smith, now, she made a fuss about the arrangements, but Mizzus Bassett, she said she was the one in charge and that Mizzus Smith should tend to her own knitting. Then Mizzus Purvis comes along and *she* tried to run things, too. I hear it was quite a sight. Quite a sight."

Delphi sniffed angrily. "Pack of busybodies," she said.

The stout gentleman craned to add something to his news, but stopped when he spotted Sophie. Up until then she'd been half-hidden behind Mr. Conner's bulk and Delphi's breadth. At the sight of her, the stranger blinked, then grinned and abruptly retreated.

Though she'd tried not to notice the interest her arrival had generated, Sophie was uncomfortably aware of the occasional murmured asides and the curious glances thrown their way.

She shut her eyes and tried to pretend she was safe at home in her room with the doors locked and the windows drawn. It didn't work. She could feel Zeke's presence like a thunderstorm on the horizon.

Her eyes snapped open. She shouldn't have thought about thunderstorms.

It might have been easier if there hadn't been several thousand watermelons stacked up not too far away.

It had to be her imagination, of course, but she would have sworn she could smell them, despite all the people in between.

"Would you look at that Adelaide Smith," Delphi said with undisguised disgust. "You'd think she was standing on an ant pile the way she's dancing around. *Most* undignified, but then, what can you expect?"

In spite of herself, Sophie turned to see what was going on.

Delphi was right. Mrs. Smith was hopping around and gesturing toward Zeke and Mrs. Bassett like a demented puppet.

And Delphi wasn't the only one who'd noticed.

Zeke had never been more confused in his entire life. Quite aside from the mortifying terror of having to eat in front of what seemed like hundreds of curious and unreasonably interested people, now Mrs. Smith was trying to tell him something, and he hadn't the slightest idea what it was.

At least he assumed she was trying to tell him something. He couldn't think of any other explanation for her mad antics.

It didn't help that he'd spent the first ten minutes blindly swallowing mouthful after mouthful of food while trying to spot Sophie without appearing to look, then, after he'd found her, spent the next ten minutes trying to pretend he didn't even notice her existence. Having her so close, yet so totally unapproachable wasn't good for his addled wits.

Of course, he'd seen the red yarn and its unmistakable number "seven" the minute he'd stepped behind the table. It was attached to a chocolate layer cake with a ragged hunk torn from one side—the four ladies who'd remained behind to keep an eye on things while everyone else was at the races had evidently been off sampling a watermelon when the raiders struck.

The missing hunk of cake didn't bother Zeke so much as the four large bites of cake he'd consumed before he'd realized that something was amiss.

It was a good cake, but it wasn't Sophie's chocolate cake. At least it didn't taste like it. In fact, he'd have sworn the cinnamon bread he'd tried earlier was just like Sophie's, right down to its sweet, honey flavor.

But there was the cake, and there was the scrap of red yarn with its lucky number "seven," all clearly attached to the plate with the chocolate cake. He had to be mistaken. Annie had been too insistent.

It was enough to drive a sane man mad, and under the circumstances, Zeke wasn't sure he qualified as sane.

He glanced at Sophie, then as quickly looked away. He couldn't bear to look at her while they were still divided by a table, a dozen cakes, and two rows of people. Soon. Mrs. Smith swore her plan would work, and a matchmaker with her experience couldn't possibly be wrong. Could she?

"Well, now, Mr. Jeffries!" Mrs. Bassett startled Zeke out of his thoughts by snatching the half-empty plate of cherry pie out of his hands. She set it to the side with the rest of the plates and turned back to the expectant crowd. "That's the last entry, and I'd have to say you've done the ladies proud with all you've eaten of their good cooking. Wouldn't you folks agree?"

The crowd clapped enthusiastic agreement. Mrs. Bassett took advantage of the noise to shoot a warning glace at Mrs. Smith, then held up her hands for quiet. The crowd stilled.

"And now, Mr. Jeffries," Mrs. Bassett said, just as if she were announcing the next major attraction in the circus ring, "who . . . is . . . the winner?"

Zeke closed his eyes. Now he knew what Custer must have felt like at the Little Big Horn.

He took a deep breath and forced his eyes open.

A hundred faces stared back at him, but all he could see was hers.

It had to be his imagination, but he would have sworn he could hear Sophie's heart beat.

Beating for him. He had to believe that.

His gaze dropped to the array of food before him. There was the chocolate cake with its red yarn tag, and there, six plates away, was the cinnamon bread that tasted of honey. His mouth tingled with the remembered taste. Honey . . . and Sophie.

He touched the red yarn with its tag. Lucky seven. Yet there was the bread. Sophie's bread. He was sure of it.

His fingers tightened over the yarn even as he started to reach across the table toward the bread.

Mrs. Bassett snatched the yarn out of his fingers. "I don't even have to look to see whose cake *that* is!" she announced for all the world to hear. "I saw Annie Talbot put it there myself!"

Zeke jerked back. *Annie's* cake?

From somewhere on the edge of the crowd, Zeke could hear a couple of dogs barking, then shouts, then more dogs barking. He glanced at Annie, but the look of horrified disbelief on her face was all the assurance he needed. It was the marauding, cake-eating boys who'd messed things up.

More shouts and barking. The crowd was shifting, trying to spot the cause of the commotion. Even Mrs. Bassett, red yarn dangling from her fingers, turned to see.

Zeke didn't care. He reached for the loaf of bread.

His fingers closed on it just as a blur of cat jumped onto the table, then leaped over the lemon meringue pie and into the crowd on the other side. Two mongrel dogs darted under the table and after the cat. Another mongrel charged into the fray, yapping madly. Mrs. Bassett shrieked and jumped aside. She hit the edge of the table at the same time some of the people in the front row of the crowd dodged away from the stampeding dogs.

Cakes, pies, cookies, and plates went flying.

Zeke's hat went sailing. He didn't stop.

He thought he heard someone in the crowd shriek-
ing, "Oh, no! It's Adelaide, the Cat!" but he might
have been mistaken. He didn't care.

All he cared about was Sophie, and she was slipping
away from him.

Zeke leapt over the mangled remains of the table
and charged after her. "Sophie, wait! *Wait!*"

Behind him, another voice shrieked, "Who are *you*
calling a cat?" but he didn't stop for that, either.

He caught Sophie at the far edge of the grove. He
grabbed her arm, then pulled her against him.

"Let me go!" She tried to jerk free.

He pulled her tighter against him, and then, because
he couldn't help himself, he kissed her.

And then he kissed her again.

All his empty days, all the long, lonely nights vanished as if they'd never been. The two of them fitted
together as perfectly as he remembered. Better.

Zeke groaned and pulled her closer still and kissed
her again. And again.

Sophie sighed and melted against him, warm and
vital and as hungry for his kisses as he was for hers.

"Oh, Zeke," she whispered an eternity later.

She arched away from him. Not far, not enough to
break free of his hold on her, but enough so she could
tilt her head back and look up at him. She laughed,
and her laugh held a faint touch of madness. "Do you
realize you're squishing what's left of my loaf of
bread?"

"I am?" Zeke blinked and held up the loaf. He'd
held on to it, in spite of everything. There were probably traces of it pressed into the back of Sophie's dress,
but he wasn't going to waste time checking.

"Marry me, Sophie!"

Sophie stared up at him, dazed.

"Please say you'll marry me! I'm not letting you go,
so you might as well." He gave her a little shake.
"Say it!"

"How'd you know it was my bread?" she demanded, ignoring his peremptory commands.

"Sophie!" It was a plea, not a protest. He couldn't endure the doubt.

"Tell me! How'd you know it was my bread?"

Zeke looked at the ruined loaf of bread, then at her, at his beautiful, beautiful Sophie.

"It tasted of you," he said at last. "It tasted of your kisses."

She sucked in a breath and held it, eyes golden with wonder.

"But now I realize I was wrong." Zeke tossed the bread away and bent back to her. "It wasn't near as sweet. Not anywhere near as sweet."

"Oh, Zeke." Sophie sniffed—it was a most inelegant sniff—and started to cry. "That's the most romantic thing I've ever heard!"

Zeke laughed. "Well?"

Sophie blinked. "Well, what?"

"Sophie!" For one mad moment, Zeke wondered if it was possible for a man to explode from mingled desire and doubt. "Will you marry me? Will you?"

She said yes. Zeke was sure she said yes.

At least, he thought she said yes.

He was so lost in the hungry, demanding kiss she claimed that he was incapable of any rational thought. All he knew was that he loved her, and she loved him, and that they would have a lifetime of honey-sweet kisses to prove it.

Epilogue

Tuesday, June 5, 1894

It was a long night and no mistake, but I don't think I ever saw a prettier dawn. But maybe that's because I've never been a father before.

Father.

That has quite a ring to it.

I have to admit, I get choked up just thinking about it. My chest swells and my throat gets thick and I get this funny, sort of sick, sort of excited feeling in the pit of my stomach, just like I used to get when Miss Ashford would call on me to give a recitation in class, knowing I'd worked harder than anyone else in the whole school to get it right, but afraid I'd make a mess of it, no matter what. Well, same feeling about being a father. Only ten times worse . . . and a hundred times better.

When I tried to explain it to Sophie, she laughed and asked why my head hadn't swelled up, too. That was easy. I told her it had been swelled up ever since she told me about the baby coming almost eight months ago.

Actually, babies, as it turned out. Sophie had twins. Two girls, both bald and fat and pink and beautiful. I was worried about telling them apart, but my Sophie knew how to manage, just like she always does. She had me fish a ribbon out of her sewing box—a little pink one, just the color of a ripe melon—and she tied it around the wrist of one of them in the cutest little bow you ever saw.

I told Sophie I was for sure willing to learn about changing diapers and bathing babies, but I hoped she wasn't going to insist I learn to tie a bow like that. There are limits, after all, and that's one of them. She just smiled up at me and looked wise, and I couldn't help wondering what else she had in store for me.

I guess that's part of the excitement, really, knowing there'll always be something new coming down the road. So long as she's there with me, I don't worry. We've both learned a few things, and I'd be willing to bet—me! who doesn't gamble—that we'll have a fair amount more to learn in the years ahead.

Kind of nice prospect, if you think about it.

For a while there, I wasn't sure we *had* any prospects. I'd heard tales about what women go through to have babies, but I never had any idea it was as bad as it is. Sophie bore up just fine, but there were times I thought I'd give up. I couldn't stand the pain she was suffering, especially knowing I was responsible and now there was nothing I could do about it, and nothing I could do for her except hold her hand.

I didn't leave her the whole time. Doc Simmons wasn't too happy about that at first, but Sophie insisted she wanted me there, no matter what he or anyone else thought. She just reared right up in bed and told him, straight-out and no-nonsense. Well, his mouth dropped, and then he grumbled some, but in the end he had to admit it worked out all right.

We had old Mrs. Farnham in to help since she's had lots of experience with the ladies and their babies 'round about. I managed to keep Delphi and Adelaide and Sarah Jane out, though I have to say, it *was* a struggle. Delphi insisted she had a right to be there since she was Sophie's mother, of course, but Sophie soothed her down somehow. Probably by telling her she needed her to keep an eye on Adelaide and the silver spoons, though that might be a bit of an ~~exajera exagura~~ that might not be quite the way things went.

Hiram and Mr. Conner helped out by taking care of the farm chores for me last night, and Patrick and Tom drove out to do them this morning. They took

Sarah Jane home with them when they left. Don't know that having the O'Boyle family out was such a good idea, though. As they drove away, Tom was wanting to know when Patrick and Sarah Jane were going to give *him* a baby sister. You could have seen the red on their faces a mile away, I swear. But I'm also pretty sure that Tom will be getting his wish one day soon. The two of them had that look in their eyes. A fellow would have to be blind not to see it.

Hiram said he'd be back tonight, too, which I probably should have said no to, given all he's done to help. I just said thanks though, since I'm almost as tuckered out as Sophie.

She's sleeping right now. Has been for a while. I crept in a little bit ago, careful not to wake her *or* the babies, and just sat there beside her, watching her sleep.

She was so beautiful. I wish I had the words to describe just how beautiful she was . . . how beautiful she *is* . . . but I don't have them, and I guess there's no sense trying to find them. I could fill this whole journal and then some, and still not manage to say what I mean.

What I do know is, if I could have gotten any happier, I'd have burst, right then and there. It's just not possible for a man to be any happier or prouder or more in love than I am, and that's the truth.

Maybe someday I'll have all the right words to explain it to Sophie. But then again, maybe I won't.

And I think maybe she knows, anyway.

Oh! Just realized I clear forgot to say what we named them. The babies, I mean. The first one out is Jane, after a heroine in one of Sophie's books. The other is Elizabeth. After another lady in another book, of course. Sophie said now I'll *have* to read those books, just to find out what's what. But I didn't make any rash promises.

We didn't even consider Delphi and Adelaide.

A Note to the Readers

George Swink really did exist. He first came to Colorado and the area of the "rocky ford" over the Arkansas River in 1870. The following year he, along with his partner, Asa Russell, established a trading post by the ford to serve travelers headed south to Santa Fe. His family joined him in Colorado in 1874. His daughter, Mattie, the first child born in Rocky Ford, arrived a few months later.

Swink is generally regarded as the founder of the melon industry that eventually made Rocky Ford watermelons and cantaloupes famous from coast to coast. He planted his first watermelon crop in 1878. That harvest was so bountiful, he invited everyone in the area to share in a feast at his store. Guests, hungry for a taste of sweet, juicy melon, even came by train so they'd be sure to get a taste! That first Watermelon Day has become a yearly tradition in Rocky Ford. Just as in years past, it's held on the tree claim Swink developed in the 1880s, though these days it's part of the Arkansas Valley's annual fair.

Gee Ging, the gentleman to whom Zeke forgot to take his dirty laundry, ran a hand-laundry service out of the back of a barbershop on Walnut Avenue from 1888 to 1901, when he returned to China because, according to a report in a local paper of the time, he couldn't compete with J.D. Wolf's new steam laundry.

Rocky Ford really *did* inaugurate a new racetrack in 1893. The festivities as presented here are entirely my own fabrication, but the Fair Board at the time recorded gate receipts of $2,050, which was almost a third of the total capital investment in the track, barns, and other improvements to that time.

Although some of the fictional characters Sophie refers to are truly "fictional" for this book, Mrs. Southworth really existed. The popular author's works were available in a variety of editions through the Montgomery Ward & Company catalog and, later, through the Sears, Roebuck & Company catalog. Montgomery Ward offered all Mrs. Southworth's books in a set of forty-three bound volumes for $10 the set, or $.27 each, with postage $.10 extra per volume. Some of her popular titles were *Curse of Clifton, How He Won Her, Fatal Marriage,* and *Prince of Darkness.* Bertha M. Clay came a great deal cheaper. She could be had for a mere $.08 per volume through the Ideal Library's extensive list of popular, paperbound titles. Shipping cost $.02 extra. Her books—including, to my delight, *Her Only Sin*—carried titles like *The Duke's Secret, Wife in Name Only,* and *Her Sister's Betrothed.* Miss Mulock's library-bound volumes, including *Plain Speaking,* were a great deal pricier—$.90 each, though Montgomery Ward offered them at $.65, a substantial discount, even counting the $.10 postage. Perhaps the elevated tone of her titles had something to do with their higher cost—*A Brave Lady* strikes a much grander note than, say, Mrs. Clay's *Foiled by Loving.*

Perfumes at the time were pure extracts rather than the blended mixes we are accustomed to today. Fragrances available to the feminine shopper included Lilac Blossoms, Musk, Ylang Ylang, English Violet, Lily of the Valley, and yes (Honest! I didn't make it up!), New Mown Hay. I tried, but couldn't quite work in the Pink Pills for Pale People that were also available for $.25 a box. I'd like to order some myself. Among other wonders, they were reputed to be excellent against "Rheumatism and all diseases arising from mental worry, overwork, early decay, etc." Quite frankly, it's the early decay, etc. that interests me.

Everything and everyone else in the story—the characters, the Ladies Missionary Society, the bake contest, the opening ceremonies for the racetrack, the Fourth of July celebration that Miss Annie graces—are all creations of my own imagination.

Well, not quite. There is a photo of a slightly later Independence Day parade in Rocky Ford that shows two "Roman chariots" proudly rolling down the street, just as I've described them for Sophie's parade. I couldn't bear to exclude them or the kids with their pets because one of my own favorite memories is of decorating my tricycle (I was five) with crepe paper streamers for a Crowley County Days parade in Ordway, Colorado, the town where my mother was born and I managed to get through first grade. (I don't think it was my school record that caused my family to move to Pueblo before I started second grade, but I wouldn't want to swear to it.)

Colorado history has fascinated me ever since my aunt took me to see the first excavations on Bent's Fort, near La Junta, Colorado. The state's history is a rich and wonderful blend of the famous, the infamous, and the relatively unknown. *Summer Fancy* was a chance for me to explore one small part of that history.

My next book explores an entirely different facet of Colorado's past—its early tourist industry and its early tourists, including European nobility, wealthy business magnates, government potentates . . . and those who were just pretending to be one of the three for their own, often no-quite-legal ends!

The story is set in Glenwood Springs, Colorado, a town famous for its mineral hot springs and, in June 1893, the opening of one of the most luxurious hotels in the United States at the time. The Hotel Colorado was built on the fortunes that silver made, but it survived silver's disastrous plunge two months later because the wealthy still had money to spend, and they were quite willing to spend it playing tourist in all the traditional ways—climbing mountains, playing croquet, soaking in steaming mineral baths, or exploring mineral caves lit by—imagine!—electric lights. And that doesn't even begin to cover the evenings' entertainments.

Among the hotel's visitors are a wealthy magnate who survived the fall of silver (or so he says), a beautiful Italian countess who wants to see the sights (or so *she* says), and a compellingly handsome man who doesn't say much at all. Together, the three of them play tourist and their own, private games to the hilt—and to the confusion of just about everyone!

I enjoy hearing from readers. My address is Anne Avery, P.O. Box 62533, Colorado Springs, CO 80962-2533. A self-addressed, stamped envelope would be appreciated.

Sincerely,
Anne Avery

◆ TOPAZ

LOVE AND DANGER . . .

☐ **STOLEN HEARTS by Melinda McRae.** Death was his enemy, and Stephen Ashworth fought it with all his skill as a surgeon, though his methods made some call him a devil. Lady Linette Gregory felt the young doctor must be stopped, and she was the woman to do it. Linette and Stephen were rivals—yet when they were thrust together to save a young girl's life, a tenderness blossomed . . .   (406117—$5.50)

☐ **DARLING ANNIE by Raine Cantrell.** When the likes of Kell York, leanly built, lazily handsome with a dangerous streak, meets up with the beautiful barefoot girl Annie Muldoon, she is not what he expected. Neither was the gun she pointed between his eyes when he insisted he and his "soiled doves" be allowed to move into Annie's boarding house. But both of them soon learn that true love changes everything.
                                                              (405145—$4.99)

☐ **DAWN SHADOWS by Susannah Leigh.** Maria McClintock is as beautiful and free-spirited as the windswept Hawaiian island of Maui where she was born and raised. And soon she catches the eye and wakes the lust of powerful planter Royall Perralt, who traps her in a web of lies and manipulations to get what he wants.   (405102—$4.99)

*Prices slightly higher in Canada

Buy them at your local bookstore or use this convenient coupon for ordering.

PENGUIN USA
P.O. Box 999 — Dept. #17109
Bergenfield, New Jersey 07621

Please send me the books I have checked above.
I am enclosing $_____ (please add $2.00 to cover postage and handling). Send check or money order (no cash or C.O.D.'s) or charge by Mastercard or VISA (with a $15.00 minimum). Prices and numbers are subject to change without notice.

Card #_____ Exp. Date _____
Signature_____
Name_____
Address_____
City _____ State _____ Zip Code _____

For faster service when ordering by credit card call **1-800-253-6476**

Allow a minimum of 4-6 weeks for delivery. This offer is subject to change without notice.

ROMANTIC TIMES MAGAZINE

*the magazine for romance novels
...and the women who read them!*

"WAITING TO EXHALE" CATAPULTS ETHNIC ROMANCE!

Romantic Times MAGAZINE

Marilyn Campbell's
DOUBLE DELIGHT

OVER 150 ROMANCE NOVELS REVIEWED

Also Available in
Bookstores & Newsstands!

♥ *EACH MONTHLY ISSUE* features over 120 Reviews & Ratings, saving you time and money when browsing at the bookstores!

ALSO INCLUDES...
♥ Fun Readers Section
♥ Author Profiles
♥ News & Gossip

PLUS...

♥ Interviews with the <u>Hottest Hunk Cover Models</u> in romance like Fabio, Michael O'Hearn, & many more!

♥ Order a <u>SAMPLE COPY</u> Now! ♥
COST: $2.00 (includes postage & handling)
CALL 1-800-989-8816*
*800 Number for credit card orders only
Visa ● MC ● AMEX ● Discover Accepted!

♥ BY MAIL: Make check payable to: **Romantic Times Magazine**, 55 Bergen Street, Brooklyn, NY 11201
♥ PHONE: 718-237-1097   ♥ FAX: 718-624-4231

♥ E-MAIL: RTmag1 @ aol.com

VISIT OUR WEBSITE: http://www.rt-online.com